COWBOYS AND INDIANS

SCOTT CULLEN BOOK 7

ED JAMES

To Ginty, Dawn, Kay, Ed, Jon, Ron, Kim, Sam, Barford, Flocky, Rich, Jim, Stef, Mandy, Spencer, Tizzard, Mose, Liana, David, Stephen, Mike, Mike, Andy, Rakesh, Hang, Marion, Karen, Caroline, Steve, Mark, Lee, Alan, Graham, Tom, Arthur, Angus, Isobel, Alex, Shagger, Derek, Brian, Séan, Gary, Willis, James, Damian, Andrew, Welshy, Jarrod, Kirsty, Lisa, Joan, Lucy, Peter, Graeme, Mark, Daegal, Richie, Jon and all the other survivors of IT programmes I've worked on.

OTHER BOOKS BY ED JAMES

SCOTT CULLEN MYSTERIES SERIES

1. GHOST IN THE MACHINE
2. DEVIL IN THE DETAIL
3. FIRE IN THE BLOOD
4. STAB IN THE DARK
5. COPS & ROBBERS
6. LIARS & THIEVES
7. COWBOYS & INDIANS
8. HEROES & VILLAINS

CULLEN & BAIN NOVELLAS

1. CITY OF THE DEAD (Coming March 2020)

CRAIG HUNTER SERIES

1. MISSING
2. HUNTED
3. THE BLACK ISLE

DS VICKY DODDS

1. TOOTH & CLAW

DI SIMON FENCHURCH SERIES

1. THE HOPE THAT KILLS
2. WORTH KILLING FOR
3. WHAT DOESN'T KILL YOU
4. IN FOR THE KILL
5. KILL WITH KINDNESS
6. KILL THE MESSENGER

MAX CARTER SERIES

1. TELL ME LIES

SUPERNATURE SERIES

1. BAD BLOOD
2. COLD BLOOD

DAY 1

Saturday
17th May

1

Detective Sergeant Scott Cullen barged through the crowd at the bar, clutching a metal tray. Six tumblers rattled as he carried them, each containing sparkling amber and a shot glass filled with black liquid. A bleary-eyed man in a tight shirt nudged into him, spilling some. Cullen glared at him and walked on, dumping the drinks on the high table. 'Here we go. Jägerbombs all round.'

Acting DI Sharon McNeill grabbed one and kissed Cullen on the lips, her familiar taste mixing with Red Bull. She tugged her purple top, showing off her bare arms, almost stick thin. Her ponytail smoothed out the worry lines on her forehead. Could get away without wearing a bra these days. She raised the glass, her gaze wandering around the busy club. 'Cheers.'

Four other hands snatched a drink.

Cullen raised the last one in the air. 'One, two, three!' He necked it, the shot glass chinking off his teeth, the contents blending with the Red Bull, and slammed it on the table. 'First!' He wiped the dribble on his chin.

Sharon finished hers next and winked at him. She leaned over to peck him on the cheek. 'Cheers, Scott.'

Cullen leaned in close. 'You think he's here?'

'Not sure yet.' She peered around the bar again, nudging her empty tumbler across the table. 'That's a great idea, by the way.'

'What, Coke instead of Jägermeister?'

'Thank Budgie for me.' She nodded back to the bar, the queue three deep, an array of tenners in the air. 'Hope our guy's not working with the bar staff.'

'You've interviewed them, what's your take?'

'I think they're as worried as we are.' She raised her eyebrows at a man near them, grinding away at the edge of the dance floor. 'What about him?'

Tall and lithe, maybe late twenties. Fists pumping the air in time with the beat. Skinny jeans, patterned shirt open to the waist, a thin line of hair tracing down his flat stomach. His sculpted beard would take more effort every morning than Cullen spent in a month.

Cullen rubbed his chin and sniffed. 'More likely he's a potential victim. He's out of his tree.'

'Drink or drugs?'

'Maybe both.'

The man spun around, moving away from them, stomping his feet in time to the song's heavy thud. He stopped by a pair of men — rich students, judging by their jeans and jumpers. Both tall and athletic-looking. He worked one of them away from the other, like a lion separating a gazelle from the herd. Got in the guy's face, shouting the song's lyrics at him. He grabbed his hand and led him across the dance floor. Stopped at the bar and raised a finger at the barman.

'Nice queue jumping.' Sharon leaned in to Cullen, her perfume cloying. 'This is looking possible. Do you think he's being helped?'

'Let's see.' Cullen watched their target take two shot glasses and lead his prey towards a booth, his hand passing across the top of a glass. What the hell was that? 'Shite, he's put something in one of them.'

Sharon spun round to her team — two men and two women. 'Think we've got a suspect. You know the drill.' She marched across the crowded club.

Cullen followed her. The first pair of officers headed to the front door, the other towards the toilets.

The men reclined next to each other on a red banquette, the fake leather frayed in a few places. The older one slapped a hand on his prey's thigh and raised his glass, glowing in the UV light.

'DI Sharon McNeill.' She held up her warrant card. 'Police Scotland Sexual Assault Unit. I'm detaining you under—'

Liquid splashed across her face.

Cullen reached into the back of his jeans and snapped out his baton.

The older man leapt towards him. His skull thudded into Cullen's forehead. He tumbled backwards, slipping on the floor and collapsing on the sticky tiles.

He made it up onto all fours, blood spurting down his face, covering his mouth.

Black trainers darted away from him through the crowd.

The younger man cowered in the booth. 'What happened?'

'You had a narrow escape.' Cullen got to his feet and pointed at the glass, rubbing his bleeding nose. 'Don't drink that.' He jogged through the gap in the crowd as it parted further, nostrils stinging.

DC McKeown hunched over by the bar, hands over his groin, eyes screwed up.

Cullen shook his shoulder. 'Did he get you?'

'What do you think?'

'Where did he go?'

'Out the front. Rhona's gone after him.'

Cullen shot off towards the front door, passing the cloakroom. The other two officers overtook him and barged past the gorillas on the door. He climbed up the steps into the warm night air and stopped on the pavement, getting out his Airwave. 'Control, this is DS Cullen. Requesting immediate support outside the Liquid Lounge on George Street.'

'Receiving. DS Lorimer and DC Lindsay are in pursuit of a suspect down Frederick Street, heading towards the New Town.'

'On my way.' Cullen wove between crowds of staggering drinkers and confused tourists and slid round the corner. He wiped his bloody nose.

The two who'd outflanked him in the club were chasing a man down the hill, footsteps and shouts echoing off the grand buildings.

Cullen squinted at their target. Definitely him. 'Control, suspect's now on Queen Street.'

'Received. Alpha fifteen are attending an incident on Great King Street. Want me to redirect them to support you?'

'Affirmative.'

'Acknowledged.'

Cullen sprinted across Queen Street, his outstretched warrant card stopping the long queue of evening traffic. He powered on down the hill, passing the darkness of Queen Street Gardens on his right. No sign of his quarry or the other officers. 'Control, need an update.'

'Suspect has entered Jamaica Street.'

Shite. Cullen bolted past Howe Street's Georgian town houses and swung a left into a side road. Boxy sixties concrete lit up in sodium yellow. Footsteps clattered from the right. He curved round the bend to a row of stone mews houses.

One of Sharon's male officers lay on the ground, blood bubbling from his mouth. 'Fucker got me.'

'Support's on its way.' Cullen raised his baton and jogged on.

His target punched out, cracking a fist into Rhona's face. She tumbled backwards, her head crunching against the pavement.

Cullen wheeled round to him, baton poised just as a uniformed officer stormed round the corner. He swung out, thwacking the backs of the suspect's knees.

The man fell forward, hands slapping against the cobbles. 'You bastard!'

Cullen stuck a knee in his back and applied his cuffs. 'What's your name?'

The man from the club twisted his head round, as if he was sucking it into his neck. 'No comment.'

Cullen nodded at the uniform. 'Thanks for the help, Si.'

'Let me help in future, mate.' PC Simon Buxton unclipped his stab-proof vest and let it hang open. 'This weighs a ton.' He ran a hand through his full beard, then across his shaved head, the dark stubble ending in a line with the tops of his ears. His forehead creased. 'You know you're bleeding, right?'

Cullen put a hand to his nose. Wet. Warm. 'Christ.'

'This your guy?'

'I think so.' Cullen hauled the suspect to his feet, grip tight on the cuffs. 'Let's read him his rights down the station.'

2

Cullen smoothed down the plaster across his nose, blinking at the lights on the ground floor of Leith Walk station. 'This can't be doing anything, can it?'

Buxton winked. 'Might hold your brains in.'

Cullen reached over and tugged at Buxton's hairy chin. 'You're such a fashion victim.'

Buxton jerked his head back. 'I've grown quite attached to it.'

'See you in a bit, hipster.' Cullen patted his aching nose as Buxton entered the uniform locker room.

'Here, Sundance!'

Cullen clenched his jaw, catching his tongue between his teeth. He swivelled round, hands balled into fists. And breathed out.

Just Gary Mullen, the Desk Sergeant.

Cullen glared at him. 'I told you to quit that. It's bad enough when Buxton does it.'

'Gets you every time.' Mullen cleared his throat. Took a few goes. 'Got a text off Bain, by the way. Boy was asking how you were doing. Well, whether you'd made a mess of anything.'

'We've seen and heard the last of him. Let's keep it that way.'

'Suit yourself.' Mullen thumbed into the public reception. 'Wondering if you could escort your lad's lawyer up to the room.'

'Fine. Got a name for the suspect yet?'

'Kyle Graham.'

'You owe me one.' Cullen wandered over to the waiting area. He stopped and sucked in a breath.

Campbell McLintock stared up from his leather-bound legal pad, covered in scribbles. He wore a navy suit with pale yellow chalk stripes. Must've chosen the green shirt and purple tie in the dark. His charcoal hair was a couple of shades too dark for his grey skin.

'You're his lawyer?'

'Mr Graham's father received a personal recommendation.' McLintock lumbered to his feet, kneading his back. 'You could do with some new chairs in here. I've a mind to sue.'

'Austerity's a bitch.' Cullen led him through the station towards the interview rooms. 'Been a while, Campbell. Not long enough.'

'Need to thank you, Cullen. Billables have been through the roof thanks to your efforts in January.'

'If I'd known my work would line your pockets, I wouldn't have bothered.'

'That's the way of the world, Sergeant.'

'Isn't it just.' Cullen swiped through and held open the security door

Sharon stood in the corridor, swapping her phone to the other hand. She nodded at the door to room four. 'In there.'

McLintock entered and nudged the door shut behind him.

It bounced off Cullen's foot. 'Keep it open, there's a good boy.'

'Very well.' McLintock dumped his pad on the desk and sat next to his client.

Kyle Graham leaned forward, massaging his forehead. His shirt was now done up to the top button.

Sharon stabbed her mobile with a finger and pocketed it. 'That us good to go?'

Cullen glanced into the room, McLintock whispering into his client's ear. 'Give them a minute.'

She brushed a hand over his nose. 'That's going to be some shiner.'

'I'm sure you'll soothe it better when we get home.' He stroked her bare arm. 'You didn't give chase.'

'Someone had to stop the target from leaving. Name's Alistair Jeffries. His drink's clear, in case you were wondering.'

'So this Graham wasn't trying to date rape him?'

'He threw the contents of Alistair's glass at me.'

'Right. Any roofie symptoms?'

'The duty doctor's with him just now.'

'What if he's not your guy?'

'*Our* guy.'

'This isn't my case, Sharon. Crystal told me to provide brute force and ignorance. That's it.'

'Just how you make love, my dear.' Sharon entered the room and sat opposite McLintock. 'Good evening, Campbell.'

Cullen followed her in, staying by the door as it clicked shut.

Sharon leaned forward to the microphone. 'Interview commenced at twenty-three oh six on Saturday the seventeenth of May, 2014. Present are DI Sharon McNeill and DS Scott Cullen. Kyle Owen Graham is also present along with his lawyer, Campbell McLintock. Mr Graham, can you please confirm your whereabouts earlier this evening.'

Graham nibbled his top lip, stretching the skin out. 'I was out for a drink with a few friends. They left about half nine.'

'So you went to the Liquid Lounge on your own?'

'That's right.'

Cullen folded his arms. 'You have a good dance in there?'

Graham shrugged, eyes on Cullen. 'No comment.'

'You weren't trying to pick up one Alistair Jeffries, were you?'

'Excuse me?'

Cullen waved at him. 'I see you've buttoned up your shirt.'

'It's cold in here.'

'Tell us about Alistair Jeffries.'

Graham sniffed. 'I knew him from university.'

'You're a fair bit older than him, though.'

'I'm a lecturer. Alistair was in one of my tutorials last year. He got a first in that class.'

'We'll check with him. In case you're wondering, he's pretty shaken up by what's happened. Our colleagues are speaking to him right now. Quite a lengthy statement he's giving.'

'He'll tell you the same story as mine. I bought him a drink. That's it.'

'Was it Rohypnol you dropped in it?'

'What?' Graham scraped the chair back over the carpet tiles and stood up. '*Rohypnol?*'

'Did you spike Mr Jeffies' drink?'

'Of course I didn't.'

Sharon ran a hand across her top. 'It ended up all over me. There wasn't enough to sample. That's convenient for you.'

'Are you going to let me go?'

'You assaulted three officers.'

'And you've assaulted my client, Inspector.' McLintock leaned forward. 'Given he has committed no crimes, I'd say that's a score draw.'

Sharon ignored the lawyer. 'Edinburgh has a lot of bars for gay men to meet in.'

'I'm not gay.'

'Of course you're not.' Sharon untied her ponytail, letting her hair hang loose. She flicked one side behind her ear. 'So, Mr Jeffries will confirm your story, right?'

'I've done nothing wrong.' Graham narrowed his eyes. 'Wait a sec. You're fitting me up for a crime because you think I'm gay?'

Cullen crouched down next to him, voice just loud enough for the microphone to pick up. 'Mr Graham, someone's attacking young men in Edinburgh. They spike their drinks and take them home. They rape them. Brutally. Each victim's suffered serious injury.'

Graham swallowed, his Adam's apple bulging. 'It's not me.'

'Three of the victims met their assailant in the Liquid Lounge.'

'So?'

'You bought Mr Jeffries a drink in there. Spiked it with Rohypnol. You were going to take him home and rape him, weren't you?'

McLintock gripped Cullen's wrist. 'Sergeant, given you've no evidence supporting these fanciful claims, I suggest you release my client.'

Sharon bunched up her hair. 'Mr Graham, we're holding you while we obtain further evidence.'

'You've got to let me go. My wife doesn't know I'm here!'

'Your *wife?*'

Graham snorted and looked away. 'Beth.'

Cullen shook off McLintock's grip and stood up straight, his knees clicking. 'Maybe we should have a word with her and see what she's got to say about your nocturnal activities?'

Graham shrugged. 'I don't care, so long as you let her know I'm safe.'

~

SHARON STORMED into the meeting room and locked eyes with Cullen, letting out a deep sigh. 'Another barman who doesn't know anything.'

'Complete sodding waste of time.' DI Colin Methven loomed over Cullen, jangling keys in his trouser pocket. The other hand rested on his forehead, his eyebrows shorn to stubble. 'I don't need this. It's half past sodding eleven and I'm doing a triathlon in the morning.'

'I'll try to avoid detaining suspects at inconvenient times in future.' Sharon leaned against the wall. 'This is going to be a long night. Kyle's wife's coming in soon.'

Methven nodded. 'I'm sure your own officers can support you.'

'What's that supposed to mean?'

'If we're not charging him, we shouldn't be holding him. He's not a terrorist.'

'So you're washing your hands of this case?' Sharon snorted, jaws clamped together. 'He's a suspect for three rapes.'

'I have to agree with Campbell McLintock.' Methven scowled at the door. 'You've got precious little to go on, Inspector. DS Lorimer's still in hospital, DS Cullen and DC McKeown both have bloody noses and DC Lindsay is having his nether regions probed by the duty doctor.'

'Do you prefer it when it's your own bollocks getting battered, Colin?'

'You're trying my patience, *Sharon*.'

'I've got to conduct another dozen interviews like that. That eats up resource.'

'If you arrest him, you can investigate his flat. That's your most likely source of evidence.'

'I'm aware of how to do my job, *Colin*. I'm just not arresting him yet.'

'You've got insufficient evidence. He was hitting on men in a nightclub. It's not a crime.'

'He's not likely to stash Rohypnol in his house. His *wife* might find it.' Sharon crossed her arms. 'This is nothing to do with you being mates with Mr McLintock, is it?'

'Excuse me?'

'He always seems to know what's going on here.'

'I'd suggest keeping that to yourself in future.'

Sharon held up her phone, the screen flashing up. 'His wife's just arrived, so I'll bid you adieu.' She tugged the glass door shut behind her, the mechanism clattering as she stormed across the empty office space.

Methven glared at Cullen. 'Sergeant, I need you to extricate yourself from this case.'

'Excuse me?'

'I've had strong reservations about seconding you to an investigation your — I hesitate to say "better" half — an investigation your *other* half's running.'

Cullen sat forward, the chair creaking. He sucked in air reeking of whiteboard pen and Methven's deodorant. 'I trust you to manage me in the correct way, sir.'

'And I do. Supporting a task force with our present resource shortage is a tall order. Luckily, we've suffered no detrimental effect to our own work stack. I'll be reallocating you on Monday morning.'

'Looking forward to it.' Cullen got up and left the room, shutting the door. He trudged across the office, passing an army of locked computers all showing the Police Scotland screensaver.

The door to the Ladies screeched open. Sharon emerged from inside, scowling at it. 'Someone needs to get that fixed.'

Cullen shrugged. 'I suspect a can of WD40'll break the budget.'

'True.' She chuckled as she looked back at the meeting room. 'How'd it go with Crystal?'

'Thanks for leaving me with him.'

'He's your boss. I just used him to borrow you.'

'Well, I think you've lost me and the other two. Better hope Graham's your guy.'

'Brilliant.' She dabbed her eyebrow and winced again. 'You heading home?'

'I'm meeting Buxton for a pint.'

'Scott ...'

'It'll be a soft drink, don't worry. I'll head after that.'

3

C ullen scanned around the newly refurbished Elm. Oak panelling, subtle spotlights and granite surfaces, craft beer taps lining the wall behind the bar. The serving hatch flopped down and a man with a thick beard passed a burger on a wooden chopping board to the barman. A pair of students sat at the piano, playing some Cockney music hall numbers.

Buxton was fiddling with his phone at the table by the window, a half-full glass of beer fizzing in front of him. He waved at Cullen and joined him at the bar, clutching his glass. 'Evening, squire.'

'Pint?'

'Caesar Augustus, cheers.' Buxton took a long drink. 'You having one?'

'Wish I was, mate.' Cullen stared at the taps behind the bar and focused on the barman. 'Is the ginger beer alcohol-free?'

'Brewed it myself. It's all about the sugar.'

'Ginger beer and a pint of Caesar, then.'

The barman nodded and started pouring, facing away from them.

'What's that, five months now?' Buxton took a sip. 'It's not like you were an alcoholic, though, is it?'

Cullen avoided eye contact, instead waving a hand at the piano. 'That's your sort of music, isn't it?'

'Takes me back to Lambeth, me old China.' Buxton finished

his pint and set the glass on the bar. 'Your doctor didn't tell you to stop?'

'Sharon did.'

'How does it feel?'

'Odd. The weirdest thing is, I miss that ... presentness, if that's a word. Being in the moment. My head's so full of shit these days. I'm worrying about what's happened, what hasn't happened.'

Buxton scratched his beard. 'Not a problem I've got.'

'Didn't think it would be. Sharon says I should try mindfulness.'

'And you call *me* a hipster.'

Cullen handed over a tenner and took his change. He grabbed his ginger.

Buxton led to his table, sipping his fresh pint, getting foam all over his beard. He slurped it off. 'That's lovely. Sure you don't want any?'

Cullen perched on a stool. 'I'm fine. How's being back on the beat?'

'Thinking about jacking it in, to be honest.'

Cullen sipped his ginger beer. Sharp and full of elderflower. He hated elderflower. 'You serious?'

'I'm not winding you up, mate. Being back in uniform after two years as Acting DC? It's not good.'

'Wait till you see what happens with this new permanent DC gig, mate.' Cullen swirled his glass around, the ice cubes tinkling. 'You did apply for it?'

'That form took ages.'

'But you finished it?'

'Sent it to HR with, like, an hour to spare.' Another sip. 'Thought I'd get my tenure when you got your DS.'

'Methven had to soak up the cost, didn't he? We've been two heads short for a year and the criminals don't take it any easier. New financial year and it's just getting worse.'

'What, more cops on the beat?'

'Got it in one. Fewer detective jobs. Political shite galore.'

Buxton fixed a glare on Cullen. 'I really need that job, mate.'

'Leave it with me.' Cullen grimaced through another sip of ginger beer. 'Confident QPR'll win the play-off final?'

~

CULLEN SHOVED his leather jacket on top of his fleece on the coat rack.

'Ma-wow!' Fluffy sat in the sitting room doorway, glaring up at Cullen. 'Ma-wow!'

Cullen crouched down and tickled his chin. 'I take it that's cat for "feed me, you bastard".'

Fluffy reared up and rubbed against his cheek. 'Ma-wow!'

'So you do like me?' Cullen stood up, knees creaking. He went into the kitchen area and flicked on the TV. Lower-league English football highlights played out on BBC One. He got a can of cat food from the fridge and forked it into a bowl on the counter. He hefted Fluffy up. 'You're not getting any lighter, mister.'

Fluffy spread out on all fours, furry pom-poms sticking out as he ate, purring away.

The flat door thunked open. Heels clicked on the laminate.

Cullen leaned back against the counter. 'That you?'

Shoes thudded to the floor and Sharon stomped through the flat. 'No, it's the Easter bunny.'

'Take it the interviews didn't go as planned?'

Sharon reached into the fridge for a half-drunk bottle of wine. 'Could say that.'

'You've released him?'

'I don't care what Crystal bloody Methven says.' She sniffed the wine, poured out a glass and took a long drink. 'This is my case and I'll charge who I want, when I want.'

'Good luck with that.'

Fluffy chomped at a splodge of cat food. Half of it dropped onto the counter.

Cullen stared at her wine. 'You back in tomorrow?'

'No. I've asked Rhona to lead.'

'Take it you're not that convinced of his guilt?'

Her shoulders slumped. 'Is it that obvious?'

'Hey, hey.' He went behind her and massaged her upper back, thumbs attacking tight flesh. 'I'm almost cutting myself on your shoulder blades.'

'Scott...'

'You're taking this too personally.'

'And to think I used to worry about you doing the same.'

Cullen pecked her on the neck, wrapping his arms around her. 'You'll get this sick bastard, you know you will.'

'Scott.'

Another kiss, further up. Hands on her hips. 'Mm?'

She flinched. 'Stop.'

'Stop what?'

'That.' She stepped forward and smacked the glass down on the counter. 'I'm not in the mood.'

Cullen raised his hands. 'Sorry.'

'*Sorry?*'

'What's up?'

'What do you think, Scott?'

'The baby?'

'Of course it's the baby.'

'It's been over a year.'

'Scott, she'd be six months old now.' She shut her eyes. 'It takes years to get over something like that.'

'Most people try again. Most people want it in the first place.'

'What the hell's that supposed to mean?'

'Nothing. I want you to be okay.'

'I still feel—' She glared at him. 'I don't know...'

'You're disgusted by me, right?'

'It's not you, Scott. It's just ... sex.'

He swallowed. 'I don't want to force myself on you.'

'It's not like that.'

'What is it, then?'

'I just don't know. There's just so much crap in my head. Stuff I can't pick out from all the noise.' She nibbled at a fingernail and took another sip of wine. 'Can't believe I let myself get into that situation in the first place.'

'Situation? Having a kid with me's a situation?'

'Isn't it?'

'Come on, we've both got good jobs. It's not like we'd be bringing her up on benefits or whatever.'

'I can't believe I let myself get pregnant.'

'That takes two, you know. It's my fault as much as yours.'

She pinched her nose. 'Look, I need to work out how I feel, okay?'

'Sorry, I just thought, you know...' He shrugged.

'It's okay.' She stroked his cheek. 'Let's try again in the morning. We're both off work.'

He grabbed her in his arms, kissing her on the top of her head. 'Take all the time you need, okay?'

DAY 2

Sunday
18th May

4

Cullen blinked at the light, sun streaming through the bedroom window. Warm skin caressed his back, fresh perfume. The firm stub of a nipple dug into his shoulder blade. 'You're awake, then?'

Sharon pecked him on the neck. 'Do you need more sleep?'

'It's okay.' Cullen spotted the alarm clock. 07:53. Way too early. He rolled over and put an arm around her.

Hair tied up. Some makeup. Lipstick glistened in the light. She leaned forward, eyes closing, and kissed him. Wet lips on his.

He pulled her close, his cock already erect, brushing her thigh through his shorts. Bursting for a piss. He sucked her nipple. Then lay back. 'I need to go to the toilet.'

She leaned back on the pillow, hand on her forehead. 'I just cleaned the sink yesterday.'

'Very good.' Cullen hopped through, his abdomen tingling. He sat on the seat, still warm. Urine splashed on the porcelain. He let out a breath. That's better.

His phone blasted out from the hall, clattering drums and jangling guitar. *Crystal* by New Order. He wandered through and checked the display.

Methven calling...

Stared at the bedroom door for a second before answering it. 'Sir.'

'Cullen, I need you to attend a crime scene at Dean Bridge.'

'Supposed to be my day off.'

'Mine too. Had to cancel my sodding triathlon.'

Cullen let out a sigh. 'What's happened?'

'There's a body.'

'I'll be about an hour.'

'Now, Sergeant.'

'I'll be as quick as I can. What's—'

The line clicked dead.

'—happened?' Cullen sighed as he ended the call. He dumped the phone back on the ledge in the hall and stomped through to the bedroom, perching on the edge of the bed. 'I've got to go to work.'

Sharon pulled the duvet up to her neck. 'Right.'

'I'm sorry. You know what it's like.'

'Don't I just.'

~

CULLEN PULLED up at the side of the road, leaving just enough room for the Bell's Brae traffic to scrape past Sharon's orange Focus. Still hadn't replaced the battered Golf he'd totalled last year. He got out and traipsed down the cobbles, damp from the morning's rain. He turned right and trudged past wild trees, cars and a mill building. The water of Leith thundered on the left, heavy after a week-long deluge. Typical for an Edinburgh May.

A SOCO van filled the gap at the end. On the left, a few uniforms took statements on benches around an old millstone. Up ahead, police tape sealed off an old turreted building.

He flashed his warrant card at the uniform guarding access. 'DS Cullen.'

'Right you are, Sarge.' He handed over a clipboard. 'DI Methven said you're to get through there ASAP.'

As he signed, Cullen glanced up at the curved bridge above them, maybe twenty metres away. Then at the SOCO tent below it, the perimeter's guardian in full-on Smurf suit. 'Take it we've got a faller.'

'That's what I heard, Sarge.'

'Cheers.' Cullen plodded across the tarmac towards the tent and grabbed a suit from the adjacent pile.

A figure stormed out of the white and blue fabric and tugged the mask down. Methven. 'Try harder, Mr Deeley. This is clearly a murder.'

Jimmy Deeley, the city's chief pathologist, followed Methven out of the tent and dumped his medical bag on the ground. He tore off his romper suit. Silver hair gelled into spikes, red trousers hiding underneath a Harris tweed coat with elbow patches. 'That's not for me to say, Colin. Let me do my job and you can do yours.'

'I wish you'd do it with a tad more haste, that's all.'

Cullen put a leg into his SOCO suit.

'Sarge?' The voice came from behind. DC Chantal Jain folded her arms, her jacket crumpling. Salon-perfect hair, pale lipstick clashing with her hot-chocolate skin. 'How's it hanging?'

'Straight down the middle, as ever.' Cullen zipped up the front of his suit, shaking his head at Methven and Deeley as they jabbed fingers at each other. 'Haven't spoken to our Lord and Master yet.'

'That can only be a good thing.' Jain's zip caught halfway up. She tugged at it, freeing the mechanism. 'Is that Sharon's car back there?'

'She's off today.'

'Bet she's happy about you being in.'

'Is that sarcasm?' Cullen charged off towards Methven. 'Sir.'

'Cullen, right. Good.' Methven focused on Cullen and Jain. 'Thanks for your prompt arrival.'

'Is the guy still alive?'

Deeley grimaced. 'Landed on his head and neck. Fractured his spine. Snapped the carotid artery and bled out internally, though he'd have been unconscious for most of it.'

'Poor guy.' Cullen stared up at the bridge. 'It's not a big fall from up there, though.'

'This boy's just been unlucky.' Deeley dumped his suit in the discard pile. 'I'll be off, Colin.'

Methven took a step back and clasped his hands. 'I'll speak to you later, Jimmy.'

'You won't.'

'What?'

'It's my son's wedding today. I need to be in my kilt at twelve. Katherine's on her way in. She'll do the PM for you.'

'Then we'll catch up tomorrow.'

Deeley gave a salute. 'I'll look forward to it.'

Cullen signed him and Jain into the crime scene. 'Any idea who it is?'

'Not yet.' Methven led over to the tent's entrance and pointed inside. 'Uniform responded to a call from a jogger this morning. Local CID handed it to us half an hour ago.'

'So it's suspicious?' Cullen nudged him aside to get a better look inside.

A middle-aged man lay on his front, naked except for white Calvin Kleins. Rolled over on one side, a deep tan stopping at his waist, heavy belly clinging to the tarmac. Long hair hauled back over a thinning patch, still in place.

Methven lifted the left hand and pushed out the ring finger. 'He's married.'

Two suited figures hauled the body over onto his back. The face was a riot of blood, the jaw hanging open, dead eyes half closed.

Methven walked over to the perimeter and unzipped his suit. 'All we've got is six foot one IC1 male in his forties with a heavy build. Doesn't match any active MisPers. No tattoos or other distinguishing features at present. Deeley reckons the time of death was four a.m.'

'Where do you want us to start?'

'Anderson's getting DNA traces, fingerprints, dental and blood tests arranged.' Methven let the suit flap down his back. 'I want you to identify this chap.'

Over by the body, Jain crouched down and held her metallic HTC phone over the victim's face, her click giving a blast of flash. She wandered over, eyes on the screen. 'This'll give us something to go on.'

Cullen stared at the mangled body. 'We can't show a photo of him looking like that to anyone.'

'So describe it. We know what he looks like.' She stabbed at the screen. 'Sent it to you, anyway.'

Cullen focused on Methven. 'Any danger we could get a facial composite analyst in?'

'Let me see what I can do.' Methven dumped his suit in the discard pile and stormed off. 'Dig into what's happened. Get me an ID.'

CULLEN STAGGERED ACROSS DEAN BRIDGE, shielding himself against the battering gale as it sucked air from his lungs. Cars crawled in both directions. The ancient mill buildings of Dean village sprawled below them, contrasting with the New Town grandness on the hill to the left and mansions to the right. In the river below, a fake otter sat on the rocks just metres from the SOCO tent. Cullen pulled up his shirt collar. 'Bloody wind.'

Jain stopped partway across the bridge, just above the tent, and tapped the stubby metal spikes, rising a couple of inches from the stone wall. 'These won't stop anyone from falling, will they?'

'Did he fall or was he pushed?'

Jain peered over at the church to their right, its squat spire gouging the overcast sky. 'Tenner says pushed.'

'You're probably right. If he jumped, it'd be a couple of uniform going door to door.' Cullen folded his arms, resting his elbows on the cold spikes. 'You don't get an MIT out unless you're certain it's a murder.'

'Whatever. The guy's in his pants. That's not your typical suicide.'

Farther over, a skinny man leaned over the edge, the wind ballooning his hoodie, baggy jeans flapping in the breeze. Shaved head, the ridges of his skull visible.

Next to him, a tall woman in a blue leather jacket clicked away with an SLR, a telephoto lens resting between the spikes.

Cullen walked over and tapped him on the shoulder from behind. 'Police. Richard McAlpine, I need you to come with me.'

Rich stood up straight, still facing away, hands in the air. 'I'm just doing my job!'

'I understand.' Cullen grinned at Jain. 'Still need the contents of that memory card and a word with you down the station.'

Rich turned around, his shoulders pinched tight. 'Skinky.' He let out a breath. 'For fuck's sake.'

'I've not seen you in months, mate. This isn't Features.'

'I do whatever gets paid.'

'I need you to clear off.'

Rich leaned against the wall. 'Can I get a quote?'

'I'm not *a police source*, okay? I'm not *revealing* anything to you. Any links between you and me in this case and we'll have words. Serious words. Lots of sweary ones.'

'Can I expect a press release soon?'

'We'll see.

'Suit yourself.' Rich smirked at the photographer and started off towards the city centre. 'Come on, Ali.'

Cullen gripped his shoulder again. 'Have you got something?'

Rich spun round. 'Working on a few leads, Skinky. Nothing worth sharing yet.'

'Let's have a chat later.'

Rich looked him up and down. 'As long as you show me yours first.'

'Have you any idea who it is?'

'That's interesting...'

'Do you?'

'Nope.' Rich nodded at the photographer and wandered off. 'See you later, Skinks.'

Jain watched them go. 'Who was that?'

'Ex-flatmate. Known him since school.'

'You'd better watch your arse, Scott. If Methven gets wind of you knowing a journalist...' She made a scissors motion with her fingers, aimed it at his balls. 'Snippety snip...'

Cullen gripped the stone and peered over the edge. 'Someone must've seen something. We need to get out speaking to people.'

5

Buxton jogged to catch up, his uniform rattling. 'Why are we over this side?'

Cullen passed the Gothic church and stopped outside the first town house on Buckingham Terrace. 'Assuming someone's not dumped him there, his state of undress means he's not far from home.'

'You'll make Sergeant one day.'

'Cheeky sod.'

Buxton thumbed behind them. 'So why not start on the other side?'

'Luck of the draw. Chantal and her uniform might get a result.'

'Her uniform?' Buxton rubbed a hand against his forehead and swooned. 'Is that all I am to you?'

'Don't push it.' Cullen pressed the first buzzer. Three storeys of bay windows, a small balcony on the top. Probably not used in a hundred years.

The door slid open. A man peered out, head tilted, his cravat crinkling. 'Yes?'

'Police, sir.' Buxton cleared his throat, thumbs tucked into his stab-proof vest. 'We're wondering if you were aware of an incident on the bridge in the early hours of the morning?'

'I wasn't in, I'm afraid.'

'We're investigating the death of a man in his forties. Approximately six foot one with dark hair.'

The man glared at him. 'I don't know anyone fitting that description.'

'Really?'

'Not around here, anyway.'

'Are there any other flats inside?'

'Flats?' He glowered at them. 'This is a town house.'

'Do you live alone?'

'Yes, I do. Last time I checked, that wasn't a crime?'

'Thank you for your time, sir.'

He slammed the door.

Cullen rolled his eyes at Buxton. 'I'm wishing we'd taken Dean village.'

~

CULLEN CHECKED his watch as they sauntered back down the hill. 12:32. 'You've felt the last six in your water.'

'Don't I know it.' Buxton glanced at his Airwave. 'Four hours and bugger all to show for it.'

'And you miss being a DC.' Cullen crossed the small lane. 'This should remind you what it's like.'

'Beats moving on vomiters every Saturday night, mate.' Buxton shook his head. 'This city's supposed to be civilised.'

Cullen spotted the rest of his team by the crime scene.

Surrounded by uniforms, DC Eva Law tapped her gelled quiff, dyed bright red, and frowned down at Jain, a few inches shorter. She folded her arms tight to her chest, stretching her top to its limits. 'Sarge.'

'You guys having a break or something?'

Jain tossed a roll at Cullen. 'Crystal got us some sandwiches.'

Cullen leaned against the wall and unwrapped the cellophane. He sniffed the contents. 'Last Tuesday's egg mayonnaise. Smashing.'

Buxton raised his. 'I've got ham.'

'Swap?'

'Piss off.'

Cullen took a bite, hunger just about greater than revulsion. 'Take it we've got nothing?'

'Just had updates from all five teams.' Jain tossed over an Ordnance Survey map. 'Except yours.'

Cullen unfolded it and marked their lack of progress. He checked the streets on Jain's side of the river. 'This is, what, about forty per cent?'

'Less than half, anyway.'

Cullen took another bite and chewed. 'We need to speed up.'

∿

METHVEN DUMPED the map on his Range Rover's dashboard. 'You need to speed up.'

Cullen snatched it back and folded it in half. 'We're trying our hardest, sir.'

'When I supported your promotion, it was because I thought I could rely on you for a result. Don't let me down.'

'Wasn't planning on it.'

'Good.' Methven held out a wad of paper. 'Here.'

Cullen took it, checked the top sheet. A man's face, a computer image. 'That was quick.'

'The facial composite analyst in Stirling owed me a favour.' Methven twisted the key in the ignition and the car growled. 'The press release went out, too. Should be on TV and radio at the top of the hour.'

Cullen opened his door. 'Reckon we'll get anything from it?'

'I live in hope.' Methven smiled at him. 'I appreciate you doing the legwork on this case.'

'Thanks, sir. That's ten days straight I've been in, though.'

'Noted.'

Cullen hopped out and leaned back in. 'If you want us to speed up, extra resource would help.'

∿

'AND I CAN'T GET my Fiat 500 parked because of the bins outside.' Catherine Brown folded her arms across her chest. Long silver hair flowed down to her cardigan. Tight skirt, shiny, sequinned, magenta. Knee-high boots. 'It still doesn't stop my neighbours dumping bin bags onto the pavement. I mean, have you ever walked home from the opera and seen a fox ratting at a tin of beans? This is Learmonth, for crying out loud. Stewart's Melville is just down the road.'

Cullen inspected the first-floor living room, adjusting his shirt against the stifling heat. The drone of Queensferry Road pulsed through the open window. Everything except the walls was pink, various shades from faint rose to acrylic purple. The upholstery, the sofa, the cushions, the tables, the mantelpiece. Even the wooden cabinet housing the TV and the pink stereo. Tiny porcelain figures. He checked his watch again. 15:47. 'It's something we'll look into, Mrs Brown.'

'I should think so, too.'

'All I want to know is whether you saw or heard anything suspicious during the night?'

'I'm a sound sleeper, I can assure you. My white-noise generator sees to that.'

Cullen stood, handing her a business card. 'Give me a call if you recall anything about what happened last night.'

'Of course.' She stared at the small sheet, as if it might answer her refuse collection issues. 'Can you make your own way out?'

'We will.' Buxton led them through the flat and the bright pink front door into the dim stairwell. 'If I ever see any pink again, it'll be too soon.'

'It was like being in a womb.' Cullen trotted down the steps. 'She was, what, sixty?'

'Think so, yeah.'

'An older woman who dresses young. Right up your street, Si.'

'Piss. Off.'

'She's about the same as ... what's her name? The one you danced with at Christmas?'

'Surprised it's taken you this long to start the Cullen bollocks machine up.'

'Touched a nerve?'

'Less said about Geraldine the better.'

Cullen's Airwave chattered. 'Control to DS Cullen.'

'Receiving.'

'DI Methven's asked me to pass the first hit on the press release to you.'

'Go on.'

'Received a sighting of a man in his pants on Dean Bridge last night.'

6

Buxton powered the pool Vauxhall along Barnton Park Gardens, most of the bungalows disfigured by attic conversions. They rocked over another speed bump. 'Which one is it?'

Cullen pointed down the street. 'Last house.'

'The other way would've been quicker.'

'Six and two threes.' Cullen pointed at a squat triangle in white harling, a more recent second floor overhanging the side entrance. 'That's it there.'

Buxton pulled into a long space and let his seatbelt whizz up. He got out and plipped the car locks.

Cullen crossed the road, pressed the doorbell and took a step back, warrant card out.

Buxton reset his cap and tightened his stab-proof vest.

The door scraped open. A white blur burst out, yapping at their feet.

'Russell, stop that!' A plump woman in a green summer dress crouched down to pick up the dog.

'DS Scott Cullen. Constable Simon Buxton. I presume you're Mrs Suzanne Marshall?'

'That's correct.' She smiled at them, her long earrings twinkling in the breeze. 'Come on in.'

Cullen followed her into a living room, vertical blinds

obscuring the view of the street. White walls filled with photos of a family. A TV showed the *EastEnders* omnibus, the picture paused. He sat on a three-seater sofa and rested his notebook on his lap.

Suzanne collapsed into an armchair facing the settee, resting the squirming dog on her lap. 'Is this about the phone call?'

'We understand you saw a man on Dean Bridge in the early hours of this morning?'

'That's correct. It was about half past three.'

'Can you be any more precise?'

'Maybe just before.' She clicked her fingers. 'Three twenty-seven. I looked at the clock when that song came on.' She hummed a tune, unrecognisable. 'Do you know it?'

'Afraid not.' Cullen smiled as he noted down the time. 'What were you doing in town at that time?'

'I was giving my son a lift home from a nightclub.'

Cullen glanced at Buxton. 'Which one?'

'The eighties one on Lothian Road. Next to what used to be the Caley Palais. You know, I saw The Smiths there when I was fifteen. I was a wild child back then.'

'Does your son live at home?'

'He's just finished his sixth year exams. Off to Bristol in September.'

'And you gave him a lift home from a nightclub?'

'I don't sleep at all well when he's out, I'm afraid. Lord knows what I'll be like when he's in Bristol.'

'What did you see on the bridge?'

'There's no easy way to say this.' Suzanne clamped her jaw and cupped a hand round her mouth, whispering. 'I saw a man in his underpants.'

Cullen handed her the photofit. 'Was this who you saw?'

'I didn't get *that* good a look at him.' She stared at the face for a few seconds. 'It's possible. The news just before *EastEnders* jogged my memory. Last night, I just wanted to get home. You see all sorts in Edinburgh at that time of the morning.'

Cullen took the sheet back. 'Any idea who he is?'

'None at all, I'm afraid.'

'Could your son corroborate this story?'

Suzanne frowned. 'What do you mean corroborate?'

'Well, we get a lot of phone calls in response to press releases. If there's anything we—'

She clutched a hand to her chest. 'I'm not a liar.'

Cullen smiled. 'Much as I'd like to take your word for it, we do need this backed up.'

Suzanne held his gaze. Then stood and bellowed. 'Isaac, can you come down here for a minute, please?' She frowned at the thumps coming from above. 'He's such a bright boy.'

Cullen tapped his pen off his notebook.

Suzanne put the dog on the carpet and shuffled to her feet. 'I shall return.' She marched into the hall.

Cullen leaned forward, trying to distinguish the voices mumbling in the hall. Nothing.

'Lucky bastard.' Buxton slumped back on the sofa. 'Getting picked up from a club in town at the crack of sparrow fart... Bet she fried up some chips when they got back.'

A lanky boy in a dressing gown padded into the room, yawning wide. 'Sorry, I'm just up.' Deep voice, hair all over the place. 'Mum said you wanted a word?'

Cullen glanced at Suzanne, waiting in the doorway. 'Did you see anything on the way home last night?'

'Saw a man on Dean Bridge.' Isaac sprawled out in his mother's seat. 'Just wearing his pants. Pretty freaky, like.'

Cullen passed him the identikit. 'Is this him?'

'Maybe. Boy was pretty tall. Had dark hair.'

'You're sure?'

'Totes. Not too sure about the other punter.'

Cullen clenched his jaw. 'There was someone with him?'

'Shorter than him.'

'Male or female?'

'Think it was a woman. Wore this big freaky cloak, man.'

'What colour?'

'Think it was red but it was dark and I'd, you know, had a few.'

Cullen glanced over at his mother. 'Did you see this person?'

'Now Isaac mentions it, yes.' She beamed at the boy. 'I didn't get a good look at her face, though.'

Cullen handed her a card. 'Call me if you remember anything else.'

'JESUS, SI. SLOW DOWN *EARLIER*.' Cullen braced himself against the dashboard, his left wrist bending back. He tightened his right fingers around the Airwave.

Buxton snorted, eyes on the glowing brake lights of the cars in front. 'Sorry.'

'Are you okay, Scott?'

'We're fine, Chantal. Simon can't find the brakes in this new Vectra.'

'So, is that all you were after?'

'Hang on.' Cullen checked the scribbles on the map, a thick line now scored through Stockbridge. 'Think so. Just needed a status update.'

'Does that mean you're letting me get back to my job?'

'Goodbye.' Cullen ended the call. 'Does everyone get this much aggro from her?'

'Just you.' Buxton switched into the outside lane, the boxy houses of Queensferry Road blurring past. 'How's it looking?'

'Like I need to speak to Methven again.' Cullen dialled the DI's badge number on his Airwave. 'Sir, it's Cullen. We're heading back from that sighting.'

Methven huffed into the microphone, out of breath. Birds tweeted in the background. 'Anything to report?'

'Her son confirmed it. Our guy was definitely on the bridge.'

'Unless they're both lying.'

'We've no evidence to support that, sir.'

'No, I suppose not.'

'Our guy wasn't alone. He was speaking to a woman in a red cloak.'

'A cloak?'

'That's what the son said. The mother got a look at the face.'

'That's peculiar.'

'The facial composite was helpful. Can you send the analyst round there to get a photofit of the woman?'

'Not a problem.' The car engine droned in the background. 'I'm just back from the post mortem with some more sandwiches.'

'Anything?'

'The blue Stilton and sweet chilli chutney's excellent.'

'I meant at the PM.'

Another sigh. 'Well, Katherine Sweeney confirmed everything Deeley told us this morning. Cause and time of death. There are traces of sperm on the underpants.'

'His own?'

'They were on the front, so we think so. Anderson's running a DNA test. Lucky he fell on the footpath and not in the river.'

'Not for him. He might've survived that fall.'

Methven ignored him. 'How's the door-to-door progressing?'

Cullen flipped the map over. 'I think we've done about seventy-five, eighty per cent of the area in question.'

'And you've got nothing?'

'So far.'

Another sigh, deeper.

'Do you want us to keep going?'

'Crack on, please. Finish the initial area, then move into those surrounding. If he's not from round there, then someone's dumped him. Out.'

Cullen tossed the handset in the air and caught it. 'Guy does my head in.'

Buxton swung the car around the bend at Orchard Brae, heading towards their search area. 'There are worse DIs out there.'

'Aye, but that one isn't a DI anymore.'

19:04. Cullen blinked away tiredness, leaning against the wall next to a garage. Rothesay Mews, a tight corridor of old stables converted into yuppie apartments. Almost at the bottom of the hill. Why anyone would want to live there...

He let out a sigh and yawned. 'Still no ID and we've checked pretty much every house within a square mile of that bridge.'

Buxton crouched and stretched out his arms, biceps straining his T-shirt. 'Chin up, me old mucker.' He sprang to his feet. 'You're supposed to be keeping me motivated here, not the other way round.'

'Crystal will batter me, not you.'

'I've missed doing this. Proper graft.' Buxton ran a hand across his scalp. 'I thought I'd left walking the beat behind me.'

'And people say I moan.'

A car trundled over the cobbles.

Cullen squinted against the glare, just at the right height to dazzle. A Volvo's sash on the radiator grille, stopped just outside the garage doors. 'That house is one of our gaps.'

A man got out, grey hair slicked back, the rumble of the engine fighting with the bass voices on the radio. He flinched when he saw them. 'Christ, you frightened me there.'

'Police, sir.' Cullen held out his warrant card. 'Just wondering if you can help us with an incident on Dean Bridge last night.'

He frowned. 'I'd love to help, but I was down in Melrose with the rugby club.'

'We believe the victim may live around here.' Cullen handed him the facial composite. 'Do you recognise him?'

He took a look at the image and shut his eyes, nodding. 'I know him.' He sucked in a breath. 'Think I've played squash with him once or twice. Miles better than me. Clearly on his way to the top of the ladder.'

'What's his name?'

'Can't remember, son. He's a member of the sports club down the hill.'

THE DOOR CHIMED as Cullen entered Edinburgh Sports Club.

Cullen took in the small space, the acrid smell of chlorine wafting from a swimming pool somewhere. Squeaking shoes on a squash court. Nobody on the desk. Another door led deep into the building. 'Police! Anyone here?'

A toilet flushed to the left and a tanned youth slouched out, the legs of his shell-suit bottoms thwapping against each other. He frowned at Cullen's warrant card. 'Who're you?'

'DS Cullen and PC Buxton. Need to speak to you about one of your members.' Cullen held out the sheet of paper. 'Do you recognise him?'

The youth swallowed as he collapsed onto a plastic chair behind the desk and shrugged at the photofit. 'Never seen the punter, sorry.'

Cullen gritted his teeth. 'Are you sure?'

'I'm not in the habit of lying to the pi— police. Besides, only been here a couple of months, like.'

'Is there someone in charge here?'

'Think Adie's about, aye.'

'Adie?'

'Adrian Tronci.' He slid fingers through his hair. 'I'll give him a buzz.' He got out his phone, a chunky Nokia thing with a Windows logo, and stuck it to his skull. 'Aye, Adie, it's Paul. Police want to speak to you. Aye, okay. Will do. Cheers.' He put the mobile on the counter. 'He's just in his office. Second on the left.'

'Thanks.' Cullen pushed through the security door and marched down the corridor. He knocked on the door. *A. Tronci, Manager* stencilled into a plastic strip.

'Come in!'

Cullen entered the room, warrant card out. Double windows looked out over the tennis courts, floodlights shining on a game of mixed doubles, the wind blowing the ball around. 'DS Cullen, PC Buxton.'

'Adrian Tronci.' Accent purest Morningside. Tall and lean, like he spent a few hours a day on the treadmill. A large iMac filled most of the desktop space. He pointed to a pair of chairs in front. 'How can I help?'

'We're investigating a murder. We believe the victim played squash here.' Still standing, Cullen passed him the facial composite. 'Do you recognise this man?'

Tronci stared at the sheet for a few seconds and waved across the tennis courts. 'Plays in the squash ladder, I think. Swims a couple of mornings a week, too.'

'So he's a member?'

'His name's Jonathan van de Merwe.'

7

'You try running in full uniform, mate.' Buxton stopped next to Cullen, doubling over and sucking in breath. 'I'm fucked.'

Cullen stopped outside a derelict office, breathing hard. Dean Bridge and the church were now lit up across the river. A row of Georgian town houses led up to Queensferry Road. The street sign listed two streets, Lynedoch Place sitting below Belford Road, for no reason he could identify. He checked the numbers — twenty-three was a seventies brick extension to the end house. 'Is it that one?'

Buxton wiped a hand across his beard. 'Nah, over there.'

Cullen followed his gaze. 'Aye, you're right.' He trotted down the street, passing antique lighting, and stopped by a squat town house second from the end, three dark windows wide. Deformed dormers on the third storey, unlike the beige sandstone of the neighbours' top floors. Black railings around a garden maybe ten metres deep. 'Doesn't look like anyone's in.'

Buxton tried the gate. 'Shall we?'

A couple of squad cars pulled in by the bollards blocking the road at the end, followed by a Range Rover. Four uniforms got out and jogged after Methven.

Cullen waved at them and pointed at the house. 'In here, sir.'

Methven stared up at the building, rubbing his eyebrows. 'You're positive it's this one?'

'That's what the sports club manager told us.' Cullen waved at two of the uniforms. 'Check with the neighbours.'

They nodded. One went up the path on the left and knocked on the door. A woman answered it, a cat swirling round her feet. The other jogged over to the sprawl next door.

Cullen glanced at Methven. 'Have we got the Enforcer if we need it?'

Methven folded his arms. 'Torphichen Place lent us theirs.'

'Are you approving its use, sir?'

'If needs be.'

The first uniform returned, shaking his head. 'She doesn't know who lives there.'

'Typical Edinburgh.' Methven looked over. 'Sergeant, this is your operation.'

'Let's get in there.' Cullen waved at Buxton to lead. 'After you.'

'Of course.' Buxton flipped open his Body-Worn Video camera. 'PC Simon Buxton and DS Scott Cullen reporting to the last-known address of the deceased.'

Cullen followed him up the path, flagstones cut from the same stone as the buildings. Six steps led up to a grey door, a dark overlight above. He knocked, the sound echoing inside. 'This is the police requesting entry.'

Nothing.

Cullen stared around at Methven. 'Sir, we need the Enfo—'

'Sarge.' Buxton pushed the door wide. 'Wasn't even shut, let alone locked.'

Cullen frowned at it. 'What?'

Buxton switched on his torch and nudged the door against the wall. He sniffed as he entered the hall. 'Doesn't smell funny.'

Black and white marble chequerboard led over to a staircase rising up into the house. A long dresser pressed against the magnolia walls on the left. Two doors to the right.

'Doesn't look like it's been subdivided.' Cullen pointed at two of the uniformed officers. 'You two go upstairs.'

They marched off, fiddling with their video cameras.

Cullen gestured for Buxton to try the second door. He entered the first, Methven following.

Dim light shone across the parquet flooring. The room looked back over the Water of Leith to the church over the far side of the river valley. A black leather sofa lay opposite a curved LED television, tuned to ESPN, baseball playing on mute.

Methven marched across the room to inspect the tall bookcase, heavy and dark, lined with vintage hardbacks. 'Not much in the way of personal effects here. No photos of children or a spouse.'

'He wore a wedding ring.' Cullen walked over to the mahogany coffee table and did a double take. Two long seams of white crystals dusted the wood, next to a rolled-up fifty-pound note. 'Looks like cocaine.'

Methven scowled at the bookcase. 'Who the hell is he?'

'Chantal's looking, sir. We'll find out soon enough.'

'Get her looking at those drugs. You need a competent officer on it.'

'Will do, sir.' Cullen searched around the room for anything else. Nothing much — just some modern artworks. 'Let's try the other rooms.'

'Not so fast.' Methven swung something on the end of a rope. 'Catch.' He let go.

It arced through the air and Cullen caught it. A work pass on a blue lanyard.

Jonathan van de Merwe.

Alba Bank.

Cullen rolled the cord around the badge. 'Guess I'm going back to the bank.'

Methven tilted his head to the side. 'You've got previous there?'

'In a way of speaking. One of the suspects on the Schoolbook case a few years ago worked there.'

'All I'm asking you to do is find out about this Van de Merwe chap, not apply for a sodding mortgage.'

DEELEY SLUMPED BACK in his chair, still in full kilt, his bow tie hanging loose, chomping on spearmint gum. A sole desk lamp lit up his office. The stink of cleaning chemicals almost overpowered the stench of second-hand whisky. 'You know I shouldn't be doing this, don't you?'

Cullen frowned. 'Because you've been drinking?'

'Ducking out of my son's wedding while Katherine goes home to tend to her daughter's fevered brow... I tell you...'

'She's five.'

'True.' Deeley tugged off his bow tie and dropped it in his desk drawer. 'Off we go.'

Cullen followed him through into the hallway, a long corridor crawling under the police station, their overshoes squeaking on the floor.

Deeley eased into a room two down, banks of freezer units lining three of the walls. 'I'll take it from here.'

His assistant nodded and left them.

Deeley adjusted the dials on a unit and hauled out the drawer.

Jonathan van de Merwe stared up at the ceiling, what remained of his face ice-white. Dark hair plastered to his scalp. A green sheet covered him up to his chest, his jaw hanging open.

Cullen looked away, his buttocks clenching at the sight of the injuries, and waved a hand at the body. 'You better fix his mouth.'

'Oh, aye.' Deeley reached over and pushed Van de Merwe's jaw. It stayed open. 'Rigor bloody mortis. Jesus H. Christ.'

Someone cleared their throat behind them. 'Need I remind you we don't want any blasphemy in front of members of the public.'

Cullen wheeled round. Methven stood there, hands in pockets. 'Sorry, sir. We're just about ready.'

'Very well.' Methven left and pulled the door to.

Cullen got close to Deeley. 'Can you fix this?'

'Not without a cocktail stick or two.'

'What do you suggest?'

Deeley burped into his hand. 'I've run out of ideas, Constable.'

'Sergeant.'

'Apologies.' Deeley swallowed hard, eyes shut. 'Too much bloody champagne. And whisky.'

'Are you okay to do this?'

'I'll soldier through, as ever. Let's see if I can get this bugger fixed.'

Cullen paced over to the door, stopping to take another look at Deeley, swaying by the body. He shook his head as he tugged the handle and nodded at Methven in the corridor. 'We're ready now, sir.'

Methven waved to the man next to him. 'Mr Henderson, this is DS Cullen. One of my sergeants.'

'Alan Henderson.' Deep bags ringed his eyes. Hair fighting a losing battle against baldness, just a small tuft at the front. A racing-green jumper draped over his shoulders, tied at the neck, a crisp white shirt underneath. Designer scuffs on the knees of his jeans. Rimless specs and salt-and-pepper hair, chin shaved even on a Sunday. Standard attire for financial services senior management. 'Can we get on with this, please?'

Methven led inside, hovering a few feet from them. 'This is James Deeley, the city's chief pathologist.'

Henderson locked eyes on the body, now covered in a sheet. 'Is that him?'

Deeley frowned. 'Sorry, who are you?'

'Alan Henderson. Jonathan works for me.' Henderson thumbed at Cullen. 'Your colleague's call was diverted to me.'

'I got that.' Deeley grinned. 'I mean what do you do at the bank?'

'I'm the COO of Alba Bank. Sorry, Chief Operating Officer.'

Deeley beamed. 'My number one son works there. In Alba Corporate.'

'I'm sure he's a credit to the business.' Henderson snorted. 'Now, can I see this body?'

'Of course.' Deeley pulled back the sheet, Van de Merwe's mouth now pressed shut. 'Do you recognise—'

Henderson gasped. 'That's Jonathan.'

Methven raised a trimmed eyebrow. 'Jonathan van de Merwe?'

Henderson leaned against a freezer, arms folded. 'Aye, it's him.' He rubbed his face. 'Do you need anything else from me?'

'Do you know his next of kin?'

'Not off the top of my head. I'll have to put one of my team on to that. Seldom use PeopleSoft myself, but I can get you a print of his employee record.'

Deeley stood up tall. 'I've got some paperwork, if you'll just follow me.' He wobbled as he led Henderson from the room.

Methven let out a breath. 'Is Jimmy okay?'

'As long as someone drops him back at the wedding.'

DEELEY YAWNED as he stood and snatched the form from Henderson. 'I'll leave you gents to it.'

'Cheers.' Cullen smiled at Henderson and pushed away from the filing cabinet now imprinted in his side. 'I need to ask you some questions about Mr Van de Merwe's death.'

'That's fine.' Henderson picked up a steaming mug, the reek of instant coffee filling the room. 'You think he was murdered?'

'We've reason to believe so, yes.'

Henderson shut his eyes. 'Good God.'

'You said he worked for you?'

'That's correct. I'm the Chief Operating Officer. Fourth in line to the throne, I guess.' Henderson swallowed. 'I own HR, IT, Corporate Functions and Operations.'

'Own?'

'I'm responsible for them. VDM ran OPT for me.'

'It's been a while since I worked in financial services. Can you enlighten me on what OPT stands for?'

'Operational Transformation Programme.' Henderson collapsed back in his seat and drummed a tattoo on the table with his thumbs. 'We're building on the integrations I've delivered over the last ten years. It's a three hundred million pound programme.'

'That's a lot of money.'

'Full delivery will gain us almost one billion a year in cost savings.'

'So there's a lot of pressure to deliver?'

'And then some. All on VDM's broad shoulders.'

Cullen circled *VDM*. 'You said "full delivery". Does that mean you've already completed some of it?'

Henderson looked away and sniffed. 'Not as yet. The first drop's due in January next year. It's been running two years now.'

'That's a long time with no pay-off.'

'You're telling me. That said, we're on schedule. The plan of record indicates a 2016 finish.'

'So another two years for this full delivery, then?'

'Just over. August's the date, I believe.'

'Any idea why he'd be on Dean Bridge at half past three wearing only his underpants?'

Henderson coughed his coffee up. He held the mug in front of his face and sneezed. 'None at all.'

'Why the reaction?'

Henderson locked eyes again. 'Just shows how little you know the people who work for you, doesn't it?'

Cullen noted it. 'Were you close to Mr Van de Merwe?'

'I'll be honest, VDM was just an employee. He guarded his private life. I can tell you his CV, but that's about it.'

'He's married, isn't he? We can't find his wife.'

'They divorced last year, I gather. Never knew her name.'

'Any children?'

'I've no idea. Sorry. He never mentioned any family.'

'Give us the CV stuff, then.'

'VDM was born in South Africa. Durban.' Henderson frowned. 'Sorry, I'm conscious of the fact I'm using his nickname.'

'That's okay, just don't use any of mine.'

Henderson laughed and took another drink of coffee. 'He grew up in London. Studied at Oxford, if I remember right. Went into consultancy. The usual suspects — IBM, Accenture, Deloitte. Then he moved into industry, as they call it, and took up a position at HSBC in Canary Wharf. They'd headhunted him.'

'So he moved up from London?'

'He was the perfect man for the job. He's delivered countless programmes at many other institutions.'

'Is his apartment part of the package?'

'That's confidential.'

'It's a large property, Mr Henderson.'

'The apartment's a drop in the ocean. VDM earned a million a year.'

Cullen whistled. 'That's a hell of a lot of money.'

'It's the London rate. Half of that's performance-related bonus, but we paid it both years. Once this referendum nonsense is out of the way, Scotland'll be on fire. I'm sure you understand, given your FS background?'

'I answered phones and typed up insurance applications.'

Another sip of coffee. 'I see.'

'Could Mr Van de Merwe have been the subject of blackmail?'

Henderson licked his lips. 'Not that I heard.'

'Did he have any enemies at work?'

'VDM was well liked in the bank. Never heard of anything he'd done to annoy anyone more than was necessary. Nobody who'd want to kill him.'

'But he annoyed people?'

'To deliver this programme, we need buy-in from three other divisions, as well as the areas I own.'

'So you're saying he butted heads with a few people?'

'Just some friendly jousting over the conference room table.'

JAIN SLAMMED the phone in the cradle. 'Thanks for nothing.'

Cullen frowned at her, cramped tight in the DCs' office space. 'Tell me you've got something on Van de Merwe.'

'Eh?'

'Did you check his background, like I asked?'

'Methven told me to look into the coke on his coffee table.'

'Christ on a bike.' Cullen rubbed his forehead. 'The background check's the priority.'

'Holdsworth gave me an action. I'm not pissing about with him again.'

'Where is he?'

'Crystal's got him setting up an Incident Room.'

Cullen shook his head. 'Nothing like focusing on admin.'

'Who's in charge? You or Crystal?'

'I'm in charge of you.'

'Well, what do you want, O wise one?'

Cullen tightened his grip on his notebook. 'Start with a PNC check on Van de Merwe?'

'Boss.' Jain logged into her machine and hammered the keys. 'Pretty sure you could've done that on your Airwave...'

Cullen looked around again. A female DC he vaguely recognised sat at the other end of the room. 'Where's Eva?'

'Don't know. I'm not her boss. Is that Jonathan with an A or an O?'

'Eh?'

'At the end. A or O?'

'A.' Cullen folded his arms. 'Do people spell it with an O?'

'I've heard it happen.' A click of the mouse and Jain ran her finger across the screen. 'Here we go. Oh. Got his wife listed here. Elsbeth van de Merwe.'

Cullen leaned closer. 'They're divorced.'

Jain battered the keys. 'Right. Different address.'

8

'Bloody hell.' Jain took a right along a high-walled avenue, lined with parked cars. 'I always think of Polwarth as the shitty flats.'

'They're hardly shitty.' Cullen glanced over at her, silhouetted in the evening light, catching glimpses of grand houses set back from the road. 'More than I'll ever afford.'

'Doesn't JK Rowling live round here?'

'Among others.' Cullen counted the numbers, still at least ten away. 'I'm still not happy with you.'

'What? Christ, Scott, you're getting so much like Bain.'

'Shut up.'

'You know something I don't get? You deal with murderers and rapists all the time, but Bain's the one you hate.'

Cullen checked the house numbers, still too low. 'These people usually get justice for what they've done. With exceptions.'

'Like Dean Vardy?'

'Can't believe he got off.'

'So, your problem is Bain hasn't been done for anything?'

'The number of times he's wriggled out of serious shit. He should be in prison or off the force at least.'

'You've not got any sympathy for him?'

'He got dumped out of our team because he tried to batter

Turnbull for prosecuting his son. His guilty son. Glasgow's welcome to him.'

'Crystal's in the same ballpark.'

'Not even close.' Cullen tapped the glass. Number twenty-four. A Georgian mansion lined with trees, lights on downstairs. 'Here we go.'

Jain pulled in and got out without a word. She tightened her coat against the wind. 'Want me to lead?'

'Aye, go on.'

She marched up the drive and stopped at an estate agent's sign. 'Place is for sale.' She knocked on the door, tossing her hair as she waited.

A woman opened the door. Looked late thirties, blonde hair out of a bottle. Navy jeans and white blouse. 'Can I help?' Forty-a-day croak, Home Counties accent. Plummy, whatever that meant.

'Elsbeth van de Merwe?'

'And you are?'

'We need to speak to you about your husband.'

'Jon no longer lives here.'

'We know. It's a matter of urgency.'

She frowned. 'What's he done?'

'Can we come in.'

Elsbeth shut her eyes and ran her hand over her forehead. No rings. 'He's dead, isn't he?'

'I'm afraid so.'

'Come in, then.' Elsbeth led through a white-painted hall filled with artworks of varying styles, heels clicking off the flagstones. She went into a kitchen, dark oak cabinets and marble worktops, and grabbed a glass of red wine, downing it in one. 'Good Lord.' She collapsed onto a stool at a breakfast bar and refilled the glass. 'What happened to him?'

'He fell from Dean Bridge in the early hours of this morning and died as a result of his injuries. We believe he was murdered.'

'Jesus. I was in London with my sister. Just got back an hour ago.' Elsbeth took another drink, clearing half of the glass. 'How can I help catch whoever did this to him?'

'Let's start with the last time you saw him.'

'Two weeks ago. Sunday.' Elsbeth swirled the wine around the glass, the liquid staining the sides. 'We had a coffee in that place on Marchmont Road. Near the top.'

'I know it. Think it's called Toast.' Jain got out her notebook and made a note. 'Why were you meeting up?'

'A few reasons. We're trying to sell this place. I moved here with him from London but I want to move back home. I've bought a place in the Cotswolds. There's a long chain and the market's quite slow. All this independence nonsense.'

'What else were you talking about?'

'Jon was behind on my maintenance payment.'

'From your divorce?'

'That's correct.' Elsbeth sucked down more wine. 'I won't lie to you, our divorce was acrimonious. It took months to settle. Finally came through in November.'

'Why'd it take so long?'

'The sums didn't add up. I believe Jon'd hidden a lot of money overseas.'

'Do you have any evidence?'

'Well, I enlisted a private investigator but he didn't find much actual proof. It was hidden in some obscure jurisdiction. The Caymans or British Virgin Isles. Something like that.'

'You got a maintenance order?'

'With the disputed overseas cash, the judge couldn't calculate the clean-break amount. I accepted a modest lump sum, this place and a maintenance order.'

Cullen jotted down *Offshore account*. 'Do you know if you're in his will?'

'I doubt it.'

'Any insurance policies in your name?'

'We adjusted our protection when we divorced. I'm the only life insured against this place.'

'Must be quite an expensive mortgage.'

'Not helped by Jonathan not bothering to pay me for the last three months.' Another slug of wine. 'He's not been good at paying up despite all the money he earns.'

Jain smiled at her. 'Why did you divorce?'

'I don't have to answer that.'

'It might help this case.'

'I fail to see how.'

'Did your husband have many friends?'

'Just work colleagues. Jon was a workaholic. Used to embody the whole work hard, play hard thing. You know how it is.' Elsbeth drained her glass and grabbed the bottle, something French and expensive. 'He'd be in the office until late most nights. Then a beer or two and a cab home. Usually be home around ten.'

'Who would he have these beers with?'

'Wayne Broussard and William Yardley. They're colleagues, I think.'

Cullen made a note. 'No other friends?'

'Not to my knowledge. Jonathan kept that part of his life secret.'

'What about any other friends? Maybe the best man at your wedding?'

'Morgan Allason. Knew Jonathan from university. We met at his wedding.'

'You got a number for him?'

'Died in 2009. A car crash.'

'I'm sorry to hear that.' Jain flipped over the page. 'Do you have any children?'

Elsbeth nibbled her lip. 'Jon never had time even though I wanted them.'

'What about his family? Any brothers and sisters?'

'He's an only child. Both of his parents died in 2011.'

'The same year?'

'His father didn't last long after his mother passed.'

Jain cleared her throat, eyes narrowed. 'Ms Van de Merwe, we found your ex-husband wearing only his underpants.'

'Jesus Christ.' She sipped more wine and tugged her hair. 'Bloody bitch.'

Jain scowled. 'Excuse me?'

Elsbeth's eyes clamped shut. 'Not you.'

'Who?'

'Amber.' Elsbeth topped up her glass. 'Jon was having an affair. It's why we divorced.'

'That must've been hard to take.'

'You don't know the half of it. It broke my heart. She's *eighteen*. Traded me in for a younger model. Such a cliché.'

'Was he still seeing her?'

'To my knowledge, yes.'

'Why did you say "bloody bitch"? Think she could've killed him?'

'I wouldn't put anything past her.'

'Do you know her surname?'

'Jesus.'

'What's up?' Jain pushed past Cullen. 'Sudden urge for a drink?'

'Hardly. This place has changed a hell of a lot.' He waved around the Southern's bar area, stripped back from a rugger-bugger hellhole to a modern style bar. White walls filled with framed photos — black and white film stills, fifties noir book covers. Burgers served on wooden chopping boards. Craft beer on tap. Just like the Elm. 'Big change since my student days.'

'I'll leave you to reminisce, while I do some work.' Jain sashayed over, winking at a pair of muscle men near the bar. She nodded at a barman, thin face lost beneath a wiry beard. 'Looking for an Amber Turner.'

'Who's asking?'

A flash of her warrant card. 'DC Chantal Jain.'

'Sit over in the snug, hen. I'll just fetch her.'

Cullen followed Jain over to the small area at the far side, shaking his head as she bumped into one of the muscle boys. He settled into a booth and waited for her to finish apologising with a business card. 'Nice work.'

'Always on the lookout for a pretty boy like that.'

'You'll eat him alive.'

'That's part of the fun.'

'What's wrong with Buxton?'

Jain burst into laughter. 'Aye, right.'

'Not your type?'

'Looks the part but I try not to shit where I eat.'

'Charming.'

A girl leaned into the small room. Blonde hair, girl's face, woman's body — cut-off denim shorts and a Ramones T-shirt, ripped to show cleavage, tied off to show a flat stomach. 'Chantelle?'

'Chantal.' Jain smiled. 'Amber?'

'Aye.'

Cullen made space for her. 'Here you go.'

'Cheers.' She sat, her bare thigh brushing against his leg. 'What do youse want to know?' Niddrie accent, with a snarl to go with it.

'Do you know a Jonathan van de Merwe?'

Her mouth hung open. Braces covered her teeth. 'Right, I'll see youse later.' She got up.

Cullen grabbed her arm. 'Here or at the station. We're not far from St Leonard's.'

'Youse arresting me?'

'Have you done something?'

'No.'

'Then why leave us when we mention his name?'

'Because I'm not speaking about that arsehole. Haven't heard from him in months, anyway. What's this about?'

'He's dead.'

Amber blinked hard and collapsed back onto the bench. 'What?'

'We found his body this morning.'

'Shite.'

'Where were you last night?'

'I was working. Here.'

'So your mate at the bar'll confirm it?'

'He wasn't in. Shug was. He's not in tonight.'

'Tell us about your relationship with Mr Van de Merwe.'

'Met him about a year ago. Thought he was my white knight, you know?'

'What do you mean by that?'

'I met him on sugardaddies dot com. It's a site where young girls like me can hook up with older guys like him.' She ran her hands down her torso. 'You know how long I spend in the gym every day to look this good?'

'I can imagine. What happened?'

'Met up with him a few times. He took me for dinner each time.'

'Did you sleep with him?'

'You're not supposed to.'

'But you did, right?'

A shrug. 'He seemed nice. But he just fucked me. Didn't let me move in with him. Look for him on there, lots of girls mention him on the blacklist page.'

'What did you do next?'

'I checked him out. Found out he was married, so I told his wife. She kicked him out. This was last summer.'

'When was the last time you saw him?'

Amber smirked. 'When she was hurling his suits across their front garden.'

'WAIT FOR IT.' Jain switched off the engine, holding up her hand till the final groan. 'There it is. Told you, these cars are all knackered.'

Cullen let his seatbelt ride up, staring at the garage wall, pale concrete pillars holding the police station up.

Across the car park, Methven clambered into his Range Rover.

Cullen sighed. 'I was hoping to catch Crystal, but he's foxtrotting oscar.'

Jain turned off the car. 'Want me to do some digging into Amber?'

'Please. What do you think of her?'

'Doesn't sound like she's been involved with him for a while.'

'Got a motive, though. He didn't follow through on what he promised.'

'Maybe. Enough to kill him, though?'

'Elsbeth seemed to think so.' Cullen let out a sigh. 'Do some more digging into her as well.'

'As if I've not got enough to do. We need more men, Scott.'

'Aye, I know. I'll sort it.'

'The joys of your extra stripe.'

9

'Sharon?' Cullen dumped his wallet and keys on the chest of drawers in the hall, knocking a pile of unread post onto the floor. 'Shite.' He bent down to pick it up. It was all his. He yawned. 'I'm home!'

'Through here.'

He frowned. The bedroom? He slipped off his shoes and padded across the laminate.

Candles flickered against the cream walls. A rose petal lay on Cullen's pillow.

'Sharon?'

Thin arms tightened around his torso from behind. Teeth nibbled his neck. 'Hello.'

Cullen let his head drop. 'Hello.'

Kisses up his neck. Tongue in his ear. 'I've been waiting for you *all day*.'

Cullen yawned as she tore off his shirt, dropping it on the floor. 'Been a hell of a day.'

'Lie down.'

'Have you been reading *Fifty Shades of Grey* again?'

'I'm on the third one now.'

'That's about my dad's greyhounds—'

'Lie. Down.' She shoved him forward.

His knees clattered against the bed frame. He tumbled face down onto the duvet.

She straddled his back. Tight leg muscles against his soft flesh. 'Sharon, watch it.'

Slap on the bum. 'Shut up.'

He blinked away tiredness. 'Look, I'm exhausted and I haven't—'

Another slap. Searing pain.

'Jesus, what's up with you?' He tried to wriggle free. Couldn't. 'I'm not in the mood.'

'Yes, you are.' She pinched his side. 'Don't make me get my whip out.'

'Seriously, I'm knackered.'

'You're a very bad boy. Taking my car from me.'

'Knock it off. Come on.'

She hauled him over and straddled him, wearing some kind of bodice, pink frills against purple satin. She kissed his chin. Then his neck, then his chest. Kept going down. Rubbing his cock through his jeans. 'Wakey, wakey.'

'I told you, I'm kna—'

A finger covered his mouth. 'Shhh.'

She snapped his belt off, the buckle clanking off the wooden floor. Pulled down the top button. Then unzipped his fly and hauled down his trousers. Then reached into his trunks. Wet lips over his flaccid cock.

∿

A SLAP STUNG Cullen's cheek. 'Huh?'

Another slap. 'Scott, wake up.'

He blinked at the dim light. Candles. Rose petals. His head throbbed, mouth dry. Eyes stinging, his contacts dry. 'What happened?'

'You fell asleep while I was giving you a blow job.'

He rubbed his eyes. 'Sorry.'

She propped herself up on an elbow, left boob hanging out of the bodice. 'Do you want me to punish you?'

'Seriously, knock it off. I've had a shite day.'

She tucked herself back in and hauled herself into a sitting position, resting against the headboard. 'Two rejections in twenty-four hours.'

'Not my fault I got called to work.' He paused. 'Not like the old days, is it? Used to be two or three times a night. Now we can't seem to synchronise our libidos.'

'What's the matter with you?' She glowered at him. 'Last night, you were all over me like Buxton at a wedding.'

'And you were shattered. Now it's my turn.' He yawned. 'Look, I've been out on the bloody streets all day, trying to identify a body.'

'You don't find me attractive anymore, do you?'

Cullen ran a hand through his hair, his eyes watering. 'It's not that, at all.'

'What is it, then?'

'I'm exhausted. Really.'

'It's been months since you've been interested in me.'

'What about last night?'

'That's different.'

'How?'

'It just is.'

'Sharon, I still find you sexy as hell.'

She looked away. 'Right.'

'I mean it. What's going on in your head?'

'I've been bored out of my mind. Doing work on my day off. Then I started reading that book...' She shrugged. 'Scott, I don't want to put you under pressure, but I think we should move. Put it all behind us.'

'It?'

Her eyes darted around the room. 'This is where...'

'Shit, right.' Cullen grabbed her hand and stroked her palm with a finger. 'Let's talk about this tomorrow.'

'Maybe.'

'Please?'

'Try harder.'

'Pretty please? Sugar on top and chocolate diamonds.'

'Okay.' She laughed and stabbed a finger at him. 'Tomorrow.'

'Sorry. It was nice what you were trying to do, but I am knack-ered.' He ran a finger along the underside of his eyes. 'Look at my bags.'

'That's hay fever. It's oil seed rape season just now.'
'I don't get hay fever.'
'Then it's too much coffee.'
'Man's got to have a vice.'
She knelt and hauled off her bodice, showing ribs and tight stomach. 'Go to sleep, Scott.'

DAY 3

Monday
19th May

10

Methven held up his notebook and glowered around the Incident Room. 'Next is the Jonathan van de Merwe case, fresh in yesterday. First point to note is DCI Cargill is the Senior Investigating Officer.' He glanced over to the side. 'Alison, would you like a word?'

'Thanks, Colin.' DCI Alison Cargill stood by the entrance, dappled by early morning glare. Hands on wide hips. Forehead creased below her short fringe, the red hair not much longer than shoulder length. 'We need to focus on getting our ducks in a row pretty quickly. Identifying the body so late has put us behind the curve, but I know you can do it. There will be press interest in this case, lots of it.' She flashed a smile at Methven. 'You should all note DI Methven's Deputy SIO on this and I expect him to take point on the case. Understood?'

Cullen gave a nod. Standard fare. He gazed around the room, his team spread out. Jain at the far side and Eva between them. 'Any progress overnight, sir?'

Methven checked his notebook. 'The SOCOs are still going through Mr Van de Merwe's residence.'

'They've had twelve hours.'

'As I'm sure you'll recall from yesterday, it is a town house.' Methven narrowed his eyes. 'A large one at that. They're struggling to finish it in a standard timeframe.'

'Have they found anything?'

'Nothing of note.' Methven drew a breath through his nose. 'His front door wasn't just unlocked, it was open. From the lack of obvious signs of disturbance, we think it'd been that way since the early hours of the morning.'

'I'd say that rules out suicide.' Cullen rubbed his hands together. 'Someone's snatched him from his house in the middle of the night.'

'Agreed. Determining who killed him is the primary activity of your team today.' Methven focused on Cullen and nodded. 'We have two possible suspects. Mr Van de Merwe's ex-wife, Elsbeth, and an Amber Turner, the cause of his divorce. DS Cullen?'

'DC Jain's going to do some more digging, time permitting, but I'd say they're fairly low priority. Of the two, Elsbeth's looking more likely. He's missed a few alimony payments and she thinks he hid money in some offshore accounts.'

'That's interesting. Follow the money, as they say.'

'Quite. She mentioned a couple of colleagues, might be useful to speak to them. William Yardley and Wayne Broussard.'

'Do it.' Methven held up the front page of that morning's *Edinburgh Argus*, the Scottish independence referendum taking second billing for once. Jonathan van de Merwe beamed out of the cover, dressed in a navy suit with red tie, looking presidential. 'Our friends in the press have also identified the body. I much prefer dictating terms to our friends in the fourth estate. Our facial composite of his cloaked companion was supposed to go out with this.' He folded his arms. 'I'm not convinced this is independent of our investigation.'

Cargill paced over and snatched the paper. 'Are you saying we've got a leak?'

'The byline is a Richard McAlpine.' Methven looked around the room. 'Does anyone know him?'

Like I'd admit that here. Cullen checked his buzzing phone. A text from Sharon. *Lunch today at 1?* He typed a message to Rich. *Who's your source on VDM case?*

'DS Cullen?' Methven raised an eyebrow, a lone hair spearing up. 'I want you to visit Alba Bank. I've got James Anderson and his SOCOs analysing the office. Ask Henderson to introduce you to this Yardley and Broussard. Take DC Jain with you.' He nodded at Cargill. 'Anything else, Alison?'

'I'm good.'

'That's us. Dismissed.' Methven wandered over to the five-metre-wide whiteboard hanging from the wall.

Cullen looked around the room at his team shuffling towards him. Jain wore a dark purple outfit. Eva Law patted her quiff. 'Okay, I've been through HOLMES and sorted out our actions. Chantal, can you investigate the cocaine we found at his apartment?'

'Once the SOCOs finish, aye.' Jain scribbled in her notebook. 'Must be a hundred grand of coke in that bowl of his. I'll round up some dealers, if you want?'

'Wait for the forensics. Check into our suspects first.' Cullen tilted his head at Eva. 'And support DC Law with family and friends.'

'As well as chum you to Alba Bank?' Jain glanced at Eva. 'Anything else?'

'I'll get you out of it. You're supervising the street teams.'

'We finished yesterday, Scott.'

'Now we've got an ID, we should speak to everyone again.' Cullen stifled a yawn. 'A name and a photograph might jog people's memories better than my description.'

Jain gave a salute. 'Okay, boss.'

'Cheers.' Cullen joined Methven at the whiteboard, trying to decipher the scribbles and arrows. Most of his cases on the right-hand side were green, just a couple of reds. 'We need more resource, sir. Stuart Murray's still on leave. Leaves me two short.'

Methven crouched to write something at the bottom. 'Alison and I are on it.'

'I'd like them before I head to Alba Bank.'

'We're going through proper channels, Sergeant. I'll send them over to you if and when we secure any.'

'Fine.' Cullen crossed his arms. 'I'm not taking Chantal with me to Alba Bank.'

'You're down to two leads. I want her backing you up there.'

'Come on, sir. We've got—'

'You've got a team. Use it.'

DS Holdsworth lumbered over, clutching a printout. 'Sir, I need to have a word.'

'I'll see you later.' Cullen made to leave.

Holdsworth blocked his exit. 'Not so fast. It's about you.'

'What have I done now?'

Holdsworth handed the actions sheet to Methven, glaring at Cullen. 'His actions and resources aren't balanced.'

'Is that a surprise?'

'You need to balance them, you buffoon.'

'Buffoon?' Cullen spun round to Methven. 'You see what I'm dealing with here? I'm two heads short, means I can't balance anything. Prioritising the team based on your instructions is as good as I can do.'

Methven scanned down the list. 'All of this needs worked on.' He handed the sheet to Cullen. 'Get on it.'

'I can't. I've got no resource to play with.'

Methven held Cullen's gaze, looking away first. 'Leave it with us.'

Cullen started away from the board and felt his phone buzz.

A text from Rich. *If you read the article, you'd see the source is close to the case.*

He tapped out a reply. *Police?* Waited for the reply.

Two more guesses, caller.

He stepped back towards Methven, glaring at the retreating Holdsworth. 'Sir, there's something else. Rich McAlpine used to be my flatmate.'

'Sodding hell.' Methven closed his eyes for a few seconds. 'Did you leak the identity?'

'Of course I didn't. But really, would I tell you if I did?'

'Sergeant, you need to reassure me your cowboy days are behind you.'

Cullen held out his hands. 'I'm a signed-up sheriff's deputy, sir.'

'You'd better be.' Methven replaced the cap on the pen. 'So where did your chum get the story from?'

'I'll find out.'

11

'Sergeant?'

Cullen got to his feet and held out a hand.

Alan Henderson marched across the Alba Bank reception area, paw outstretched, green eyes darting around. Shirtsleeves rolled up, suit jacket hung over a shoulder. Firm grip of the ex-military. 'We meet again.'

'This is DC Jain.' Cullen gestured at her. 'We wanted to speak to a William Yardley or Wayne Broussard.'

'Let's take a walk upstairs.'

Cullen followed him down the corridor, Jain scowling at him.

Henderson smiled at a few people in the winding queue outside Caffè Nero. The south face of the Alba Bank pyramid towered above their heads, the glass specked with early morning rain. A six-storey brick building dotted with windows met the peak above them. Four lifts ran up and down. He got in and hammered the button for Four.

Cullen leaned against the back wall. The elevator ground up, looking out across Register House and the pair of hotels guarding North Bridge. 'Quite some view.'

'Comes at a cost.' Henderson shook his head, his tongue darting over dry lips. 'We're considering selling up and relocating out west. John Lewis have first dibs on this site.'

'Should you be telling us this?'

'It's an open secret.' Henderson shrugged, swiping his ID badge through the lift door and striding across the tiled floor. 'This is the pinnacle of the building for most of us. Sir Ronald has the top floor, Bill and Ailsa the one above this.' He stopped by some police tape blocking the way and pointed round the corner. 'This was VDM's office. Don't know what you're expecting.'

Cullen peered through the floor-to-ceiling glass at a team of SOCOs working away inside and glanced at Jain. 'And Mr Yardley or Broussard?'

Henderson waved down the corridor. 'Lorna, can you come here?'

A woman in her thirties strode over, dark hair tucked behind one ear. Knee-length skirt and leather boots, blouse done up to the second-top button. She smiled at Henderson. 'What is it, sir?' West-coast accent, maybe North Lanarkshire.

'Lorna, can you arrange for William to come here?'

'Will do, sir.'

Henderson shook out his jacket and put it on. 'I'll have to love you and leave you, I'm afraid. Got a meeting.'

'Of course.' Cullen folded his arms, watching Henderson pace away from them, fiddling with his BlackBerry.

Lorna frowned at Cullen and offered a hand. 'Lorna Gilmour. I'm Jonathan's PA.'

'DS Cullen.' He shook her hand. 'This is DC Chantal Jain. We'll need to have a word with you in due course.'

'Certainly. I'll just round up William.' She walked back over to her desk in the corridor and picked up a phone.

Cullen pointed at her desk, shaking his head. 'Imagine having to sit there all day.'

Jain smirked. 'Beats sitting next to some mouth breather in an office.'

'True.'

Lorna reappeared. 'Mr Yardley should be on his way over.'

'Thanks.' Cullen pocketed the sheet and stared into the room. A Smurf hoovered up the carpet contents near the door. 'Think they'll—'

'Stop!' A heavy man stormed down the corridor towards them, the paintings on the wall shaking with each bound. He stood huffing, hands resting on his hips, a chunky gold band on his left ring finger. Thin red hair scraped over in a parting, skin only a few shades lighter. Eyes shooting around the officers outside the room. 'What the hell's going on here?' Southern American accent, maybe Louisiana. Deep voice. 'Well?'

'DS Scott Cullen.' He got out his warrant card. 'And you are?'

'William Yardley.'

'We're investigating Mr Van de Merwe's death. Can we have a word in private?'

'What's happening to Jon's office?'

'We're performing standard forensic analysis. If you're a regular in there, we'll need a DNA sample from you.'

Yardley glared at him, eyes tiny slits. 'You'd better come to my office.' He stomped off down the corridor and eased a door open. 'In here.' He leaned against the wall behind his desk and crossed his arms, his suit bulging at the chest. 'Well?'

Jain stood in the doorway.

Cullen took his time sitting in front of the desk and unfolded his notebook. 'Thanks for agreeing to see us, sir.'

'I've not agreed shit. Jon's lying on a slab and you punks are speaking to *me*?'

'Us *punks* are trying to find out who killed him.'

'Oh, yeah? And how you doing that?'

'I've got two teams of forensic analysts working at his home and in his office. Another press release will go out soon. We've identified two possible suspects and we've got twenty officers scouring the streets near where he was found.'

'Again, why are you speaking to me?'

'We spoke to Elsbeth van de Merwe last night. She mentioned you were a close friend of his.'

'We were colleagues, that was it.' Yardley tore off his suit jacket and placed it on his coat rack. 'You know how much pressure's on my shoulders, now Jon's gone?'

'I can imagine. Is there anything in Mr Van de Merwe's private life we should be aware of?'

'Such as?'

'Any notable friends or acquaintances we should be speaking to?'

'None spring to mind. Most of his friends are here, working for him. With him. He was like that.'

'Mr Van de Merwe was behind on his spousal maintenance payments.'

'Jon never talked about his private life.'

'What about his financial arrangements?'

'Look, buddy, I worked with him and played squash with him, that's it.' Yardley shut his eyes. Then stared over at the wall. 'Wiped the court with me a few months back. Thought I was gonna have a heart attack.'

'Witnesses place Mr Van de Merwe on Dean Bridge at half past three yesterday morning. Wandering around in his underpants.'

Yardley's mouth slackened. 'What?' He crumpled back against the wall, hammering a finger against his eyebrow. He blinked hard a couple of times. 'I don't believe it.'

'Why would he be out of his house in the middle of the night, dressed like that?'

'I've no idea.'

'We found his front door unlocked.' Jain jotted another note. 'It's likely someone coerced him from his home.'

'He's an IT Programme Director. It's not like he can open the vault at a branch.'

'Does he have access to any security protocols?'

Yardley shook his head. 'Jon couldn't log on without Lorna.'

'Could anyone have blackmailed him?'

'Nobody's going to blackmail him over his weak backhand.'

'There's no dark secrets in his closet?'

'Like I say, he was a private man.'

'Does the name Amber Turner mean anything to you?'

'Who?'

'Mr van de Merwe had an affair with her. It ended his marriage.'

'Means nothing to me.'

'We found a large amount of what we believe to be cocaine in his living room. Do you know anything about it?'

'Nothing at all.'

'How long have you worked with him?'

'Six years.'

'And you've never talked about your private lives in all that time?'

'That's correct. Guys don't talk like that, least not where I'm from.'

'Mrs Van de Merwe mentioned a Wayne Broussard. Do you know him?'

'Him and Jon go back longer than anyone I know. He heads up Schneider Consulting here, our Delivery Partner. Good ol' American firm. One of the big five.'

'Can we speak to him?'

'Wayne's bear hunting in the US just now.'

Jain arched an eyebrow. 'Bear hunting?'

'Yeah.' Yardley let out a breath. 'He likes to go off-grid in the Rockies every year for a couple of weeks. No BlackBerry, no laptop. Says it keeps him fresh.'

'Can you get a message to him?'

'He's off-grid. All I know is he's somewhere in Colorado. I could get someone to drive from Mexico up to Canada and see if they can find him, but it's a long shot.'

'Don't get smart with me.'

'I'm just saying. We won't know where he is until we hear from him.' Yardley finished his cup and tossed it into a bin in the corner. 'You could speak to his second in command. Guy called Oliver Cranston.'

'Let me think about it.' Cullen made a note — *Why so cagey?* 'Tell us about your relationship.'

'I met Jon at HSBC in London. Delivered a two hundred million finance programme under budget. He brought me here as Head of Delivery. I do everything — installing the new apps, designing the data feeds and establishing the architecture. You name it.'

Jain scribbled in her notebook. 'Was Mr Van de Merwe popular here?'

'Nobody's popular here.'

'What's that supposed to mean?'

'I imagine working in the police is a dream. All on the same side, singing from the same hymn sheet.' Yardley leaned forward, still resting against the wall. 'Jon had enemies here. Sure. Anyone who'd kill him? No way.'

'So there's nobody else we should speak to here?'

'Like who?'

'Anyone with a grudge, that kind of thing.'

'Well, I don't think the guy killed him but it might be worth you talking to Vivek Sadozai. He–'

'How do you spell that?'

'V-I-V-E-K S-A-D-O-Z- A-I.'

Cullen scribbled the name. 'Why him?'

'He works for our offshore development partner. Things aren't going well.' Yardley grimaced. 'Not entirely their fault, but Jon had a few run-ins with Vivek.'

'What kind of thing?'

'Speak to him.' Yardley glanced up at the clock. 'Look, I'm running late for the morning prayers.'

'Take us to him and you can run off and kneel down.'

'Lorna'll help.'

～

LORNA OPENED A GLASS DOOR, the steel frame catching on the carpet. Another shove and it settled. 'I've booked this room for the rest of the morning. Give me a shout if you don't need it anymore.'

Cullen dumped his notebook on the table, eight seats clustering around. Just a conference phone in the middle. A whiteboard hung off a picture rail, framed watercolours of fruit and flowers either side. 'Mr Yardley suggested we speak to a Vivek Sadozai.'

'Yeah, he called me. His flight's delayed.'

Cullen checked his watch. 'His flight?'

'He lives in London. Flies up on the red eye every Monday morning.'

Cullen tried for a sympathetic smile. 'Were you close to Mr Van de Merwe?'

'He was my boss, that's it. Bit arrogant and aloof at times, but I've had much worse.'

Jain winked at Cullen. 'Hope he's better than mine.'

Lorna smirked. 'They all expect us to fetch their coffees while they run off to meetings. I still can't believe what's happened, though.' She ran a hand through her hair and stared into the middle distance. 'I keep expecting Jon to just walk up and ask for a latte.'

'So you're on first name terms with him?'

She blushed. 'It's what he asked me to call him. Never Mr Van de Merwe.'

'Alan Henderson called him VDM.'

'Jon didn't really like that. He let Al and a few others do it.'

'I'll give you a shout if we need anything else.' Cullen sat, getting a squeak as he crunched down. He dropped his mobile and Airwave on the table and watched Lorna scurry down the corridor. Wrote *Lorna Gilmour* in his notebook.

Jain got out her lipstick and reapplied it. 'She likes you, Scott.'

Cullen stayed focused on the page. 'What do you think of her?'

'Her boss has just died. She's barely holding it together.'

An Indian man stood in the doorway. 'Sergeant Cullen?'

'Vivek?'

He nodded. Not much over five foot. Moisture dripped from his forehead, misting his chunky glasses. Black hair soaked through. His armpits were damp, several shades darker than the rest of his shirt's pale-blue fabric. A small potbelly poked over his brown trousers. No jacket. 'What's this about?'

'Police Scotland.' Cullen held out his warrant card. 'Need a word with you.'

Vivek trundled his suitcase into the room, breathing hard and wiping his brow. 'Sorry, I ran up the stairs from the taxi.' English accent, London. Middlesex, maybe. 'Do you know what "haar" is?'

'I'm intimate with it.' Cullen smiled, eyeing the blue wisps encircling the pyramid outside. And it was so nice earlier... 'They call it "Scotch mist" down south. That why your flight was delayed?'

'We were circling round for an hour. I've never seen so much bloody rain since I worked in Pune. At least you don't have the traffic here.'

Cullen sat next to Jain. 'This is my colleague, DC Chantal Jain.'

'A pleasure.' Vivek winked at her before collapsing into a chair, tugging at his shirt fabric and blowing air up his face. 'How can I help?'

'You're aware of Mr Van de Merwe's death?'

Vivek's eyes darted between them. 'I heard.'

'What was your relationship with him like?'

'Purely professional. We had the occasional dinner, but that's client entertainment. I've never socialised with him beyond sustaining our involvement in this programme.'

'What do you do here?'

'I'm responsible for the application development and management of all configuration on the apps. I work for IMC. We're the third largest IT consultancy in the subcontinent. We bring industry best prac—'

'What does IMC stand for?'

'Indian Metals and Computers.'

'Shouldn't all that development be IT's responsibility?'

'On a big project like this, best practise is to outsource. Keep costs down and scale up. We've delivered similar programmes several times—'

'I'll take your word for it. Where were you yesterday morning at four a.m.?'

'I was in Mahiki.'

'Is that in India?'

'It's a club in London.' Vivek grinned. 'Why do you ask?'

'Mr Van de Merwe was wandering around Edinburgh half-naked at that time.'

Vivek flicked up his hands. 'I just have a professional relationship with him.'

Cullen made a note. 'What's this programme been like?'

'Well, it's not what we call a "meat grinder". This is not the most aggressive delivery culture I've ever experienced.'

'So it's going well?'

'Not really. I've had a lot of staff turnover. Worse than usual.'

'Was Mr Van de Merwe well-liked here?'

'Better than most we deal with.'

'Did he have many enemies? Anybody who'd want him gone from the job?'

'Can't think of anybody, I'm afraid.'

'What about you? We gather you had some arguments with him.'

'There've been a few slip-ups here and there. Technology aren't playing ball.' Vivek licked his lips. 'They're a separate part of the business. Their agenda isn't in sync with the programme. I've kept escalating it to Jon but he couldn't fix the problem.'

'So you argued with him?'

'He shouted at me. I took it.'

'How did that make you feel?'

'It's not the worst treatment I've ever had.'

'You didn't hold a grudge?'

'Listen, I'm paid to soak up the anger while my team delivers the project. That's it. Unlike some others.'

Cullen narrowed his eyes. 'What do you mean by that?'

'Look, there's an old boys' network here, you know? VDM goes back a long way with Yardley and Broussard.'

'Corruption?'

'I'm saying you should speak to these other guys.'

'Mr Broussard's in America.'

'You might want to speak to Michaela Queen.'

'Who's she?'

'She heads up the Programme Management Office. Runs Financial Control, as well. She knows a few things about what's going on.' Vivek stood and grabbed the handle of his luggage. 'Do you mind if I catch up with my team?'

'Sure, be my guest.' Cullen watched him leave the room and jog down the corridor, iPhone clamped to his head. 'Can't quite put my finger on it, but there's something odd here.'

Jain looked over. 'Think that IT stuff's related?'

Cullen got up. 'Let's go speak to Yardley again.'

12

'Christ, that takes me back.' Cullen stopped outside the office.

Through the textured glass, Yardley stood at a whiteboard mounted on the wall, doodling away.

'An idiot at a whiteboard.' Jain laughed. 'Good old Bain...'

'The same.' Cullen pushed open the door and knocked on the glass. 'Mr Yardley?'

He stayed focused on his drawing, pen hovering over the surface. A series of boxes and arrows ran top to bottom, each one artfully sketchy, the lines barely connecting. 'Mm?'

Cullen cleared his throat. 'We need another word, sir.'

'I'm busy here.' Yardley glanced around, jaw clenched. 'The morning prayers dredged up an issue with the system architecture. I'm trying to fix it now.'

Cullen sat at the meeting table just inside the door and gestured for Jain to shut it. 'Don't you have people for that?'

'They need guidance.'

'Is that part of your role, as well?'

'I wish it was.' Yardley fixed his gaze on a point halfway up the wall. 'Throwing myself into my work's how I deal with things. How I handled my second divorce and the death of my parents.'

The door thudded open.

Lorna stepped into the room and handed Yardley a tall Caffè Nero cup. 'Here you go.'

Yardley sucked coffee through the lid. 'Thanks.'

'Need anything else?'

'No, that's all.'

Cullen smiled, eyebrow raised. 'Could've got us one.'

'Sorry.' Lorna folded her arms. 'What can I get you?'

'It's fine.' Cullen nodded at the door. 'I'll let you get back.'

She shut it behind her, gaze lingering on Jain.

Cullen joined Yardley at the whiteboard. 'We've spoken to Mr Sadozai. He insinuated an "old boys' network" here.'

'God damn it.' Yardley pinched the bridge of his nose with his free hand. 'That punk needs to learn to keep his mouth shut.'

'Is there anything in it?'

'What he's referring to is Jon's loyalty.' Yardley took a deep breath. 'Programme delivery's based on trust. You've got to believe in the guys working for you. Jon's built up a team over the years, people he can trust to deliver.'

'That's all it is?'

'There's nothing sinister here.' Yardley tore off the lid and gulped the mid-brown liquid. 'Whoever killed Jon does *not* work here, I swear.'

'He mentioned a Michaela Queen.'

'Michaela's on leave.'

'Have you got her number?'

Yardley got out his BlackBerry, hammering his left thumb against the joystick in the middle. 'Here you go.'

Cullen jotted down a note, flicked back a page and spotted a note about IT. 'I'm struggling to find anyone here who had an axe to grind against Mr Van de Merwe. That sound right?'

'It's quite a collegiate environment here. Big programmes aren't always like this.'

'So, everyone's everyone else's best friend?'

'That's right.'

'Mr Sadozai intimated some issues with IT?'

'Always one bad apple, I suppose. Jon was at loggerheads with them. They kept blaming us for lack of servers and infrastructure. Everything's either late or just broken. And it's never their fault, always ours.'

'So this was a professional disagreement?'

'They used to go off the deep end at each other at the weekly status meeting and the architecture forum.'

'Why didn't you mention this earlier?'

'Because it slipped my mind. Listen, Jon's tried to sack the lead for chronic lack of delivery.' Yardley glanced at the clock. 'I spoke to Rob at morning prayers. He's free at eleven if you want to chat to him.'

'Rob?'

'The IT Delivery Lead. Rob Thomson.'

Cullen clenched his fists, digging nails into his palms. 'Rob Thomson?'

'You know him?'

Cullen scribbled his name down, a bead of sweat trickling down his back. 'The name's familiar.'

BEEEP! 'You've reached the voicemail of Colin Methven. Please leave a message after the tone.' Beeep!

Cullen tightened his grip on the phone and stared through the glass to the Alba corridor outside, a hulking local man and an Asian woman walking past. 'Sir, with reference to my last voicemail, I really need your help.' He ended the call and stared over at Jain. 'Getting anywhere?'

'Michaela Queen's not answering.' Jain shrugged as she pocketed her mobile. 'I saw you shit a brick back there when he mentioned Rob Thomson.'

'Was I that obvious?'

'You were.' Jain sucked air through her teeth. 'The Schoolbook case, right?'

'Forgot you worked it. Thomson's ex-wife was victim number one. Then Buxton found his girlfriend's body in his flat, him next to it. Not sure how well he'll react to us pitching up.' Cullen got out his throbbing mobile. 'This'll be Crystal.'

Text from Rich: *A lady never names her sources.*

He hammered out a reply. *Is it Tom?*

Just a zipped mouth icon in response.

He scowled at it for a few seconds, then texted Tom. *Did you tell Rich about what happened at Alba Bank?* He waited a few seconds.

A text popped up. *Alba? What do you mean? What's happened?*

Cullen tapped out another text to Rich. *Need to know your source.*

A knock on the door. Lorna tugged her hair behind her ear. 'I had to collect one of your colleagues from downstairs?'

Buxton entered the room, wearing a business suit. No beard. 'Sarge.'

Cullen smiled at Lorna. 'Can you give us a minute?'

'Sure thing.' She shut the door, the metal digging into the carpet.

'Where's the beard, Si?'

'Must've lost it.' Buxton rubbed a hand over his smooth face. 'Four months of growth down the sink. Literally.'

Jain snapped her compact shut. 'You look a lot younger without it.'

'Cheers.' Buxton grinned at Cullen. 'Did an Abraham Lincoln on the way down.'

'It's either that or a Metallica, right?'

Jain rolled her eyes. 'Did Methven send you over?'

'Grabbed me before I started my shift. Says I'm a short-term loan as an ADC. "Don't get used to it, Constable." Guy knows how to make a man feel wanted.'

Cullen nodded at Jain. 'Chantal, can you get back to base and get stuck into the drugs?'

'Got a tenner I can roll up?'

'Very funny. Annoy Anderson till he gives you what you want.'

Jain pretended to scrawl in her notebook. 'Take a leaf out of Scott's book.'

Buxton roared with laughter. 'Brilliant.'

Cullen winced. 'And get everything you can on Elsbeth and Amber.'

'Will do.' Jain hefted up her handbag and left them to it.

The door rattled open. Methven perched on the edge of the desk, staring into space. 'I got your voicemail, Sergeant. You're telling me you've got previous with this Robert Thomson?'

Cullen wrapped his hands around a cooling coffee beaker, looking

away across the meeting room to the corridor outside. A group of Alba
Bank employees chatted. 'The Schoolbook guy killed his fiancée and
ex-wife. Must be almost three years ago. We tried to frame him.'
'*We* did?' Methven dropped his pen onto the rim under the
whiteboard. 'Was this your cowboy antics?'
'Not mine, sir. My DI at the time.'
Methven glanced at the door and winced. 'Bain?'
'Him.' Cullen folded his arms and exhaled. 'Rob sued Lothian
& Borders, as was.'
Buxton cleared his throat. 'He settled out of court, though,
Sarge.'
Methven shot him a glare. 'Why do we need to speak to
Thomson?'
'He's a suspect. Sounds like Van de Merwe was trying to sack
him.' Cullen took a slug of lukewarm coffee. 'I'm worried about
what'll happen if I speak to him.'
Buxton raised his eyebrows. 'I'm happy to—'
'Back-up's here, Sundance.'
Cullen clamped his jaw shut, his stomach lurching. What the
fuck?
DS Brian Bain leered at him from the doorway. He'd regrown
his moustache, thicker than when Cullen worked for him. His hair
had filled in from a skinhead, enough for a little flick at the front.
Still the same reptilian menace in his dull eyes. He handed a
coffee to Methven and sucked on his own. 'What're you fuckin' up
now?'
'Jesus Christ.'
Methven nodded thanks. 'DCI Cargill went cap in hand to
DCS Soutar. She got Glasgow South MIT to free up DS Bain and
DC McCrea—'
Cullen shifted his gaze between Methven and Bain. 'With all
due respect, sir, what the hell are you doing?'
'I beg your pardon?'
'Come on, Sundance. Haven't you missed me?'
'This'll just throw petrol on the fire, sir.' Cullen couldn't look at
Bain, locked his eyes on the floor. 'He's the reason Thomson sued
us, sir.'
'Can't you fuckin' look at me when you speak about me?'
'This is me trying.'

'Sergeants!' Methven held out his free hand. 'You are to work together, do you understand?'

Cullen finished his coffee and dumped the container in the basket. 'Sod it. I'll go see Thomson myself.' He stabbed a finger at Bain. 'Keep him up here.'

13

Rob Thomson stretched back in his chair, headset clamped to his skull. Still looked like he would know his way round a combine harvester.

Cullen let out a deep sigh and shut his eyes for a few seconds. He reopened them and sucked in a breath as he knocked on the door.

'Come!'

Cullen pushed through the door, heart fluttering.

Thomson switched his focus from the Caffè Nero across the wide corridor to glance over at Cullen. He did a double take. Then held out the microphone. 'Sorry, Pauline, something's come up and I need to dial out. I'll catch up offline.' He stabbed a finger at the phone, tossing the headset onto the desk as he stood. 'What the fuck are you doing here?'

Cullen raised his hands. 'The alternative's much worse, believe me.'

Thomson slumped down in his chair, the leather creaking. He focused on the floor and raised his gaze. Shot it back down again. 'Why the fuck should I help *you*?'

Cullen collapsed into the seat opposite. 'Because I fought tooth and nail to clear your name.'

'Bullshit.'

'Almost lost my job over it. I found out who killed your fiancée and ex-wife. That got you off. Because of what I did, he's over in Shotts for the next forty years.'

'They've got names. Kim and Caroline.'

'I know.'

'You expect me to believe this tale?'

'I don't care if you do or don't. It's the truth.' Cullen took out his notebook. 'Do you ever visit him?'

'Every month. On the third. Just to see that fucker inside there, suffering. It'll never be enough but it takes a tiny bit of the sting away.'

'How's your son?'

Thomson picked up a packet of Rizlas from his desk and rolled a cigarette, tipping in tobacco from a pouch. 'Jack's living with Caroline's folks up in Carnoustie. I still see him when I visit my parents.'

'It's good you're back at work.'

'Only way I could cope.' Thomson licked the underside of the paper and folded it over. 'You can't act like we're fucking mates, pal.'

'I'm sorry about what happened.' Cullen gazed at the smooth ceiling for a few seconds, then focused on Thomson, his eyes watering. 'I was involved with a girl at the time. He took her and tortured her. I saved her, but it broke her apart.'

Thomson put the roll-up in the pouch. 'Am I supposed to applaud you?'

'I lost a colleague.'

'Well done, hero cop. That's what the papers called you, right?' Thomson pushed his cigarettes away. 'You never reached out to me. Why bother now?'

'I need to speak to you as part of our investigation. Got a few questions about Jonathan van de Merwe.'

'That wanker.' Thomson shook his head. 'Good riddance.'

Keep him talking... Cullen narrowed his eyes. 'When was the last time you saw him?'

'Friday's status meeting.' Thomson rubbed his neck. 'Had a big ding dong with him.'

'About what?'

'Usual shite. Guy was a complete wanker.'

'So you've no idea why he'd be in his underpants on Dean Bridge at—'

Thomson burst out laughing. 'What?'

'You think it's funny?'

'I've got a different view on the world these days.' Thomson fiddled with his headset, righting it on the desk. 'Look, I hated the guy. He was a bully and a liar, but I didn't kill him.'

'Why all the antagonism?'

'Because that daft bastard kept pushing things too far. Kept cutting our budget and headcount. They gave us shite requirements and we were supp—'

'Who did?'

'That American prick Broussard. Has no idea what the fuck he's doing.'

'What's a requirement when it's at home?'

'It's how the business tell us what they want the system to do.'

'The business?'

Thomson flicked up his eyebrows. 'It's what we call the end users.'

'I see. Go on.'

'It'll be things like, it must let them search by name, put a valid postcode in, validate age from date of birth. All that stuff.'

'With you now. What do you do with them?'

'We use them to design and build a system. We try to do things properly here, but IMC and the previous idiots were complete cowboys. No requirements or just the most minimal rubbish you've ever seen. '

'Why is that bad?'

'Because they cut corners. Speed things up.' Thomson jabbed a finger in the air. 'And don't get me started on Schneiders, either. They're a bunch of yes men charging three grand a day for the privilege of lying to us. If you wonder why we've overspent, look at them.'

'You've overspent?'

'I haven't. Van de Merwe had. I know a few people in the PMO—'

'That's Michaela Queen's team, right?'

'Good luck getting hold of her.' Thomson flicked up his eyebrows. 'She gave him some bad news, so he told her to go on holiday.' He reached for his tobacco. 'The IMC bill was higher than he'd expected. Like, a lot. I heard Van de Merwe was thinking about sacking IMC, even though they've only been here since January.'

'What?'

'Yup. They're supposed to save money and deliver faster. What these clowns never get with offshoring is you can't replace one UK-based guy on four hundred quid a day with an Indian guy on a hundred. You need at least four offshore for every one they replace here. You need more guys onshore to manage the whole process. My costs have *doubled*.'

'Really?'

'Aye. And those Indian clowns are utter shite. Look, I'm not being racist here, okay? If you tried to offshore from India to here it'd be the same. It's a fool's game.'

'So why offshore?'

'Because it worked for some American bank in 1996, when it was ten quid a day for Indian resource. And you could get the pick of them. Ever since then, it's been a law of diminishing returns. Unless you throw something massive at them, you'll get piss-poor resources back.'

Cullen jotted it down. 'While we're talking about rumours, I heard your position's under threat.'

'That's bullshit. I'm a permanent member of staff and my boss knows how much of a disaster this programme is.'

'Thought it was a success...'

'Pissing four hundred million against a wall isn't success.'

'Alan Henderson told me the total budget was three hundred million.'

'So, you see what I'm dealing with here.' Thomson rolled his eyes. 'They're rushing things and it's just not working. Why do you think this programme keeps slipping? They've massively over-spent and now they're forced to do it on a shoestring. It's completely fucked.'

'Yardley suggested you had a grudge against Mr Van de Merwe.'

Thomson bellowed with laughter. 'That's brilliant. The only thing I'd do is go to *Private Eye* about this clusterfuck. Tell them how much money we've pissed up the wall on this disaster.'

'Why don't you?'

'Because I believe in this bank. I want to do everything possible to deliver this programme.'

'So who'd want him out of the way?'

'Vivek Sadozai.'

'Why?'

'If they lose a fifty million quid contract, it's his bollocks on the chopping block.'

CULLEN GOT BACK to the meeting room and opened the door so hard he hit the wall. No Bain or Methven, just Buxton fiddling with his phone. 'On your lonesome?'

'You'll break the glass if you're not careful.' Buxton dropped his mobile on the desk. 'Bain and Crystal are speaking to Henderson again. Get anything?'

'A few nuggets. Second time Vivek's name has come up.' Cullen checked the seats for one to collapse into.

A knock on the door followed by the carpet digging up.

'Morning, boys.' James Anderson scowled up at Cullen, a good six inches shorter than him, patches of stubble along his jawline flanking his greying goatee. His curtains haircut needed a good wash. A SOCO suit hung from his waist, flapping behind him. 'Heard you were here. Quite the big boy, now you've got your extra stripe.'

Cullen tried to stand up even taller. 'Found anything in his office?'

'Might get some DNA and prints. Sent the computer off to Charlie Kidd.'

'He'll love that.'

'Your wee Indian lassie's been nipping my boys' heads.'

'That's what I asked her to do.'

'You're a fu—'

Another knock on the door, still open. Vivek. He stepped into the room, his hair now dry. 'Sergeant, you called me?'

Cullen motioned towards a seat. 'We've got some questions, if you don't mind?'

'Right.' Anderson wandered off.

Vivek sat in the chair, arms folded. 'What do you want to know?'

'We understand IMC were in danger of losing the contract here.'

'That's incorrect. We're the only ones VDM could rely on to deliver.'

'So why am I hearing these rumours?'

'That's what happens here.' Vivek took off his glasses and misted the lenses, rubbing them against his shirt. 'The programme is red.'

'Red as in red, amber, green?'

'Like traffic lights. Red means it's in bad way.'

'So, it's stopped?'

'It's in danger of slipping. All the milestones are red.'

'What's a milestone?'

Vivek snorted. 'We mark out tasks on the plan. Some of them we call milestones. It lets us track progress. The key dates have delayed at least six months since we started here. It'll take another year, at least. Which means a lot more money.'

'Why?'

'The requirements we got from Cranston were terrible. We couldn't do anything with them. I called it out at VDM's status meeting. He told us to just get on with it.'

'Have you got any proof of this?'

'I could dig out the minutes.'

'That might help.' Cullen made a note — *Follow up.* 'Was there any other reason?'

'The environments from IT were always late.'

'Environments?'

'I mean the server where we do our development. IT provide these to us. Supposed to be on Alba Bank kit, but we had to use the cloud to meet the timescales. Bringing them back in will add months to the programme end date.'

'I'll take your word for it. Did Rob Thomson handle this?'

'Yes.' Vivek shook his head. 'He kept blaming us. VDM just told us both to shut up and get on with it.'

'You seem to have a lot of resentment towards him.'

'VDM said do things cheaper and faster. All the time. Every

single assumption we'd made blew up. Everything took longer. There's no governance on this programme.'

'What do you mean by that?'

'Someone has to look after all the cowboys. Make sure milestones are met. Manage the risks and issues. Deliver dependencies on time.'

'Whose job should that be?'

'Michaela Queen.'

'And she's not around.' Cullen made a couple of notes next to her name, just about running out of space. 'So you'd say she's not doing her job?'

'Van de Merwe and Yardley got in her way, put so many obstacles in the way that she *couldn't* do it.'

'Why didn't you mention any of this earlier?'

'I can only apologise.'

'We'll need this in a statement.' Cullen handed him a card. 'I trust you can find your way to Leith Walk police station?'

'Of course.' Vivek left them to it, eyes locked on the card.

Buxton sat on the edge of the table. 'What the fuck's going on in this place?'

'They all hate each other. And they're all covering their arses.'

'You got any suspects?'

'I've not ruled anyone out yet.'

An alert chimed on Cullen's phone. He checked it — *Lunch with Sharon at 1*. 'Ah, shite.'

14

'You missing the beard?' Cullen marched down Leith Walk, flickers of sunshine clearing the mid-May gloom.

Buxton ran a hand across his smooth face. 'I'm just glad it's not December, mate.'

Cullen passed the posh furniture shop and café, glimpsing the station round the corner, the glass and chrome glinting.

Sharon stood outside, a brown paper bag in her hands. 'Get away from me!'

'Let him go!' A woman in her early twenties stabbed a pudgy finger in the air at Sharon. She wore a tight dress, white with red polka dots, hugging her chubby body. Barely five foot tall, she looked at least that wide. 'He's done nothing!'

'I'm warning you, I will arrest you for assault if you persist with this.'

The woman slapped a hand across Sharon's face. 'You bitch!'

'Shite!' Cullen sprinted down the street.

'That's it.' Sharon dropped her shoulder bag and grabbed her attacker by the wrist. She pushed down with her other forearm, digging into her triceps. The woman swivelled round in front of her, landing face down on the ground. Sharon put a knee in her back. 'I warned you!'

Cullen stopped a few feet away. 'Do you need any help?'

Sharon pointed at two nearby uniformed officers with her free hand. 'Arrest her!'

They jogged over and hauled the woman to her feet. 'Come on.'

Sharon dusted herself down and crouched to collect both bags. 'Shite, I've got tea all over my bloody sandwich.'

'Let's go to a café.' Cullen helped her up. 'My treat.'

'Fine.' Sharon nodded at Buxton. 'Weird seeing you back in a suit. I miss the beard.'

'Don't get used to it.' Buxton grimaced as he took the spoiled bag from her. 'What am I supposed to do with this?'

'Bin it.' Cullen pointed up at the station. 'Get the team together for quarter past two, will you?'

'Sure thing, boss.' Buxton trotted up the steps.

Cullen gripped Sharon's hand and led her back up the street. 'Who was that?'

'Beth Graham. Kyle's darling wife. Doesn't believe her husband's been raping young men.'

'That's a hard message to take.' Cullen opened the door to the café and clocked a pair of stools in the window. He offered her the pick of the seats and sat next to her, grabbing a menu. 'This where you got your lunch from?'

'Last ham salad, too. Think I'll have a soup.'

Cullen checked the sign above the counter. Tomato and bean. He caught a passing waitress's eye. 'Two soups, please.'

She scribbled in her pad and walked off.

Cullen put the menu down again. 'How's it going?'

'We're not getting anywhere with Graham.'

'He's still denying it?'

'Until the end of time. I agreed an extension with Campbell but we need to arrest him today. Methven got round to telling me you're off the case.'

'Doesn't waste any time, does he?'

Sharon reached into her bag and took out a wad of papers. 'Finally got a profile of our rapist.'

He flicked through the pages. 'Wouldn't mind having a look at this.'

'Even though you're no longer on the case?'

'I'm still interested.'

'What's Crystal got you working on?'

'This banker's death.'

'Must be hard to have sympathy for the victim.'

'Sympathy for the devil, more like. Spent a morning up at Alba Bank getting the square root of hee-haw done. They all hated him.'

'Least you've got Budgie back, though.'

'Keeps me out of mischief, I suppose.' He took his bowl of soup from the waitress. Beans and sprigs of parsley sat on a red splurge, a slice of seeded bread hanging off the side of the plate. 'When I was there, I met Rob Thomson.'

She dropped her spoon. Red splashed up. 'You're kidding.'

'Nope. Brought a lot of stuff back.'

'You okay?'

'I'll live. And Crystal's rustled up Bain.'

'Scott, quit it. I don't believe you.'

'I'm serious. Him and McCrea, though I've not seen him yet, thank God.' Cullen dipped his bread into the soup. 'When do you think you'll finish tonight?'

'Next Wednesday.'

~

Buxton waved a hand in front of Cullen's face. 'Thanks for turning up on time, Sarge.'

Cullen looked up from Sharon's profile. His team stood there, Buxton, Eva and Chantal Jain. 'Shite, the update.' He folded up the profile and took a second to think as they sat. 'You should all know we've got Simon working for us on secondment for a few days. Let's get straight into your updates. Eva?'

She flipped open her notebook and reattached the elastic at the bottom. 'Chantal asked me to look into Elsbeth van de Merwe. Don't think there's much there, though. Before Edinburgh, she lived in London. Three last-known addresses all check out.'

'And Amber?'

'Going to check the alibi this afternoon.' She turned the page. 'The street team have spoken to his neighbours and people at the sports club. They've re-interviewed everyone we did yesterday. Neighbours say he kept himself to himself.'

'This is a summary.' Jain passed over a sheet of paper. 'Guy doesn't have many friends.'

'Tallies with what I hear.' Cullen checked the page. 'Three lines?'

'There's just not a lot on this guy.'

'Have we got anyone running over his Schoolbook profile? Twitter? LinkedIn?'

'Charlie Kidd's pulling Schoolbook for me.' Jain adjusted her scrunchy. 'I've had a look at the others this morning. My sister posts absolutely everything that happens to her. Photos, updates, location, the whole lot. Van de Merwe's the complete opposite.'

'So he's quiet?'

'No Twitter account. LinkedIn has three hundred-odd contacts, but it's all recruitment agents, that kind of thing.'

'Can you and Eva dig into that? Just see if there's anything anomalous.' Cullen noted the action. 'What about his drugs?'

'Still with the SOCOs for analysis. They're confident we can track them back to a dealer.'

'That's unusually bold for them.'

'That Owen guy bored the tits off me about this new machine the drug squad paid for. I'll let you know when they get anything.'

'What else?'

'I've looked through his bank accounts.' Jain held up another sheet. 'The only thing was a payment for a hundred grand, later reversed.'

'Where did it come from?'

'Don't know. Could be a genuine error.'

'Could be something else, though. We know he might've been messing about with offshore accounts.'

'Still nowhere on that.'

'Right. Keep digging.' Cullen glanced over at Eva. 'Have you got hold of Michaela Queen yet?'

'Nowhere on that, Sarge. Her and this Wayne Broussard.'

Cullen stared at Eva. 'Have you called him?'

'The number you gave me went straight to voicemail. Message was recent, though, said it was a week ago last Friday.'

'Thanks for that.' Cullen stood up and stretched out. 'Another update at six, okay?'

Jain folded her arms. 'What have you two got to share?'

'Basically, Van de Merwe was running a big IT project. Nine-figure budget. Lots of staff, including two third-party suppliers. Don't think there's much in it, with the possible exception of our old chum Rob Thomson.' Cullen nodded at Buxton. 'Simon can tell you all about it. I need to update Methven.'

'Anything else you want from us, Sarge?'

'Get me copies of the street team's statements. Cheers.'

Jain made a note. 'I'll see what your last slave died of.'

~

BAIN FINISHED the last of his energy drink, "WakeyWakey" graffi-tied in green on the side. He crushed it and chucked it at Methven's office bin. A spray dribbled across the carpet. 'Doesn't feel like you're doing much, Sundance.'

Cullen held his gaze, fists clenched. 'I seem to be the only one doing anything.'

'Same old fuckin' Messiah complex.' Bain scratched his moustache, flakes of skin wafting up into the air conditioning. 'Got your work cut out with this boy, Col.'

'Keep your opinions to yourself, Brian.' Methven got up from his desk and strolled over to the whiteboard. 'Can we go through our list of suspects, please?'

'That's the thing, sir.' Cullen leaned back in his chair. 'They're all suspects.'

'They can't *all* be.'

'Every single person we've met at Alba Bank has some kind of a grudge against Van de Merwe.'

'You've got motives, Sundance. Just fuckin' missing the means and opportunity.'

'I'm serious. We've been there all morning...' Cullen drummed his fingers on the desk. 'There's something going on. Haven't got to the bottom of it. But we will.'

Methven uncapped a pen. 'Start with the basics.'

'Well, it sounds like the programme's in a mess, for starters. Delays to the schedule, arguments over ownership and delivery. Fights with IT and the delivery partner. Sounds like Van de Merwe was pushing things too far.'

Methven clenched his eyes shut. He opened them, narrow slits.

'Neither Mr Yardley nor Mr Henderson mentioned this when we spoke to them.'

'They're not likely to. We got this from Vivek Sadozai and Rob Thomson.'

'Why are we hearing different opinions?'

'That's what I'm trying to work out, sir.' Cullen glanced at Bain. 'We need to speak to Michaela Queen, their equivalent of DS Holdsworth.'

Bain narrowed his eyes. 'What else's that Thomson boy been saying?'

'Just how bad it's been.'

'That's fuckin' helpful.'

Methven smacked the pen down on the board's rim. 'Brian, do you ever stop swearing?'

Bain smirked. 'Just in front of brass, Col.'

Cullen gritted his teeth. 'Thomson told us Van de Merwe was trying to sack IMC, the offshore company.'

Methven jotted it on the board. 'That can't be drilling, can it?'

Bain coughed into his hand, eyes betraying a laugh. 'Offshore IT development, Col.'

'Right, right.' Methven noted it, his ears reddening. 'What did this Vivek have to say on the matter?'

'He blamed the mess on Schneider Consulting and Rob Thomson.'

Methven tapped the pen against his teeth. 'Well, I can see where you're coming from. Lots of angles here.'

'Van de Merwe's management team is full of people he's worked with before. Jobs for the boys.'

'Not necessarily a bad thing, Sergeant.'

'It's open to abuse, though. Lots of conflicts of interest.' Cullen checked his notebook. 'Deeley's still ruling out suicide?'

'Like that case we had at New Year, we're lacking a note, amongst other things.'

'There are easier ways to top yourself than taking a header off that fuckin' bridge.' Bain stood up and leaned against the wall, hands in pockets. 'Lot of people have survived that fall over the years.'

'Indeed.' Methven prodded the whiteboard, eyes on Cullen. 'What's next, Sergeant?'

'Still need to speak to Wayne Broussard.' Cullen glanced round at Bain, fiddling with his phone. 'What about you?'

'DS Bain wanted to review the crime scene and the body before we move on.'

Bain tapped his nose. 'How I like to work, Sundance.'

Cullen clenched his teeth. 'Well, I'll see what evidence I can rustle up here.'

15

Cullen powered across the station's top floor, heading for the Forensic Support Unit. A flash of white hair to the right caught his eye.

Eva Law was chatting to a wiry man, fizzing with energy. Tommy Smith, Phone Squad.

Cullen tapped him on the shoulder. 'Are you trying to get her to join your poetry club, Tommy?'

He spun round and grinned. 'She's already a member.'

She shrugged. 'I did English lit at university.'

Cullen raised his eyebrows. 'So did I. Doesn't mean I want to hear Tommy reciting Burns every week.'

Eva pointed at Smith's desk, a bagged mobile connected to a laptop. 'Tommy's pulling the calls from Van de Merwe's personal and work phones. We'll get the call log by six o'clock.'

Smith winked at her. 'Always pays to keep a pretty young lady in your debt.'

She batted his arm. 'Tommy!'

Cullen thumbed over to the back of the room. 'Need you else-where, Eva.'

'Right, sure.' She raised her eyebrows and followed Cullen across the room. 'Tommy's a good guy.'

'Just don't endure a bottle of whisky with him. And keep on top of him.'

'I prefer doggy style, Sarge.'

'Jesus Christ.'

Charlie Kidd rolled his eyes at their approach. He shook out his ponytail, greasy dark hair willowing out. His black T-shirt showed an egg shouting *"Come and have a go if you think you're soft enough"* in pink lettering. 'You can get to fuck, Cullen.'

He grinned at him. 'No way to treat an old friend.'

'Piss off. I'm always in the shite whenever you're around.' Kidd folded his arms across the egg's face. 'The Schoolbook extract's already running. I'll send it down once it's finished, okay?'

'Sounds good.'

'It's not just that we're after.' Cullen rested on the edge of the desk. 'You guys are Forensic Support, right?'

'Oh, here we go.' Kidd let out a deep sigh. 'Aye.'

'So if I needed to trace some offshore money...'

'Big Paul's the liaison with City of London police.' Kidd sniffed. 'But I'll see what I can do, so long as I don't have to speak to you, Cullen.'

'Charming. Eva's your man. Woman.'

Eva smiled at Kidd. 'Mrs Van de Merwe reckons he had some offshore accounts.'

'I'll see what I can dig up.'

'Good man.' Cullen play-punched his shoulder. 'Have you got his computers in yet?'

'Just going through his personal laptop. It's a monster. Might see if I can acquire it after we're finished with it.'

'Got anything off it?'

'Emails should be with Eva in about an hour.' Kidd winked at her. 'He gives you all the good jobs, eh?'

She flicked up her eyebrows. 'Don't I know it.'

Cullen scanned around the desk. No sign of it... 'What about the work computer?'

'Eh?'

'He works in an office, Charlie.' Cullen folded his arms. 'Anderson said he sent his work machine up here.'

Kidd logged onto his machine and tapped the keyboard. 'Well, our SOCO chums haven't delivered it yet.'

WEASEL BOB LOOKED up from his clipboard, bum fluff covering his pointy face. He grimaced. 'If you're trying to hassle Anderson, he's not here.'

Cullen leaned against the counter. 'Where is he?'

'I could tell you, but it'll cost you.'

'Quit with the games.'

'I'm serious.' Bob thumbed behind him. 'Get your wee lassie to clear off.'

Cullen glanced over at Eva. 'She's right here?'

'I mean Chantal, you numpty. She's annoying young Owen through the back.'

Cullen hefted up the partition and stormed through to the lab round the corner.

Jain skulked in the window, scowling at a male SOCO. She glanced at Cullen. 'Sarge, he's not playing nice.'

'*I'm* not playing nice?' Owen ran a hand over his bald head. 'You'll get the drugs analysis once I've finished the priority work.'

Cullen kept his focus on Jain. 'What's higher than this?'

'Drug squad work.' Owen shrugged. 'Orders came down from the Chief Constable.'

'How long's it going to take?'

'At least until the weekend.'

Cullen folded his arms. 'We've not got that long.'

Owen scratched the back of his head. 'Tough shite, mate.'

'This could be important. Any chance you could speed it up?'

'Your patter's still shite, Cullen.' Owen glowered at him. 'I'll see what I can do.'

'Charlie Kidd's not received Van de Merwe's work laptop yet.'

'Better shift that forward.' Owen scrawled on a yellow notepad. 'You lot owe me, I swear.'

'Is Anderson back there?'

'You're going over my head?'

Cullen raised his palms. 'It's about something else.'

'What?'

'The office search, for starters.' Cullen shrugged. 'Weas— Bob said he was here.'

Owen frowned and clicked his fingers. 'Think he went out to the boy's house.'

'Why?'

'Closing things off with Crystal and the wanker.'

'The wanker?'

'Your old mate Bain.'

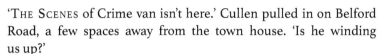

'THE SCENES of Crime van isn't here.' Cullen pulled in on Belford Road, a few spaces away from the town house. 'Is he winding us up?'

'Think they buggered the suspension in the other two.' Jain let her seatbelt ride up. 'Chief won't sign off on repairs until the second half of the year.'

'What's this force coming to?'

'Can't be called a police service if our techies can't get to crime scenes, can it?'

Cullen got out onto the street and set off towards the house, school kids screaming and shouting nearby, the reek of the brewery pungent from a couple of miles away.

Chantal stopped by the gate.

Cullen's mobile blasted out New Order. He mouthed 'Methven' at Jain as he put it to his head. 'Afternoon, sir.'

'Where the sodding hell are you?'

'I'm back at the crime scene.'

'And what the hell are you doing there?'

'Looking for Anderson.'

'Why?'

'We're running low on leads, sir. I've not got an update on the office.'

'Bain and I have just left there. He was planning on finishing the town house this evening. I need to tally up some statements with you.'

'Can we catch up afterwards?'

'Back of six.'

'Fine...' Cullen killed the call and pocketed his phone, glaring at Jain. 'You'll tell me when I start irritating the living shit out of everyone about not getting a DI post, right?'

'Like that'll stop you.' Jain grinned. 'Working for Crystal that much fun?'

'And then some.' Cullen gazed up at the house. 'Might as well have a proper look around while we're here.'

Jain opened the front door, markers dotting the entrance hall, cataloguing stains on the tiles. 'What the hell's this supposed to show?'

'Work creation?' Cullen looked up at the dark staircase, polished cherrywood. 'I only searched downstairs yesterday. Let's try upstairs.'

'That massive bowl of coke still makes me laugh.'

Cullen glanced over as he climbed up, the wood creaking beneath his feet. 'Laugh how?'

'Guy's having a midlife crisis.' Jain giggled. 'Enough coke to burn out his septum. Eva said he's got a Ferrari.'

Cullen stopped at the top of the stairs. 'Shut up.'

'They're looking at it down in Fettes.'

'What, for coke hidden in the chassis?'

'Hardly. Just in case there's any DNA in there.'

'Figures.' Cullen stared down the long hall. An antique chair looked out across north Edinburgh. The stairs at the end crept up into the attic conversion, two doors on each side. 'Can't believe this is all for one guy.'

'Money, money, money. Crystal said he was on a million a year?'

'That's right.' Cullen opened the first door on the right. 'I'll take this side.'

'Sure.' She wandered off down the corridor.

He entered an office, cables and wires entwining a large desk in the middle. Where his laptop had been. IKEA filing cabinets lined the walls. He tried a few of them. Nothing much to see.

'Scott!'

He shot back into the hall.

'In here!' Jain's voice came from the first room. He pushed into it. She sprawled on the bed, head pressed against the wall.

Cullen joined her, clocking a series of scores on the metal frame. 'What's up?'

'I can hear something from the next room.'

'Did you check the door?'

'Aye, it didn't open.'

'Locked?'

'That or the handle's just a facing. Like when windows got boarded up years ago.'

Cullen looked around. A tall closet towered next to the bed. He opened it. Just suits, shirts and—

'Wait a minute.' He stepped inside. A dark panel filled the left side, two metres tall. He tried to nudge it open. Nothing happened. Gave it a harder push.

It slid up.

Anderson blinked at the light, his SOCO suit trailing from his waist, sweat dripping from his forehead. The walls and floor in the room behind him were painted jet black. 'Thank Christ.'

16

Cullen stepped inside the room, his Tyvek suit crinkling. The mask misted against his breath. His shoes touched something spongy. 'Always said you'd end up in a padded cell.'

Anderson snorted. 'Cheeky bastard.'

Cullen shone his torch across the wall. 'What's all that stuff?'

'Leather covered in rubberised paint. You can get it all from ScrewFix or B&Q.'

'Shite.' Cullen shuffled forward to let Jain in and ran a hand across the surface. 'What were you doing in here after you got trapped?'

'Banging the walls, phoning people.' Anderson held up his mobile. 'Bloody thing's a Faraday cage. No mobile signal. Guy wants to get away from— Don't let that door SHUT!'

Jain caught it. 'Calm down, boys.' She shook her head as she wedged a drawer in the panel. 'Crystal and Bain are on their way back.'

Anderson let her past and flicked on his light. 'Can't believe that prick's back. He's even worse than you, Cullen.'

'You're a charmer.' Cullen scanned around the dark space. 'No lights in here?'

'Nope. Think there's a load of candle wax around the edges.'

'You better hope it's wax.'

Anderson smirked. 'Oh. Watch it with my black light.' He held up another device. A dull purple glow shone out of a stubby torch, splash patterns glimmering on the walls and floors, pink against the bruised glow. 'That's spunk.'

Cullen felt his stomach lurch. 'So he's had sex in here?'

'And then some. Come with me.' Anderson switched back to the torch and traipsed across the room. A stepladder leaned against the far wall. He shone up, white light flashing off an open hatch in the ceiling and started climbing the steps. 'You won't believe this.'

'I still think I'm dreaming.' Cullen let Jain go first. 'Be glad he switched off the black light.'

Jain lifted her fingers off the ladder. 'Jesus, Scott.'

'I'm joking.'

'He's right.' Anderson shone the light down from the roof. 'That ladder's like a plasterer's radio.'

Jain clamped gloved hands onto the metal. 'I'm just glad we've got these suits on.'

Cullen waited for her to clear the top of the ladder, then hauled himself up. Another dark room, cracks of light spilling in around gaps in the dormer's tiles. 'This better be worth braving that spunky ladder.'

Anderson flicked a switch and the room lit up. Four large shelving units lined the walls, crammed with BDSM equipment. Leather straps, whips, chains, ball gags.

Cullen held up a ring. 'What the hell's all this?'

Anderson swatted it from his grip. 'That's one of many cock rings.'

'Oh, Jesus.'

'You should've seen that Van de Merwe boy on the slab. Needed every extra millimetre he could get. Fucking tiny cock.'

Jain smirked at him. 'You shouldn't be looking.'

'Couldn't help it. I've got a photo if you—'

'I'm cool.' Jain got up from a crouch. 'So this is a sex room?'

Anderson switched back to the torch. 'Think it was a panic room. You know, for rich idiots to hide in when they get burgled. But he's repurposed it for BDSM activities.'

'You don't go to all this trouble for a bit of missionary.' Jain frowned. 'I can never remember what it stands for.'

Anderson dropped a ball gag. 'Bondage, Domination, Sadism and Masochism.'

'Quite the expert.'

'Piss off, Chantal.' Anderson snorted. 'Anyway, I did an inventory while I was waiting. Got straitjackets, dildos, butt plugs, corsets, hoods. Loads of ropes. An A-frame, which looks new. And enough leather gear to kit out a Hell's Angels chapter.'

Shouts came from below. 'Cullen!'

Cullen stared down the ladder. Lights flickered in the room. He rattled down the steps. 'Wait!'

Methven peered through the panel from the bright bedroom, crouched in the closet. 'Cullen?'

'Stay there.'

'I can't hear you!'

Cullen blocked off the entrance and pulled down his mask. 'I said, stay there.'

'What the fuck's going on, Sundance?' Bain clasped a hand on Methven's shoulder. 'You having a sex party up there?'

'Van de Merwe was.' Cullen pushed through into the bedroom and collapsed onto the bed, hauling off the mask. 'There's a sex room through there. Anderson got trapped when he found it. Chantal and I rescued him. Suit up if you're going in. There's an attic extension with lots of BDSM gear on the wall. Whips and chains and ball gags.'

Buxton appeared behind Bain and laughed. 'That must be where yours went, Scott.'

Bain frowned. 'Eh?'

'Someone got him a ball gag for Secret Santa.'

Bain tilted his head back and bellowed. 'That's a fuckin' classic!'

'First time he's shut up about his promotion in years.'

'Gentlemen!' Methven scowled at them. 'A little decorum, please?'

'Aye, sorry, Col.' Bain sniffed. 'So what do we think of this?'

Cullen unzipped the suit and let it drape across the bed. 'He's into BDSM. That's about ten grand's worth of equipment up there. Not to mention the cost of converting the room.'

'Plot fuckin' thickens, Col.'

Methven nodded at Cullen. 'Find out if anyone knows anything about these proclivities.'

∼

ELSBETH VAN DE MERWE opened the front door and let out a deep sigh. 'What now?'

Cullen folded his arms. 'Just wondering if I could have a word.'

'I'm busy. Can you come back later?'

'We hopefully won't be too long.'

'I'm showing some buyers around.'

'We can wait.'

'Fine.' Elsbeth led them into the house.

Cullen followed Jain into the kitchen. 'Where are your buyers?'

'Upstairs.' Elsbeth took a sip from a teacup. 'What do you want to know?'

'There's no easy way to say this.' Jain plonked herself on a stool at the breakfast bar. 'We found a sex room in your husband's house. It contained a lot of BDSM equipment.'

Elsbeth clattered the teacup back on the saucer. 'Have you spoken to Amber?'

'She backed up your story. I could ask her about whether she and your husband were into BDSM.'

She gasped. 'Listen. It's not a crime.'

'I'm not saying it is. Trouble is, it might be the reason for his death.'

'And it might not.'

'That's true. I prefer to rule things out, though.' Jain smiled. 'Did you participate in it?'

'No comment.'

'Mrs Van de Merwe, you're a suspect in a murder case. We need your cooperation. Here or down the station.'

Another sip of tea. 'There was a ... group we both used to go to. It was for consenting adults. We tied each other up. Experimented.'

'This was back in London?'

'Correct.'

'Not here?'

'For a while. Until we divorced.'

Footsteps thundered down the stairs. A man in jeans appeared, followed by a woman in a business suit. She smiled at Elsbeth. 'Thanks for letting us look around. You've got a beautiful home.'

'Is there anything else I can help with?'

'No, that's good. Bye.' They hurried through the front door.

Elsbeth glared at Jain. 'You've lost me that sale.'

'This place is on at over a million. The police being in your house won't affect the sale.'

'I need you to leave.'

'Did your ex-husband engage in these acts?'

She poured another cup of tea from a china pot. 'That's none of your business.'

'I'm not sure that's the case. He's been murdered near his home and now we find a secret sex room there.'

'How dare you?'

'How dare I what?'

'Prying into his life like this. Assuming everything's sordid and seamy. Jon could be a loving man.'

'But he did like to engage in BDSM?'

'Fine, okay. Yes, he did. Happy?'

'Was there anyone else involved in this?'

'Not in Edinburgh, no.'

'What about London?'

'I suggest you ask William or Wayne.' Elsbeth tipped her cup into the sink and dumped it on the drainer. 'Now, do you need anything else?'

'That'll do, I suppose.' Jain led the way out of the house.

Cullen smiled at Elsbeth and followed Jain out, pulling the door shut behind him. 'Well?'

'She's never going to sell it.'

'I meant about him.'

'Dirty bastard. I think I should speak to Amber again.'

'I might have another word with Yardley.'

'Going to drop me off?'

~

'THANKS FOR SEEING US AGAIN, SIR.' Cullen sipped bitter coffee through the lid and looked around William Yardley's office. Bain was staring at the confusion on the whiteboard, the number of lines and boxes more than double since the morning. 'Looks like you've been busy.'

Yardley shrugged. 'No rest for the wicked.'

Cullen rested the cup on the edge of the desk. 'We discovered a sex room in Mr Van de Merwe's home.'

Yardley tugged his earlobe. 'A sex room?'

'Full of gimp masks and what have you.' Bain swallowed some WakeyWakey. 'You and he never talked about it?'

'Never came up.' Yardley wiped a bead of sweat from his forehead. 'We didn't have that sort of relationship, I'm afraid.'

'You hiding something?'

Yardley raised his hands. 'I swear I'm not.'

'What's with the sweating?'

'I don't know what you're talking about.'

Bain stood up. 'Let's take this down the station.'

'Wait.' Yardley gripped his desk. 'I don't know anything about this.'

'Really?' Bain took a step towards Yardley, leaning over him, and folded his arms. 'Mr Van de Merwe never talked about his sex life?'

'Like I said, it was just work. Always work. Never time for anything else. He made me miss my son's birthday last year to review the offshore partner pitches. Jon liked me because I made things happen.' Yardley pulled a paper tissue out of his drawer and mopped his forehead. 'He'd come in here at half six every night and we'd talk about who'd let us down. We'd formulate plans for the next day. That's it. I swear.'

'So you didn't socialise together?'

'Just when it suited him. He delegated things like client entertainment to me.' Yardley slicked back his hair, soaked through. 'He'd get me to go to functions put on by Schneider or IMC or other suppliers. Some bank stuff.'

'Never went for a pint?'

'Jon was much more of a wine and whisky man.'

'Elsbeth van de Merwe suggested you drank with him after work in London.'

'That was always shop talk.'

'No women on the scene?'

'Not that I knew.'

'Mr Yardley.' Cullen leaned across the desk and rubbed his hands together. 'There's a team of forensic analysts round there just now. If your DNA's in one of those rooms, we'll find it.'

'Jon kept his private life private, okay?'

'Elsbeth suggested we speak to you.'

'What Jon and Elsbeth did in their own time is no business of mine.'

'You weren't party to these activities?'

'God damn it, no. I'm a happily married man.'

Cullen glanced at Bain draining his can. 'We've still not heard from Wayne Broussard. Reckon he'll know anything about it?'

'Those guys go back to college. Wayne was a Rhodes scholar during his Masters at Princeton. Jon was an undergrad at Oxford. They met at some ball or something.'

Cullen stared at the ceiling. Sounded plausible. 'Have you any idea when Mr Broussard's due in?'

'Check with Lorna.'

~

CULLEN STOPPED around the corner from Yardley's office and glanced at his phone.

A text from Tom. *Aye, OK. Give me 10mins. Canteen downstairs.*

He pocketed it and glared at Bain. 'You weren't much use back there.'

'Got the prick to talk, didn't I?' Bain dropped his can into a bin set into a bench. 'Sweaty bastard.'

'Think he's lying?'

'That or he's feeling the heat. Big man's gone, he's on the fuckin' hook for this shite until they bring in someone competent.'

'What was Crystal wanting to check with me earlier?'

'Fuck knows, Sundance.' Bain got out his mobile and checked the display. 'Fuckin' years till I get back home. Apinya's going fuckin' mental.'

'Thought you'd separated from your mail-order bride?'

'Shut your fuckin' mouth.'

'Sorry.' Cullen raised his hands. 'You'd split up, though, right?'

'Well, we're back together. Expecting a boy in August.'

'You ever see your other son?'

Bain took a step forward, almost touching his forehead to Cullen's. 'I've not got a son, okay?'

Cullen stepped back. 'If that's how you deal with it.'

'That's the only fuckin' way.' Bain shook his head. 'We need to find this Broussard prick.'

'Agreed.' Cullen started off down the corridor. 'Got an idea of someone who might know.'

Around the bend, Lorna stuffed her iPad into a flower-patterned handbag. She looked up. 'Do you still need that meeting room?'

'I don't think so. Can we have a word?'

'I've really got to dash.'

'It's urgent.'

Lorna shrugged on her coat. 'Make it quick.'

'His speciality.' Bain grinned and held out a hand. 'DS Brian Bain.'

She shook it, a smile flickering across her lips. 'What's up?'

Cullen gave him a scowl. 'Do you know when Mr Broussard's due back?'

'Not till next week. Can we do this tomorrow?'

'Why tomorrow?'

'I need to speak to the Schneider guys. They go back to their offices at the other end of George Street every night.'

'Why's everyone here so evasive?'

'You get used to it.'

'How close were you and Mr Van de Merwe?'

'Distant, like I told you.'

'We found a sex room in his house.'

'Oh my God.' She clamped a hand over her mouth. 'Really?'

'I take it he didn't talk about it?'

'No!'

Cullen smiled. 'I'll let you go, then.'

'Thanks.' She grabbed her keys and trotted along the corridor, heels clicking on the flagstones.

'Well worked there, Sundance.' Bain watched her go. 'Doesn't have a fuckin' clue, does she?' He narrowed his eyes. 'Wouldn't kick her out of bed for farting, mind.'

'You reminded me of Keith Miller there.'

'Fuck off, Sundance. She's getting on a bit, though.'

'She's about my age. How old's your missus?'

'Twenty.' Bain shook his head at him. 'Right, what's next?'

'Do you want to update Crystal?'

'What're you going to do?'

'Got a potential lead.'

'You're still a sneaky little fucker.'

17

'They must be doing well.' Cullen stared across the empty street, the Alba Bank pyramid towering above. He swapped his phone to the other hand. 'There's nobody here at six o'clock.'

Jain sighed down the line. 'One of their execs has just died, Scott. Give them a break.'

'How's it going back there?'

'Waiting on our Lord and Master to return.'

'Isn't Methven there?'

'Not him, you. You wanted to catch up before you speak to Crystal.'

'Shite. Can you speak to him and push it back to half past?'

'Christ, Scott, you need a PA.'

'Don't I just. How'd it go with Amber?'

'She wasn't there. Neither was her alibi.'

'Suspicious?'

'Maybe. Got another delay on the drugs.'

'Even after I spoke to that Owen guy?'

'Maybe because. It's Monday at the earliest now.'

'I'll speak to Anderson. Anything else going on?'

'Got copies of the statements from the street teams for you.'

'Anything in them?

'Nobody saw a man in his pants.'

'Well, it was half three in the morning.' Cullen spotted a familiar figure trudging down the corridor. 'Look, I'd better go. See you soon.' He pocketed his phone and got up, hand out. 'Evening, sir.'

'Hey.' Tom Jameson thudded down on the wooden seat, the material groaning. Didn't shake his hand, just dropped his laptop bag to the floor. He let his suit button go and his belly unfolded. 'You're looking well, Skinky.'

'Can't say the same about you.'

'Need to get back on that diet.' Tom glanced down at his gut. 'Why is it you only get in touch when you need something?'

'It's not like that.'

'Of course it is. I've not spoken to you in months. Since you moved out of the flat, you've become the Scarlet Pimpernel.'

'I've been busy.'

'Being a sergeant.' Tom shrugged off his coat. 'What are all these texts about?'

'Did you see the paper this morning?'

'Rich's big scoop? Barely speak to him, Skinky.'

'But you share a flat.'

'He's a tenant, that's it.'

'You didn't leak it to him?'

'I didn't find out about this guy's death until I got briefed at our daily stand-up.'

'I don't even want to know what that is. So it's not going well with Rich?'

'We've got into a groove where he pays me his rent and we keep away from each other.'

'It's that bad?'

'I'm just winding you up. We get on fine. He came for a drink at a team night out a couple of weeks ago.'

Cullen frowned, tilting his head. 'Who was there?'

'Like, fifty people.'

'Did he speak to any of them?'

'Tried it on with one of the guys in the mailroom.' Tom smirked. 'Why do you want to know?'

'Because someone's leaking stories. I just wondered if that's where he found them.'

'Well, I don't think Post Jimmy's got anything to leak.'

Cullen cracked his knuckles. 'How's he been?'

'Busy. Stressing out about getting sacked. Working on a book as well as doing his day job.'

'Crime fiction, right?'

'Don't pay much attention, to be honest. Says it's like *The Wire* but set in London.' A frown flickered across Tom's forehead. 'Why the meeting?'

'Wanted to pick your brain about this Van de Merwe guy.'

'Mate of mine got chucked onto that programme. Works for Rob Thomson. From what I hear, Van de Merwe was a total wanker. Not well liked. At all. Could sell sand to the Arabs, though.'

'Ever hear anything about BDSM?'

'BD-what?'

'Sado-masochism.'

'Nope.' Tom frowned. 'Why?'

Cullen glanced around the empty space. 'I didn't tell you this, but we found a sex room in his house.'

Tom shook his head. 'What a guy.'

'Never hear anything sordid about him?'

'Not about that.'

'What have you heard?'

'My mate got this from one of the Schneider guys. When they were pitching for this, they took Van de Merwe out in London for the weekend. Went to a Chelsea match — corporate box and all that jazz. Few boozers in Soho, then a titty bar. Think they had some coke and the like. Van de Merwe was out of his skull and fired into a lap dancer at some place in Mayfair. Kicked up a stink about wanting to have sex with her.'

'Sounds like an idiot.'

'Then they took him to their hotel. Got a few girls in from a brothel.'

'Jesus Christ.' Cullen jotted down a note. 'And they just told you this?'

'My mate, remember. Not me. Got it after a few shandies, when the truth serum kicked in.'

Cullen underlined *Brothel*. 'Anything else?'

'There was a corporate gig Schneider ran up at the Caledonian for their Edinburgh clients. "Scottish Consultancy of the Year

Awards" or some nonsense like that back in February. Anyway, Van de Merwe turned up with this girl on his arm. Local, dolled up. Next week, Schneider hosted another one, a kickback for some clients. Lower key. Bottles of prosecco and decent red. Nibbles. Van de Merwe got Yardley to go instead. He pitched up with Van de Merwe's girl.'

'Seriously?'

'Couple of their directors were at both events.'

'Isn't Yardley married?'

'Wife lives down in Peebles with his kids. He's got a flat in the New Town.'

'Dirty bastard.' Cullen tapped his pen off the page. 'Was this girl called Amber?'

'Cindy, something like that. She's an escort. Guy said she was a lap dancer. Works in a bar on Lothian Road. Don't know which one.'

'Classy.' Cullen shook his head as he made a note. 'I need to get this in a statement.'

'He'll not speak.'

'I meant from you.'

'Oh, for fuck's sake.'

'Tom, get down the station soon.'

'THIS'LL DO.' Buxton pulled in on some double-yellows on Lothian Road, just across from the Filmhouse. Stuck an "On Official Police Business" sign on the dashboard. 'Which one do you think?'

Cullen looked out at the three lap-dancing bars. Bottoms Up and Wonderland on the street level, the Ambassador sauna on the first floor. 'Eeny, meeny, miny, moe.'

Buxton cleared his throat. 'Careful there, Mr Clarkson.'

'Eh?'

'Someone leaked Jeremy Clarkson using the N-word on a *Top Gear* rehearsal the other night.'

'I'm not falling for that.'

'Don't you read the news?'

'Try not to.'

'Bloody hell.' Buxton got out his phone. 'Here, I'll—'

'It's okay, I believe you.' Cullen stared at the bars again. 'The sauna's the least likely one, right?'

'Best place for a hand job, not a lap dance. Bottoms Up's less classy than Wonderland.' Buxton pointed down the street. 'Club Rouge down there.'

'There's a couple of places at the end of Princes Street. And the pubic triangle.'

'Quite the expert.'

'Shut up.' Cullen chuckled, narrowing his eyes as he calculated. 'I'm thinking Wonderland. It's the newest and most upmarket. A big shot would go there.' He frowned. 'Used to be a model shop, didn't it? Radio-controlled cars and train sets.'

'Different type of models now.'

'Boom, boom.' Cullen got out onto the street, busy with Monday-night drinkers.

Buxton walked up to the door and nodded at the bouncer. 'Evening.'

The doorman gave a curt nod and stepped aside for them, looking about five stone lighter than the usual front-of-house security. 'In you go, gents. Pay on the left, please.'

Cullen followed Buxton up to the counter.

A woman sat behind it, chomping on gum. 'Ten quid, boys. Each.'

'Police.' Cullen showed his warrant card. 'Wouldn't mind having a word with your staff.'

'What about?'

'It's in connection with a case.'

'Heard that before.' She rolled her eyes and pressed a button. 'Head through the turnstiles.'

Cullen nudged it. The metal dug into his thigh before it gave. He pushed through a door into a long hall, a stage filling the wall facing the street, booths lining another two. An empty dance floor flashed in the far corner.

He made for the bar.

A lumbering giant was cleaning some glasses, a pint of Guinness settling in front of him, thin arms poking out of a designer T-shirt, stretched tight across a large pot belly. His beard was a series of pencil dashes, his neck shaved. 'What can I get you, like?' Polish accent mangled by Edinburgh patois.

'Police.' Cullen held up his warrant card, then switched to a print of Van de Merwe. 'Has this man ever visited here?'

The barman inspected the photo. 'Looks very familiar. Definitely been in.'

'His name's Jonathan van de Merwe.'

'Got it.' The barman frowned at the photo again and clicked his fingers. 'Mr VDM. That's what he asked us to call him. Mr VDM. Used to come in at least once a week. Big player. Bought lots of champagne.'

'Did he have any favourite girls?'

'Everybody likes everybody in here.'

'What about a Cindy?'

'Cindy? Don't have a Cindy here.'

Cullen glanced at Buxton. 'Thanks for your time.'

'Could it be Candy?'

Cullen spun round. 'She ever dance with him?'

'Couple of times.' A leer. 'More than a couple of times.'

'She on tonight?'

He pointed over at the booths. 'Second from the left.'

'Cheers.' Cullen nodded and left him to his drying cloth, wandering over to a table at the far end surrounded by chatting girls. 'Candy?'

'That's me.' A woman raised a hand in the gloom, head and shoulders above the other girls. Tanned legs and arms, dark hair in pigtails. Red school tie, white blouse struggling to contain her chest. Very Britney Spears. 'You pair don't look like you're paying for anything.' Fife accent, long vowels masked by pronouncing the Ts. 'Cops?'

'Very insightful.' Another flash of the warrant card. 'Wondering if we could have a word with you about Jonathan van de Merwe.'

She sniffed. 'What about him?'

'When was the last time he was here?'

'Can't remember.'

'Need to speak to you in relation to his murder.'

She frowned. 'His *murder*?'

'We found his body yesterday morning.'

'Jesus Christ.' She kneaded her forehead. One of her colleagues massaged an arm. 'I'm saying nothing.'

'It's just a few questions.'

'And I told you I'm saying nothing.'

'Right, let's head down the station.'

'Suits me.' Candy gave a shrug. 'I'll call my lawyer first, though.'

18

Cullen stopped in the doorway and stared across the Incident Room. Virtually empty, just Holdsworth by the whiteboard. He nodded at Buxton, as he sat at the meeting table. 'Where is everyone?'

'Bain ordered them back out on the street. Bet you regret moaning about resource.'

'I needed it for me, not for him to arse about with.'

'He must have photos of Soutar and a donkey or something.'

'Don't say that out loud again, Si.' Cullen retrieved his notebook. 'Where the hell's my team?'

Buxton prodded his phone's screen and put it to his head. 'Yeah. In the Incident Room. See you soon.' He dumped the phone on the table. 'Just finishing up an interview.'

Cullen stretched out and looked through his notebook. 'My actions list never seems to go down.'

'How do you cope?'

'Prioritise the ones Crystal will chew my balls over.'

'Fair enough.'

'It's not. I need to get more organised.'

The door flew open and Jain stomped across the room, Eva following. She sat next to him and opened her orange notebook. 'Where've you two been?'

'Just up at a lap-dancing bar.'

Eva frowned. 'Are you serious?'

Buxton smirked. 'Got a suspect in number Three waiting for her lawyer.'

'While we're waiting, I need an update from you lot.' Cullen smiled at Jain. 'Anything on Amber?'

'Finally got hold of her.' Jain flicked through her notebook. 'Spoke to her colleague as well. She's in the clear. Alibi checks out. Doesn't know anything about cock rings and ball gags.'

'Our suspect was seen at an event with Van de Merwe. Was he seeing Amber then?'

'They were finished by August, Sarge.'

'Fine. What about Elsbeth?'

'Looks clear. Sister confirmed the alibi with some Met officers.'

'Good.' Cullen scanned through his notes. 'Anyone found Michaela Queen?'

'Not yet.' Eva darted her eyes between Buxton and Jain. 'Got another angle that might work.'

'What about Schoolbook?'

'I'm looking at the stuff from Charlie, but I'm not getting anywhere.'

Jain dumped her notebook on the table. 'We were just interviewing a Tom Jameson.'

'Thanks for doing that.'

Jain clicked a finger. 'He's why you were up Lothian Road?'

'Yup.' Cullen switched his gaze to Eva. 'What about the mobile stuff from Tommy Smith?'

'Still waiting for that.'

'Need me to chase it up?'

'Said it'll be first thing tomorrow. Drug squad found a load of burners. Orders from the Chief.'

'Fine.'

Buxton stood to answer a call, turning away.

Cullen turned the page, spotting just one open item. 'What about the offshore accounts?'

Eva nodded. 'Reached out to the City of London lot a couple of hours ago.'

'You reached out?'

Eva blushed. 'Sorry. I spoke to a DI Coulson. Said he's confident he'll get it back to me tomorrow.'

'Good work.'

Buxton held up his mobile. 'That's the lawyer turned up.'

'CANDY, CANDY, CANDY...' Cullen got up and paced the interview room. He stopped by the door and locked eyes with the Custody Officer, a mountain of scar tissue and thread veins, thin rivers of red filling his cheeks. Then switched focus to Candy. 'You need to speak to us.'

She twitched a nostril. 'I'm saying nothing.'

'You've not even given your real name.'

'I'll remind you that's not an offence.' Alistair Reynolds looked barely out of high school, let alone a qualified lawyer. A fresh welt of acne covered his face. 'You've yet to charge my client with anything, so I suggest you let her leave.'

'We need to validate statements we've received concerning her—'

'—involvement with a murder case.' Reynolds yawned. 'I know, I know. She doesn't have to comply with your requests, though.'

Cullen thumped the desk. 'A man's been murdered.'

She looked up, grinning. 'That supposed to frighten me?'

'Candy, I just want to find out who killed him.'

'You think I did?'

'Have we said that?'

'Not yet. I didn't kill him.'

Cullen sat, leaning back in the chair. 'I need you to help us out.'

'What's in it for me?'

'If you comply, you get out of here.' Cullen checked his watch. 'It's half seven. I imagine Mr Reynolds will give you a lift to your place of work.'

Reynolds nodded at her. 'If that's what you want to do.'

Candy let her body sag, tanned arms hanging by her side. 'Fine.'

'We understand you accompanied Mr Van de Merwe to a business function.'

'Maybe.'

'I'd prefer a straight answer.'

'VDM asked me along to some corporate thing at the bank.'

'VDM?'

'What he told me to call him. He liked me. Had a few dances every couple of nights.'

'He ever try to pay for anything else?'

She narrowed her eyes. 'I'm a dancer, not a *whore*.'

'What about William Yardley?'

'Who?'

'We gather you attended another corporate event on his arm.'

'*Him*? His wife was out of town. VDM suggested he take me. Got five hundred quid for it.'

'Did you do anything with him?'

'I was his escort. Nothing more.'

'You sure?'

'Positive.'

'Did either man try it on? Wandering hands, that kind of thing?'

'They were perfect gentlemen.'

'You ever see them again?'

'Not Yardley.'

'But you saw Mr Van de Merwe?'

She lowered her gaze to the table. 'VDM kept coming into the club. Stopped about six weeks ago.'

'Did he ever mention anything kinky to you?' Buxton coughed. 'Handcuffs, bondage?'

'I'm. A. Dancer.' She let out a deep breath. 'What is it with you two?'

'You never visited his house?'

'Once.' She nibbled her lip. 'Before we went to this thing at the Caley hotel, we had a cocktail at his house. Nice place.'

'Did he suggest doing anything? Sex? Drugs?'

'Wee bit of rock 'n' roll. Boy played a mean sax.'

'Very good. Did you ever see any drug paraphernalia?'

Candy flicked her hair out. 'He snorted a line when I was there.'

'Cocaine?'

'It looked like it. Didn't have any, though. I'm a good girl.'

'Did you have sex with him?'

'We've been over this...'

'You just went there for a cocktail in his living room?'

'That's what I said.'

'Where were you on Saturday night, Sunday morning?'

'Until when?'

'Let's focus on half past three.'

'I was in bed.'

'Can anyone confirm that?'

'I'd need to figure that out.'

'What do you mean by that? Thought you're just a dancer.'

'And I am, it's just...' She looked away.

'Sounds like you're making it up.'

'It's ... complicated.'

Cullen waved over to the Custody Officer. 'Take her down to Holding, would you? Charge her with—'

'Wait!'

'—obstruction.' Cullen stood up. 'I've got to brief my DI.'

'I said wait.'

He sat again. 'I'm listening.'

'Look, I'm not being funny here. I don't want to lie to you. I think my boyfriend was with me, I need to check with him.'

'So he can give you an alibi?'

'Look, I was at my flat. Do you want the address?'

'Sergeant.' Reynolds leaned across the table. 'If you want to question my client as a suspect, you need to detain her. She's losing income while you keep her here for spurious reasons.'

Cullen glanced at Buxton and got a shrug. 'Fine, but I want you back here tomorrow morning, okay? First thing, with an alibi we can start to tear apart.' He smiled at Reynolds. 'You can take your client to work.' He left the room, smiling at the Custody Officer. 'I'll let you escort her out.'

The Custody Officer grunted in reply.

Cullen waited for Buxton to shut the door. 'Well?'

Buxton raised his hands in the air. 'Don't think she's involved.'

'Dead end?'

'Probably. At least we know the coke's his. Other than that, she seems clean.'

'*Seems.* Check out her background, aye?'

'Do you need anything else from me, sir?' Cullen got up, snapping his notebook shut.

'Just to say I'm impressed with your progress in the role so far.' Methven leaned back in his office chair and stared up at Cullen. 'I knew it was the right move to promote you.'

Cullen rubbed at the fire in his ears. 'Thanks.'

'Unlike DS Bain, who's done nothing other than take up all my sodding time.' Methven pursed his lips. 'The only thing he's achieved is obtaining a second witness statement placing Mr Van de Merwe on the bridge at half three.'

'That's the first I've heard.'

'That's what I wanted to speak to you about earlier.'

'Right, I see.'

'A drunkard from Orchard Brae saw him with this figure in the cloak. Thinks it was a woman but he wasn't the most sober. The facial composite going out hasn't jogged anyone's memory, either.'

Cullen sucked air through his teeth. 'His wife wasn't in Edinburgh. Amber was at work.'

'They confirmed this bondage stuff, though?'

'Elsbeth did. Don't know where that leaves us. Neither are suspects, sir. Besides Candy, we've got nobody else.'

'Candy? Why would she do it?'

'No idea. Buxton's looking into her background.'

'It seems a tad far-fetched.' A spotlight caught one of Methven's stray eyebrows as he turned to the side. 'Look, I've got a hell of a day tomorrow. Can I ask you to deputise the DC interviews?'

Cullen frowned. 'Is that allowed?'

'It's the art of delegation, Sergeant. I'll lend you some books on the subject.'

'What I mean is, I'm Buxton's sponsor.'

'And I need you to be impartial, Sergeant. I can trust you on this, I know it.'

'Well, I'll see what I can do.'

Methven patted Cullen on the shoulder. 'Go home, fresh in for seven.'

'Sir.'

'And make sure we rule out this Candy girl ASAP.'

19

'Jesus, Si.' Cullen rested his forehead against the wall in the corridor, tempted to headbutt it. 'What do you mean she's gone?'

'I'm at Wonderland just now.' Buxton's footsteps clattered off slabs. 'Candy never turned up.'

'What happened after she left here?'

'I spoke to the PCSO. Big Chris. Said her lawyer drove her off. I called Reynolds, says he dropped her outside Wonderland.'

'Shite.' Cullen thunked his head off the plaster a couple of times. 'Call me when you find her.'

'Will do, Sarge.'

'Cheers.' Cullen pocketed his phone and wandered into the empty Obs Suite. Collapsed into the chair in front of the bank of monitors. On the leftmost screen, Sharon and DC McKeown were interviewing the woman from earlier, the one who'd slapped Sharon. What was her name? Beth Graham? Head down, eyes shut, make-up slithering down her chubby cheeks.

'Mrs Graham, I need you to confirm your statement here.' Sharon looked up from her notebook. 'Shall I read it back to you?'

Beth raised a shoulder. 'Whatever.'

'My client wishes you to proceed to reading out the statement.' Her lawyer let his glasses drop to the chain around his neck. 'Please.'

'Very well. Your husband, one Kyle Graham of Meadowfield Terrace, Edinburgh, was present with you on the evenings of the twenty-fifth of April, the thirtieth of April and the third of May. You were, respectively, at the cinema, watching a DVD and walking on the beach at Portobello on the dates in question.'

Beth gave a slight nod, wiping a tear from her cheek. 'That's right.'

'You're aware this is an official police document. If this alibi is later proven to be false, you will be prosecuted.'

'I get that. I'm not lying.'

'Thanks for your time.' Sharon rose to her feet and walked over to the door. 'You'll be escorted out.'

'I'm sorry.'

Sharon frowned. 'What for?'

'Slapping you. It's been a difficult few days. I'm trying to get pregnant and it's not working.'

'Apology accepted.' Sharon slammed the door behind her.

Cullen waited for the equal and opposite explosion of the Obs Suite door opening. It smacked off the filing cabinet. 'That went well.'

'For Christ's sake.' Sharon collapsed into the seat next to him. 'She's given him an alibi for all of the rapes.'

'But you still think he did it?'

'He's gay and she's in denial. You saw what he was up to in that club on Saturday.'

'You didn't answer the question. Being gay doesn't mean he's raped anyone, does it?'

'No. We've got to let him go.'

'Back to square one?'

'Aye.' She held his hand. 'How's your day been?'

'Buxton took me to a lap-dancing establishment.'

She let go of his hand. 'Scott, you'd better be winding me up.'

'It's part of the case.'

'It had bloody better be. Don't want me to fire up the lathe, do you?'

'I thought we'd had enough *Fifty Shades* stuff.'

'How's Bain been?'

'Keeping his powder dry. I'm just waiting for the eruption.'

Cullen pinched his nose. 'Crystal's asked me— Sorry, he's *told* me to do the interviews for this DC position.'

'The one Budgie's going for?'

'Aye.'

'Methven can be such a fanny.'

'What do you mean "can be"?'

DAY 4

Tuesday
20th May

20

Buxton dumped a coffee on the desk. 'Here you go, Sarge.'

Cullen lifted it up. Black cup with white lid, a red star etched in marker. 'What's this?'

'My treat. Got you a posh one from that place on Broughton Street.'

'Why?'

'For getting me off the beat.'

'Right, so you've still not found Candy?'

'Rumbled.' Buxton leaned against the desk and took a sip. 'They've got nothing on her at Wonderland. Nobody there knows much about her.'

'Shite. She's cleared off, hasn't she?'

'Well, I spoke to six of her colleagues. Nobody heard about spanking or rogue fingers from Van de Merwe.'

'Quite the gentleman. What about those escort gigs?'

'All they know about is her attending the functions.'

Cullen tore off the lid. The latte's delicate feathering had remained mostly intact despite the walk over. 'Cheers for this. Even though I don't like lattes.'

'Shite.'

'It's cool. I need to get more calcium.' Cullen rubbed his teeth. 'My gums are receding.'

'Is that going to fix it?'

'Dr Google said so.'

'Classic.' Buxton sipped through the lid. 'I've got my interview at eleven.'

Cullen hid his face behind the cup and stared over at the whiteboard as he swallowed. 'For the DC gig?'

'Yeah. Shitting myself.'

'You'll be fine.' Cullen checked his notebook, open at the actions page. 'Did you get the meeting minutes from Vivek?'

'He sent them over last night. Went through them after I got back from Wonderland.'

'Anyone would think you're trying to impress.'

'Nobody was here, though.' Buxton shuffled through a wad of papers on the desk. 'Dry reading, mate. Poor guy kept on calling out the low standard of requirements.'

'What do you mean by "kept on"?'

'Every single meeting.' Buxton waved the papers. 'Thirteen different occasions. Guy's a broken record.'

'But they've been there since the start of the year. That's once a week, isn't it?'

'Looks like that.'

'Who was there befo—'

'Cullen!'

He swung around.

Methven stormed across the Incident Room, waving a copy of the *Argus*. 'What the sodding hell's this?'

Cullen caught it, the folded paper connecting with his throat:

Banker Death — Sex Dungeon Link

Cullen checked the byline. Rich again. 'I swear this has nothing to do with me.'

'You used to share a flat with him, didn't you?'

'Up to a year ago, aye. We're both from Dalhousie, if you want to throw that one at me, as well.'

'Don't you sodding get smart with me.'

'Look, you honestly think I'd mess up my career just so he gets a story?'

'I've seen it happen.'

'You're not seeing it happen here, okay?'

Methven jangled keys in his pockets. 'I've asked DS Bain to bring this Richard McAlpine in for questioning.'

'You sure that's wise?'

'Unless you've got another idea of where this juicy little tidbit's come from?'

'He's not answering my calls or texts anymore.'

'We need to make sure there's nothing sinister going on here.' Methven folded his arms. 'DS Bain's our best bet.'

'What, are you—'

'I've cancelled this morning's briefing. Have you got a statement from Candy yet?'

'Si's just tracking her down.'

Methven stabbed a finger in the air. 'I want her in an interview room by lunchtime.'

'I'm not promising anything.' Cullen watched him stomp off across the room and glanced round at Buxton. 'Think the stress is getting to him?'

'Maybe. Not sure you should be pushing him, though.'

'No, you're probably right.' Cullen grabbed his coffee and a sheaf of papers. 'Be back at lunchtime. I've got to see someone about something.'

'Let me guess, a man about a dog?'

'Not really.'

'Who?'

'Never mind. Just find Candy.'

PEN IN MOUTH, Cullen pushed the other CVs to the far side of the table and sifted through the police records of the candidates. Helen Armitage had been a naughty girl in her teens. Surprised she'd been let into the force. He scribbled a note in the margin of the interview questions pack and sat back to look around the canteen. The queue was as short as it'd get this early. Another coffee wouldn't go amiss.

'What do you mean I'm barred?' Bain gripped the counter at the front. 'This is supposed to be a service!'

Barbara stabbed a finger at him. 'Cut out the swearing and I'll let you back.'

'Oh, for fu—'

'See? Can't stop yourself!' She pointed to the door. 'Out!'

Bain headed over to Cullen, hands in pocket, scowling at everyone he passed. 'Morning, Sundance.' He hovered by the table, arms folded. 'It was a bastard getting through here for seven. Can't believe that fucker canned the briefing. Could've done with another hour in my scratcher.'

'Tell it to someone who cares.'

'You cheeky scamp.' Bain dropped a two pound coin on the table. 'Any danger you could get me a coffee?'

'You sound like a wee ned outside an off-licence.'

'That bitch makes me feel like it.' Bain sat next to him. 'Can't believe this case. All that effort for a fuckin' *banker*.'

'Even bankers are human beings.'

'You reckon?'

'Someone's been killed. Our job's to find out who did it.'

'If all you want's a puzzle, Sundance, you should take up crosswords.'

'Does it matter if it's a heroin addict in Wester Hailes or a Lord Advocate out in North Berwick? If someone's dead, we—'

'—need to find out who did it. Aye, I get it. Fucking bastards took down the economy, Sundance.' Bain stared at the papers. 'What's that?'

'Crystal's asked me to do the DC interviews.'

'Aw, look at you all grown up.' Bain grabbed a sheet. Held it at arm's reach. 'Think I know this bird.'

Cullen snatched it back. 'Stop mucking about.'

'Who's the favourite?'

'Buxton. Two years as ADC. The best of the others has six months.'

'Two years and he didn't fuckin' make it, though.' Bain laughed. 'Your boyfriend's shite, Sundance.'

'Times have been tough. They didn't replace me when I got this DS gig.'

'Aye, that's cos that prick Turnbull nicked it off McCrea.'

'It's not all bad. He took a stripe off you.'

'Shut it.' Bain sneered at him. 'Buxton's your mate. How are you going to handle that?'

'I'll treat everyone fairly.'

'Can't believe he's getting away with pulling this sort of clown shite.'

'Take it you're not getting on well with him?'

'Methven's a fuckin' arsehole, pure and simple. Running around pretending he knows what he's fuckin' doing. Told him last night I've got fifteen years as a DI if he wants any coaching.'

'How'd he take that?'

Bain picked up his coin. 'Told me to go home.'

'How do you feel about your demotion?'

'Shut it.'

'Come on. He was behind it, not Turnbull.'

'I asked for it, you know.'

'Bollocks.'

'I'm fed up of the politics, Sundance. I just want to solve cases. Likes of Methven are welcome to play *Game of fuckin' Thrones*.'

'I don't believe you.'

'DS wage plus overtime's enough for me. Got my pension locked in at the DI rate and got them to include my OT.'

'Wonders'll never cease.'

Bain looked at the counter. 'Right, that fuckin' battleaxe's gone on her break.'

DONNA NICHOLS LOOKED up from her interview pack, eyes lined. Hair in a bun, trouser suit. 'Can you describe a time when you've had to take on a leadership position?'

PC Helen Armitage let her eyes wander around the room. Dark hair, severe glare. Clenched jaw. Perfume, something generic. Lots of it. 'Okay. I worked six months as ADC in DS McMann's team. There were a few times when he asked me to give the status update at DI Lamb's morning briefing.'

Cullen jotted down a few words. *No leadership skills shown.* 'I see on your record how you were arrest—'

'I'm asking the questions, Sergeant.' Donna smiled at Armitage. 'How often was this?'

CULLEN DRUMMED his fingers on the table. 'PC Buxton, why aren't you wearing your uniform?'

Buxton flashed a frown. 'Because I've been seconded to work plainclothes in the MIT.'

'Before we go through the competency-based part of the interview, can you tell us why you think you're suited for the DC role?'

'I had two years as an ADC in DSI Turnbull's Edinburgh Major Investigation Team.'

'But that's only been in operation since April last year.'

'That's right. Nine months in the MIT. Fifteen in Lothian and Borders CID.'

'Why didn't you get a full tenure?'

'There was a reorganisation and austerity cuts.' Buxton cleared his throat, the frown deepening. 'My record's solid.'

⌁

DONNA SMILED ACROSS THE TABLE, eyes cold. 'PC Allison, can you outline how working for traffic makes you suitable for a detective role?'

'Aye, eh.' Ginger-haired, mouth slack and open with his tongue hanging out. A few spots dotted around his acne scars. He coughed. Sniffed. 'I deal with a lot of crimes and, eh, manage my caseload.'

⌁

WILL TRAYNOR WAS BARELY twenty but stubble dotted his bald skull. At least six foot six. 'Does that answer the question?'

Cullen sat back in his chair and glanced at Donna, shaking her head. He smiled at Traynor. 'That's fine. Do you have any questions for us?'

Traynor got to his feet. 'That's good, eh?'

Cullen nodded. 'Thanks for your time.' The door wobbled shut. 'Jesus Christ.'

Donna clicked her pen and dropped it on her interview pack. 'What a shower.'

'Buxton's the clear favourite.'

'You think?'

'Don't you?'

'I'm not sure about his record. Two years as ADC is a long period without full tenure.'

'It's a lot of valid experience in a trying time. Shows commitment.'

'The first one impressed me the most.' Donna shuffled through the papers. 'PC Armitage.'

'She's got a criminal record.'

'Which we addressed when she joined the force eight years ago.'

'I don't think she even passed the interview, let alone deserves a full tenure. Can't imagine having her in my team.'

'PC Buxton worked for you, didn't he?'

'That doesn't stop me recommending him.'

'What do you mean?'

'I'll send an email to the board when I get back to my desk.'

'Sergeant, we're interviewing three more candidates tomorrow.'

21

'Think I've stretched my stomach.' Cullen pushed his plate away across the table, red lasagna grease glistening, and nudged the china against the hard wood tray. 'That was too much for lunch.'

Sharon looked up from her own plate as she speared a shard of iceberg with her fork. 'You could've had a salad.'

'Should've done.'

She bit into the lettuce. 'How's your morning been?'

'Interviews. Buxton was the best candidate by a country mile, but—'

'But you're sponsoring him and you need to be impartial?'

'That.'

'I'm sure you'll sort something out.' She chewed on the iceberg. 'Methven's given me some more of your time. Another victim interview at three o'clock.'

'Jesus Christ. I've got my own caseload as well as these bloody interviews.'

'He didn't seem to mind.'

'Why me?'

'Rhona's in hospital. Maternity check. She did get clattered on Saturday night.'

Cullen reached across the table to caress her hand. 'You okay about that?'

'She's had more sexual offences interview training than you, so of course I'm not happy.'

'I meant about her going for a check on her baby.'

She sipped her coffee. 'I'll talk when I'm ready, Scott.'

'You used to get on at me for not talking about what happened with Keith and Mandy and ... Alison.'

'And you talked. Well done. You don't have to change Fluffy's cat litter for the next month. Happy?'

He glanced around the canteen at the healthy-eating slogans, then at her blouse, arms lost in baggy fabric. 'We should've swapped lunches.'

Sharon's fork clunked to the plate. 'What's that supposed to mean?'

'You're getting too thin.'

'Is that why you don't want to fuck me?'

He shut his eyes and rubbed them. Then stared at her. 'Of course I still want to ... make love to you.'

'You sound like a Barry White B-side.'

'I want to make love *with* you.' Another glance at her arms. 'It's just ... I'm worried about you.'

'I'm glad somebody is.'

'Look, I'm being serious. I want you to talk about losing a baby.'

'It's not that, Scott.' Water welled in her eyes. 'That's not all there is.'

'Are you keeping something from me?'

She looked away, gasping against the tears. 'No.'

'Come on, Sharon. Be honest with me.'

She wiped the back of her hand across her face. 'Not here.'

'Let's get a meeting room. Or go to a pub or sit in your car.'

'I'm not in the mood.'

'Look. I want to talk to you about what's going on. We *need* to.'

She grabbed his hands, wrapping her fingers around them, cold and clammy. 'Let's go out for dinner tonight.'

Cullen frowned. 'Like a date night?'

She laughed. 'I hate the term, but aye.'

'It's a deal.'

'Remember, room three at three.' She checked her watch, the face rattling round to the back of her wrist. 'You've got an hour.'

〜

'LET ME GET THIS STRAIGHT.' Cullen leaned back in the chair and stared at the meeting room ceiling. Not one of Leith Walk's best rooms. He shut his eyes for a second, let out a breath, and looked at the team, one by one. Eva, Buxton, Jain. 'I've been flat out all morning and you're telling me we're no further on?'

Jain undid her scrunchy, her hair dropping to her shoulders. She ran a hand through it. 'We can't all be super cops like you, Scott.'

'It looks like you've waited till teacher's out of the room to start mucking about.'

'We've been busy all morning, *Sarge*.' Jain glanced at Eva, then Buxton. 'Everything on this case is blocked. One wee step forward, then we can't get any further forward for a week. You know how it is.'

'Do I?' Cullen folded his arms. 'Right, what's your biggest problem?'

Eva gave a smile. 'Charlie sent me the Schoolbook stuff. There's no fresh leads from any of it.'

'What are you telling me?'

'Here we go again.' Jain tossed her pen on the table with a clatter. 'The only thing we got is a Google+ account. It's a stub because of his Gmail account.'

'Have you requested the Gmail account?'

'Need a warrant for it.'

'So, have you asked for one?'

'I was waiting for you.'

'Chantal, can you take it up with DI Methven for me?'

She picked up the pen, clicking it and scrawling a note. 'Fine.'

Cullen focused on Eva, mainly to avoid looking at Jain, his ears burning. 'What else?'

'I've got the mobile bills from Tommy Smith. Started going through them, but there's nothing of note so far.'

'Keep going.'

'The drugs are still stalled.' Jain stared at her notebook. 'I spoke to Owen and we agreed you and Anderson still need to have a chat.'

'I'll get round to it. What about the bank accounts?'

Eva shrugged. 'Still waiting for the details from the City cops.'

'"Details" is a bit vague.'

'He's got a list of possibles. Needs me to get security clearance so I can look at them.'

'So do it.' Cullen waited for Jain to look at him. 'Chantal, can you help out with that?'

'Right, *Sarge*.'

Cullen nodded at Buxton. 'You've been quiet.'

'Had something to do this morning, as you know.'

Cullen switched his focus between them, sucking in a deep breath. 'Come on, guys. I need more application from the three of you.'

Jain arched a plucked eyebrow. 'Is that us dismissed?'

Cullen let out a sigh. 'Fine.'

Jain stormed off, Eva following close behind.

Buxton stayed. 'You should've warned me.'

Cullen looked over at him. 'About me interviewing you?'

'No, about Chantal and Eva having a lesbian fling.' Buxton shook his head. 'Of course I meant about the interview. Why didn't you tell me it was with you?'

Cullen ground his teeth, one of the molars spearing pain. He winced. 'Because Crystal threw me into it.'

'This morning?'

'Last night.'

Buxton folded his arms. 'You definitely should've told me, mate.'

'Look, Si, I've got to be professional here, okay? He told me to make sure the right candidate gets in.'

'So it's not me. Great.'

'I didn't say that. I need to show complete impartiality.'

'It's going to be that bird in McMann's team, right? Helen.'

'I'm recommending you.' Cullen leaned across the table. 'The other three were bloody awful.'

Buxton exhaled, smiling. 'Thanks, mate. That's great to hear.'

'There are more interviews tomorrow.'

'Hope they're all shit.' Buxton stood up and shoved his hands in his pockets. 'You coming?'

Cullen winked. 'Just the way I'm sitting.'

'Jesus Christ, you sound more and more like Bain by the day.'
Buxton left the room, shoving the door open.

'Just a sec, Si.'

'What?'

'Are you getting anywhere with Candy?'

'Picked it up again after the interview. Halfway through all ten
lappies in Edinburgh city centre. No sign of her.'

'Let me know as soon as you find anything.'

'Of course.' Buxton stormed off down the corridor.

The joys of rank.

Cullen felt the flutter of his phone in his pocket and fished it
out. Text from Rich. *Who's the barbarian you sent after me?*

Cullen replied. *You've got to stop printing this stuff. I'm in the shit
here.*

His phone buzzed again. *I'm saving my job, mate. Desperate times
and all that.*

Bloody hell. He tapped out another text — *Who's your source?*
— And waited for a reply, eyes locked on the mobile. He gave up
after thirty seconds.

Who was giving him this stuff?

∽

Sharon stopped outside interview room three, the light above
flickering. 'I'm leading here, okay? You're just supporting.'

Cullen squinted against the broken strip light. 'You sure you
need a DS for this?'

'I need someone competent. DC Lindsay hasn't proven himself
yet. Don't start me on McKeown.'

'You can have Chantal Jain.'

'Are you serious?'

'She's getting right on my tits.'

'Don't make that formal, because I will take her.'

'I'll think about it.' Cullen opened the door and stopped,
frowning.

Kyle Graham hunched over the side of the table, hugging his
arms around his torso.

Cullen spun round. 'Thought you let him go?'

'We did.' Sharon entered the room, taking the chair opposite

Graham. She pressed record. 'Interview commenced at fifteen oh four on Tuesday the twentieth of May, 2014. Present are myself, Acting DI Sharon McNeill, and DS Scott Cullen. Also present is Kyle Graham.'

Graham didn't look up, staying focused on the table. 'I don't need a lawyer for this, right?'

'Mr Graham, this is an interview to determine the events of last night. Thanks for agreeing to meet us.'

'I want you to catch this guy.'

Sharon smiled at Graham, eyebrows inverted. 'We're trying our hardest.'

Wasted on him, his eyes now shut.

'Please take us through what happened last night.'

'After you let me go, Beth and I went for a meal. I bumped into a couple of my mates.'

Cullen looked up from his notebook. 'What were their names?'

'Brian Craig and Will Hart.'

Sharon shot him a look, then focused on Graham. 'What happened next?'

'Beth and Keith got cabs home. Me and Will went for another drink. One turned into many. We ended up in a club.'

'Which one?'

Graham wiped his nose. 'The Liquid Lounge.'

'Again? What were you drinking?'

'Jägerbombs.'

'Then what happened?'

'Next thing I know, I woke up back in my flat. My arse felt like it'd been... There was blood all over the sheets. Fucking every-where. The pain was ... excruciating. Beth took me to the hospital. I saw Dr—'

'We'll come to that in a minute.' Sharon leaned forward on the desk. 'How did you get home?'

'I've no idea. I don't remember anything after the first drink.'

'Were you in pain the night before?'

'No.'

'Did Mr Hart see you leave?'

'I called him this morning. He left about midnight, needed to get home for work.'

'You don't remember seeing him?'

'Nope.'

'What were you doing when he left?'

'I can't remember. He said I was dancing.'

Cullen's phone thrummed in his pocket, on mute. He let it ring out. 'Do you remember speaking to anyone else last night? Bar staff? Bouncers? Someone in the toilet? At the next table, maybe?'

'I don't remember much in the club. Just doing shots. I've had flashes of dancing. Bits of music.' Graham glared at him. 'Someone spiked my drink. The doctor did a blood test. Can't remember what she called it, but it's basically Rohypnol.'

'Mr Graham, what else happened at the hospital?'

He sat back and exhaled. 'She did a rape kit on me.'

'Did they find anything?'

'Just spermicide.'

'So your rapist used a condom?'

'He tore my anus!' Graham shut his eyes, fingers hammering his eyebrows. 'I could've bled out in my bed.'

'You've no recollection of getting home?'

'None at all.'

'What about your wife?'

'She said she heard me get back at about two, maybe later.'

'You were on your own?'

'I've no idea.' Graham flared his nostrils and glowered at Sharon. 'If you'd caught whoever did this to the others, they'd not have got me.'

'I understand your anger, Mr Graham. We're doing—'

'You really should've caught him!'

'Believe me, we're doing all we can to catch him.'

Graham stood, fingers gripping the edge of the table. 'Look, if —' He sighed. 'If there's anything else you need from me, call my wife. I need to ... I need to do something else. I'm sorry.' He staggered over to the door, clutching his buttocks.

The man-mountain Custody Officer put a hand to his chest. 'Mr Graham, please sit down.'

'I'm finished here.'

He glanced at Sharon, receiving a shrug. 'You'll have to accompany me out of the station, sir.'

One last glare from Graham and he was gone.

'Interview terminated at fifteen eighteen.' Sharon ended the recording and leaned back in her seat. 'What the hell's going on with my case?'

Cullen exhaled. 'Think he's trying to throw us off the scent?'

'How easy is it to do those injuries to yourself?'

Cullen crossed his arms. 'I suppose you could lower yourself—'

'Yeah, yeah, I get it.' She shook her head. 'He'll be the death of me. Can't believe he went back to the Liquid Lounge.'

'Right place, wrong time.' Cullen held up his notebook. 'You need any of my interview notes?'

'Email me them. I'll get Rhona to speak to his doctor, given she's at the hospital.'

Cullen checked his phone. The missed call was from Buxton. 'That me done?'

'That's all for now. Send Chantal next time.'

'Charming.' Cullen got out his ringing phone. 'Si, what is it?'

'Get your dancing trousers on, Scotty. Think I've found her.'

22

'Don't see why I need my dancing trousers.' Cullen stepped out of the pool car. Looked around the beige tenements of East Newington Place.

'Cheer up, you dozy bastard.' Buxton plipped the Vauxhall and nodded at the stone façade of the tenement. 'That's her flat up there. Top floor.'

'You should've gone through me to get the warrant.'

'You were too busy doing God knows what.' Buxton crossed the road, jammed with parked cars. Buses hissed past at the end of the street. He jabbed a finger against the intercom. 'Where were you?'

'Helping Sharon.'

'Doing what?'

'Never mind.' Cullen put his thumb over the buzzer. 'She's not in, is she?'

'Doesn't look like it.'

Cullen moved his thumb to the ground-floor flat. 'We'll get in there and kick the door down.'

Static blasted out of the intercom. *'Hello?'*

'This is the police. We need access to the stairwell.'

'In you come.'

Cullen pushed the buzzing door and entered the stairwell, thick with cigarette smoke.

A small tabby cat shot up the spiral stairs, stopping to hiss back at them.

Cullen flashed his warrant card at the pair of glasses staring out of the ground-floor flat. 'DS Scott Cullen. ADC Simon Buxton. We need to speak to one of your neighbours.'

'The tart on the top floor?' The woman stepped out of the doorway and sniffed. 'Trollop has her wares always on display. Comes and goes at all hours.'

'Candy?'

'That what they call her?' She snorted and retreated into her flat.

Cullen raced up, following the tabby to the top floor, before it disappeared into a cat flap with a final hiss. 'That our flat?'

'Nah, this one.' Buxton hammered on the other door. 'Candy? It's the police. Open up.'

Nothing.

Cullen thumped the door. 'Candy, we need to access your property.'

Nothing again.

He let out a sigh, spotting the tabby peering through the flap at them. 'Have you got her real name?'

'Christine Broadhurst.' Buxton clattered the door again. 'Comes from — not sure how to say this — Lochgelly in Fife.'

'Brutal.'

'That how you say it?'

'That's right. Ex-mining town. Hard as nails there.'

'Well, this is the address she gave Sergeant Mullen when we brought her in the other night.'

'Open it.'

Buxton took a step back and launched his shoulder at the door. Crunch. It twisted on the hinge and fell forward onto the clear lino. He entered the flat, snapping out his baton. 'Dark in here.'

Cullen followed him in. Six doors led off the wide hallway. 'Let's stick together.'

Buxton flicked his baton against the first handle. An ironing board clattered out of a cupboard, bouncing off the opposite wall. He knelt down to pick it up and stuffed it back in. 'Right, next.'

Cullen snapped on a pair of nitrile gloves and tried the next handle. A bathroom, musty and dark. He nodded at the next door.

Buxton opened it. An empty kitchen. Next, an empty living room. A bathroom at the end. 'This is great fun.'

'Aye, smashing. Go on, Si. Through the last door.'

Buxton flicked his baton. 'Finally, a bedroom.'

'Wait here.' Cullen trudged into the room. A wide, metal-framed bed with white sheets. Louvre-doored cupboards. Dark wood chest of drawers. Alarm clock showing the time in green. He opened the closet. Just clothes. Dresses, skirts, blouses, jeans. A flash of red.

He pulled apart a dress and a kimono. Tore the red cloak off the hanger and held it up. 'Here we go.'

Buxton squirmed. 'What's that all over it?'

Cullen turned it round. The back side was covered in a white crusty stain. He sniffed it. 'It's semen.'

CULLEN KICKED THE DOOR SHUT, killing the noise from the rest of the crime scene lab. 'Time to pull your finger out.'

Anderson swung round from staring at his laptop, eyebrows raised. 'Your finger's still up your own arse, Cullen.'

'I'm waiting on two crime scene reports — three if you separate out the sex room. And there's our drug trace.'

'Never ends with you lot, does it?'

Cullen handed him the cloak, wrapped in an evidence bag. 'Check this, will you?'

'What the fuck is it?'

'A gateway to a parallel universe, what do you think? It's a red cloak.'

'What's that on it?'

'Spunk, I think. Run a DNA test, if you can.'

'Look, son, your boss and his little Rottweiler are doing my head in.'

'Bain?'

'Aye, fucking Bain. The pair of them keep switching my priorities every five minutes. Van de Merwe's office. The drugs. Van de

Merwe's house. His sex dungeon.' He shook his head. 'You lot need to make your minds up, okay?'

'I've been crystal clear about what I want you to focus on, haven't I?'

'You're only a DS, Cullen. A new one at that. Get your chiefs to agree with you, or at least toe the party line.'

'How's the house going?'

'Got twelve rooms to report on. Still waiting for the DNA exclusion.'

'Any early results?'

'I like to keep everything to myself, so I can hamper the investigation as much as possible.' Anderson shot daggers at him. 'Of course there's nothing.'

'What about the office?'

'Different matter, entirely. There's a million and fucking one DNA traces in there. It's going to take weeks. Even then, it's unlikely you'll get a result from it. Guy had meetings with every man and his dog in there, they're probably not suspects. Besides, it's not like he died in there.'

'Keep at it.'

'Where's it sit in the priority list? Bain had it top.'

Cullen sucked in a deep breath. 'Put it at the bottom, okay?'

'You need Methven to sign off on this.'

'Just do it. Seriously.'

'Your grave, son.'

'What about the sex room?' Cullen smirked. 'Now you've escaped, of course.'

'Get to fuck.' Anderson shut his eyes and chuckled. Then cleared his throat. 'I did a fair amount of work on that before Bain told me to refocus.'

'And?'

'Lots of DNA traces to process.' Anderson reached into a desk drawer, producing a magazine, which flopped open at a page. 'You see this?'

Cullen snatched it off him. A dark room filled with seats, splashes of purples and light blues. 'What's this?'

'It's a black light test in a San Francisco porn cinema.'

Cullen shut his eyes, his stomach lurching. 'This is horrific.'

'Well, you saw what I found at the house. It's on that scale. Bottom end, mind, but there's a fuckton of jizz in that place.'

Cullen dropped the magazine on the desk. 'You're saying a lot of people have used the room?'

'Aye.'

'So, an orgy?'

'Stands to reason he'd have one there. It's that or your pal Van de Merwe was at it every night. Boy only took over the place a year and a half ago. That's a ton of spu—'

'I get it.' Cullen got up. 'Hurry, please. And check reprioritisation with me first, okay?'

'You're the boss.'

~

METHVEN DUMPED his keys on the desk, at least twenty hanging off a silver M stamped with "Iron Man Triathlete". 'Thanks for the update, Sergeant. I want her found.'

'We're trying, sir. ADC Buxton's stepped it up.' Cullen couldn't take his eyes off the keys. 'What've you been doing?'

'Bain spoke to that journalist. Your ex-flatmate.' Methven leaned against the wall, arms folded. 'He's cleared him of spying on an active police investigation.' He thrust his hands deep into his pockets and rattled his keys. 'We don't want any more headlines like this morning.'

'And I've said I'm not stupid enough to leak leads to him.'

'Is there anything else from your team?'

'We're struggling with the numbers we've got, sir.'

'You still need more resource?'

'Stuart Murray's coming back from his holiday tomorrow. Supporting the rape unit's a real bottleneck. We didn't have any big cases when they asked for assistance. Now, we're swamped.'

Methven frowned. 'Could we give her ADC Buxton?'

'We'd have to explain to Sergeant Mullen why we've shunted one of his seconded resources onto another investigation.'

'True.'

'We could give her DC Jain.'

'She's your most senior DC, Sergeant.'

'Murray's got more experience. Besides, she's demonstrated a competency for DS activities. Let her flourish.'

'Are you suggesting we should make her an Acting DS?'

'I'm suggesting you second her and see how she gets on.'

'This is nothing to do with you not getting on with her, is it?'

'She'll do a better job on that case than this one, sir. That's all.'

JAIN CROSSED HER LEGS, arms folded, eyes darting around the canteen. 'Is being in Bollocking Corner a bad sign?'

'We're here because the meeting rooms are all busy.' Cullen glanced over at the counter, the early birds of the back shift queuing for all-day breakfasts. The salad bar was empty. 'I've got some good news for you.'

'Oh aye?'

'You're seconded to Sharon's team.'

'The rape unit?' Her forehead twitched. 'You want rid of me?'

'It's nothing to do with that.'

'Is this an Acting DS position?'

'No, but if you play your cards right...' Sweat trickled down Cullen's back. 'We deemed it inappropriate to have me support Sharon given our relationship status.'

'You've been doing this all month, though. It's not like you just started seeing each other.' She leaned forward. 'You don't rate me, do you?'

'I think you're a good officer.'

'Nothing to do with you telling Sharon I'm being a nightmare?'

He clenched his fists. 'That's one of your more positive traits, Chantal.'

'Right. Bullshit.'

'Don't talk to me like that. You need to remember I'm your line manager, not your mate down the pub.'

'After the way you spoke to Bain over the last few years?'

'Do as I say, not as I do.'

'Right.'

'I've been losing time supporting a case not on the MIT books.'

'Jesus, you're sounding more and more like Crystal.'

'Makes an improvement on sounding like Bain.' Cullen fluffed up his shirt, now soaked through. 'Come on, this is good for you. These task forces are high priority just now. If you do a good job here, well...'

'Dangling a carrot, eh? Remember how much of a bitch you were about that, Scott?'

'Chantal...'

'Wouldn't stop moaning about it. All the shite me and Angela had to put up with.' She made hand puppets and screwed up her face. 'All that, "I passed my sergeant's exams and caught a million serial killers and they didn't promote me." Fuck sake, Scott, it was boring. And annoying.'

Cullen nibbled his lip, drawing blood. 'Look, this is a development opportunity.'

'Piss off. This is me doing your dirty work while you take the glory on this case.'

'Stuart Murray's back tomorrow morning. Want me to give it to him?'

Jain scraped the chair across the lino and got to her feet. 'I'll give Sharon a call, okay?'

23

'And here's yours, sir.'

'Thanks.' Cullen sucked in the smell of the spicy meat of his pizza, trying to drown out the drone of the restaurant. 'Looks good.'

Sharon sighed at her plate and smiled at the waiter, eyes cold. 'I ordered the chicken Caesar salad *without* the dressing.'

The waiter frowned. Then nodded. 'Why, of course.' He whisked her plate away.

'I hate it when that happens.' Sharon took a sip of wine. 'Worse if they turn up with non-decaf coffee, I suppose.'

'I don't get the point in decaf coffee.'

'You wouldn't.' Sharon pushed the wine glass across the table's pale wood. 'Don't wait for me.'

'You sure?'

'Go for it.'

Cullen sliced into the edge of the pizza, snaring two pepperoni slices and some onion. He bit into it. 'This is good.'

Sharon stared at a point between them. 'I'm glad.'

His fork hovered in the air. 'Do you want some?'

She focused on him. 'No, I'm fine.'

'What's up?'

'Just distracted by my case, I suppose.'

'You get anywhere with our friend Mr Graham?' Cullen took another bite.

'Not as such. His hospital story checks out.'

Cullen winced. 'Poor guy.'

'Doctor couldn't say whether he'd done it to himself or not. Definitely had Rohypnol in his system.'

'Jesus Christ. You've still got his wife's alibis for the other assaults, though, yeah?'

'Aye.' She smiled over Cullen's left shoulder.

The waiter presented her replacement salad.

'Thanks.' She speared a chunk of chicken and ate it, chewing slowly. 'He's in the clear on the other ones. I've got two DCs looking into his movements over the last week and interviewing the bar staff again.'

'Reckon you'll get anything?'

'We'll see.'

'You could thank me for giving you Chantal, you know.'

'Yeah, whatever.'

'Seriously? I gave you my best officer and you say "whatever"?'

'You've given me her because she's a pain in the hoop. I've got to manage her.'

'At least she's your mate.'

'Never manage friends. Worst time in my career was when you worked for me.'

'You reported to Bain, though.'

She laughed. 'True.'

He folded up a wedge of pizza and took a bite, swallowing it down with some lemonade. 'What's happening to us?'

'I don't know, Scott. Has something happened?'

'I'm struggling with all this.' Cullen dropped his cutlery. 'You're just so cold these days.'

'Is that what you think?'

'Deny it.'

'What about the other night? When you came back from work?'

'That's because I guilted you into it.'

'You honestly believe that?'

'It's the truth. I can count on one hand how many times we've had sex this year.'

'So it's having sex now, is it?' She ate a clump of lettuce. 'At lunchtime, it was making love.'

'That's almost three years we've been together. I'm wondering if we've run out of track.'

'I don't know. Have we?'

'Do you still love me?'

'Of course I—'

'I mean it, Sharon. Don't just say you do, okay? At least give me that.'

'I still love you, Scott.' She stabbed her fork into a piece of chicken, shutting her eyes as she exhaled through her nostrils. 'It's just ... hard.'

'What is?'

'I thought you'd say "not my cock" there.'

'I'm not that bad, am I?' He sipped some more lemonade, the ice cube tinkling in the glass. 'I want to help. Whatever it is. However you feel. You're not alone.'

She took a big dent out of her wine. 'Last year, I went to the—'

Her phone rang. The Velvet Underground, *Sweet Jane*.

'Sorry.' She picked it up and answered. 'DI McNeill.' Stared across the restaurant.

Cullen ate a wedge of pizza in one go.

What the hell was happening to them? She couldn't even talk to him.

Sharon pushed her plate away and stood, chucking her mobile in her purse. 'There's been another rape.'

CULLEN DROVE ON, rumbling over the cobbles on the Leith Shore, coming to a halt outside Fisher's. A rounded turret climbed four floors out of the ground-floor restaurant. The car sucked in the aroma of fish frying in butter and garlic. 'It's up there?'

'So she said.' Sharon glanced over at him and hiccuped. 'Shouldn't have drunk that wine.'

'You were off duty.'

'And now I'm not.' She let the seatbelt ride up and dug out her phone. 'Can't see her anywhere.'

The light had a thundery feel to it, sunlight bleaching the old

Malmaison building, the next-door yuppie flats set in a deep gloom.

'Must cost a pretty packet.' He looked over as Sharon stuffed the phone in her purse. 'Anything?'

She stumbled out of the car. 'Flat six.'

Cullen followed her across to the stairwell door, cream frame surrounding the black-painted wood. He hit the buzzer marked six. *C. Egan.* Gazed at the tables outside the pub. A couple near them tucked into posh burgers, foaming pints of Peroni making him salivate.

'Up you come.'

Cullen let Sharon go up first.

The flat door hung open. Jain came out into the stairwell, a grim expression on her face as she pulled the door to. 'Wish I was still on Scott's case, Shaz. This is brutal.'

'Nobody said it was going to be pretty.' Sharon covered her mouth with her fist and yawned. 'What've we got?'

'Guy says he was date raped.' Jain thumbed into the flat. 'Come on.'

Cullen waited by the living room door near the kitchen area, looking like it was the only room in the flat. Expensive stereo, wall-mounted flatscreen, Apple laptop. The bedsit for the twenty-first century.

Jain sat on the edge of the sofa by the cooker. 'Callum, we're going to need you to go through your statement again. Is that okay?'

Egan sat on the four-poster bed, kneading his temples. A long fringe swept across his forehead. Blue gingham shirt, the top four buttons open. Navy jeans and dark sandals. His hands shook as he nodded. 'That's fine.'

'You believe you were raped?'

Egan took his fingers off his skin. 'Last Friday.'

'Where were you?'

'I was out for a drink after work. Guy I sit next to. Turned into a pretty heavy night and we ended up in the Liquid Lounge on George Street.'

Jain exchanged a look with Sharon. 'What happened?'

'Someone spiked my drink. I don't remember anything after a Jägerbomb. That's usually the sign, right?'

'What happened after?'

'Someone brought me back here and raped me.'

'You didn't consent?'

'Look, the state I was in, there's no way I could've.' Egan nibbled at a fingernail. 'I'm in a relationship. My boyfriend's in Singapore on business.'

Sharon glanced at Cullen, a frown on her face. 'You're homosexual?'

'That's correct.'

'Were you flirting with any men in the club?'

'No way. I'm not the type to have no-strings sex while he's away.'

'When did you realise you'd been raped?'

'That morning. I know what it feels like to have an injury ... there.' Egan crossed his arms. 'I went to A & E.'

'You didn't report rape?'

'I was embarrassed enough.'

'So why report it now?'

He waved over at his laptop. 'I was looking at my Feedly and saw a news story.'

Cullen frowned. 'What's Fee—'

Sharon raised a hand. 'You realised you fit the pattern?'

'That's right.'

'Okay.' Sharon led out into the corridor, Cullen and Jain following. 'What do you think, Scott?'

'Time for another alibi from Kyle Graham.'

'Agreed. Chantal?'

'I'm with Scott on that. We should check with the hospital.'

'Taxis.' Cullen sniffed. 'Someone's brought him here. I'd find out if it was in a cab.' Cullen glanced back at Egan, now tapping on his iPhone. 'I think you need to have another word with the Procurator Fiscal about shutting that place down. The CCTV search isn't getting us anywhere.'

'We've not identified a suspect yet who spoke to any of the victims and was there more than once. It's got to be an inside job.'

'So we've no proof any of these guys were picked up there?' Jain scowled at Cullen. 'I can see why you dumped this onto me.'

Sharon rummaged through her bag for her phone. 'Okay,

Chantal, let's wrap up his statement, then meet the team at Leith Walk.'

Jain approached Egan, notebook out.

Cullen leaned against the wall. 'Take it you don't need me?'

Sharon shook her head. 'You'll be a spare part.'

'What about that chat?'

'Think I'll be in till all hours. When I get in.'

'Right, I'll catch the bus. Need to get into the car, though.'

'Why?'

'My pizza's in a doggy bag on the back seat.'

24

Cullen entered the busy Incident Room carrying his morning coffee, blinking against the bright lights as he collapsed into a spare seat. His phone buzzed. He reached into his pocket and checked it.

Text from Sharon: *Wanted to talk but didn't get in till two. You were sound asleep. C U tonight. Luv S*

Look forward to it. He sighed and pocketed his mobile.

'That's the mother of all sighs, Cullen.' DC Stuart Murray reached down to brush his polished brogues, stamped with an elaborate pattern. He stood up and stuffed his hands in his jeans pockets.

'You've stopped calling me "Sarge"?'

'Better start again.' Murray slumped against the wall. 'Crystal says I'm reporting to you on this banker case.'

'Shuffling the deckchairs on the *Titanic*.' Cullen caught himself before he sighed again. 'How was your holiday?'

'A distant memory now. But aye, Menorca was—'

Shouting came from the opposite side of the room.

'Listen to me, princess, I don't fuckin' care who you work for, okay? You tell *me*. Now!'

Murray frowned. 'Is that *Bain*?'

'And then some.' Cullen jogged over to the centre of the storm. 'What's going on?'

Bain swung round and focused on Cullen. Then Murray. He snorted. 'Ho ho! Look what the fuckin' cat's dragged in. Not seen you since you made a mess of that case out in banjo country.'

'Banjo country?'

'East fuckin' Lothian. Still can't get the sound of pigs squealing out of my fuckin' head, pal. Where's your boyf—'

'Brian.' Cullen stepped between them. 'What are you doing?'

Bain frowned at Cullen. 'Eh?'

'Why are you shouting at one of my officers?'

'You're not progressing anything, so I need to find out what the fuck your team are up to.'

'We've got a briefing in ten minutes to go over that.'

'And you think I'm waiting? Fuckin' pull the other one, it's got—'

'Quit hassling my team and let me speak to them. Okay?'

Bain got in his face, sickly breath washing over Cullen's skin. He licked his lips. 'We're not fuckin' done here.'

'No, we are. Piss off and get out of my way.'

'Are you going to grass to teacher again?'

'Don't tempt me.'

Bain took a step back and laughed in Eva's face. 'Be thankful for your shite in nining armour, sweetheart.'

Cullen stepped forward. 'Any problems with my staff, you speak to me. Okay?'

'Fine.' Bain wandered off, whistling a Bowie tune — "Young Americans".

Cullen nodded at Eva. 'Don't take any notice of him.'

She folded her arms. 'I can fight my own battles.'

'You shouldn't have to.' Cullen watched Bain grab his suit jacket and leave the room. 'Why was he pestering you?'

'Because I was looking for you. Needed to get another warrant for his emails.'

'Still need any help with it?'

'I'm a big girl now, Sarge. I can handle it.'

Cullen took a deep breath. 'So what was he going mental about?'

'Remember how Chantal asked me to look for Michaela Queen? She's just called me. Returning to work today.'

'When does she get in?'

'Early. Drives up from Galashiels or something. Had to stop her boring me to death about traffic.'

Cullen locked eyes with Murray. 'Stuart, can you cover me at the briefing?'

Murray slumped his shoulders. 'But I've only just—'

'Tough luck, mate.'

'WHAT DO you mean *I'm* out of order?' Cullen marched down the corridor, storming ahead of Bain. Alba Bank just after seven o'clock in the morning was as quiet as at six at night. 'You were the one bullying my staff.'

'Fuck's sake, Sundance, I wasn't bullying her.'

Cullen stopped and glared at Bain. 'I don't care what you think you were doing. She wasn't happy.'

'Stupid little princess. I'll fuckin'—'

'She's not a bad officer.'

'I meant you.'

'Any more of that and I *will* take you to Methven.'

'Now the hard man talk comes out. I'm shitting myself, Sundance.'

A man in a business suit powered past them.

Cullen got in close and lowered his voice. 'Do you want me to boot the shit out of you?'

'Quite the big man, aren't you?'

'I'm just not a bully.'

'Oh aye? Reckon you're taking on someone your own size?'

'I know that's not your style, but I'm up for it.'

'Fuck off, Sundance.' Bain strolled off down the corridor, a grin on his face.

Cullen trudged after him. Total wanker.

Bain stopped outside an office.

A woman was staring at a laptop on her desk, glasses perched on her nose. Hair streaked with white. Grey trouser suit, a blue and maroon striped shirt underneath. She reached for a tall coffee beaker, a kiss of red lipstick around the hole in the lid.

Bain rapped on the door frame, warrant card out. 'You Michaela Queen?'

'That's me.' She looked round and frowned at his credentials. 'And you are?' Northern English accent. Liverpool, Manchester area. Maybe even Leeds.

'DS Brian Bain. This is DC Scott Cullen.'

'*DS* Scott Cullen.'

Bain frowned. 'That's right. You got promoted, eh?'

Michaela sat back in her chair and took a drink, her lipstick glistening under the spotlights. 'How can I help you, gentlemen?'

'We're looking to speak to the direct reports of Jonathan van de Merwe.' Cullen nudged the door shut behind him. 'You're aware of his death?'

She nodded. 'I received a few texts on holiday.'

'We've been trying to reach you.'

She shrugged. 'Well, nothing came through about that.'

Cullen sat opposite, leaving Bain by the entrance. 'Were you well acquainted with him?'

'Not in any way, shape, manner or form. We had a purely professional relationship, though that's stretching his competence somewhat.'

'You didn't get on?'

Michaela smirked. 'Is it that obvious?'

'The man's dead.'

'I don't see many people grieving for him, do you?'

Cullen got out his notebook. 'You're being very candid with us.'

'That's what I do here. I keep everyone honest.'

'And everything on track?'

'How wonderfully innocent a view that is.' She put her coffee down and placed her hands flat on the table. 'I'm the one who watches all the deadlines whiz past and the annual budget shatter after two months of the year.'

'So things aren't going well?'

'People will write MBAs on this programme for the next fifty years.'

'It's that bad?'

'It's rumbled on too long to cancel it. If they'd kicked Jonathan out, Alan Henderson and others would have dirt on their hands.

Better to let it trundle on in the vain hope he delivered or his contract ran out.'

'I take it he wasn't delivering, then?'

'All he'd have delivered is spending a billion.'

'A billion?'

She smiled. 'Do you need me to speak up?'

'No, I thought the budget was two hundred million.'

Michaela tore the lid off her coffee, latte foam almost to the top. 'It might've been, but they spent that in the first year.'

Cullen glanced at Bain. 'So people are lying to us?'

'Who've you been speaking to?'

'William Yardley, Vivek—'

'I'll stop you there.' She raised her cup. 'Bill Yardley lies when he orders coffee.'

'What the hell's going on here?'

'I wish I knew. They've got me on the mushroom diet.'

Bain smirked. 'What, kept in the dark and fed shite?'

'I wouldn't be so crass, but yes.'

'Someone intimated Mr Van de Merwe had let you go.'

'Is that what you heard?' She ran a hand through her hair, smiling. 'Listen, we weren't on great terms. Jonathan sacked my last Financial Controller from under me.'

'When was this?'

'December. I only joined in November.'

'Why?'

'Jonathan didn't like what he'd put in a presentation. They'd over-spent and under-delivered. The Unholy Grail of project delivery. Every day you slip puts your costs up even more. Martin put together a presentation showing the projected spend was going to be seven hundred million.'

'Thought you said it was a billion?'

'Well, it's gone up another three hundred since then. Every week that whooshes by, we slip another three.'

'Christ.' Cullen let out a sigh. 'You said Martin?'

'Martin Ferguson. Sadly, he took the fag packet they wrote the programme budget on with him.'

'Can I see this presentation?'

'You'll need a warrant, I'm afraid.'

'This is a mur—'

'I know. The information's commercially sensitive.'

'But if we speak to him?'

She gave a wink. 'He might still have it.'

'Do you know where Martin is?'

25

A man stood by the floor-to-ceiling window, staring across the sprawl of the Alba Bank complex, a chunky old BlackBerry clamped to his ear, doing more listening than talking. He wore a mint shirt with rolled-up sleeves and a pair of tight navy trousers. His eyes were weighed down by heavy bags, his face lined. He turned away from Cullen. 'Yep. Keep going.'

Bain stuck his warrant card in his face and got a fresh glare. 'Mr Proctor, we need a word.'

He raised a finger and turned to the window, forehead almost touching the glass. 'I actually do need to call you back, Miles. Sorry about this. No, it's fine. Thanks.' He stabbed his BlackBerry. 'What?'

Bain held out a hand. 'DS Brian Bain.'

'Harrison Proctor.' He shook it, gaze resting on Cullen. 'And you are?'

'DS Scott Cullen.'

Proctor steepled his fingers and narrowed his eyes at Bain. 'What's this about?'

'We wanted to speak to Martin Ferguson. We understand he's not in.'

'That's right.' Proctor shrugged a shoulder, stared out of the window. 'He's been off for the last two weeks.'

'Nothing serious, I hope.'

'Stress.'

'That a common thing with him?'

'Hardly. Martin's a contractor here. He doesn't get paid if he doesn't come in.'

'What's his role here?'

'I'm the head of Group Project Tracking. He's one of my deputies.'

'Wish I knew what that meant.' Bain grinned. 'Not going to ask us to sit?'

'I prefer to stand. It helps my back. Is Martin in trouble?'

'I hope not. You heard about the death of Jonathan van de Merwe?'

'There was an announcement yesterday morning.'

'Did you know him?'

'We had some dealings. I wanted to keep an eye on him, so I brought Martin here from OTP.'

'Poacher turned gamekeeper?'

'Quite. Martin knows where the bodies are buried on that particular mess.'

'So you were responsible for the financials on OTP?'

Proctor held up a finger. 'That mess was Mr Van de Merwe's sole responsibility. My role's to approve budgets and report to the board when programmes fail to adhere to them.'

Cullen jumped in. 'I suspect you've done a lot of that recently.'

'I want to cancel the whole bloody thing.'

'Why?'

'Because we're spending a fortune and getting no benefit for our stakeholders.'

'But you can't cancel it?'

'Correct. Jonathan's charm seduced the executive.'

'What did you mean by Mr Ferguson knowing where the bodies were buried?'

'You'd need to speak to Martin about that.'

'Do you know where we can find him?'

'I'm afraid not.'

CULLEN LEANED against the wall in the meeting room and stared at the corridor outside, phone dialling against his ear.

'I'm sorry but the caller is unavailable. Please leave a message after the tone.'

'This is Detective Sergeant Scott Cullen of Police Scotland. I'm looking to speak to a Martin Ferguson in relation to an ongoing inquiry. Please call back on 101, asking for me. Thanks.'

Bain looked up from his own phone. 'That both numbers?'

'Aye. Voicemail on both. Found out where he lives?'

'West Linton.'

'Do you want to head down there?'

'It's a bit of a fuckin' stretch, Sundance. Not sure we should bother.'

'Why?'

'I'm thinking it's just Michaela Queen causing mischief.'

'She seemed a bit too forthcoming.'

'Made my Spidey-sense tingle, Sundance.'

'Bet you wish you'd used that a few times over the years.'

'I'm exactly where I fuckin' want to be.' Bain walked over to the window overlooking the corridor, his breath misting the glass. 'Think Queen's on the level?'

'I don't see why she'd lie. I've heard from a few people that the programme's—'

'—fucked?'

'Not so explicitly, mind, but aye. How forthcoming she's been is suspicious, though.'

'Never trust a confession you don't have to batter out of someone.'

'What would she gain from telling us how bad it is?'

'It's like with our team, Sundance. Everyone's grabbing at the fuckin' ladder, trying to climb it.'

'You slid down a snake.'

'Fuck off, Cullen.' Bain stepped forward. 'You know what I'm saying, though. These wankers are just the same as Turnbull and Cargill and Crystal fuckin' Methven. They'd shit on anyone else just to climb up a couple of steps.'

'You think she's trying to gain some advantage by talking to us?'

'The big man's gone. Stands to reason she's got the chance to take out a few rivals, right? Didn't have a nice word to say about Yardley, did she?'

Cullen's phone rang. 'DS Cullen.'

'Scott, it's Maggie in Bilston. Got an Elaine Ferguson on the line for you?'

'Cheers for that. Put her through.' Cullen waited for the line to click. 'This is DS Cullen. Thanks for calling me back.'

'What's Martin done now?'

'We need to speak to him in relation to an ongoing investigation.'

'Well, he no longer lives here.' A sigh down the line. 'We're going through a separation.'

'Do you know where he is staying?'

'I hope it's Hell, but I suspect it's with one of his cronies.'

'You've no idea at all?'

'Harrison Proctor would be my first choice.'

'We've just spoken to him.'

'Might be a hotel, then.'

'Call me back if he gets in touch.'

'Very well.' The line went dead.

Bain placed his fist against the wall, shouting into his Airwave. 'The guy's not fuckin' here! Get a lookout on him, okay?'

Cullen sat at the table. Who was Bain shouting at now? He picked up his phone and called Tom.

'What *now*, Skinky?'

'Ever heard of a Martin Ferguson?'

A long pause. 'Where are you?'

'I'm at Alba Bank.'

'Meet me down in the canteen. Five minutes.'

~

'WHO WERE YOU SHOUTING AT?'

Bain barged through to the stairwell. 'Eh?'

Cullen trotted down. 'You were going ballistic at someone.'

'That idiot McCrea. What's the point in having a DC if he never does any fuckin' work?'

Cullen held open the ground-floor door, espresso machines

hissing. The bittersweet tang of the coffee hit his nostrils. 'Don't start me on DCs.'

'I'm growing to like this DS Cullen.' Bain wandered across the Caffè Nero, rubbing his hands together. 'Who are we looking for?'

'A contact.'

'This that prick I had to interview yesterday?'

'Rich? No, it's someone else.' Cullen clocked Tom at the other side of the café. A big man sat opposite, his back to them. 'Morning, Tom.'

Rob Thomson twisted his neck round and locked eyes with Cullen. Then Bain. He sprang to his feet and stomped across the tiles. Grabbed Bain by the throat. 'You motherfucker!'

Bain clawed at his hands, choking. 'Get the fuck off me!'

'You should fucking die for what you did to me!'

Cullen got between them, Thomson's fingers clawing his shirt, Bain's spit flecking his cheek. 'Quit it!'

'He tried to fucking frame me!'

'You can fuck off, son!'

Cullen turned his back to Thomson and pushed Bain back. 'Go to the meeting room!'

'I'm not fu—'

'Now!'

Bain took a step back and snarled at Thomson. Then walked off towards the stairwell, dusting himself off.

Cullen felt the fingers ease off and wheeled round. 'You okay?'

Thomson tracked Bain's progress across the café. 'How the fuck's he still got a job?'

'I ask myself that every single day.' Cullen clapped him on the shoulder. 'I'm sorry about that.'

'Didn't expect to see that motherfucker again.'

Tom patted him on the back. 'Do you want another coffee, Rob?'

Thomson collapsed into a seat, a spotlight reflecting off his shaved head. 'Latte.'

Cullen leaned in close to Tom. 'What the fuck?'

'He knows Martin Ferguson. Thought it might help you.'

Cullen stared at Thomson, now with hands over his eyes, then focused on Tom. 'Is he your contact on the programme?'

'No. Can I get you a coffee?'

'Americano, black. Cheers.'

'Coming right up.' Tom strolled over to join the queue winding down the street.

Cullen sucked in breath and checked his shirt. Nothing torn this time. He sat in Tom's chair, the wood still warm. He smiled at Thomson. 'You okay?'

'What do you think?' Thomson clenched his jaw. 'If that fucker'd got his way, I'd be in prison now.'

'There was evidence pointing to your guilt.'

Thomson shot his gaze up at Cullen. 'Are you *defending* him?'

'Look, he did what he thought was right. He was wrong and he's been disciplined for that. Got demoted to sergeant.'

'Because of what happened to me?'

'That and a few other things.' Cullen shrugged. 'Tom said you know a Martin Ferguson.'

Thomson widened his eyes. 'You really expect me to help you?'

'He's a possible lead on Mr Van de Merwe's death. Were you close to him?'

'A bit. We'd been out for a beer or two.'

'Wouldn't mind a word with him.'

'Martin's not replying to my texts.' Thomson snorted, fists clenched on the table. 'His wife kicked him out. Someone told me he'd left his wife for a secretary. Turned into a bit of a sex pest.'

'Harrison Proctor said he's on sick leave. Stress. Didn't know where he is.'

'That's a good one.'

Cullen stretched out his legs under the table. 'What's that supposed to mean?'

Thomson nodded at Tom as he approached with three coffee beakers. 'Ferguson's staying in Harrison Proctor's spare room.'

26

Cullen stared out of the window at the sandstone mansion peeking over tall walls, the front protected by a thick hedge. He folded one arm, his free hand clamping his phone to his ear. Still ringing. He ended the call. 'Mobile's just ringing out.'

Bain smirked as he clunked off his seatbelt. 'You wanting to lead?'

'Be my guest.' Cullen got out and tapped the roof of the purple Mondeo. 'You've not had this car nicked in a while, have you?'

'Fuck off, Sundance.' Bain plipped the locks.

Cullen screeched open the gate, mossed flagstones leading up to the house. 'Nice place.'

'Tell you, Sundance, we're in the wrong game.'

'You'll be on the market soon enough.' Cullen looked around at the neighbouring properties, almost all butchered by extensions. Proctor's house retained the original front entrance, a gloss white door. 'This guy must be on serious money — the rest are all subdivided into flats.'

'You reckon?' Bain looked around and sniffed. 'Don't fancy doing that boy's job?'

Cullen stomped up to the door and rang the bell. 'Not even for a house like this.'

Bain thumped the door. 'Mr Ferguson! Can you open up!'

Cullen jogged onto the cricket-crease lawn, perfect tramlines in the grass. He checked the windows — lights burned in the lounge. 'There's someone in.' He trotted back to the door.

Bain hammered again. 'Open up!'

A voice boomed through the door. 'You can't do this to me!'

'Do what?'

'Harass me at home. You've done enough at work!'

'It's the police, Mr Ferguson. We're not from Alba Bank.'

A long pause. 'I'm not letting you in without a search warrant!'

'I wish they'd fuckin' stop TV programmes educating these arseholes.' Bain crouched down and poked a finger at the brass letterbox, the metal grinding. 'We just need a word with you, Mr Ferguson.'

'What about?'

'The death of Jonathan van de Merwe.'

'What?' Another long pause. 'You think I've killed him?'

'Have you?'

'Of course not.'

'Do you want me to get a load of six-footers to come batter down your mate's antique door?'

It clicked open. Martin Ferguson was hefting a cricket bat. Short with a dyed-black goatee, he had Phil Collins hair, a long ridge of dark stubble coming to a widow's peak. Ruddy cheeks betrayed a love of port or whisky. Maybe both. Adidas tracky bottoms and brown moccasins, the seventies punk band logo on his T-shirt losing a battle with the washing machine. 'Can I see some credentials?'

Cullen walked up to the door, warrant card out. 'DS Scott Cullen. This is DS Bain.'

'You'd better come in.' Ferguson led them through the house, footsteps echoing off cream walls and stripped-wood floorboards, into a lounge on the right. The overhead light, blazing through a spherical lantern, bounced off framed artworks. Widescreen TV in an antique cabinet. 'Have a seat.'

Cullen collapsed into one of two Chesterfield sofas positioned at right angles to each other. He got out his notebook and rested it on the scarred surface of a coffee table between them. 'Nice place he's got.'

Ferguson perched at the opposite end of the other settee from

Bain. 'Let's cut the crap. I don't like being here. My wife kicked me out.'

'We need to speak to you about Jonathan van de Merwe's death.'

'There's nothing I can tell you. They moved me off the programme in December. I report to Harrison Proctor now.' Ferguson slumped back in the seat. 'I'm on sick leave, though.'

'But you did work for Mr Van de Merwe?'

'I was the Financial Controller. Ran a team of two. We controlled all expenses, managed the contract negotiations with suppliers and tracked expenditure. Budgets, forecasts, plans.'

'Slow down, pal.' Bain waved his hands in the air. 'What exactly did you do?'

'I looked after all the money. Tried to make sure the delivery parts of the programme weren't overspending.'

Cullen wrote the words down. 'We understand your contract wasn't renewed?'

'They sacked me. I had the temerity to tell Mr Van de Merwe his programme was in a mess. I was the third in the role. Same reason each time. We kept telling him it was a disaster.'

'Why was it a disaster?'

'Let me explain it to you.' Ferguson licked his lips, leaving a trail of saliva above his thick goatee. 'That programme had fixed costs, such as the computer servers and software licences.'

'You're going to have to bear with me, what with me being a thick copper and everything.' Bain smirked. 'What's a server?'

'It's what the applications are installed on. They do some development and they—'

'Sounds like you don't really know yourself.'

Ferguson fiddled with his T-shirt. 'I'm just a bean counter, really.'

'You were saying?'

'Right. After servers and software, there are the staffing costs — permanent, contract and those of our suppliers.'

'Pretend I'm following you.'

'What I did was chart the burn-down rate and how long we had left.'

Bain leaned forward on the sofa. 'This is going to take a hell of a long time if you keep using fifty quid words.'

'Look, I was tracking how much we were spending every day. Multiply the day rates of staff by their time sheets.'

Bain frowned. 'Right, I used to do that kind of thing.'

'Now you're with me. Next, I got copies of the plans from the PMO—'

'That's Michaela Queen, right?'

'Correct. Well, it was John Fisher before her but yes. That area. I had to make some assumptions, but I projected the costs until completion.'

'And?'

'We'd spent the whole budget but hadn't delivered even a fifth of the project.'

'And this was why he sacked you?'

'No. This was in October. The start of it all. Jonathan's genius idea to save cash was to get rid of the delivery partner and offshore it to IMC.'

'It didn't work?'

'Costs went up and productivity took a severe dip. The end date jumped a year in one go because of the transition. People dropped off the programme with information in their heads, none of it written down.'

'So why were you sacked?'

'I gave Jonathan a pack asking the board for more money. He didn't like the figures. Said the owners wouldn't be happy.'

'Isn't Alba Bank a PLC?'

'A hedge fund bought us outright when the shares tanked last year. They believe they can quadruple the value. OTP's part of that journey.'

'Mr Proctor hired you because you "know where the bodies are buried", to use his words.'

'That and we played rugby together at university. I've told you all I know. The programme's finances were in a horrendous state. I suspect they're worse now.'

'Michaela Queen implied you had wind of something illegal going on.'

Ferguson smacked a fist off the leather arm. 'I'm not saying anything without a lawyer.'

'Come on, sir. This is a murder inquiry.'

'That's everything I know.'

'I don't believe you.' Cullen lounged back on the settee. 'Mr Ferguson, we can do this down the station. Holding stuff back from us doesn't look good for you.'

'Fine.' Ferguson licked his lips. 'There were rumours Mr Van de Merwe received payments from delivery partners.'

'Bungs?'

'That's correct.'

'Where did you hear this?'

'A friend.'

'Going to need to back this up with a statement from your friend. Can we get his number?'

'Okay, there's no friend. I found some documents on a printer outlining payments Jonathan received from our suppliers.'

'Which ones?'

'They'd redacted the detail.'

'Do you have any copies?'

'I'd have to dig them out. They were among the possessions my wife scattered around West Linton.'

'Call me when you find them.' Cullen handed him a business card.

Ferguson stared at it. 'I will do.'

Cullen leaned back in the chair. 'Can I just say you don't seem particularly stressed.'

'I'm on very strong medication.'

'Because of what you were doing with the secretary?'

'Excuse me?'

'We heard about your affair.'

Ferguson looked away. 'They're terminating my contract because of it.'

'What happened?'

'I fell in love. When I informed my wife she...' Ferguson snorted. 'She cut up my suits. Threw my possessions onto the street.'

'So why are you living here and not with this secretary?'

'When I told her, she said she wasn't interested.'

'Excuse me?'

'She'd just been leading me on.'

'So you hadn't been an item?'

'I thought we were.' Ferguson rubbed his hair – guy clearly

had nits or OCD. 'I wanted to do the right thing. Get out of my marriage before committing to her.'

'That doesn't sound too bad.'

'The witch took me to HR. She didn't love me.'

'What's her name?'

'Lorna Gilmour.'

27

Cullen barged past Bain into the Alba Bank corridor. 'What do you think?'

'Your interview skills are getting better, Sundance. Clearly learned a lot from working for me.'

'I meant about Ferguson.'

'What a fuckin' idiot. Very noble and everything, but what a tool.'

Cullen stopped by Lorna's desk, an iPad plugged into the computer's base unit. A notepad filled with detailed columns of text. Three piles of blank Post-its. He grabbed one and scribbled a note.

Please come to the meeting room. DS Cullen.

He yawned, his stomach rumbling. 'Haven't eaten anything all day.'

'I never have breakfast.' Bain patted his stomach. 'How I keep in shape.'

Lorna pushed through the nearest office door and slumped in her chair, glancing at the Post-It. 'Are you looking for me?'

Cullen nodded. 'Need a word with you.'

Lorna crossed her legs, an impish grin on her face. 'I'm not in trouble, am I?'

Not that bad a figure on second inspection. Cullen shook his head. Quit it with that shit. 'Depends on your definition of trouble. We understand you had an affair with Martin Ferguson.'

She rolled her eyes and let out a laugh. 'That's a load of bollocks. I wouldn't let him near me.'

'He said he left his wife for you.'

'Look, we worked closely for a while. He got the wrong idea. That's it. I took him to HR.'

'Aren't you allowed relationships between staff here?'

She folded her arms. 'I told him to back off, but he was being clingy and weird. It frightened me. The next step was going to the police.'

'When was this?'

'Three weeks ago.'

'You don't work together anymore, though.'

'Exactly. He wouldn't leave me alone. That's why I took him to HR. Jenny Stanton was progressing the case for me.'

'He never tried anything sinister?'

'Martin's a lovely guy, don't get me wrong, but I was terrified. I was worried he'd stick me in a dungeon like that guy in Austria.'

Cullen jotted a note — *Get Lorna/Ferguson emails.* 'Can you pass the emails to me? The address is on my business card. And could you set up an interview with this Jenny Stanton?'

'Will do.'

Cullen led Bain away from her desk and put his face up to the meeting room door. Harrison Proctor sat with Murray.

'Is that McLean prick from banjo land your latest chimp, Sundance?'

'My latest chimp? Jesus. His name is Murray. You're still getting him confused with Ewan McLaren. Unbelievable.' Cullen chapped on the window and waved for Murray to come out, waiting in the corridor. 'How's that interview going?'

'Proctor's backing up your story. The project's fucked.'

'Programme.'

'Why do they call it that?'

'Sounds better, I suppose.'

'Aye, well, the *programme's* fucked.'

Bain glared at Murray. 'McCrea's supposed to be in there with you. Where the fuck is he?'

Murray gave a shrug. 'No idea.'

Inside the room, Proctor nodded at Murray and opened the door wide, eyes dancing between Cullen and Bain. 'Officers.'

Cullen blocked his passage. 'Before you go, sir, I'd like to ask a supplementary question.'

Proctor raised an eyebrow. 'Fire away.'

'Why didn't you tell us Mr Ferguson was sleeping at your house?'

Proctor looked away. 'He swore me to privacy. Martin's going through a difficult patch. He's one of my oldest friends. I didn't want you pushing him over the edge. He's been suicidal since ... what happened.'

Cullen glanced at Bain. 'Suicidal?'

'I've had to get his stomach pumped twice in the last fortnight.'

'We've just spoken to him.'

Proctor's eyes bulged. 'Christ.' He tapped the keys on his Black-Berry, stuck it to his ear and raced off.

Bain put his hands on his hips. 'Come back here!'

Proctor turned, hand raised. 'I need to go!'

Bain started off after him. 'Wait for me!'

Murray leaned against the rattling glass. 'What an arsehole?'

'Can you dig into this story about Van de Merwe taking bungs.'

'Sure thing.'

'And do some more digging into Martin Ferguson. And Michaela Queen. Find someone who knows what the hell's going on.'

CULLEN BIT INTO THE ROLL. Too much butter, too little cheese. And someone'd had the bright idea of putting cinnamon in the pickle. Still, beggars couldn't be choosers. He took a slug of coffee and turned to the interview pack in front of him.

'That looks like fun.'

Cullen looked up.

DI Bill Lamb strummed his thick moustache, tickling the downward-pointing triangle underneath. Ran a hand through salt and pepper hair. Dark suit, navy shirt. 'Interviews, right?'

'Aye.' Cullen slumped back in the seat. 'Round two.'

'Rather you than me.' Lamb dumped his tray, wisps of steam wafting from his soup. The chair squeaked as he sat. 'Must be a good sign if we're hiring again.'

'It's only because one of the sergeants will jump off the top of the building if we keep going like this.'

'True.' Lamb tore off a chunk of bread and dunked it in the beige gloop. 'Your mate Buxton's up for one, isn't he?'

'That he is.'

'Decent officer. Puts you in a difficult position.'

'DI Methven's fond of that.'

'Isn't he just. Did I hear the dulcet tones of DI Bain earlier?'

'DS Bain. And aye, he's back here. Seem to have him attached to my side.'

'How's that working out?'

'Complete disaster.'

'That good?'

'You know what he's like.'

Lamb chewed his bread. Swallowed, his eyes tight slits. 'More than most.'

'Must be happy you've swapped ranks with him, though.'

'That part's okay, I suppose. The bump in pay means Angela doesn't think she'll come back from maternity.'

'Really?'

'She hates working. We've both made some cash out of selling houses. Barely got a mortgage on the new place.'

'Wish I was the same.'

'You'll get there, Scott.'

'Aye, maybe. How's she been?'

'She's going stir crazy.'

'Young Keith as bad as Jamie?'

'Worse. Little pair of sods.' Another dunk. 'Seen your other half around the place. How's she doing?'

Cullen rubbed his eyes. 'I'm worried about her.'

'She's a good officer. Needs to learn to take more care of herself.'

'I don't know what to do, Bill. She's so busy all the time. I can't get through to her.'

'Speak to her. Show her you care. That's the only way.' Lamb got soup stuck on his moustache. 'I take it you don't want Angela to head out and see her?'

'Not with your boys.'

'Quite. Let me know if there's anything I can do. I mean it.'

'Cheers, Bill.' Cullen took another bite of his roll and gathered up the papers. 'Need to get on with this. Interviews start in half an hour and I've got nowhere with it.'

'Just wing it. You'll be fine.' Lamb wiped the soup away. 'You want my advice on your wee problem?'

'Aye, go on.'

'Forget about Buxton being your mate, okay? Put the best candidate forward.'

'Planned to do that anyway.'

~

PC SCOTT SOUTAR cleared his throat. At least the thirtieth time in an hour. He fiddled with his uniform T-shirt, his index finger tugging at the epaulet on his left shoulder. 'Does that answer it?'

Cullen glanced over at Donna Nichols and nodded. 'That's fine.'

Donna rested her pen, massaging her writing hand. 'Have you got any questions for us?'

'Eh, what's the money?'

Donna frowned. 'It's the same as your current salary as a PC, though there's opportunity for overtime.'

'Oh.' Soutar sniffed. Got to his feet. 'Cheers, eh?'

'We'll be in touch via your sponsoring officer.' Donna watched him leave the room and slumped back. 'Useless.'

'Worst yet.' Cullen checked the interview sheet. 'I take it he's not related to DCS Soutar.'

'It's her nephew.'

'You're kidding?'

'Deadly serious. We've used him as proof against nepotism in the force.'

~

MALC BREWSTER COLLAPSED into the chair. Snorted, then rubbed his ruddy face. 'Nightmare the day. Busy as hell, man.'

Donna tapped her watch. 'You're forty minutes late.'

'Aye. Traffic's murder.'

~

BRIAN OGILVIE SIPPED from his water, blinking hard as he stared at the ceiling. Shaved head, looked like he worked out. Deep scar under his left eye, running down to his jawline. 'Okay. Under the PACE Act, the court has to exclude confessions obtained by coercion. The lawyer should only advise clients and carry out their instructions. Therefore, he should've objected to the leading questions asked in the interview. In your example, the confession should stand.'

Donna grinned at him. 'Excellent answer, Constable.'

Ogilvie nodded, a blush creeping up his cheek. 'Thank you.'

~

CULLEN WATCHED the door trundle shut before letting out a sigh. 'Well, that's us down to three candidates.'

Donna folded over her interview pack, scoring the paper with a painted nail. 'Selecting the right candidate's the hard part.'

'It should be Buxton.'

'I've noted your opinion.'

'You done with me?'

She nodded. 'For now.'

'What's that supposed to mean?'

'The agreement between me and DI Methven was for you to attend the interviews.'

'What happens next?'

'The interview panel meets to decide on the successful candidate.'

'Thank God I'm not involved in that.'

~

CULLEN HANDED over a tenner and picked up his coffee. 'Thought you said this building was shutting down.'

'That was a rumour, Scott my boy.' Barbara blew air up her face as she handed him his change. 'Never pay any attention to them.'

'There's a load of guys shifted up from Fettes, so it's looking less likely.'

'They'll sell that place off for housing. Just mark my words.'

'I'll bear it in mind.' Cullen left her to tackle the queue and wound his way over to a seat by the window. He shrugged off his jacket and checked his watch. How the hell did it get to half five?

'There you are.'

Cullen twisted round as he sat. Buxton. 'Been busy, Si.'

He flopped down opposite. 'Not seen you all day, mate.'

'Alba Bank fun and games.' Cullen flicked off the lid and sipped the coffee. 'Found Candy?'

'Not yet.'

'You're kidding me.'

'Wish I was, mate.' Buxton sighed. 'Got the results back from Anderson on that cloak, though. Turns out it's Van de Merwe's spunk.'

Cullen inhaled his coffee's aroma. 'Right, step this up. I want a BOLO out on her, okay?'

'Will do.'

'Methven'll fuck me for letting her walk out of here.'

'There's nothing else we can do.' Buxton folded his arms. 'You been doing more interviews?'

Cullen let out a laugh. 'Si, you know I can't tell you.'

'Come on, mate.'

'Look, things are different now. I'm a DS. Crystal's asked me to do this. If I leak anything, I'll get a doing from the HR woman.'

'You know she's Cargill's missus, right?'

'As in—'

'Yeah. Our boss. Civil partnership and everything.'

'Christ.' Cullen gulped coffee, scalding his tongue. 'I've got to watch myself even more. Anything I've said to her's already gone to the Ice Queen and she'll have told Crystal.'

'Mate. I'm desperate. I need this.'

'Si, I've been there, remember?'

'Soon as we get a result on this, I'll be back in bloody uniform.'

Cullen's mobile blared out.

He fished it out of his pocket. Anderson. 'Si, I need to take this.'

'Come on, mate.'

'I'm serious. My balls are on the block if I tell you anything.'

'Thanks for nothing.' Buxton screeched to his feet and stormed across the canteen.

Cullen put the phone to his ear. 'Go on.'

'Been looking for you all afternoon. Wondering if you could give us a wee hand down here.'

'What about?'

'Bain's been reprioritising me. Again. Told us to check the boy's car. It's clean as a whistle.'

'For crying out loud.'

'So, priority?'

'Number one's the drugs. Anything else, speak to me first before stopping it. Okay?'

28

C ullen swallowed the crispy pancake in one go. Still a bit frozen in the middle. They pre-cooked them, though. Right? He took a mouthful of peas and a couple of chips, soaked in vinegar.

Fluffy crouched on the arm of the sofa, elbows like pompoms, eyes locked on the peas.

Cullen put one in front of him.

Fluffy ate it.

'Weird cat.' He gave him another one and flicked the TV channel until he got the roar of a football crowd and the nasal drone of the commentator. Hibs beating Hamilton two nil in the Scottish Championship play-off. Yawnsville.

The flat door rattled. 'You in?'

'Can't you tell by the noise?'

'And all the lights being on.' Sharon dumped her coat in the hall and traipsed through to collapse on the sofa next to him. She reached across to pat Fluffy. 'Is he ratting again?'

'At *peas*. Your cat's a freak.'

'I must have a thing for freaks.'

'Charming.' Another pancake, less frozen.

'Are you watching this?'

'Not really.' Cullen flicked it off. 'When did you get in last night?'

'Just after two, like I told you in my text. You were a grumpy shite. Grabbed all the duvet. You were speaking in your sleep again. The carrots were very definitely on fire.'

'Again? When are they going to put them out?' Cullen blushed as he munched on a chip. 'There's more in the oven. Might've defrosted by now.'

'I'm not hungry.'

Cullen stared at her. Time to push it? He took another mouthful of peas. 'How's the case going?'

'Mm.' She grabbed a chip off his plate. 'Thanks for Chantal.'

'Don't mention it.'

'It's good having someone I can rely on. Don't suppose you could lend us another ten like her?'

'I've only got three in total. Two and a half, more like.'

'Spent six hours interviewing Kyle Graham's wife again.'

'Any more slapping?'

'Not today. She's still adamant he's straight. Couldn't explain why he was flirting with men in the club, though.'

'Take it she's given him an alibi for that guy you saw last night?'

Another chip. 'They were having a romantic evening at home.'

'Convenient. Reckon he's in the clear?'

'No idea. Wasted a load of time speaking to taxi firms.' Another chip. 'Got them logging all trips in more detail than usual.'

'Probably a complete waste of time, but you never know.'

'Don't disagree. Spoke to the bar staff again. Still think someone's at it there.' Another chip. 'Be glad you don't drink anymore, Scott.'

'Why?'

'Someone's raping young men who can't control themselves.'

'Your guy's going for skinny young guys. I'm too fat and old.'

'You're not so bad.' She patted his belly. 'That's a lot flatter than it used to be.'

Cullen finished the last chip and pushed the peas to the edge nearest Fluffy. 'In the restaurant, you were saying something about going somewhere.'

She bit her lip and shut her eyes, tears welling behind the lids. 'I need some food.'

Cullen grabbed her arm as she got up. 'You can tell me.'

She stared at his hand.

He let go and flicked up his hands. 'Sorry. I'm just ... sick of you avoiding talking.'

She slumped onto the coffee table. Facing him, tears running down her cheeks. 'Scott, after I lost...' She gasped. 'After I lost *Becky*, I went to the doctor.'

He frowned. 'I was with you, remember?'

'You didn't come in. I don't know how—' She gasped. 'Scott, I can't have kids.'

Cullen stared at his palms. Clenched his hands into fists. Tightened, pulled the nails against flesh. Looked up at bleary eyes. 'Why didn't you tell me?'

'Because I knew you'd be angry. Like this.'

He looked away, throat thick. 'I'm not angry.'

'Look at me.'

He stared at the kitchen area. The extractor whirring above the hob. The oven display flashing. Pile of plates in the sink. A carton of cranberry juice open on the counter.

'Scott, look at me.'

He sucked in breath. Twisted his head round, focusing on her eyes, dark pools. He exhaled through his nose. 'I'm not sure I want kids.'

'You *do* want them. I've never seen you happier than when I told you.'

'What about when you got me the 3DS?'

'Scott, stop fucking about. This is serious.'

'Sorry.' He covered his eyes with his hands. 'Look, you didn't tell me—'

'Scott, I—'

'That's been over a year.'

She swallowed and tugged hair behind her ear. 'I know.'

'Why did you keep it from me?'

'Because I— I just don't— When I came out of the doctor's, I tried telling you. I couldn't get the words out. Then it became this big thing. I couldn't let it out.'

Cullen leaned forward, reaching out with his hand to stroke her arms. 'I'm worried about you.'

She flinched away. 'I feel so horrible.'

'Why?'

'Because I can't have kids. I'm not much of a woman, am I?'

'Jesus, Sharon, do you think my mind works like that?'

'Doesn't it?'

He let out a deep breath. 'I love you. Okay? I've spent the best three years of my life with you.'

She stared at her hands.

'Sharon.'

Eyes shut, tears streaking her cheeks.

'Sharon.'

'Are you leaving me?'

'What?'

'Are you leaving me?'

'No. Why would I?' Cullen thumbed at the cat over his shoulder, chewing on peas. 'Unless you're replacing me with him.'

'I told you to be serious.'

'I feel very threatened by him.'

She laughed, snot bubbling in her nose. 'Scott. I can't have kids. That's serious.'

'Sharon, it's—'

'You're thirty-two. That's a long life without kids.'

'It's a lot longer without you.'

'That supposed to sound poetic or something?'

'Sharon. Quit it with this, okay? I want you and only you.'

'You need to think long and hard about it, okay?' She got up. 'Goodnight.'

DAY 5

Thursday
22nd May

29

Bain joined Methven at the whiteboard. 'I said, me and DC McCrea have completed the evidence trail against Martin Ferguson.'

Cullen smirked. 'You mean you stopped him committing suicide?'

'Aye, well. Uniform had caused a clusterfu— Sorry, a massive mess by the time we got there. Once we'd calmed the boy down, he gave us permission to speak to his GP. Took a statement about his health. Mr Ferguson's on some nuclear meds for depression. His words, not mine.'

'So you think Ferguson's on the level?'

'I do. He's adamant there's corrupt shite going on at this place.'

'Which we'll come to in DS Cullen's update.' Methven jotted a note on the board. 'Now, is there anything else to report?'

'That's it, Col.'

'There must be more, surely?'

'Had a hell of an afternoon with the Ferguson boy.' Bain sniffed and cleared his throat. 'That's all I've got, sir.'

'DS Cullen.' Methven wheeled round, menace flickering in his eyes. 'Can you give your update?'

Cullen looked around at his team. Buxton and Eva perched on a desk. No sign of Murray. 'First up, the SOCOs will finally process the drugs we found in Mr Van de Merwe's flat today.'

Methven tapped the pen off the board, jotting it down. 'That's good news, for once.'

'Anderson's aiming for first thing tomorrow.' Cullen checked his notebook. 'Next, we've closed both the phones and social media. No leads.'

'Sodding hell.'

'Eva, anything on the emails?'

'Got the work ones back from Charlie. There's one from someone who worked in Group Internal Audit. Think that's like our Complaints.' She tugged her hair behind her ears. 'From what I can gather, they met to go over corruption allegations. I'll do more digging today.'

'Thanks.' Cullen nodded at Methven. 'Sir, that's it.'

'Got a couple of things, guv.' Buxton flicked through his notebook. 'I'm still looking into this lap dancer Van de Merwe was at it with.'

Methven glowered at Cullen. 'There's still no sign of her?'

'We found a cloak at her flat, but she's gone to ground.'

'Get her in here.'

Cullen glanced at Buxton. 'I'll sort this out, sir.'

'Dismissed.'

Cullen went over to his desk and slumped in the seat.

'Sarge?'

He looked round.

'Found something.' Murray stopped by his desk, out of breath. 'Got in early this morning to get stuck into the bank accounts. Remember the payment Chantal found in Van de Merwe's personal account?'

'The one that was refunded?'

'Came from an Indian company.' Murray grinned. 'An IMC subsidiary.'

~

CULLEN STOPPED outside Vivek Sadozai's office and held out his hand for Murray to hang fire on knocking. Shouting boomed through the door. He couldn't make out the figures behind the frosted glass window.

'Viv, we need to make sure these guys are playing the same game as us!'

'But we're not playing their game, Chris! That's the problem!'

'That's Vivek.' Cullen put his ear to the door. 'Who the hell's Chris?'

'—get them playing our game. We're open to Broussard swooping in and stopping progress as he usually does.'

'We'll be the ones stopping progress if we pull our resource.'

'I don't want to, but we're running out of options, Viv. Unpaid invoices are not going unnoticed.'

Cullen rapped on the door and pushed it open.

Vivek leaned back in his chair, boots on the desk, glasses on the top of his head. He shifted his feet off and stood. 'Sergeant Cullen.'

A squat man lurked in the window area, morning light silhouetting him. He looked like he'd been in one too many scrums — cauliflower ears ready to pop. Beefy arms and belly stretched his black shirt, the buttons straining. 'Christian Xavier.' Expensive accent — public school, Oxbridge, military service. Officer grade. 'How can we help?'

Cullen gave a smile, eyes narrow. 'You could start with telling me who you are.'

'Vivek works for me.' Xavier thrust out a hand, his round face twisting into a grin. 'I'm in charge of IMC's UK-based onshore staff.'

'Nice to meet you.' Cullen shook his hand and perched on the edge of a cabinet. He nodded at Murray to shut the door. 'We just need a word with Mr Sadozai.'

Vivek slumped into his chair and tugged on his glasses, frowning at Xavier. 'How can I help?'

'I need to remain present, I'm afraid.' Xavier raised a hand. 'We'll need to involve our lawyers if this relates to our commercial activities.'

'Suits me.' Cullen tossed a sheet of paper onto the desk. 'Have a look at this.'

Vivek gave it a glance. 'Looks like a bank statement.'

'The account belongs to Mr Van de Merwe.'

'Viv, I think we should get Legal in here.'

Vivek slid the page back across the desk. 'I don't know what this relates to.'

'That true?' Cullen pointed at the transaction highlighted in yellow. 'That payment came from an IMC subsidiary.'

Xavier left the window, getting between Cullen and Vivek. 'We definitely need to take legal advice.'

'If that's how you want to play it.' Cullen took a step towards the door and swung around. 'This doesn't reflect well on your company.'

Xavier snatched up the page. 'Are you accusing us of something?'

Cullen held up his hands. 'I'm gathering information here for a murder case. If you can't explain that transaction...'

'Look.' Xavier jabbed a finger at the sheet. 'We reversed the transaction. See?'

'So it's just an error?'

'That's all I can suggest.'

'I'm intrigued by Mr Van de Merwe receiving a hefty payment from one of his new suppliers.'

'I swear I know nothing about it.'

'That your final answer?'

'Of course it is, Sergeant.'

Cullen nudged Murray aside and opened the door. Whispered into his ear. 'Play along here.' He spun round. 'Now I think about it, do you mind if we do this down the station?'

'That's fine.' Vivek got up and buttoned his suit jacket. 'Lead on.'

Xavier put a hand to his chest. 'I need to insist on legal representation.'

'Your corporate lawyers won't know anything about criminal defence.'

'Criminal defence?' Xavier shifted his focus to Vivek. Then the floor. 'Okay, fine.'

'Fine, what? We can interview Mr Sadozai?'

Xavier looked Cullen in the eye. 'This can't go on the record, okay?'

'Why?'

'Because it relates to our commercial interests.'

'So you're accepting responsibility for the transaction?'

'No.'

'Then what are you doing?'

'Avoiding dim light shining on IMC. That's all.'

'DC Murray and I are Murder Squad. I just want to find who killed Mr Van de Merwe. That's it.'

'You swear?'

'Stuart, step out of the room.'

'Sure.' Murray left them to it, pulling the door shut.

Cullen leaned against the wall. 'Anything we discuss now's inadmissible in court.'

'So what do you want to know?'

'Just the truth, Mr Xavier. Always a good place to start.'

'This was an admin error. That transaction should've gone to one of Mr Van de Merwe's offshore accounts but they put it into a personal account.'

'So it's a backhander?'

Xavier stared at the window. 'The cost of doing business.'

'That's quite a high cost.'

'We're making a lot of money out of the engagement.'

'Fifty million, I heard.'

'That's only the start of it.' Xavier thumped down onto the edge of Vivek's desk. 'Look, if you want real dirt on this programme, I suggest—'

'Woah, woah, woah!' Cullen held up his hands. 'Are you trying to deflect the blame?'

'We're trying to, ah, assist your investigation.'

'Is that all it is?'

'Listen, you should speak to the previous delivery partner. There was some corrupt shit going on there.'

'What sort of thing?'

'All I can offer is hearsay.'

'We're off the record here.'

'Fraud is what I hear. Just speak to them. The name is UC Partners.'

~

'SARGE, HAVE YOU GOT A SEC?' Murray grabbed a sheaf of papers and walked over, dumping them on Cullen's desk. 'Take a look at this.'

Cullen looked at the front page. The UK Companies House logo loomed above a table of data. 'What is it?'

'This is UC Partners LLP. Dissolved in January this year.'

'What does that mean?'

'They're no longer trading.'

'Who are the partners?'

'Don't even know how many partners there are. Found an address in deepest, darkest Middlesex.'

'Great. Another one for the City of London guys. Is Eva getting anywhere on the bank accounts?' Cullen leaned forward, resting his elbows on the desk. Couldn't see her. 'Van de Merwe's wife thought he had offshore accounts. IMC said they paid it into one.'

Eva pounded back into the room, clutching a coffee.

'Eva!'

She marched over. 'Sorry, Sarge, did you want one?'

'I've got one, cheers.' He took a sip. 'When you were looking through the offshore accounts, did you come across the name UC Partners?'

'Still waiting on them.'

'Bloody hell.'

Murray tapped his monitor. 'I'm Batman!'

'Then I don't want to see Robin. What is it?'

'Got an Edinburgh address for them.'

30

Cullen parked the pool car on Rutland Square. Two men in dark suits bellowed at each other, grins on their faces. He glanced over at Bain as his seatbelt slumped into his lap. 'Wouldn't know this was here.'

'Been here a few times over the years.' Bain waved a hand in front of them. 'Our old mate Campbell McLintock moved his firm somewhere round here.'

'Let's not firebomb them today.'

'Well, we are here...'

Cullen got out into the cool air of the street. An aggressive breeze cut through him. 'Methven gave you a bit of a shoeing at the briefing.'

'That wasn't a fuckin' shoeing, Sundance.'

'You're not his favourite officer, are you?'

'Didn't sponsor me through a promotion, unlike some.'

Cullen tried to ignore the wave of heat on his neck.

'Young McLean didn't seem too happy to be cast aside like that, by the way.'

'Murray.'

'Fuck's sake.' Bain folded his arms, grinning away. 'Doing all that work only for Crystal to ask a proper cop to attend with you.'

'Shame he had to send you instead.' Cullen looked up at the

town house. Steps led up to the door, ornate columns either side. 'Place looks empty.'

Bain squinted at it. 'What's that say?'

'You're getting old.' Cullen squinted at the cream signs in the windows. 'It says, "The new home for Nelson and Parker". We shut them down in January. Dodgy bastards.'

Bain knocked on the door. 'Let's see if anyone's in.'

A man in tweeds limped along the pavement towards them, sunlight catching his bald head, heart-attack red. 'Can I help?'

'Police.' Cullen flashed his warrant card. 'DS Scott Cullen and DS Brian Bain.'

'John Carston. I work for Rutland Commercial Property. We own this side of the square. How can I help?'

'Need to ask a few questions about the tenants here. UC Partners.'

'Them.' Carston's jaw tightened. 'Still owe us rent for their last quarter. And we haven't managed to replace them. Just upped and left in January.'

'Do you mind if we have a look inside?'

'Come on in.' He barged Bain out of the way and unhooked a heavy keychain from his belt, slotting a large brass key into the lock and twisting. 'After you.'

Cullen entered first. A threadbare carpet led through to a curved reception desk, no mail on the floor. Whitewashed walls, cheap office furniture. A cream door blocked off the rest of the building. 'If you don't mind me saying, it's quite grotty.'

'Location's what sells this place. Clients just want a blank canvas.' Carston shrugged. 'Besides, your lot left in something of a hurry. Loads of furniture was still here, but they'd repainted the whiteboards on the walls.'

'Why not just wipe them clean?'

'I'm not an expert, Sergeant.'

Bain thumped the door. 'Got any mail for them?'

'Over here.' Carston limped across the carpet and reached into a cabinet, stuffed with post. He dumped it all on the desk. 'Here you go. This is all since they flitted.'

Cullen sifted through it. 'Do you mind if we take this as evidence?'

'It's just going into recycling when someone else moves in.'

Cullen paused at one letter. Alba Bank logo in red at the top right. URGENT. He tore at the seal and skimmed it.

'What's that, Sun— Sergeant?'

Cullen showed it to Bain. 'It's from Martin Ferguson last November. Says Alba Bank won't pay UC's invoice.'

~

CULLEN TOOK the coffee from Martin Ferguson, the acrid aroma of instant drifting across the sitting room, undissolved granules floating on the surface. 'Thanks.' He set it on the coffee table.

Ferguson handed another cup to Bain. 'Here's yours.'

Bain slurped at it. 'That's better.'

Ferguson sat on a Chesterfield sofa, legs crossed, and grabbed the last mug from the tray. 'I trust you're not here to further investigate my mental state?'

Cullen glanced at Bain and smiled at Ferguson. 'Sorry, sir, we didn't mean to cause—'

'It's fine.' Ferguson waved a hand in the air, eyes bulging. 'I understand your concern yesterday, but I'm fine. Talking to you got a lot off my chest. Made me think of going back to work.'

Quick turnaround... Cullen frowned. 'I thought they terminated your employment?'

'I'm thinking of fighting it.'

Cullen reached into his pocket for the letter to UC Partners and passed it to Ferguson. 'Do you recognise this?'

'Give me a second.' Ferguson put on a pair of glasses, one of the legs all bent, and scanned through the sheet. 'Yes, I sent this. I was acting on Mr Van de Merwe's express instructions.'

'We've just got your word on the matter.'

'I retained a copy of the email instructing me to cease.' Ferguson glugged his coffee and set the empty mug on the tray. 'It pays to save emails putting any blame on another party.'

'Can we see it?'

'That shouldn't be a problem.'

'Here's my email address.' Cullen held out a business card. 'Did they reply to this letter?'

'We received no further bills.' Ferguson didn't take the card, instead clenching his hands around his thighs. 'But, before I was moved off the programme, Jonathan and I arranged a meeting on their territory.'

'Rutland Square?'

'Yes. The place was empty. This was November. The twentieth, I think.'

Cullen flapped the sheet. 'So they turned their backs on twenty million pounds?'

'They'd received over one hundred and fifty million by that point. Against my will, I should add. Jonathan forced me to sign off their invoices. He would come into my office when I refused, screaming and shouting. I just made sure I had his instructions in an email to cover myself.'

'So he was a bully?'

'Of the worst kind.'

Cullen exchanged a look with Bain, getting a shrug in reply. 'Why was he bullying? What were UC Partners up to?'

Ferguson reclined on the Chesterfield and stretched his arms along the back. 'It's complicated.'

Bain dumped his mug on the antique table, missing the tray by a foot. 'We've got time, pal.'

Ferguson smoothed down his goatee yet again, like he had lice. 'A management consultancy like Schneider trains up skilled resources and charges them out at a high rate, say a thousand pounds a day for the lowest rung of the ladder. They report to managers, who report to senior managers to directors, who report to partners like Wayne Broussard. Basically, a pyramid scheme.'

'What's the charge-out rate for a partner?'

'Five thousand a day.'

'A *day*?' Bain shook his head. 'Definitely in the wrong job.'

Cullen leaned forward. 'What are you getting at here?'

'UC employed the same model. Except, instead of one thousand a day for an analyst-level employee, they'd invoice two grand.'

'Definitely in the wrong—'

Cullen butted in. 'Is the resource twice as good?'

'See, that's the thing. What they were doing was back-charging contractors as consultants. They'd bring in self-employed resource, similar to myself.'

Bain snorted. 'I'm not following you, pal.'

'I contract myself directly with the bank, through my limited company. Cuts on their pension costs and so on.'

'And you earn more money?'

'Well, there is that.'

'Definitely in the wrong—'

Cullen clenched his fists. 'So were they any better?'

'Don't get me wrong, some of them were excellent, but there's just not the same consistency as with the Big Five.'

'They're better?'

'And they have a chain of command. I can ask someone to do something and they'll just do it.' Ferguson rubbed his temples. 'Listen, after they paid the contractors the market rate, UC scalped the profit off the top.'

'How much would these people cost?'

'The market rate's five hundred a day.'

'Definitely in the wrong game.'

Cullen shot another glare at Bain. 'Right, so they took in two grand and paid out five hundred.' He frowned. 'They were creaming off fifteen hundred a day in profit?'

'That's right.'

Ferguson nodded. 'And they had over two hundred onboard.'

Bain whistled. 'Ten grand each and every day.'

Cullen cleared his throat. 'A hundred grand.'

'Jesus.' Bain shot up an eyebrow. 'A *hundred*?'

Cullen got to his feet. 'Was Mr Van de Merwe involved?'

'The rumour was, VDM owned a third of UC.'

'Thirty-odd grand a day from his own programme?' Cullen frowned at Ferguson. 'Who else owned UC?'

'I've no idea.'

'Who might know?'

'William Yardley.'

'We need this on the record.' Cullen folded his arms. 'Can you accompany us down to the station?'

Ferguson checked his watch. 'Look, I'm supposed to meet my lawyer soon. It'll be after five before I'm finished.'

'Ask for me at the front desk at Leith Walk station as soon as you're done. Call me if you can't make it.'

31

A man in an Alba Bank polo shirt was swiping a mop across a brown puddle on the sandstone. The smell of cleaning fluid mixed with the sweet tang of cola. He glanced up at Cullen and Bain, before going back to his work.

The corridor opened into an open-plan area at the end. A sign swung from the ceiling, blown about by air-conditioning breeze. Operational Transformation Programme.

Bain crushed his can of WakeyWakey. 'What's up, Sundance?'

'You did better with Ferguson than last time. He didn't try to kill himself.'

'Cheeky fucker.'

'You keeping quiet helped us get what we needed out of him.'

'Come on, give me that invoice and I'll show you how it's fuckin' done.' Bain snatched the sheet and strode across the wet flagstones, leaving a trail of damp footprints on the dry floor.

Cullen followed, raising his hands to the cleaner. 'Sorry about that.'

Bain was leaning over Lorna's desk. 'Morning.'

She tilted her head to the side. 'Can I help?'

'Mr Yardley's not in his office.'

'He'll be in a meeting.'

'Any danger you could track him down for us?'

'Sure.' She glanced at Cullen. 'I've set up some time with Jenny Stanton about that … stuff.'

'Can you arrange it with one of my DCs?' Cullen scribbled his number on the back of a business card. 'His name's Stuart Murray.'

'Will do.' She took the card, carefully placing it by her iPad. 'Oh, I spoke to Oliver Cranston.'

Bain snorted. 'Who's he?'

'Wayne Broussard's number two. He got a call from him last night.'

'Where is he?'

Lorna pointed at the room next to theirs. 'That office there.'

'Cheers.' Bain powered across the corridor and knocked on the frosted-glass door. He pushed it open, not waiting for a response. 'Mr Cranston, we need to speak to you.'

Cullen followed him into the office and lurked near the entrance. A square meeting space, twenty young men and women sitting around a table covered in laptops. Sharp suits, salon hair.

Oliver Cranston nodded at his team around the table, eyes blazing at Bain. More than a passing resemblance to Ewan McGregor.

Oliver grinned at his team. 'Guys, can you give us the room?' An indistinct accent, traces of Belfast.

The man next to him led the others out, laptop under his arm.

Bain nodded over. 'This is DS Cullen.'

Oliver offered a hand. 'Pleased to meet you.'

Cullen shook it — not quite the ex-forces grind of Alan Henderson, but not far off — and took his seat, still warm. After-shave and perfume mixed, ocean smells blending with spices.

Bain sat opposite, sandwiching Oliver between them. 'Gather you've had word from your boss?'

Oliver snapped his laptop shut. 'Last night. Broussard's cancelled my holiday.' Clicked his fingers. 'Just like that.'

'Why?'

'Does there have to be a reason?' Nervous laugh. 'I'm pissed off. It'll pass, I suppose.'

'He's done this before?'

'A few times, usually for no reason. Thinks he's doing me a

favour. Developing my career. Putting me in front of the other partners.'

Bain folded his arms. 'So, in response to my question, I take it you have heard from him?'

'I passed on the message to call you guys.'

'Any idea when he'll be gracing us with his presence?'

'He'll be here sometime next week.'

'That's not soon enough.' Bain got out his notebook. 'He wouldn't have anything to do with Mr Van de Merwe's death, would he?'

'Excuse me?'

'Think about it. His old best mate dies in mysterious circumstances. Guy's pissed off at how much your boss is charging. Nobody knows where he is, supposed to be hunting bears or wrestling crocodiles or whatever. Sounds like someone running away from something.'

Oliver reached into a briefcase for a sheet of paper. He slid it over to Bain. 'His PA dug out the flight manifests for the eighteenth of April. Wayne flew from Edinburgh to NYC. Into JFK. BA. First Class.'

'That's convenient.'

'Wayne expected this. He *was* on that flight.'

Bain pocketed the sheet. 'Let's talk about UC Partners.' He got out the UC letter, already dog-eared and tattered. 'You know anything about this?'

'Before my time, I'm afraid. I rolled on in January when we took over from UC.'

'But Mr Broussard was here before that?'

'He had a team of five supporting him. He was advising Sir Ronald on delivery and helping with some other matters.'

'Such as?'

'Providing industry best practice.'

'Broussard was an old mate of Mr Van de Merwe, right?'

'They knew each other, yes.'

'Were they in cahoots?'

'Of course not. Look, Wayne used their connection as a route in to Sir Ronald. It worked.'

'Did Broussard kick this UC lot off?'

'Wayne wasn't happy with them.' Oliver closed his laptop. 'He kept pressuring VDM to sack them.'

'And did he?'

'Wayne took his concerns to Sir Ronald in December. They were gone within a week.'

There was a knock on the door. Lorna frowned at Cullen. 'That's William back in his office now.'

∼

WILLIAM YARDLEY POUNDED a fist off his desk. Then tore his other hand through his ginger hair. 'Listen to me. I've never heard about any of this.' Full-on Southern drawl.

His office door juddered open. Lorna hurried across the carpet, clutching a coffee, nodding at Cullen as she put the beaker in front of Yardley. 'Here you go.'

'Thanks.' He sucked at the cup. 'Guys, I need to attend a meeting.'

'You've just been to one.'

'Do you want to see my diary? I'm full up for the rest of the week.'

'No, you're not.' Bain blocked the door. 'You're answering our questions here or down the station. Your choice.'

'I don't have to—'

'No, you do. Do you want me to detain you? Not done it for a while, but I can still remember how to read you your rights.'

Yardley slumped into his seat. 'Ask the question again.'

'Was Mr Van de Merwe a partner in UC?'

'Look, I know nothing about that.'

'We've heard he was.'

'This is a man's life you're stomping over. His reputation. His legacy. You can't just do that.'

'He's a murder victim. We need to find out who killed him.'

Yardley slammed his cup down, sending coffee spraying through the hole in the lid. 'Did these rumours come from Martin Ferguson?'

'We can neither confirm nor deny.'

'So it was him.' Yardley shook his head at Lorna. 'What are you still doing here?'

'Facilities are hassling me about their meeting room.' She bit her lip. 'Nobody's been in there all day.'

Cullen smiled at her. 'Thought I told you to release it?'

'Oh, okay.' Lorna left the office.

Bain watched her go, narrowed eyes locked on Yardley. 'So you're saying there's nothing in these rumours?'

'To the best of my knowledge.'

'But you were here when UC were onsite, right?'

'I never met the owners, though.'

'Excuse me?' Cullen glanced at his notebook. 'You've been on the programme for two years and, in all that time, never met one of the UC partners?'

'God damn it, will you listen to me? I don't know anything about them.'

'Did they wear masks in meetings?'

Yardley yanked the lid off his coffee and flopped it down on the desk. 'My understanding is the firm's partners were silent.'

'So if the owners weren't here, who managed their resource?'

'They had a guy onsite. He was managing the entire programme. Big Scotch guy. Used to come to all of the meetings. I think his title was Delivery Manager or something.'

'Was he a partner in the firm?'

'Not that I know. I mean, he could've been.'

'What was his name?'

'Stephen Nicks. I don't have his number.'

Cullen got up and paced the room. 'And all this time, they were creaming off a few hundred thousand a day.'

'Where did you get that?'

'Simple maths. Two hundred employees at fifteen hundred a day.'

'I'll take your word for it. I don't look after supplier management or finances. UC were fired because they weren't performing. We needed to restructure the finances of the programme as we shifted into delivery. They weren't the best fit.'

'So you moved to Schneider and IMC?'

'We swapped one firm out for two. Lowered the consultancy spend and moved our cost base overseas.'

'Was Mr Van de Merwe a partner in UC?'

'What? God no. Did Ferguson—'

'Are you?'

'God damn it! No, of course I'm not.' Yardley gulped coffee. 'This is ridiculous.'

'You should know we're looking into the ownership of the business. Two names unaccounted for. If we find out—'

'Get out of here!'

Cullen got to his feet. 'If we find out you're involved, this won't look good.'

'Get out.'

32

Cullen looked around the Incident Room. He spotted Eva at a desk near the door. 'Can you do me a favour?'

She turned to a fresh page in her notebook. 'Go on.'

Cullen crouched down, his knees creaking with effort. 'Can you look for a Stephen Nicks? He used to work for UC Partners.'

'I'll see what I can do.'

'Cheers. Have you seen Murray or Buxton?'

'They asked Holdsworth to arrange a meeting room for them. Think it's about this City of London stuff.'

'Weren't you looking into that?'

'Stuart took it off me. They're in room Six.'

Cullen got up, his knees creaking, again.

'Sarge, wait a sec.'

He spun round. 'What's up?'

'Been going through these emails like you asked? I found one sacking UC Partners.' She handed him a sheet, stabbing a finger at a highlighted section. 'Martin Ferguson sent it to a generic email at their domain. And a Paul Vaccaro.'

'This is good work. Any idea who he is?'

'I'll add him to the hunt, Sarge.'

'Cheers. Getting anywhere with Van de Merwe's Gmail account?'

'Charlie's on it. Reckons hell's gonna freeze over before we get it.'

'Keep on him. And dig into any emails he received from Vivek Sadozai. And Wayne Broussard.'

'Aye. Still nowhere with finding him.'

'Cheers, Eva.' Cullen left the room and jogged down the corridor. He knocked and entered room Six.

Buxton and Murray were leaning against the window frame. Their eyes shot over to him.

'You pair better not be talent spotting.'

'Hardly, Sarge.' Murray laughed. 'Got a hold of our contact in the City of London Financial Crime Unit. Wanted to speak to a sergeant or above.'

'Wouldn't Methven have done?'

'Not seen him.'

Cullen sat at the end of the meeting table. 'Dial it, then.'

Murray held up his mobile and dialled a number into the conference phone on the desk. The dialling tone burst out of the speaker. Then room noise.

'*DI Coulson.*'

'Steve, it's DC Stuart Murray in Edinburgh.'

'*Afternoon, Constable. How's it up there in chilly Jockland?*'

'Thanks for agreeing to speak to us, sir. I'm with DS Scott Cullen and ADC Simon Buxton.'

'*What do you want to know?*'

'We were talking about UC Partners earlier.'

'*Ah, them. Listen, the ownership's in the Caymans.*'

'Is that a problem?'

'*It's a dead end. You're snookered, unless I can get access through my back channels.*'

'What about Jonathan van de Merwe's accounts?'

'*Got a few in the Caymans bearing his name.*'

'How come you can get that but not for UC?'

'*Don't ask to see how we make the sausage, Constable. I've got access to some of the transactions. Your guy's received a lot of cash from a company called Indus Consulting.*'

Murray nodded at Cullen. 'That's the IMC subsidiary.'

Cullen stared at the phone. 'How much are we talking?'

'Looks like an initial hundred grand, then ten a month since December.'

'What's the balance on the account?'

Coulson whistled down the line. 'A cool ten million plus change that's bigger than my pension.'

'Can you send through a copy?'

'Will do. That all you need from me?'

'For now. Thanks for your help, sir.'

'Don't mention it.' The line bleeped dead.

Cullen sprang to his feet. 'Time to update Crystal, I suppose.'

Murray winked. 'Or take credit for our work.'

'I'm not taking any credit for you doing bugger all, Stuart.'

'I love you too, Sarge.'

METHVEN CHECKED HIS WATCH. Third time in half an hour. 'You've been very informative, Sergeant.'

Cullen leaned back in the chair. 'I'll keep you posted as we go, sir.'

Methven shook his head. 'Look, what I still don't see is why someone's murdered him.'

'I'm thinking it could relate to what he was up to with UC Partners. Some rough maths and you can work out how much he's made. Where there's money, there's usually a motive.'

'If it's true.'

'I'm assuming it is. He bullied procurement, rushed through staff hiring and kept his team from speaking to UC.'

'We need evidence.'

'We'll get it, sir.'

'The City cops are notoriously slow.'

'Notoriously rigorous, too. It'll stand up in court.'

'Who are you putting in the dock, Sergeant?'

'That's another question entirely.'

'Why's he on the bridge in the first place?'

Cullen shrugged. 'Someone pays a prostitute to visit his bondage room and service him. Then she lures him out into the street.'

'If it's a hit, surely they'd do it in his house. That safe room—'

Methven smirked. 'DS Bain called it a danger room. Like in the *X-Men* comics.'

'Very good.'

'But you follow my logic? If you were killing him, you'd strangle him and leave him in the house.'

'I'd shove Bain off the Forth Road Bridge.'

'I meant sodding Van de Merwe.'

'I know, sir.' Cullen cleared his throat, covering a smile. 'But I agree. If it was a hit, we'd've found him in his suit with some shopping scattered around. Not at three a.m. in his underpants.'

'Which only adds to the mystery.' Methven checked his watch again.

'Am I keeping you from something?'

'Sorry? No, no. I've got an appointment at two and I need to get some lunch beforehand.'

'Do you think we're wasting our time looking into his background, sir?'

'Your guess is as good as mine. We could be dealing with an assassin who's leading us to think it's not a hit. We desperately need to find this person in the cloak. How are we with Candy?'

'I need to pick up with ADC Buxton.'

'Sergeant, that's been two days now.'

'I know, sir, but we're—'

Methven's Airwave thundered against the wooden desk. 'DS Bain to DI Methven.'

'Receiving.'

'Need you down in the Scenes of Crime office, Col.'

'Is it going to take long?'

'I'd say so.'

Methven sighed. 'I'll be down presently.'

Cullen got up and stepped towards the door. 'We done?'

'I need you to cover my two o'clock, Sergeant.'

'What is it?'

'Presenting Buxton's case at the panel.'

Cullen let his shoulders drop. 'Right.'

33

Cullen slumped back in the seat, gazed up at the canteen's ceiling and gripped his phone tighter. 'Crystal's put me in the shit again, Sharon.'

'He shouldn't be doing this to you. You need to sort it out.'

'You think I should go to the Police Federation?'

'I meant speak to him.'

'Oh. Right.' Cullen shifted his mobile to the other hand and glanced at the half-filled page of A4. 'I've done nothing because I thought he was presenting Si's case.'

'You think he's ready for it, though, right?'

'Been ready for eighteen months.'

'Then you'll be fine.' Pause. 'How are you feeling?'

'I'm tired. Have you thought any more about what we talked about last night?'

'Scott.... This is hard for me. I've got to go.'

'When will you be back tonight?'

'Chantal wants to go for a drink.'

'Right. Love you.' Cullen ended the call.

'Sarge.'

Cullen looked up. Buxton was looking down at him.

'Tried calling you.'

'I was on the phone to Sharon.' Cullen leaned back in the chair. 'Tell me you've found Candy.'

'Think she's disappeared.'

'People don't just disappear. Have you spoken to her parents?'

'Both dead.'

'Si, Methven's biting my bollocks about it. Find her.'

'Keep your wig on, mate. I'll bring her in.' Buxton got up. 'I liked you better when you were drinking.'

Cullen watched him wander across the canteen. Was he really detective calibre? Or was he just his mate?

A hand appeared from the side, snatching up the page.

Cullen grabbed for the hand. Missed.

'Oh, ho! Look at this.' Bain held it at arm's reach to read it. 'Aw, bless! "Simon is my boyfriend and I wuv him vewy, vewy much." You soft shite, Sundance.'

'Give me that back. Now.'

'Make me.'

'How old are you? Six?'

'Come on, Sundance. Just a little bit of fun.'

'Look, I've got to take that to a panel in five minutes.' Cullen snatched it back, folded it and put it in his pocket.

'So Crystal's dumped that on you now?'

Cullen looked away.

Bain thumped into the seat opposite. 'You regret getting the stripe?'

'All these little shitty things he gives me. I'm supposed to be running this investigation, but I've spent more time interviewing candidates or prepping for the interviews than on the case.'

'Nightmare.' Bain dumped a handful of coins onto the table and started sifting through. 'I tried to put you through the same thing.'

'What, delegating?'

'No, a promotion, you daft bastard. You were such a moaning git. Promotion this, promotion that.'

Christ. Cullen swallowed.

'This was after I lost Butch to Wilko.'

'Don't call her that.'

'Cargill knocked it back. Said you were too much of a cowboy.'

'What did you say?'

'Saw the writing on the wall and let it pass.'

'I didn't realise.'

'It's not just saving your fuckin' life you've got to thank me for, is it?'

~

CULLEN OPENED the meeting room door.

DCI Cargill and Donna Nichols were lost in conversation. Sitting close, legs almost touching. Were they really a couple?

Cargill glanced round and flashed a yellow toothy smile at Cullen. 'Ah, Sergeant. Thanks for joining us. DI Methven said you were his deputy on this.'

Cullen sat on the other side of Donna. 'Where's everyone else?'

'They'll come as and when they're needed. You're to provide assurance through the process.'

'Have a look through this.' Donna tossed a pack at him. Their interviews all typed up and bound. 'The format's twenty minutes for each candidate.'

'But we've already interviewed them.'

'And we need to hear from their sponsors.'

Cargill winked at him. 'This is what Colin and I had to do for your current position. Be thankful you avoided the interview and presentation.'

Cullen flicked through the pack. 'So, who's up first?'

~

'LET ME THINK ON THAT.' DI Bill Lamb stared at the window, stroking his moustache. He cleared his throat. 'Okay. PC Helen Armitage has worked for one of my sergeants for the last six months. In that time—'

Cargill frowned. 'But she's since returned to uniform duty?'

'That's correct. You know how the budgets are this year, ma'am.'

'Do you think she'd be a good fit for DS Cullen's team?'

Lamb raised his eyebrows at Cullen. 'Possibly not. He's already got a few inexperienced officers. DC Murray's the only one with any experience and most of that's out in East Lothian.'

'I've got DC Jain.' Cullen glared at him. 'And Eva Law's got two years as a full DC in A Division.'

'All the same, I think Helen'd be better with one of my sergeants.'

'I've got an idea.' Cargill beamed. 'We could move Geraldine Fox into DS Cullen's team. She adds a wealth of experience.'

Cullen dug his pen into his interview pack, cutting through the pages. 'That's an option.'

'DI Lamb, can you continue?'

'Anyway, Helen frequently deputised for DS McMann at my daily briefings. As you know, he's had issues with his water works all year. She's really stepped up to the plate.'

~

CULLEN LOCKED EYES WITH CARGILL. 'So, in conclusion, then, PC Simon Buxton should get the role. Full stop. In the two years he's worked both alongside and for me he's not once complained about the nature of the job or the type of activities he's undertaken. That's two years of handling murder cases and complex investigations. He's a good analyst and an experienced police officer. It has to be him.'

~

SERGEANT GARY MULLEN rubbed a hand against his chin. 'So, aye, I'm PC Brian Ogilvie's line manager.'

Cullen flicked through his original pack, finding the name just to the left of where his pen had tunnelled through. He was decent enough, but hardly a go-getter.

'He's worked for me here for about ten years, give or take. Good lad, always eager to put in a shift or do the odd bit of overtime. Gets on—'

'Just a sec, Sergeant.' Cargill frowned at her pack. 'Specialised Crime Division requires a lot more than "the odd bit of overtime". Our staff regularly work four or five additional hours.'

'That lad's coming up from Berwick every morning, ma'am. Can't expect him to stay too late.'

'Very well.' Cargill scored through a chunk of text. 'Please continue.'

~

'Aye, cheers.' Mullen slammed the door behind him.

Cargill let out a sigh and shoved her pack over to Donna. 'Well, that's a definite no on Ogilvie.'

'Agreed.' Donna collected Cullen's papers, frowning at the hole. 'Do you agree, Sergeant?'

'I already said he shouldn't have got this far.'

Cargill stood up and stretched out, the two sides of her parting at the bottom. 'So it's down to two.'

'Not really.' Donna flicked through her papers. 'Buxton's interview score was poor. It's only Hel—'

'What do you mean *poor*?' Cullen crossed his arms. 'I said he should've got it on that basis alone.'

'I marked him down on three separate points.'

'What were they?'

'Well, first—'

'Sergeant.' Cargill smiled at Cullen, head tilted to the side. 'I think you need to accept the decision. Helen Armitage is clearly the strongest candidate.'

'Come on...' Cullen jumped to his feet and paced the room. 'Lamb just wants to chuck his dead wood into my team.'

'Excuse me?'

'You know the issues he's had with the Cou— With DC Fox. He's already planted the seed to swap her with PC Armitage. This role is for my team. I should get to call the shots.'

'Sergeant, this has to be an open and transparent process. You can't just appoint your mate to the team. What'd happen if I had to second you to another investigation?'

'You're saying I should be stuck with someone who's not delivering?'

'That's an entirely separate manner, Scott.'

'Is it? You didn't sit in on the interview and listen to PC Armitage's piss-poor answers.'

'You could've challenged them.'

'I tried but I was scribing. Wasn't my job.'

'Nonsense.' Donna huffed. 'All you'd written was "No leadership skills shown". I had to write up the notes from memory.'

Cargill scowled at him. 'Is this true?'

'Look, ma'am, I've been at DI Lamb's briefings a couple of times, as you know. Armitage isn't up to it.'

'Let's go back to you thinking we should appoint your friend.'

'If he's a friend it's because we've worked together and he's earned my trust and respect.'

'You sure?'

'He's a very good officer. Professional, solid, reliable. Two years as an ADC. He's experienced and driven. Everything we need.'

'Let's have a vote.' Cargill pouted. 'Donna?'

'PC Armitage.'

'Scott?'

'Buxton.'

'Well, I say Helen Armitage. The motion's carried.'

Cullen stomped over to the door and stared back at them. 'It should be Simon.'

Cargill shut her eyes for a few seconds. 'We'll take this to DSI Turnbull.'

'So it's still open?'

'No, it's decided. Can you please inform Buxton?'

'But—'

'Just do it, Scott. Okay?'

34

Cullen slumped down in the seat next to Eva. 'Have you seen Buxton?'

'Went to Fanny Hill.'

'Don't let Methven hear you calling it that.'

'Right. HMP Cornton Vale, Sarge.'

'What's he doing up there?'

'Wouldn't say.'

'You anywhere with Paul Vaccaro yet?'

'Remind me?'

'Eva, I asked you. He worked for UC Partners, remember?'

'Right.' She scribbled in her notebook. 'I'll do some digging, Sarge.'

'It's fine, I'll get Murray to do it.'

'You sure?'

His phone blasted out. Unknown caller.

'I'm sure.' He put the mobile to his ear. 'DS Cullen.'

'This is Wayne Broussard returning your call.' Clipped American accent, polished. 'How may I be of service?'

Cullen moved away from Eva. 'Thanks for calling me back, sir. I need to—'

'What's this about?'

'I've left a couple of voicemails over the last few days explaining the situation.'

'You think I've got time to listen to voicemails, buddy?'

Cullen tightened his grip on the phone. 'We need to speak to you regarding the death of Jonathan van de Merwe.'

'What? Jon? What?'

'We found his body on Sunday morning.'

'Jesus Christ. Why didn't somebody call me?'

'We've tried, sir.'

'Yeah, not hard enough. Situations like this, you little guys should reach out to me, you know what I'm saying?'

Little guys? Cullen ground his teeth together. 'Where were you on Saturday night between three and four in the morning?'

'UK time? Sleeping, probably. I've been hunting elk in northwest Colorado.'

'I'll need a precise location.'

'We were moving about a lot. You want my GPS record?'

'That'd help.' Cullen swapped his mobile to the other hand. 'When are you back in the country?'

'I'll be there Monday. Sunday if I can get out of Buttfuck, Idaho any sooner.'

'Thought you were in Colorado?'

'We swung through Wyoming into Idaho Wednesday.'

'What about Saturday or Sunday?'

'I'll be busy. Got a pitch to run through with Ollie Cranston.'

'That's why you cancelled his holiday?'

'That what he told you?'

'I really need to speak to you about Mr Van de Merwe.'

'We're talking now.'

'Do you know if he was involved in UC Partners?'

'This again.' A sigh. 'Right. As far as I know, Jon held an equity share.'

'Definitely?'

'I'm not in the habit of being vague, son.'

'Do you have anything to back that up?'

'This is what you little guys never understand. Schneider is a multinational corporation. All we are is our reputation. Do you expect us to get into bed with a guy who could ruin that? No. We've got a dossier on Jon as thick as my twelve-inch.'

Cullen grimaced. 'Thought you guys were friends?'

'That's a good one. I'll treasure that.' A laugh, high-pitched. 'Son, if I were you, I'd be speaking to the Indians.'

'IMC? Why?'

'Let's be honest, they didn't get that gig on merit.'

'What are you talking about?'

'Follow the money.' Something clattered in the background. 'Listen, I've got to go. I'll see you when I arrive.'

'Wait—'

The line clicked dead.

'—a second.' Cullen stared at his phone. 'Bastard.' He redialled the last number.

'You've reached the voicemail—'

He killed the call. Dialled again.

'You've reached the voicemail of Wayne Broussard. Leave a message.'

'Mr Broussard, I hadn't finished. Can you please call me back at your next convenience. Thanks.' Cullen stabbed the "end call" button on his screen. 'Wanker.'

Eva appeared. 'You okay, Sarge?'

'I'll live.'

'Look, I'm sorry about that Vaccaro thing.'

'That's fine.'

'Can I get you a coffee? I was just heading down to see Anderson. Says he's finished the coke analysis.'

CULLEN HELD the ground-floor door open for Eva. Steel-on-stone grinding reverberated down the long corridor, the scent of bleach tickling his nostrils. 'What the hell's going on down there?'

'No idea.' Eva started down the corridor. 'But I hope it's happening to Bain.'

'I'd better not comment.'

'It's okay, Sarge, I won't say anything.' She knocked on the Scenes of Crime lab entrance. 'Open up, it's the police!'

The left door swivelled open. Anderson got up, hands on hips. He screwed up his face. 'Cullen and his latest gimpess.'

'Charming. We're here for our drugs, James.'

Anderson frowned. 'Thought I sent them to you, imp girl.'

'The stuff you sent isn't readable by humans.'

'How would you know?'

'Look, quit messing.' Cullen gripped the edge of the counter. 'I'm having a shite day and this isn't helping my mood any.'

'Better come on through.' Anderson led into the lab, heading for a large machine near the window. 'I'll try to only use monosyllabic words.'

'Good luck stretching your vocabulary.'

Anderson shook his head. 'I did the old cobalt thiocyanate test last night. There's definitely cocaine in there.'

Cullen tapped the machine, getting a deep ring. 'Using this?'

'What? This? No. The CT test's done on a slide.' Anderson reached into a unit next to the machine and pulled out a transparency covered in a thin wash of blue crystals. 'The blue means it's got cocaine in it.'

'Just coke?'

'Did the usual tests for opiates, barbiturates and LSD. All negative.' Anderson tapped the machine. 'This baby's our UV spectrophotometry beastie. Shows what's in it.'

'And?'

'Coke and a load of other shite.' Anderson waved at a machine visible through the glass pane in the middle of the room, a suited figure easing a tray out from it. 'Ran it through the mass spectrometer next. Aside from the charlie, there are the usual suspects. Sucrose, lactose, talc, procaine, ammonia—'

'*Ammonia?*'

'Aye. It's used as a base agent to turn it to crystals. We also got ether, whi—'

'Ether?'

'Aye. It was dried in. Shows it wasn't the best gear.' Anderson crossed his arms. 'Seeing as how I owed you one for the old sex room rescue, I had a chat with Jimmy Deeley. At the PM, he found burns on your guy's nasal passages and at the back of his throat. The ether and ammonia were burning his nose.'

Eva leaned back against a cabinet. 'They pack all that shite in to cut the actual coke content, right?'

'Aye. Less than thirty per cent in this stuff. Earns them more money, pure and simple.'

'Shouldn't he have known?'

'No danger. The procaine's in there to give the numbing effect. It's a local anaesthetic, makes them think they're getting good stuff.'

'Clever.' Cullen scribbled some notes. 'What else do you know?'

'See, this is where it gets interesting, Cullen.'

'How?'

'Well, we've been slow because drug squad got a shitload of the stuff at a raid down Leith way.'

'National Crime Agency?'

'No, your lot.'

'Who's the dealer?'

'I wish I could tell you.'

'Come on...'

'It's under their active investigation. I'm sworn to secrecy.'

'Come on, James.'

'Cullen, my hands are tied. Speak to DC Zabinski down in Fettes.'

EVA SWIPED through the security barrier at Fettes and trotted down the corridor to keep up with Cullen. 'You've been quiet, Sarge.'

'This better work out, otherwise I'll kick Anderson's arse.'

'You can understand where he's coming from, though, right?'

'He should've told us.'

Eva put a hand to his chest, stopping him halfway down the corridor. "EAST DIVISION / OPERATION VENUS" was stencilled in white on black plastic.

Eva waited till he'd gone. 'Look, if this was the other way round, you wouldn't want me sharing anything with Paula, would you?'

'Paula?'

'DC Zabinski and I went through Tulliallan together. I'm going to be one of her bridesmaids.'

'In that case, you're leading here.'

'Sarge, that's not fair.'

'Who said it was fair?' Cullen opened the door. 'After you.'

Eva marched into the crowded office space. She stopped and

gazed around, then headed towards the window. A row of cacti bathed in the sunshine, one of them waving out into the room. 'Paula.'

Zabinski sat at a laptop, hammering the keys. She looked up at her visitors. Pale blonde hair, rosy cheeks dotted with freckles. 'Eva, how the devil are you?' Accent purest Leith.

'Not bad. Boss is a bit of a wanker.' Eva winked at Cullen.

'We're not wearing gold dresses.' Zabinski folded her arms. 'That's settled.'

'It's work. This is DS Cullen. We need your help. Our murder victim had coke from the same batch you've got James Anderson looking at.'

'And?'

'It would be useful to know who's dealing this stuff.'

'I can't tell you.'

'Why?'

'Look, our investigation goes back to 2008.' Zabinski stared at her cacti and thumbed at Cullen. 'And he'll blab.'

He raised his hands. 'I'm not telling anyone, other than my superiors.'

'Your reputation precedes you. Six years of investigation could go just like that.' Zabinski snapped her fingers. 'Soon as we widen this out beyond our team, we lose control. Our suspect'll know we're on to him.'

'This is a murder case.'

'I'm very pleased for you.'

'Surely if we can nail whoever you're after for murder, then it'll be a good conviction.'

She folded her arms. 'Any evidence he did it?'

Cullen smirked. 'You need to tell us who he is first.'

Zabinski blushed. 'With all due respect, bugger off.'

Cullen kept his focus on her. She wasn't looking away. 'Look, I've never met you before, but we really need your help.'

'I can't give it to you.'

'This could be the link we need.'

'I'm not giving up our investigation.'

'Who's your DI?'

'Paul Wilkinson.'

Cullen frowned. 'Thought he was on football hooliganism?'

'Transferred over a couple of months back. Do you know him?'

'He owes me.'

'So call him.'

'Isn't he here?'

'He's at HQ today meeting the Chief.'

'Fine.' Cullen took out his Airwave and dialled Wilkinson's number from memory. 'Paul, how's it going?'

'Curran.'

How many more times... 'It's Cullen.'

'Right, right.' Sounded like he was driving. 'Been meaning to call you.'

Cullen let out a groan. 'Why?'

'Need someone to dig into a drug ring on Schoolbook.'

Cullen sighed, watching Eva lean forward to speak to Zabinski. 'I think Operation Venus is linked to a murder I'm working.'

'Can't just give information out based on you thinking something, lad.'

'Listen, if I keep the circle tight on this, would you give us some contacts?'

'I heard Brian Bain's back with you lot.'

'He is.'

'Then it's a fucking loose circle.'

'Look, sir, I'll be discreet. We'll just have a word with whoever it is. No mention of your investigation.'

'You think I can trust you?'

'Have I ever let you down?'

A pause. 'Right, speak to Paula Zabinski.'

'I'll put her on just now.' Cullen handed her the Airwave. 'DI wants a word.'

Eva smirked. 'That was impressive.'

'Let's see if she gives us anything.'

'What's it costing you?'

'The soul of my firstborn, I suspect.'

'You having kids?'

Cullen shut his eyes. 'No.'

Zabinski tossed the handset back. 'Wants another word.'

Cullen fumbled it, catching it on the second go. 'That us good?'

'Let's book out Monday morning for some Schoolbook analysis. You, me and Charlie Kidd.'

'Get the paperwork arranged first.'

'Already on my desk. See you on Monday, Curran.'

For crying out loud...

Cullen ended the call and perched on the edge of Zabinski's desk. 'So?'

'You're allowed into our magic circle.' Zabinski folded her arms tight to her chest. 'We've got a few street-level dealers selling this coke from some clubs and a few bars off Lothian Road.'

'You got any names?'

'Sure have. Eva was saying your guy's a banker?'

'That's right.'

'Sounds like a home delivery, then. We know of six kebab shops selling this stuff.'

'Who's doing it?'

'New guy on the block. Dean Vardy.'

Cullen winced, his mouth dry. 'Shite.'

Eva frowned. 'Is that name supposed to mean something to me?'

'Tried to put him away in January. Fucker wriggled out of it.'

35

C ullen shut the door to Methven's office. 'Did you get my voicemail, sir?'

'Which one?'

'Well, the one about the drug dealer.'

'Ah, the less sweary of the two.' Methven closed his eyes, the lids flickering. 'Be quick, I've got a catch-up with Alison in ten minutes.'

'I promised we'd be discreet about it.'

'As I shall be.'

'So we can't tell DS Bain.'

Methven opened his eyes again and glared at him. 'Get on with it.'

'They're investigating Dean Vardy.'

'Sodding hell.'

Cullen sat opposite the desk. 'I've left Eva there to go through their case files.'

'Very sage.' Methven slurped from a beige cup, gasping once he'd finished. 'What do you propose we do next?'

'I want to bring him in.'

'That won't happen.'

'Why?'

'I'm not risking an ongoing investigation without good reason. Especially one in which we've got previous.'

'Is that a dig at me?'

'We couldn't get any of the charges against him to stick. Need I remind you that the domestic abuse fell apart when the witness withdrew her testimony? Or Vardy's fake alibi recanted his statement and we didn't have a paper trail to support it?' Methven crumpled his cup. 'The only good thing was he dropped the lawsuit against us. This is a complex issue and I shall consult with Professional Standards.'

'We've got to speak to him. We need to find out where Van de Merwe got the drugs from.'

'There's nothing suggesting it's related.'

'Come on, sir. If he got behind on his drug payment, chucking him off the bridge would be well within their reach.'

'I'm not authorising it without any evidence.'

'Speaking to him is how we get evidence.'

'This drug investigation isn't a route to speaking to him.'

'Sir, I—'

'No buts, Sergeant. Now, is there anything else you need to apprise me of before I catch up with DCI Cargill?'

'Get her to reconsider the DC decision. Buxton'll be a real loss to our team.'

'There's nothing I can do.'

'I don't believe you, sir.'

~

'WHO's after a BLT with brown sauce?' Barbara looked around the non-existent queue. 'Ah, it'll be you, Sergeant Cullen. I can't get over how weird this roll is.'

Cullen took it off her. 'Ever had one?'

'I haven't.'

'Don't knock it, then.' Cullen carried his roll over to the window seat and watched buses, cars and taxis wrestle for a few inches of Leith Walk tarmac, horns blaring. He bit into his roll and checked his mobile.

A text from Buxton. *You rang?*

He thumbed out a reply. *In canteen.*

Another bite. The bacon tasted off but he still ate it. He looked around the place, a few of the back shift popping in.

Buxton wandered through the canteen, stopped by Cullen's table and folded his arms. 'Got a lead on Candy.'

'Sounds good.' Cullen pointed at the seat next to him. 'Care to join me?'

Buxton ran a hand over his head and stayed standing. 'Just back from Fanny Hill. She did time when she was eighteen. Just turned. Assault. Battered someone in a pub in Fife. Left him with two teeth missing and a cracked rib.'

'Jesus.'

'She's a big girl, remember?'

'Not really. So you've found her?'

'Wangled her parole officer's number from the screw.'

'Worth a punt, I suppose.'

'I've just spoken to him on the phone. Says he remembers her, but anything else needs to be face to face. Do you want me to follow it up?'

'Go for it.' Cullen took the last bite of his roll and swallowed it down. 'There's something I need to tell you.'

'Good news, I hope.'

'You didn't get the DC gig.'

A frown stretched Buxton's forehead. 'Are you winding me up?'

'No.'

'For fuck's sake.'

'I tried, Si. We can do it again next—'

'Forget it.' Buxton stomped across the canteen, shaking his head.

Jesus Christ. Cullen balled up his roll wrapper.

His phone rang. Unknown caller.

Here we go again. 'Cullen.'

'Sergeant, it's Martin Ferguson.'

'Are you downstairs?'

'I'm afraid I'm being detained here longer than I anticipated.'

'At your solicitor's?'

'That's right. It's a more complex matter than I'd, er, believed.'

'First thing tomorrow, then.'

'Of course.' Ferguson killed the call.

Cullen rocked back on the chair. Texted Sharon:

Going home. Knackered and can't be arsed with the briefing.

CLATTER.

Cullen blinked awake and looked around the living room. The white noise of a football crowd bled from the TV. Fluffy lay on the sofa back, purring. Burnt toast smell. Sore neck.

He sat up and kneaded the tendon on the left of his neck. Really tight.

Blinking at the screen, his vision cloudy. The top left showed AFG 2-1 TKN. Afghanistan beating Turkey? That can't be right. The drunken Irish drawl of the co-commentator confirmed it — Turkmenistan. Looked like a decent match.

CLATTER.

He spun around, fists clenched. Someone at the door. His heart thudded. He took a couple of steps into the hall.

CLATTER.

Cullen searched round for the baseball bat. Not there. He swallowed hard and leaned against the wall, reaching out for the snib. Twisted it without a sound.

CLATTER.

Laughter.

What the hell?

He yanked the door open.

Sharon knelt outside the door, fumbling for her keys. She looked up and laughed. 'Can you—' Burp. 'Can you help me here?'

'Jesus Christ.' Cullen hauled her to her feet. Picked up her keyring. 'What's going on?'

'Had a couple—' Another burp. 'Couple drinkies with Chantal.'

'Were you drinking Meths?'

She staggered into the flat and rested her forehead against the wall. 'Nice wine.'

'Come on, you need some water.' Cullen slammed the door and helped her into the sitting room.

Fluffy stretched out on his back in the white light the TV cast over the floorboards, one leg in the air. 'Ma-wow!'

Cullen pushed Sharon down onto the sofa. 'Have a seat.'

She sprawled out. 'Mm. I love you, Scotty boy.'

'I'm glad to hear it.' He got a glass from the draining board and filled it. A head rush clattered his skull. Too much too soon after waking. His pulse thudded in his ear. He downed the water himself, then refilled the glass and took it over. 'Here you go.'

'Mm, lovely boy.' She spilled half of it on her blouse. She rested the glass on the edge of the coffee table. 'Thanks.'

Cullen perched on the arm of the sofa and nudged the glass over. 'Changed days. You getting pissed after work instead of me.' He picked up the glass. 'Do you want another?'

'Easier just to have a shower.' She cackled and lay back. 'Oh, this is nice and warm.'

'I was asleep when you started throwing your keys around.' Cullen walked over to the kitchen and refilled the glass. Just about getting dark outside. He pinched his nose and cleared the sleep crystals from his eyes. He returned to the sofa and handed her the glass. Then lifted her legs to sit underneath. 'You should drink that.'

'I'll be peeing all night.'

'You'll be a mess in the morning.'

'I'm a mess all the time.'

Cullen clenched his teeth. 'You're not that bad.'

'That's what we talked about last night. You said—'

'I'm saying you need to talk about how you feel, okay?'

'Maybe.' She sipped the water. 'God, I shouldn't have had those shots.'

'Thought it was just wine?'

'Wine and vodka.'

'It always messes you up.' Cullen took the glass and put in on the coffee table. 'Why were you drinking?'

'Chantal wanted to talk about why you'd dumped her on me.'

'I didn't—'

'She thinks you did.'

'This is an opportunity for her.'

'I was telling her that.' Another burp. 'God, Red Bull's so gassy.'

'Vodka Red Bulls?'

'Yeah, I know.' She shut her eyes. 'We had another victim. Raped two weeks ago.'

'Jesus. What happened?'

'The guy was in hospital for a week. Another torn rectum.'

Cullen felt his eyes water. 'Aye, better not to talk about it.'

She peeked through her eyelids at him. 'Sorry for waking you up.'

'It's fine. I'm exhausted. Lost count of how many days in a row I've been on. Just thinking of the overtime.'

She opened her eyes again. 'Scott, don't do this to yourself.'

'It'll be okay. Once we get a suspect charged, it'll be paperwork central. Easy street.'

'You should take time off.'

'Don't worry about it.' Cullen massaged her left calf through her trousers. 'Buxton didn't get the job.'

'Oh, Scott.'

'I let him down. Cargill gave it to some constable who'd worked in Lamb's team for the last six months.'

'How did Budgie take it?'

'Not very well. You know how much of a princess he can be.'

'Pot, kettle.'

'Yeah, fair enough.' Cullen shifted to her right calf. 'It's the worst possible time for this to happen.'

'How do you mean?'

'Well, he's working for me. If I've let him down, his head'll drop. Will have to send him back to uniform and get Chantal back.'

'Scott...'

'I'll sort it out.' He patted her legs. 'You should get to bed.'

'Are you suggesting something?'

'Look, you really need to talk to me.'

'Scott...'

'I'm serious. You've not spoken about this for a whole year. A *year*. You know how much I hate you keeping things from me.'

'Don't.'

'Come on, Sharon. Talk.'

'Scott, you want kids. I can't give you that. We're done.'

'I don't bloody want them.'

'But you're good with them.'

'So? I've got two nieces, you've got one of each. We get the good bits. No tantrums or baths or hospital visits in the middle of the night. No school reports. Taking them swimming. Them waking us at six on a Saturday morning. No teenagers. That's *good*.'

'You're weird.'

'Like you said, I'm a freak. You, me and Fluffy.'

She collapsed onto the sofa next to him and snuggled in. 'You are a freak.'

He leaned down and kissed her on the lips. She responded for the first time in months.

DAY 6

Friday
23rd May

36

'So, in summary, then,' Cargill cast her gaze around the plainclothes and uniformed officers ramming the Incident Room, lingering on Cullen for a few seconds, 'this case has been underway for almost a week, but we're not seeing the sort of progress we demand in Police Scotland.'

'I wholeheartedly agree.' Methven drummed his fingers on the whiteboard, focusing on Cullen. 'We need to revisit all witness statements and re-interview where necessary. Redouble our efforts.'

Cullen glared back at him. How exactly do we do that? He sniffed and bit his tongue.

'We don't expect to close cases off in a day.' Methven jabbed a finger into the diagram. 'We do, however, expect to know what we're dealing with. This is a high-profile case, a red ball if you will. The death of a high-earning figure in Edinburgh society generates press interest. We can't let this go cold.'

Cullen raised a hand. 'We've got to accept it might be heading that way, sir.'

'This will *not* end up as a cold case. Sergeant, can you please update us on your activities to bring the killer to justice?'

Cullen got out his notebook, catching Bain sniggering into his WakeyWakey can. 'The drug analysis is one of the few leads we need to progress.'

'It's a dead end. '

'Sir, I'm not sure—'

'Leave it.' Methven glared at the whiteboard. 'Move on.'

Eva glanced over at Cullen, frowning. 'A dead end?'

'We'll keep it that way until we hear otherwise, sir.' Cullen tried to avoid looking at Eva. Failed. 'DC Law, did you have something to add?'

'Nothing, Sarge.'

'Okay. In other news, we're tracing the whereabouts of one Paul Vaccaro. We believe he's a co-owner of UC Partners.'

Cargill frowned at Methven. 'This is because of the alleged corruption?'

'UC were skimming money off resource on the programme. We believe Mr Van de Merwe was an equity partner. Vaccaro's the only other name we've heard.'

'How is this behaviour criminal?'

'Because Van de Merwe was abusing the system. He forced invoices through when Alba Bank should've been vetting the hires and the expenditure of a third party.'

'So he was double dipping?'

'Whatever that means.' Cullen glanced at his notebook again. 'We're getting assistance from the City of London Police to trace their involvement and hopefully identify the third partner.'

Cargill raised an eyebrow. 'Keep an eye on the budget there, Sergeant.'

'Will do. They're probing Mr Van de Merwe's offshore bank records for us, as well.'

'What for?'

'We believe he's accepted bribes from IMC in exchange for business. Maybe millions.'

'That's fascinating, but I fail to see how it's related to our case.'

'If they terminated those contracts, someone at IMC might have a grudge.'

'Keep progressing it, Sergeant.'

'Yes, ma'am. Next, we're trying to trace the lap dancer Mr Van de Merwe took to a few functions.'

Buxton coughed. 'I've spent the last—'

'Just a second.' Methven wrote *Candy* on the whiteboard. 'You think she could've killed him?'

'That's correct.' Buxton folded his arms, glaring at Cullen. 'Visited her screw in Fan—' He blushed. 'Cornton Vale last night. Said Candy was vicious in there. Notorious for running a gang. Got out after two years of a four-stretch.'

'Even though she ran a gang?'

Buxton remained focused on his notebook. 'Didn't do anything particularly naughty.'

'And she's a lap dancer even though she's been in prison?'

'The prison officer said it's all they talk about in there. Easy money if you've got the looks. They don't vet your CV like, say, Starbucks. They just look at your vital statistics.'

Cargill grinned. 'And what are yours, Constable?'

Buxton's eyes looked around the room. 'Sorry, those were her words, not mine.'

Methven cleared his throat. 'Why do you think she could've killed Mr Van de Merwe?'

'She has the means, sir.'

'Does she have an alibi for the time of death?'

'Sort of.'

Cargill tilted her head. 'Can you explain that?'

'We, uh, we—' Buxton cleared his throat. 'We've not, uh—'

'What he's trying to say, ma'am, is we've not spoken to her since the initial interview.' Cullen held her gaze. 'She missed a meeting the following morning to detail her alibi and has since gone to ground, ma'am.'

'Let me know the second she's in custody. Okay?'

Bain crushed his can. 'Should never have let her go in the first place.'

'I agree.' Cargill pressed her lips tight. 'But, we are where we are.'

'Interviewing a lassie like that needs experience, ma'am.' Bain tossed the can into the bin. 'Happy to step in if this pair manage to track her down.'

'Agreed. DS Bain, please lead the interview.'

Cullen clenched his fists. 'Ma'am, this is Simon's work.'

Cargill jerked her head round to Bain. 'Keep DS Cullen informed as to the progress of the interviews.' She nodded at Methven. 'Colin?'

'I think that concludes today's briefing. Dismissed.'

Chaos exploded around Cullen. He reached a hand out to Buxton. 'Si, wait—'

Buxton glared as he marched off, putting his phone to his ear.

Cullen leaned back against the pillar and snorted. 'Jesus Christ.'

Eva nudged his arm. 'What was that about a dead end, Sarge?'

'Politics.'

'So I should stop looking into the drugs angle?'

'Let's just keep what you're doing under the radar.'

She grinned. 'Cowboy.'

'So people keep saying. Get anything from your friend?'

'Drugs Squad have Vardy under surveillance.' She smiled. 'Six-man team in shifts round the clock.'

'Sounds like Wilkinson, all right.' Cullen stared back across the empty room. 'See if you can get close to it, okay?'

'Will do, Sarge.'

Buxton reappeared, nodding at Eva as he pocketed his phone. 'Just been on the blower to her parole officer, Sarge. Got another address for her.'

~

CULLEN STRETCHED out in the pool car and yawned up at the flat. Wind blew rubbish down the Bruntsfield side street. Heels clacked on both sides, women heading to buses and offices. 'You ready to tell me what the PO told you?'

'Candy gave her the address last night. Said it's a stopgap after that place we raided the other day.' Buxton let his seatbelt ride up. 'Where's backup?'

'You sure you're okay about what happened last night?'

'Thinking I should just leave the force and get a proper job.'

'You're not serious, are you?'

'Turned down for the job I've done for two years. Someone's trying to tell me something.'

'Come on, Si, the decision was out of my hands.'

'You see how much these banking guys are making?'

'Aye. Dealing with total arseholes all day.'

'So do we. I'd rather earn a decent amount for it.' Buxton tapped a finger against the glass. 'Here's trouble.'

A squad car pulled up, double-parking a few spaces away. Two uniforms got out, adjusting their caps against the wind.

Cullen opened the car door and jogged down the street, flashing his warrant card at them. 'DS Cullen. You're supporting us in apprehending the suspect.'

'Fine, Sarge.'

'Come on.' Cullen trotted over to the intercom, held it down and waited.

'What's up?'

'Police. Need to speak to a Christine Broadhurst.'

Static crackled out of the speaker. 'She's not here.'

'We know it's you, Candy. Let us in.'

'Candy's not here.'

'You're in serious trouble.'

'I'm not her.'

'Stop messing about.'

The handset clattered as it hit the wall.

Cullen nodded at the uniforms. 'Let's get in there.'

The bigger of the two tried the handle. The door opened. 'It's our lucky day.'

'Stay here.' Cullen entered the dank stairwell, the place stinking of mildew. 'Top floor, Si?'

'Always the top floor.'

Cullen led on up.

A door clicked above them.

'What's going on?' Cullen peered round, catching a flash of pigtails above the banister. 'Candy!'

Another door banged.

'She's gone to the other flat.' Buxton tore up the stairs, three at a time.

Cullen barged past him. Wet footprints led along the red tiles. He knocked on the door just along the corridor. 'Candy, this is the police!'

'You can't come in! This is harassment!'

'We'll charge you with obstructing an ongoing investigation.'

'Speak to my lawyer!'

'We have. He doesn't know where you are.'

'I've not done anything!'

'So why are you hiding?'

'I'm innocent.'

'We've got an arrest warrant for you. It's within our rights to break down this door.'

'What?'

'We're permitted to enter the property by any means necessary. Your friend won't be happy with that. Come with us and answer some questions.'

The door clicked open. Candy stood in a towel, a woman in a tracksuit behind her. She pulled the towel open, showing off her tanned body. Fake breasts, too round and too high up her chest. 'Maybe we can come to an arrangement, boys?'

Buxton grabbed her wrist and snapped on a pair of cuffs. 'You're not getting out of my sight.'

Candy gasped as the towel dropped to the floor. 'Can I at least get dressed first?'

~

CULLEN WANDERED THROUGH THE CANTEEN, picking at bacon stuck between his teeth. Spotted Murray sitting on his own, beasting a fry-up, and headed over. 'That looks healthy.'

'Lots of protein, Sarge.'

'And saturated fat and cholesterol. You're knackered whichever way the heart disease pendulum swings.'

Murray finished chewing. 'Yeah, good one.'

'You seen Buxton?'

'He's avoiding you. Told me he didn't get the full DC gig.'

'Where is he?'

'Bain told him to sit in the Obs Suite while he interviews Candy. Didn't seem too happy with you, though. Is this what I can expect when you sponsor me for DS?'

'You'll be lucky.' Cullen balled up his sandwich wrapper. 'You found Vaccaro yet?'

'Not quite.'

'You heard Cargill earlier. My nuts are toast if we don't make progress. And if my—'

'Yeah, I get it. Mine are too.' Murray soaked up the last of the egg yolk with his tattie scone. 'I've maybe got a lead on him from the City police boy.'

'Maybe?'

'Seems hopeful he can get something from somewhere.'

'Any danger of any precision here?'

Murray bit the mouthful, teeth clinking off the steel, and tapped his nose. 'A-ha.'

'Come on, what is it?'

'I'm not telling you until it pays off.'

'This sounds like some cowboy gamble.'

Murray smirked. 'Learning from the best.'

Cullen shook his head. 'Well, if you're going to be like that, I need you to do me a favour.'

Murray dropped his cutlery onto the plate. 'What?'

'Martin Ferguson didn't turn up to give a statement last night. Luckily Crystal forgot, otherwise he'd have another reason to bollock me at the briefing. Can you round him up?'

'And what about you, mighty Sergeant?'

'Off to watch Bain messing up an interview.'

CULLEN ENTERED THE OBS SUITE, upsetting the layer of dust on the computers and filing cabinets.

'—on, princess. The more you talk, the easier it'll be.'

Buxton glanced over at Cullen and sneered as he muted the speakers. 'Sarge.'

Cullen planted himself next to him and focused on the screen.

Bain and McCrea sat opposite Alistair Reynolds and Candy, now wearing a tracksuit.

Cullen glanced over at Buxton. 'You're doing well, Si. Your head could've dropped after the ... news.'

'You know I'm not that sort of copper.'

'I know. There'll be more roles soon.'

'They can shove them up their arses.' Buxton turned the sound back up.

'—eetheart, you need to speak to us.' Bain rubbed his moustache.

'My lawyer says I don't.'

'Do you listen to everything he says? If he says jump, do you ask how high first?'

'I'm not responding to that.'

Cullen stood. 'This isn't getting anywhere, is it?'

'Not really.' Buxton slumped forward, resting his head on his arms. 'Been like this for the last half hour.'

Cullen frowned. 'Do you think she's involved?'

'Got to be, mate. Why else would she piss us about?'

'Heard about your trick with the towel.' Bain licked his lips, thumbed at Reynolds. 'That how you're paying for this guy?'

'Inspector!'

Cullen's phone rang. Eva. He twisted away to answer it. 'Hey.'

'Sarge. Just got back the Gmail account from Charlie. You know, the personal ones? Anyway, Van de Merwe got some emails from someone called "The Lady In Red Latex".'

'Anything of interest?'

'I'd say they've been sleeping together. Looks like he was meeting her on Saturday night.'

'Just before he died... Any idea who it is?'

'None. Charlie's probed the IP address. Says it's in Edinburgh, but he can't pin it to a user without a warrant.'

'Shite.' Cullen swapped hands and stared at the monitor, Candy laughing at Bain. 'Did Charlie get a computer from either of Candy's addresses?'

'Don't think so, why?'

'What about a phone?'

'Got a Samsung thingy.'

'Get Tommy Smith to check if the emails came from her.'

'Right. He'll need a RIPSA form.'

'I'll get him a RIPSA. Just get him extracting emails while she's in the interview.'

'If it's Candy, it proves she was screwing him, right? Shows she's lied to us.'

'Maybe.' Cullen pinched his nose, still sore from the other night. He clicked his fingers. 'She's been inside, right? That means she's on the DNA database. Got to go.' He killed the call and dialled Anderson. 'James, you got a minute?'

'Aye, if you're okay with me delaying finishing off some proper work.'

'Have you finished the sex room analysis yet?'

'If you're recording this, you can get to fuck.'

'Of course I'm not.'

'Right. Well, I'm running your DNA against the NDNAD just now.'

'Have you got a match against a Christine Broadhurst?'

'Should I?'

'We think she was sleeping with Van de Merwe. Can you run her DNA against the sex room?'

'I'll need to stop this.'

'Go on.'

'You'll lose six hours of processing...'

'Just do it.'

'Okay. Starting again.' Keys clattered in the background. 'Oh, here she is. Did time, right?'

'Correct. Call me when you get the results.'

'Hold your horses. Tracing a record back to what we've found is a lot easier than what I was trying to do. Bingo. You've got a hit.'

'So she was in his sex room?'

'Aye. Hang on. Got dried saliva, vaginal lubrication and some pubes with the follicles still attached. Judging by the dates, she'd been there a few times.'

'Cheers. That's us even.' Cullen ended the call and raced out into the corridor.

'What's up?'

Cullen grinned back at Buxton. 'You'll see.' He jogged along the hallway and burst into the interview room. 'I need a word.'

Bain glared at him. 'What?'

'Pause it.' Cullen held open the door.

'We'll be back in a minute.' Bain leaned over to the microphone. 'Interview suspended at oh nine forty-two.'

Cullen waited for Bain to join him in the corridor, then shut the door.

Bain folded his arms. 'Right, Harry fuckin' Potter, what've you conjured up?'

'I can get her.'

Bain waved an imaginary wand in the air. 'Suspecticus confessicus.'

'Let me take over.'

Bain opened the door. 'Fill your fuckin' boots.'

Cullen entered the room without a backward glance and sat next to McCrea, giving him a nod.

McCrea stabbed a thick thumb onto the recorder, hefting his bulk over the table to lean into the microphone. He ran a hand across his shaved skull as he counted to five. 'Interview recommenced at nine forty-four a.m. DS Scott Cullen has entered the room and DS Bain has left.'

Cullen smiled at Candy. 'Good morning, Christine.'

She tilted her head to the side and tucked her loose hair behind her ears. 'I prefer to be called Candy.'

Cullen nodded slowly. 'Okay, I'll cut to the chase, shall I? Remember when we spoke to you the other night? You said something about going for a drink at Mr Van de Merwe's house?'

'That's right. Just a drink.'

'Well, we found a sex room in the house. Just finished—'

'I wasn't there!'

'—running the forensics. Your DNA matches at least three separate traces.'

'I wasn't there!'

'You *were* there. Having sex by the looks of things.'

'I wasn't!'

'You're in deep trouble here.'

'I never went there!'

'Now, we could do you for providing a false statement.' Cullen folded his arms. 'Or we can have another discussion about what you were *really* doing there.'

She glanced at her lawyer, then snarled at Cullen. 'What do you want to know?'

'Did you have sex with Mr Van de Merwe?'

She plucked a lash out of her eye. 'Yes.'

'When?'

'I don't know exact dates.'

'When was the last time?'

'It's not been for a while.'

'Days?'

'Weeks. Months, maybe.'

'Were you at his house on Sunday morning?'

'No.'

'Saturday night?'

'No.'

'In the interview the other night, you said someone might've been with you in your bed.'

'My boyfriend.'

'So you've got a boyfriend now?'

'Been going out a few months now. I was at his flat, sleeping.'

'While he was out with the boys?'

'That a problem?'

'Why weren't you there this morning?'

'I was staying at a pal's flat. He's been busy.'

'Why didn't you tell us you were with him when we spoke to you the other night?'

'Because.'

'Because you were with him or because you weren't?'

'Just because.'

'So, you're saying you were with him?'

'That's right.'

'What's his name, Candy?'

'Dean Vardy.'

37

C ullen stood outside the *Southside Cars* office, the harled
    wall gleaming white in the sunshine, and nodded at
    Bain, then Buxton. 'Other units in place?'

'Yeah. Vardy's not at his home, his bookies or his pub.'

Cullen looked around the small team. 'Let's go, gentlemen.'

Bain shook his head. 'Crystal's not okayed this, has he?'

'Doesn't need to. There's no crossover with the drug squad's
operation.'

'I'm glad you don't work for me anymore, Sundance.'

'Not as much as I am.' Cullen pointed for Bain and McCrea to
go round the back, then got the two uniforms to guard the silver
Škodas on the drive. A blue Subaru sat next to them, a strip at the
top of the windscreen reading DEANO. 'Come on, Si.'

He led inside the office. Fruit machine lights danced on the
left, Sky Sports News HQ on a TV mounted on the right wall.
Ahead was a wide reception desk, the door behind closed. Hip-
hop blared from somewhere, liquid bass and gnarly vocals.
Eminem.

A blonde girl looked up from her nails. 'Can I help?'

'DS Scott Cullen.' Cullen held out his warrant card. 'Is Mr
Vardy here?'

'He's not in, sorry.'

'Where is he?'

'Haven't seen him for a couple of days.'

Cullen gripped the edge of the counter. 'Look, you—' He stopped. Frowned at Buxton. There it was again — a loud snort came from somewhere. 'Can you hear that, Constable?'

Buxton pointed behind her at the locked door. 'Think it's coming from through there.'

The receptionist was on her feet. 'You can't go—'

Cullen flipped up the desk partition. 'We can.'

She slapped his arm, her palm cracking off his watch. 'You can't!'

Cullen pushed her back and knocked on the door. 'Mr Vardy, it's the police. Can you come out, please?'

No answer.

Cullen kept the receptionist at arm's reach and knocked again. 'I'm giving you a final chance. We've got reasonable cause to enter.'

Nothing again.

He nodded to his left. 'Constable.'

Buxton cracked his knuckles. Took a step back and lurched forward, kicking the door.

The lock snapped and the door toppled open.

Dean Vardy was crouched over the desk, facing away. Wide shoulders rippling with muscles, his T-shirt stretching around thick triceps. One finger over his nose, snorting up a line of white powder while Eminem rapped. He spun round. 'What the fu—'

'Mr Vardy, we need a—'

Vardy widened his eyes. '*You?*'

'—with you about—'

Vardy lashed out, his camel boot crunching into Buxton's groin. 'You fucking cunt!'

Cullen grabbed Vardy's arm. 'Mr Vardy, I'm arrest—'

Vardy launched his head forward.

Bone crunched in Cullen's face. His nose exploded in a riot of pain. A fist thumped his stomach. He tumbled to his knees. Blinded by blood and tears, he reached out. Caught Vardy's wrist. Twisted it round.

'Aargh, you fucker!'

Cullen pulled Vardy to the floor and got on his back, left knee into the spine. 'You're under arrest!'

Vardy struggled around, kicking out, lashing with his arm. He failed to connect.

Cullen pressed his forehead into the carpet.

Buxton got up, clutching his balls. He got behind Cullen.

'Si, can you cuff him?'

A black boot appeared, connecting with Vardy's groin. He screamed out. 'Fuck!'

Cullen snapped a cuff on each wrist and turned to glare at Buxton, wincing through the pain. 'What did you do that for?'

Buxton shrugged. 'He was resisting arrest, right?'

CULLEN PROWLED THE INTERVIEW ROOM, going behind Dean Vardy and Campbell McLintock. Rubbed his nose, specks of blood on the back of his hand. Second time in two days. Something felt loose in there.

He locked eyes with Buxton. 'Mr Vardy, you assaulted my colleague.'

'You boys burst into my office.' Vardy sniffed and tugged his nose, sniffing again. 'You'd no right doing that.'

'What were you doing in there? Other than lines of cheap coke?'

Vardy craned his neck to look at Cullen. 'You didn't have a warrant.'

'We had reasonable cause. You were using a Class A substance.'

Vardy stared at the desktop. 'It's for my asthma.'

'Your asthma?' Cullen winked at Buxton. 'That's a new one on me.' He leaned forward to growl into Vardy's ear. 'That coke's with our forensic team. There's a hell of a lot of a particular type on the street just now. Be a shame if it traced back to you, wouldn't it?'

'Sergeant.' McLintock rolled a tongue across his dry lips. He didn't turn to look at Cullen, just stared at his vacant seat. 'My client's instructed me to make a formal complaint about ADC Simon Buxton's conduct.'

'We'll deal with that once we've received it. If we receive it. I want to know about your client's drug use.'

'I've nothing to say to you, him or anyone.' Vardy snorted a couple of times. Grunted. 'I've done fuck all.'

'I'll take that to mean you've not done anything illegal.'

'Aye. That.'

'Mr Vardy, once we link that cocaine to the stuff being sold on the street, you'll be —'

'That stuff's for personal use.' Vardy screwed up his face. 'That's it, okay?'

'There's no personal use protection for a Class A.'

'I'm not dealing! Fuck's sake.' Vardy folded his arms, bulky at the biceps but thin at the wrist. 'What do you fucking want to know?'

'Are you dealing this stuff?'

'I've said I'm not. Are you deaf?'

'Sergeant, please can you get to the point?'

Cullen leaned on the edge of the table with both hands. 'I deal with murders and other serious crimes. I'm not part of the drug squad.'

Vardy raised an eyebrow. 'You saying they're investigating me?'

'I didn't say that.'

'So why are you raising it?'

Cullen swallowed. 'We need to—'

'Why the fuck have you got me in here?'

Cullen reached over to Buxton's papers and snatched up a photo, tossing it on the table in front of Vardy. 'Ever seen this man before?'

'Am I supposed to?'

'His name's Jonathan van de Merwe. He took a tumble off a bridge early on Sunday morning.'

'I'm very sorry to hear it.'

'Know anything about it?'

'Should I?'

'We found a bowl of cocaine in his house on Belford Road.' Cullen left a long pause, watching Vardy for any reaction. Nothing. 'Our forensic chemical analysis shows it matches a batch you're selling.'

Vardy laughed. 'I'm a legitimate businessman.'

'Ah yes. You own a pub, a bookies and a taxi firm. And you're only twenty-eight years old. I wonder where you got the cash to start that little empire.'

'Twenty-nine, mate. Birthday last month.'

'Many happy returns. Bet you're glad you weren't inside for big Shug to give you a special present.'

'What the fuck are you saying?'

'You managed to wriggle out of some serious crimes last time we spoke in January. Impressive work.'

'My client's innocence has been proven, Sergeant.'

'Not by a court of law.' Cullen switched his gaze to the lawyer, locking eyes. 'Cases collapsing due to witnesses pulling out isn't the same thing as being proven innocent.'

'You didn't even have enough to take it before a judge.'

Vardy prodded his septum. 'What's your game here?'

'Talk to us about Mr Van de Merwe and we'll see what we can do about the coke charges.'

'I don't know nothing about no coke, pal.'

'So many negatives... What about the stuff you were snorting?'

'You planted that.'

'Mr Vardy, did you kill Mr Van de Merwe because he owed you money?'

'What?'

'He's got a bowl of your coke. Lot of cash in that. Maybe five hundred grams? How much is that on the street?'

Vardy folded his hulking arms. 'I wouldn't know.'

'It's high five figures, at least. Price per gram's pretty low just now, isn't it?'

'What do you want from me?'

'Did he owe you any money?'

'I. Don't. Deal. Drugs.'

Cullen held his stare. Vardy wasn't looking away any time soon. 'Okay, tell us about Christine Broadhurst.'

'Candy?' Vardy shrugged. 'She works for me in Wonderland.'

Cullen frowned, tilting his head to the side. 'You own it?'

'Bought it off the model shop boy. Got approval to turn it into a lappy.'

'I still don't get where all the money's coming from.'

'It's all legit.'

'You been sleeping with her?'

'Maybe.'

'You're happy with her taking her clothes off for other men?'

Vardy gave a shrug. 'Beats what you do for a living.'

'Is she still working as an escort?'

'What?'

'We understand she used to accompany lonely men to functions or dinner. Maybe give them something extra.'

Vardy ran a hand across his nose. 'I'm trying to take her away from all that.'

'Does she still do extras, now she's your partner?'

'She's stopped that.'

'Did any of this work go through you?'

'Fuck you.'

'Are you going to beat her up as well?'

Vardy stabbed a finger at Cullen. 'Those charges got dropped.'

'My client will not answer any questions pertaining to other investigations.'

'I bet he won't.' Cullen reached over to Buxton's pile of papers and pulled out a document. He snapped the paper tight. 'Candy's admitted to working as an escort. Said she serviced Mr Van de Merwe on a few occasions. We've also got him paying for dances at Wonderland.'

'So?'

'I want to know where you were when he died.'

'Which is when?'

'Sunday morning, three thirty a.m.'

'That's easy.' Vardy gave a chuckle. 'I was on George Street. Just been in Tigerlily's.'

'Sure about that?'

'Of course I am.'

Cullen took his time treading the squeaking floorboards to his seat. He collapsed into it, arms folded. 'You weren't at home?'

'Nope.'

'So you weren't with Christine?'

Vardy gripped the edge of the table, his eyes narrow slits. 'What?'

'She says you were at home with her.'

'Fuck.' Vardy shut his eyes and clenched his jaw, hands covering his face. 'Right.'

'So, what was it? Cuddling up to Candy, where you've got no evidence, or outside Tigerlily, where we'll get you on CCTV?'

Vardy looked away. 'Tigerlily.'

'We've got two separate witness statements of a woman in a cloak with the deceased. In about an hour, Ms Broadhurst will go in front of two line-ups.'

'Eh?'

'Did she push Mr Van de Merwe off the bridge?'

'I don't fucking know.'

'If you help us with Candy, we'll see what we can do about the drug charges.'

Vardy leaned over to whisper into McLintock's ear and listened to the response before nodding. 'Right. Candy's pregnant.' He glanced away. 'I think this Van de Merwe cunt's the father.'

'That what she told you?'

The door burst open. Methven stomped into the room, eyes blazing. 'Sergeant. A word.'

Cullen leaned across the table. 'DI Methven has entered the room. Interview terminated at eleven eleven a.m.' He got up and nodded at Buxton. 'Stay here.'

'Not going anywhere.'

Cullen left the room, feeling Vardy's gaze burning into his back. He shut the door and braced himself for Methven's onslaught.

'Sergeant, I don't know what the sodding hell you're up to in there, but I want it to stop. Now.'

'We've burst Candy's alibi apart, sir. We've just established a motive for her to murder Van de Merwe.'

'You went over my head and progressed the drug—'

'This is a valid line of investigation.'

'Your methods leave a lot to be desired. I've just received a sodding fax about ADC Buxton's conduct. He kicked Vardy in the sodding balls!'

'It was reasonable force, sir. Vardy kneed him first. I was having difficulty subduing him.'

'This doesn't look good.'

'Look. He's a big guy. That was the only option we had.' Cullen smirked. 'I'm sure you know what it feels like.'

'You don't mention that again, Cullen. I'm lucky to be an expectant father.'

Cullen felt his stomach lurch. 'I didn't know, sir. Congratulations.'

'Thank you.' Methven rubbed his neck. 'Sergeant, DI Wilkinson visited me in person. He's taking this to DCS Soutar. This investigation is one of the Chief Constable's pet projects.'

Cullen ground his teeth together. 'We've done everything by the book, sir.'

Methven shook his head. 'I thought we were past your cowboy behaviour.'

'This is solid police work, sir.'

'Just make sure it stands up in court.'

38

C ullen stopped outside the witness interview room and nodded at Eva. 'She ready to go?'

'Aye, Sarge. Just a sec, though.' She folded her arms. 'Just got back from Fettes. Paula's got Vardy on CCTV. Vardy was in Tigerlily till three on Sunday morning, then was chatting to his mates on George Street.'

'It's definitely him?'

'We spoke to the bouncers on that night. They know him.'

'Good work.' Cullen stared at the door. 'You done a line-up before?'

'Did a couple when I was in Davenport's team.'

'You're leading, then.' Cullen followed her into the interview room and leaned against the wall. He smiled at Suzanne Marshall. 'Thanks for agreeing to do this.'

'Just doing my civil duty, Sergeant. Nothing special about that.' Suzanne adjusted her summer dress. 'I'm surprised it's taken you so long to get back in touch with me about my statement.'

Eva cued up the DVD player app on the laptop. 'Mrs Marshall, I'm going to show you a series of images of women matching the description you gave us. I need you to look at the women on the screen and tell me if you recognise any of them.'

Suzanne nodded, her earring twinkling. 'Okay.'

Eva clicked the mouse. 'Here we go.'

The VIPER logo swooshed across the display. It switched to a woman staring at the camera. Shoulder-length dark hair. Tall. Tanned. Number one at the top left, a grey wall behind her. She looked to her left. Then right. Then straight ahead again.

Suzanne blinked hard a few times. 'It's not her.'

'Okay.'

The screen switched. Another woman, number two top left. Taller, thinner. She turned to her left.

'That's her.'

Cullen narrowed his eyes. Definitely Candy.

Eva clicked the mouse again, pausing the video. 'You're sure?'

'Absolutely.'

Cullen frowned. 'You only had a glance at her.'

'Aye, but that's her.'

Cullen flicked back through his notebook. 'When we spoke to you on Sunday, you told us "I didn't get a good look at her face, though." How can you be so sure it's her?'

'I swear it is. I could see her hair. It was just like that.'

'This is a very serious matter, Mrs Marshall. When we get a conviction, you will be put on the stand and the defence will attempt to tear apart your statement.'

'It's her.'

'You don't want to look at the other six we've got?'

'That's enough for me.'

'Dean Bridge has sodium lights, Mrs Marshall. They can distort colours. You're positive it was her?'

'One hundred per cent.'

'Okay.' Cullen nodded at Eva. 'Can you get a formal statement from Mrs Marshall and escort her out, please?'

Candy tried to smile, skin flaking as her cracked lips parted. Her tongue traced across her teeth. 'What do you want to know?'

Cullen glanced at Methven, then smiled at Alistair Reynolds. 'Tell your client I'd prefer the truth.'

'Ms Broadhurst has only told the truth.'

'Right.' Cullen leaned over the desk, resting on his elbows. His phone buzzed in his pocket. 'Candy, Mr Vardy didn't back up your alibi for Sunday morning.'

Her eyes bulged. 'What?'

'At the time Mr Van de Merwe was killed, Dean was outside Tigerlily on George Street.'

'He was with me!'

'Candy, we've got him on CCTV.'

She rubbed her forehead, tears rolling down her blotchy cheeks. 'He was with me.' Her voice was tiny, barely loud enough for the mic to pick up.

'Mr Vardy believes your baby is Mr Van de Merwe's.'

'*What?*'

'So you are pregnant?'

'Three months. Just gone.' Her hand went to her belly. 'This isn't helping me slide down the pole.' She grabbed a breast through her T-shirt. 'These are bigger, though. Should get the silicone taken out.'

Cullen glared at her. 'Please take this seriously.'

'I am.'

'Where were you at that time?'

'Like I told you, I was at home. I'd been working. I'm shattered. This bloody baby...'

'Did you kill Mr Van de Merwe?'

'No fucking way. Are you serious?'

'Why, then, do we have a witness statement placing you on Dean Bridge at the time in question?'

Candy fanned her fingers against her chest. 'What?'

'You heard.' Cullen licked his lips. 'We have a sighting of Mr Van de Merwe on the bridge with a woman. A member of the public's just identified you.'

'How?'

'Remember the video you posed for?'

'Christ.'

'So, care to change your story?'

'I wasn't there. Whoever's telling you this is lying their arse off.'

'We found a cloak in your closet.'

Candy locked eyes with Cullen. 'What?'

'A red cloak. Matches the witness's description of the woman Mr Van de Merwe was with.'

'I've no idea what you're talking about.'

'Mr Van de Merwe's semen was splashed all over the cloak.'

'What?'

'We found it in your flat.'

'You'd no right going in there?'

'We had a search warrant.' Cullen glanced over at Methven. Time for another tack. 'How did Mr Vardy react to the news of the baby?'

She frowned. 'He wants to protect me.'

'Even though the baby's not his?'

Candy shook her head, staring at the wall. 'Fuck off.'

Cullen cracked his knuckles. 'Candy, Dean thinks Mr Van de Merwe is the father.'

'Right.'

'You told us you didn't have sex with him.'

'And then you found all that evidence.' She nodded, her head hardly moving. 'Fine. I had sex with him.'

'Unprotected?'

'He paid extra. I forgot to take the fucking pill. That's how I got into this shit.'

'Did you tell Mr Vardy the baby's his?'

'Of course I did.'

'To manipulate him?'

She looked away and sucked in breath. 'It might be his.'

'I'm not following you.'

'That night, I was at this party at VDM's. I went to Dean's after it. We had sex when I got in.' She ran the back of a hand across her face. 'It hurt. But Dean wanted it... I didn't refuse.'

'So you told him it's his?'

'I did.'

'Did he believe you?'

'You need to ask him that, don't you?'

'Are you arresting or charging my client yet?'

Methven thumped his notebook shut. 'That's still to be decided.'

Reynolds held up his Pebble smartwatch and tapped the screen. 'The clock's still ticking.'

Methven stood and adjusted his suit jacket. 'We're aware of the timeline.'

'We'll wait with bated breath.' Reynolds clasped Candy's hand.

'Interview terminated at twelve oh nine.' Cullen followed Methven out into the corridor, easing the door shut behind him. 'Well?'

'This is a sodding mess, Sergeant.'

'What matters is whether Vardy believed it was Van de Merwe's kid.'

'We've placed him elsewhere, though.'

'He could've paid someone. All it takes is for him to think Van de Merwe's knocked her up and get angry. He clearly thinks she's his property. Killing Van de Merwe might've been the next step.'

'I'll have another word with him.' Methven pulled out his Airwave and fiddled with the keys before putting it to his ear. 'DS Bain? Can you meet me outside interview room four? Thanks.'

'You're taking Bain in there?'

'Your fingers are dirty, Sergeant.' Methven wandered off down the corridor.

Cullen watched him go. Total wanker. He fished his phone from his pocket. A text from Rich: *Want to meet for lunch?*

39

T he waiter lugged two plates on one arm, presenting pasta to Rich and dumping a larger pizza plate in front of Cullen. 'Would you like parmigiano? Black pepper?'

Rich smiled. 'I'm good.'

'Sir?'

Cullen smiled. 'Can I have some Parmesan?'

The waiter tilted his head to the side. 'On a pizza?'

'Is that illegal?'

'One moment.' The waiter scuttled off.

Rich shook his head. 'You're still a freaky eater, Skinky.'

'It's a shame this place doesn't have doner kebab pizza.'

'It was a special last week, sir.' The waiter spooned pale flakes of cheese over his pizza, dusting it all over the sea of mozzarella, dotted with red islands of pepperoni. 'Enjoy, gentlemen.'

Cullen sliced into the crust. 'See? Freaky eaters are the future.'

Rich's gaze followed the waiter to another table. 'I'd smash his back doors in.'

'Come on, mate, I'm trying to eat.'

'Right.' Rich spiked a pasta shell. 'That's a fuckton of carbs, amigo.'

'I might find time to go for another run tonight.'

'Thought you'd given up.'

'Nah. I jog home via Portobello once a week.'

'And you don't visit?'

'You'd like me covered in sweat, would you?' Cullen chewed a mouthful of pizza. The Parmesan ruined it. 'This is on your expenses, right?'

'Depends what you give me, Skinkster.'

'What if it's nothing?'

'Then I'll need a tenner.'

'How's it going?'

'Shite. Job's going down the toilet.'

'How bad?'

'Another round of lay-offs looming. Talk of us merging with the Scotsman or the Herald. Maybe selling out to a London paper.'

'That must be tough.'

'And then some.'

'Used to think how weird it was you coming back up here. Now, I get it. You're a masochist.'

'Damn right. Sucker for punishment.'

Cullen ate another bite. 'Who gave you the story?'

'No comment.'

'Was it Tom?'

'It wasn't him.'

'A cop?'

'I'm not telling you, Scott. Jesus. I've got a source on the inside.'

'Someone Tom works with at the bank?'

'No comment.'

'I need to speak to them.'

'Why?'

'To find out what's going on there. You seem to get your info before we do.'

'What can I do, Skinky? Turn it down?' Rich picked up his fork and skewered another parcel. 'I could teach you how to do your job, if you want.'

'Just work with me, that's all I ask. I need to speak to them.'

'Let me think about it.'

Cullen sliced deep into the soggy middle. 'Thanks for not printing any stories over the last couple of days.'

'Do you want to stick the brownie points on my loyalty card?'

'Am I going to have anything to explain to my boss tomorrow?'

'Not sure.'

'So there's something brewing?'

'We'll see. I'm not telling you what.'

'Come on...'

Rich dropped his cutlery on the table, rattling around the noisy space. 'Sharon okay?'

'Not sure. Just don't know what's going on in her head sometimes.'

'Since the baby?'

'Aye.'

'You don't talk about it?'

'There's nothing else I can do about that.' Cullen folded up a wedge of pizza, hovering it in front of his mouth. 'Things are getting better.'

'Still, you've not been yourself either.'

Cullen chewed the wedge and wrapped a hand around the cold glass of water. He took a glance at his locked phone — no messages. 'Sharon told me something the other night.'

'What?'

'She...'

'Come on, Skinky, you can tell me.'

Cullen clenched his teeth. 'She can't have kids.'

'So how did she get pregnant?'

'It was when she lost the baby. Stopped her being able to have kids.'

'Shite. What are you going to do? Adopt?'

'I don't want kids.'

'Bullshit. Never met a bigger breeder than you, Skinky.'

'I'm not having kids.'

'You should've seen your face when you heard she was up the stick.'

'Up the stick?'

'You know what I mean. You looked like a pig in shit.'

Tears filled Cullen's vision. 'Christ.' He lurched to his feet and tore off across the restaurant.

'Scott?'

Cullen raised a hand. Pushed into the toilet and burst into the first cubicle. Kicked the door shut and locked it, collapsing onto his knees, tears burning his face.

Why hadn't she said anything?

A whole year?

He rested his head on the toilet seat, the wood cold and dry.

Why? Why couldn't she tell me? Am I that bad?

He rocked back onto his heels, propping his head against the stall door. He wiped a hand across his cheeks, soaked with tears.

Crying in a toilet... Get up, loser.

Need to let this out.

He clambered to his feet and unbolted the door. Leaned against the first sink, hands on the cold porcelain. He ran the tap and stared at his face, red and damp. Looking old. He splashed tepid water all over his cheeks.

Tell her I love her. It's not about the kids. It's about me and her. If she wants kids, let's adopt. Or not.

It's about the wall she built between us. Need to break it down.

He dried his face on the paper towels, harsh against his skin, and sucked in a deep breath. He smiled at the mirror then strolled back to their table, feeling a stone lighter. He sat and rolled up another wedge of pizza.

'You okay, Skinky?'

'I'm fine.'

'You were ages.'

'This is a good pizza.'

'Scott, do you want to talk about it?'

'It's nice. Even with the Parmesan.' Cullen took another bite, stabbing the home key on his phone. A text message from Murray. *Paul Vaccaro lead proving fruitful.*

'What's happened?'

'Work.' Cullen unlocked his phone and replied. *Let me know if anything comes of it.*

'Seriously, mate, your face—'

'I'm fine.'

'You're not fine. We were talking—'

'Drop it.' Cullen picked up the last wedge and bit into it. 'Why are you taking me out for lunch?'

'Can't I treat an old mate?'

'There's always something.'

'I want to see what you've got.'

'I'm in enough hot water with all the scoops you're getting.'

'At least tell me before the press release goes out.'

Cullen dropped the pizza crust to the plate. 'How did you hear this Van de Merwe boy was into a BDSM scene?'

Rich pushed his half-finished plate away and set his fork down. 'I don't name my sources.'

'Come on, mate.'

'This is off the record, okay? You're not getting me on tape like Tom.'

Cullen held up his hands. 'Fine.'

'Another guy at Alba Bank was into the scene.'

'What was his name?'

'Martin Ferguson.'

40

Cullen stopped just outside the Incident Room and spun round to face Buxton. 'So, Ferguson's not at Proctor's house?'

'Uniform had a cheeky look through the windows. Nobody in.' Buxton pocketed his Airwave. 'Also had a unit out in West Linton. Not there either.'

'So where is he?'

'No idea. Dirty bastard, though. Hiding his deviant sexual practices. Naughty, naughty.'

'Maybe.' Cullen rapped his fingertips off the wall. 'How are your bollocks?'

'Still got a twinge, mate.' Buxton grimaced. 'Serves me right for laughing at Crystal.'

'You'll be all right.'

'Once the swelling goes down. They're like fucking grapefruits.'

'Too much information, mate. Christ.' Cullen entered the Incident Room, busier than he'd expected — Eva stood by the whiteboard, while Murray was by the window, working on a laptop. He leaned against the pillar. 'Si, can you call Ferguson's wife? You've got a good relationship with the older—'

'Button it, mate.' Buxton yanked his phone from his pocket and walked off.

'Sorry.' Cullen got out his phone and called Harrison Proctor.

'Proctor.'

'It's DS Cullen. I'm looking for Martin Ferguson. He's not at your house.'

'I see.'

'Did he come home last night?'

'He's not been home, no.'

'He was supposed to give a statement last night but he didn't turn up. Now his name's turned up in relation to another part of the investigation.'

'Oh, Christ. When did you last hear from him?'

'About six last night. He was still at his solicitor's.'

'Have you—'

'They said he left at half past. Any idea where he could've gone?'

Proctor paused, footsteps echoing around a room. 'Listen, there might be something. If he had a deadline, Martin'd work until he collapsed, then check in to a hotel. Saved him the long drive down to West Linton.'

'Did he have any favourites?'

'I didn't go into specifics, I'm afraid. I'll look over his expenses, see if he put anything through us, rather than his own company.'

'Let me know.' Cullen pocketed his phone.

Buxton perched on the edge of the desk. 'His wife's not heard from him.'

'Shite.'

'Been looking through the case file for you, Sarge.' Murray tossed a folder at Cullen. 'Nothing. We're still waiting for Ferguson's bank records from Charlie Kidd.'

'Did he give you an ETA?'

'Charlie?' Murray laughed. 'Of course he didn't.'

Cullen nodded at Buxton. 'Come on, Si, let's get up there.' He trotted across the room, bumping into Methven as he entered. 'Afternoon, sir.'

'Sergeant, do you have time for a catch-up?'

'Not now, sir.'

'Where are you going?'

'Back soon.' Cullen pushed into the stairwell, taking the steps two at a time. He burped at the landing. 'Christ, that pizza's repeating on me.'

'Lucky you.' Buxton climbed up. 'I had a tuna baked tattie.'

'You're getting the local lingo, Si.' Cullen followed him across the floor, his tractor beam locked on Kidd tossing his ponytail and yawning. 'Afternoon, Charlie.'

'Here we go. Back to the Sundance ranch.'

Cullen rested on the edge of the desk and had a look around. 'No sign of any bank statements here.'

'Cos I don't bloody print everything out like you.'

'Have you done Martin Ferguson's yet?'

'Not had the time.'

'Come on, Charlie...'

'I do have other work to do, you know.'

'This is critical, okay? The guy's missing.'

'God's sake.' Kidd hammered his keyboard and tapped a finger on the screen. 'Here you go.'

Cullen peered at it. 'What's this?'

'Bank account and credit cards. Last three months' transactions. There's more if you want it.'

Cullen scanned down the screen to the bottom. Nothing with today's date. Only one with the previous day's. A wide line of data, a long number beginning 4543 in the leftmost column. 'What's this?'

'That's his credit card. That's a Tesco Bank number, I think.' Kidd copied the narrative into another window and pressed a key. The string split out into multiple columns. He tapped a column. 'It's a hotel just round the corner from Alba Bank.'

CULLEN FLASHED his card at the receptionist, the Leith Walk traffic trundling in the distance behind them. 'DS Scott Cullen. This is ADC Simon Buxton. We need some help in locating someone who might be staying here.'

The receptionist swallowed, his eyes darting around the empty vestibule. 'I'm not sure I can provide information like that.'

'Listen, he's a murder suspect. Just check he's here first, please?'

'Can I have the guest's name, sir?'

'It's Martin Ferguson.'

He put a hand over his mouth. 'Sorry, do you have a search warrant?'

'One can be arranged if you explicitly need it. I was hoping you'd cooperate without that.'

'I'm afraid I'll have to call my manager to request permission.'

'Look, we've identified a credit card transaction placing Mr Ferguson here last night. I don't like getting the runaround.'

'But I can't just give you the information.'

'Look, I'm pleading with you here. This is a murder case.'

A long breath exhaled through the nostrils. 'Fine. I'll look into it for you.' He switched back to the computer. 'Mr Ferguson's staying here. Checked in at twenty past eight last night.'

'Can we see the room?'

A glance out the front door. 'Come on.' He trotted over to a security door and swiped through.

Cullen and Buxton followed him down a long corridor. 'Why's it a zero value transaction?'

'We ask for a card to secure the room. Guests are requested to pay the balance on departure.'

'Isn't that old-fashioned?'

'That's how we work, Sergeant. We trust our guests.' He stopped halfway down. A DO NOT DISTURB sign hung from the doorknob. 'Here it is.'

Cullen knocked on the door. 'Mr Ferguson, it's DS Cullen. We need to have a word.'

No answer.

'Have you got a skeleton key?'

The receptionist nodded and produced a card.

'Wait.' Cullen stuck his head to the door. 'There's music playing.'

Buxton put his ear against the wood. 'Sounds like it's playing from a phone.'

Cullen stepped back and snapped on a pair of nitrile gloves. 'We better get in there.'

The receptionist pressed the card against the white pad on the door. 'After you.'

The door clicked. Cullen pushed it open. 'Mr Ferguson, we're coming in.'

A bathroom to the left, toiletries scattered above the sink. The end of a bed was visible round the corner. A chair lay against the window, a business suit thrown over it, work shoes tumbled on top of each other in front. "Sexual Healing" by Marvin Gaye blasted out of a Samsung mobile on top.

Cullen raised a hand. 'Wait.' He snapped out his baton and crept forward, rounding the edge of the bathroom. 'Shite.'

Martin Ferguson hung from the ceiling light by a rope. He wore a Batman costume, the grey trousers and blue trunks pulled down around his knees, his flaccid cock lost in a forest of pubic hair. A belt dug into his throat, a plastic bag over his head.

41

SOCO suit on, Cullen signed back into the crime scene, laughter pealing from inside the hotel room. He pushed the clipboard into the uniform's grasp and entered the crowded space, his overshoes squeaking and suit crinkling.

A suited figure pointed at the body still hanging from the belt. 'Fuckin' Batman's let himself go.' Bain's voice.

'Sergeant, will you sodding grow up?' Methven.

Another two figures inspected Ferguson.

Cullen got between them. 'Sir, I've given a statement to DC Law.'

'Excellent. I trust it's consistent with your notebook.'

'Aye.'

'Afternoon, Sundance.' Bain tilted his head back to the body, now gently swinging. 'I'm wondering where fuckin' Catwoman is.'

Cullen folded his arms. 'You used to call Angela Caldwell Batgirl.'

'Fuck, that takes me back.' Bain rubbed a gloved hand across his mask. 'How's she doing?'

'Not seen her in a while.'

'I asked someone to shut that sodding thing off.' Methven stomped over to the piled-up suit and stabbed a gloved finger against the phone's screen, killing the song before Marvin Gaye started singing again. 'Sodding hell. Someone look into this.'

A Smurf near the body cracked his spine. 'You guys finished your hilarity?'

'Mr Deeley.' Methven turned to face him. 'What have you got for us?'

'Time of death's twenty-three fifteen last night, plus or minus fifteen minutes.'

'Suicide?'

'I don't know. In agreement with DS Bain, I have to admit the Batman costume's a bit ... weird. Then there's this.' Deeley swung the body round. A fox tail hung out between hairy arse cheeks. 'I think it's what's known in certain circles as a butt plug.'

'What the fuck's a butt plug, Jimmy?'

Deeley shook his head. 'Brian, I thought you were a man of the world.'

'What the fuck is it? A dildo?'

'A shorter form, but aye. Don't want it travelling into the colon—'

'We get the picture.' Methven swallowed. 'Why's it there?'

'Other than sexual gratification, Inspector, I've no idea.' Deeley sniffed, the mask clouding against this face. 'Have to say, it seems a bit adventurous for masturbation.'

Cullen waved a hand up at the body. 'Shouldn't he have an orange or lemon in his mouth to bite into in case he accidentally strangled himself?'

'Good point.' Deeley looked round at the figure next to him. 'Mr Anderson, you should look for signs of other sexual partners.'

Bain patted Anderson on the shoulder. 'Make sure you've got a key card on you at all times. Wouldn't want you getting locked in again, would we?'

'Fuck off.'

Methven pointed at Cullen, then Bain, and gestured for them to follow him out of the room. 'Gentlemen, this case has just taken a turn for the ... weird. Why would he kill himself?'

'You sure this is an accident? He could've killed himself, I get that. But someone could've framed this.'

'Fine, here's what we're going to do. Cullen, can you speak to people, his wife, colleagues, that sort of thing? Find out if anyone had opportunity to kill him.'

'Sure.'

Methven glared at Bain. 'Brian, speak to the guests in adjacent rooms and the employees. Find out if anyone saw anything.'

'You wanting me to treat it as suicide, Col?'

'Let's keep our options open.'

CULLEN SQUINTED at the ornate carvings on the stone house's gable end, as West Linton traffic burled past behind them. He knocked on the door, jaw clenched as he waited. He glanced at Buxton. 'Has she been told?'

'Not to my knowledge.'

'Right.' Cullen prepared a smile as the door opened.

A thin woman leaning on a walking stick peered out. Middle-aged with dark hair, almost black — certainly dyed. Tracksuit bottoms and a plain white T-shirt. 'Yes?'

Buxton flipped out his warrant card. 'Mrs Ferguson?'

'Call me Elaine.'

'It's ADC Simon Buxton. We spoke on the phone.'

Elaine frowned, her free hand flicking her fringe. 'Is this about Martin?'

'Can we come in?'

'Is he okay? Is he dead?'

Buxton glanced at Cullen then nodded. 'I'm afraid so.'

Elaine tightened the grip on her stick and looked up at the blue sky. 'You'd better come in.'

Cullen followed her into the cottage. The vestibule led to a large kitchen filled with pale-blue units, a central Aga belching out heat.

Elaine pointed to a table that looked like it cost more than Cullen earned in a year. 'Have a seat.'

Buxton smiled at her. 'Can I get you a cup of tea?'

'Thanks for the offer, but I've just had one.' Elaine perched on a seat and rested her stick against the table. She kneaded her right leg, long motions up and down the thigh. 'What happened?'

Buxton sat next to her. 'We found your husband's body in a hotel room.'

'Death by misadventure?' She propped her stick against the table, sighing. 'It was always going to be this way.'

'We believe he was into—'

'BDSM?' Elaine nodded. 'That's why I thought his death was accidental.'

'Do you mind answering some questions?'

'You don't think he was murdered, do you?'

'We're investigating that possibility.'

Elaine picked up her stick, resting it on her lap, and let out a deep breath. 'We started engaging in those activities when we were younger. Started out with fluffy handcuffs and spanking. But Martin kept pushing it. He wanted ... *things* inserted. Got into breath control. I had to stop it when he started trying out edge play.'

'What's that?'

'When there's a genuine risk of harm.' She rubbed her leg again. 'I almost lost this when we were cutting each other. Six years ago. I was in hospital for a week. I told him I wasn't going to do it again, but he was addicted. He continued with ... others.'

'You had an open relationship?'

'Not voluntarily. He knew people and went away for weekends with them. Staying over in hotels. I'd had enough. I was terrified something like this would happen.'

'Why did you kick him out?'

'Stupid fool was messing around with girls and boys a lot younger than him.'

'I thought it was because of an affair with a Lorna Gilmour.'

'That was part of it. I just wanted out of it, to be honest.'

'Do you know anyone else involved in these groups?'

'I had nothing to do with them.'

'What about any of his friends?'

'Harrison Proctor was his only real friend.'

'Was he involved?'

'I seriously doubt it.'

～

'HE'S DEFINITELY NOT at Alba Bank, Sergeant.'

Cullen got out of the car first and stared at Proctor's mansion, Airwave clamped to his head. 'Definitely?'

'Alpha six are there now. Mr Proctor left mid-afternoon.'

Cullen checked his watch. Twenty to five. An hour to West Linton, another back. 'Okay, call me if you get an update.' He crunched up the path to the side door. 'Any sign?'

'Bugger all.' Buxton pressed the buzzer. 'Mr Proctor?' He waited a few seconds. 'It's the police.'

Cullen peered in the living room window. 'Doesn't look like he's in.'

'Bloody hell.' Buxton rapped on the window. 'Mr Proctor!'

'Do you want to get it out of your system?'

'What?'

'This aggro against me.'

'We're cool, Scott. I'll go back to the beat. Nothing's changed.'

'You sure?'

Buxton shrugged. 'Got no choice, have I?'

The door opened a crack. 'Hello?'

Buxton put his face near it. 'Mr Proctor, it's the police.'

'You can't come in.'

'We've got some questions for you.'

'My best friend's just killed himself. I need space to grieve.'

'How do you know about Mr Ferguson's death?'

'Excuse me?'

'We've not announced it.'

'Elaine told me.'

Buxton nodded. 'Mr Proctor, we need to speak to you.'

'I can't.'

'We need to determine whether your friend's death was intentional or not.'

'Murder?' The door opened wide. Proctor clutched a whisky tumbler filled with at least a couple of fingers, his pinstriped work shirt tucked into Adidas tracksuit bottoms. 'What do you want to know?'

'Where were you last night?'

'I was at the office until eight thirty. Then I came home.'

'Straight here?'

'I bought a ready meal in Waitrose. You can verify it with them.'

'Do you have a receipt?'

'I might do. Somewhere.'

'And you didn't hear from Mr Ferguson in that time?'

'No. Listen, I've no idea what happened to Martin.'

'Mr Ferguson checked into a hotel at twenty past eight last night.'

Proctor drained the glass and grimaced. 'Do you think he was murdered?'

'Do you?'

Proctor clutched the empty glass tight, inspecting the droplets of amber liquid inside. 'Anything's possible.'

'Do you know of anyone else who might've been involved?'

'Not really. He usually met them online, I think. Or using tags. A particular Stuart MacBride novel on public display on the bus. "Broken Skin", I think it's called. That sort of thing.'

'Any names?'

'Something Italian springs to mind.' Proctor toasted with his empty glass. 'Paul Vaccaro?'

∾

CULLEN PLONKED himself into the seat next to Murray in the busy Incident Room. 'There you bloody are.'

Murray looked up from his computer. 'Sarge.'

'How are you getting on with finding Vaccaro, Stuart.'

'Still nowhere. Found out he had a flat in Edinburgh, but he moved out a few months ago. No forwarding address.'

'Vaccaro's part of Martin Ferguson's dodgy BDSM ring.'

'Is there a non-dodgy one?'

'Aye, very good.' Cullen sighed. 'Look, can you get on to Vice and see if there's anything on him?'

'Right. I'll do that.'

Cullen stood up. 'Has your mate in the City got back about Van de Merwe's offshore accounts yet?'

'Going to get on to that next. Thought Vaccaro was higher priority.'

'That's Murray-ese for you've forgotten, right?'

'Piss off.'

'Sundance, there you are.'

Cullen swung round. 'I thought you were supposed to be at the hotel?'

Bain winked at him. 'Couple of bastards aren't speaking there so we brought them here to frighten them.'

'What do you want?'

'A certain DCI's looking for you. Told me to get your arse into her office.'

'What's it about?'

'Probably your boyfriend in the press.'

42

'Make yourself at home, Sergeant.' Cargill kept her eyes on her laptop. 'I'll just be a minute.'

Cullen collapsed into one of the navy leather armchairs in the corner of her office. The window looked north across the top of new-build flats and the old bus station. He glanced over as Cargill battered her laptop's keyboard.

It couldn't be about Rich, surely? All that shite about leaking stories to the press?

'Now.' Cargill sat in the matching armchair, resting her hands on chunky thighs. 'How's it going on this case?'

'You've been in the briefings, ma'am. It's not the easiest I've ever worked.'

'I want to know how it's really going, not what DI Methven spoon-feeds me.'

'We're getting nowhere, ma'am.' Cullen's neck started to burn and sweat trickled down his back. 'Nothing's making any sense.'

'That's a common occurrence, Scott.' She smiled, lips opening wide, showing rows of sharp teeth, gums bleeding top right. 'How are you finding life as a DS?'

'It's good. I mean, it's no walk in the park. Having to juggle the day job stuff with the side things, like the DC interviews and so on. It's difficult, but I'm enjoying it.'

'That's good to hear.' She frowned. 'How are you getting on with DI Methven?'

Cullen shrugged. 'Fine, ma'am. I appreciate him giving me this opportunity.'

'And DS Bain?'

Cullen looked away. 'Less said about him the better.'

'Quite.' She gave another flash of her teeth. 'I thought we'd seen the last of him.'

'More lives than a cat.' Cullen clasped his hands. 'How does he still have a job?'

'Connections, pure and simple. He goes way back with Carolyn Soutar. Having the DCS on your side's a powerful thing. Something you should learn from.'

The heat warmed his cheeks now. 'I'm not following?'

'Scott, I need to know everything about these newspaper leaks.'

'I swear it's nothing to do with me.'

'Leaking information to the press is a serious matter. If we—'

'You don't have to tell me, ma'am.' Cullen clenched his fists, nails digging into his palms. 'I used to share a flat with the journalist in question. Trust me on this — I've no idea where the information's coming from.'

'You need to persuade me.'

Cullen stifled a sigh. 'Look, I met Rich at lunch today. He's not giving up his source. He gave us some information which led us to finding Martin Ferguson.'

'An unfortunate event. Your other flatmate, Tom, works at Alba Bank, doesn't he?'

'He's not the source. He's given me some useful tips Rich hasn't published.'

She licked her lips. 'Should we bring Mr McAlpine in for further questioning?'

'DS Bain's already spoken to him.'

'Would it help if you and I did?'

'I don't know, ma'am. He's not obliged to provide the information. The only good I can see coming from it is if Rich agrees to run the stories past us.'

'And I can't see that happening.' Cargill flicked her hair behind her ear and gave another flash of teeth. 'Now, I wondered if you wanted some coaching.'

'On what?'

'Sponsoring a uniformed constable to a DC role.'

Cullen raised his eyebrows and looked away. 'It would've helped before yesterday, ma'am.'

'Ah yes. Simon Buxton.'

'I don't feel comfortable about what happened there. Simon's a friend and I was put—'

'You acted with the utmost professionalism.'

'Are you saying it was a test?'

'Not as such. Scott, when we promoted you, we took a gamble. We've worked together for, what, two years? In that time, I've seen the good and bad in you. Your maverick streak, while it's prone to getting you into hot water, is your greatest strength. You care about this job. If I had ten officers like you, my life'd be much easier.'

'I'd hate to see the complaints, though.'

She grinned. 'You can't make an omelette without breaking eggs.'

'I let Simon down. Should've tried harder.'

'Scott, Donna Nichols lauded your actions throughout the interview process. We go way back, you know. She said you were professional to the hilt.'

'Really?'

'Weren't you?'

'Well, I wish we could've given Simon the role.'

'It's a shame we had to give the existing role to another candidate.'

Cullen frowned. 'Existing?'

'DC Angela Caldwell resigned this morning.' Cargill grinned. 'I've been scratching DCS Soutar's back and she's given me an additional DC in my headcount over and above the one already approved.'

'I'm not following you.'

'We wish to avoid the cost of another round of interviews with the same candidates.' She reached across and patted his shoulder. 'Scott, please inform Simon Buxton of his two-year tenure as Detective Constable.'

CULLEN SWUNG into the Observation Suite, Bain and Buxton interviewing a man with Wolverine sideburns on the monitor in front of Eva. He perched next to her and tapped the screen. 'There he is.'

'Bain?'

'No, Buxton. Need a word with him.'

'Bain's got him interviewing those guests from the hotel. It's been half an hour and they're nowhere.'

He squinted at the screen. 'What are you doing?'

She shrugged. 'He told me to watch.'

'Bloody hell.' Cullen went back into the corridor and entered the interview room, shut the door behind him and leaned against it.

Bain snorted. 'For the record, DS Cullen has joined the room.' He focused on Wolverine. 'You're in a lot of shite here, son. You swear you've no idea who Martin Ferguson is?'

'Should I?'

'Of course you should. You killed him, didn't you? Met him at his hotel, strangled him. Made it look like accidental death.'

'I don't know what you're talking about, mate.'

'Come on, sonny. You should open—'

'Sergeant, that's enough.' Campbell McLintock prodded a finger in the air, inches from Bain's face. 'My client will take his time to consider his testimony on this matter.'

'I don't think so, Campbell.'

'You're not getting anywhere with these bully-boy antics. Take a step back and let me work it out.'

'You've got two minutes.' Bain leaned over the table, eyes locked on the suspect. 'Interview terminated at seventeen forty-six.' He clicked stop on the recorder and left the room, leaving the door open.

Cullen followed him out and shut the door.

Bain hit his head against the wall. 'Fuckin' bastard.'

'This you getting somewhere?'

Bain swung round. 'Piss off, Sundance. We'll get him.'

'Who is he?'

'Boy stayed in the room across the hall from Ferguson in that fuckin' hotel. Not playing ball so far.'

'You got anything pointing to him killing Ferguson?'

'Doesn't mean he's not done it.'

'Typical.' Cullen opened the door and thumbed at Buxton. 'Simon, I need a word.'

'Sundance, he's my officer for this interview.'

'It'll only be a minute. You gave Campbell two.' Cullen nodded at Buxton and started off down the corridor. 'Come on.'

'Fuckin' get back here!'

Cullen twisted round as he walked, flicking the Vs at Bain. 'Use Eva.'

'Fuckin' hell.' Bain stormed off towards the Obs Suite.

'Well played, Scott.'

'Don't know what the hell he's up to. As ever.' Cullen tried the door to the first meeting room they came to. Empty. 'Right, in here.'

Buxton took the farthest-away seat. 'Must be bad if we're in a room.'

'How's it going in that interview?'

'You called it. We're getting nowhere.' Buxton crossed his arms. 'Typical Bain.'

'How are you feeling about not getting this DC gig?'

Buxton looked away. 'Pissed off.'

'Understood. Glad you're confronting it. Your head's not dropped.'

'Right.'

'What if I was to say you'd got it?'

Buxton tilted his head. 'What?'

'I just spoke to Cargill.' Cullen pushed a piece of paper across the desk. 'DC Simon Buxton, welcome to Specialised Crime Division.'

'If this is a wind-up...' Buxton scanned the sheet and looked up, eyebrow raised. 'Two years?'

'That's pretty good. I got that with my DS role.'

Buxton folded it up, face blank. 'Let's get a beer.'

'I stopped drinking.'

'You sure? Come on, mate, just one. You didn't celebrate your own DS promotion.'

'We had a Mexican at that place on Cockburn Street.'

'This time, let's have some lovely craft beer.'

Cullen stared at the grain on the table. 'Fuck it, aye.'

Buxton put the paper in his jacket pocket. 'Give me a chance to finish up this calamity, then we'll head across the road, all right?'

'Fine.' Cullen watched him leave the room.

Drinking again. Really?

He fished out his phone. No messages. He dialled Sharon's number.

'Hey. How's it going?'

'Good and bad. You?'

'Bad and worse. The hangover's not great. What's your good?'

'Buxton got his tenure.'

'I thought you had to knock him back.'

'Angela Caldwell quit.'

'Nice for some.'

'Tell me about it.' Cullen tightened his grip on the phone. 'Do you mind if I go out for a pint with him?'

'Drinking?'

'Aye, drinking.'

'Drinking as in drinking drinking?'

'Is that okay?'

'Scott, it's been five months without a drop.'

'It'll be fine. I've got my head screwed on properly now.'

A pause, then a huff. 'Just don't be late.'

'I'm working tomorrow. It'll just be a couple of jars. Wouldn't catch me doing what you did last night.'

'*Love you.*'

'Do you want to—'

The line went dead. He tossed his mobile on the table.

Just a couple. Nothing more.

Cullen felt a thrum in his pocket. He stabbed a finger at his phone. 'Cullen.'

'Aye, it's DC McCrea. I'm interviewing an eyewitness at the hotel, but they're not talking.'

'So? Can't DS Bain do it?'

'The witness asked for you. Says Methven's okayed it.'

43

C ullen followed the dark hotel corridor round, storming past a cleaning trolley. A door hung open, Coldplay blasting out of a phone inside the room, tinny and brittle-sounding. A woman folded sheets, humming along. He glanced at the next door. Room Twenty-three.

Must be round the corner.

Started off again. Took a right turn.

McCrea stood outside a hotel room. He nodded at Cullen and stepped under the crime scene tape. 'Thanks for coming.'

Cullen frowned. 'Care to enlighten me?'

McCrea folded his arms. 'This guy's been out all day and just got back. He's being ultra-evasive.'

'So do you need an adult to show you how it's done?'

'Shut up.' McCrea cracked his knuckles, left then right. 'I'll let you lead.' He entered the room.

Cullen followed him into the gloom. Curtains drawn, lights on low, press clippings taped to the walls. He glared at McCrea and stepped back outside. 'What's all that on the wall?'

'You'll see.' McCrea smirked as he sat on the only chair, facing the man on the bed, overweight and balding. Dressed in a white hotel dressing gown.

Cullen settled on the edge of the wooden desk, covered in books, newspapers and journals. A Microsoft Surface flashed through its screensaver. He flicked a light switch, casting the room in darkness. Tried another. Full light.

McCrea gave a smile. 'Mr Porteous, I'd like you to meet one of my colleagues.'

He looked at Cullen and his eyes lit up. 'Jesus Christ!' He put a hand to his mouth. 'You're Scott Cullen!'

'That's right.' Cullen scowled at McCrea. 'Why's that imp—'

'Oh. My. God. You caught him!'

'Who?' Cullen checked out the walls.

Schoolbook Killer Caught!
Hero Cop Scott Cullen: In Profile.

He stifled a groan. 'Well, I was on the team.'

'I'm writing a book on the Schoolbook killer. Can I interview you?'

'Join the queue...' Cullen held up a hand. 'I'll maybe sit down with you if you talk to us.'

'Okay.'

'Mr Porteous, were you here last night?'

'Of course.' Porteous nibbled his lips. 'I'd been out in Portobello all afternoon. A kind lady showed me where you'd—'

'Did you see or hear anything?'

'Well, I was writing on my laptop and I heard muffled screams through the walls.'

'When was this?'

'About half past eleven?'

'So what did you do?'

'It was putting me off my stride. I'm not one for writing with headphones on. I need absolute calm and focus to get into the flow state.'

'So?'

'I hammered on the door.' Porteous re-crossed his legs, chunky and shaved smooth. 'A woman came out into the corridor and apologised. Said she was watching a horror film.'

Cullen let out a breath. 'Did you believe her?'

'I saw no reason not to.'

'Did you see into the room?'

'She'd pulled the door to behind her.'

'Did you hear anything after that?'

'It was deathly quiet.' Porteous frowned. 'Well, I heard the door going about an hour later.'

'Did she leave?'

'I think so.' Porteous sniffed. 'I feel really bad about this. I didn't know you'd found a body. I've been out in Livingston all day. Schoolbook had given me access to—'

'Yeah, yeah, we get it, pal.'

'Listen, I only found out what happened when your colleague knocked on the door half an hour ago.'

'Can you describe the woman you spoke to?'

Porteous shrugged. 'It was dark.'

Cullen held up his phone and found a photo of Candy. 'Was this her?'

'It could've been. It was dark in the corridor, you know. The night lights were on.'

Cullen got up. 'Thanks for your time.'

'Can I get that interview with you?'

'Speak to the press office.'

∼

BAIN CRACKED HIS KNUCKLES. 'I need you to open up a wee bit here, darling.'

Candy sniffed, eyes locked on Reynolds. 'When do I get out of here, Al?'

'Not my place to decide.' The lawyer shrugged. 'I can only point out how close to the wire they're running.'

Cullen leaned forward to the microphone. 'Interview paused at nineteen forty-one.' He got up, nodded at Bain and left the room.

Bain slammed the door behind them and stared down the empty corridor. 'This is another fuckin' disaster.'

'You're telling me.' Cullen rested against the wall, cold plaster on his palms. 'Might be worth cutting down on the oblique questioning. Keep it straight.'

'Cheeky bastard. How would you fuckin' handle it?'

'Don't ask stuff like, why did you do it? Why did you kill him? Keep it specific. You've not even mentioned Ferguson yet. I thought that was the whole point of us being here.'

'I'm fuckin' getting there, Sundance. That punter at the hotel said it was her. I'm just leading her down a path before I catch her in a lie.'

Cullen folded his arms. 'We've nothing linking her to Ferguson.'

Bain ran a hand across his scalp. 'Look. We've got her fuckin' this banker boy. Might be up the duff to him.'

'So why kill Ferguson?'

Bain shot his gaze to the door. 'We need to find that out.'

'There's no link.'

'She was fuckin' *there*, Sundance.'

'Come on. I'm taking over.'

Bain opened the door. 'Fill your fuckin' boots.'

Cullen entered the room and sat opposite Candy. He started the recorder. 'Interview recommenced at nineteen forty-four. Candy, do you know a Martin Ferguson?'

'Means nothing to me.'

'That true?'

'Don't even know who you're talking about.'

Bain tossed a photograph of Ferguson across the desk. 'You don't recognise him?'

'He looks like a million guys I've shown my tits to.'

'You didn't, say, murder him last night?'

'What?' Candy grabbed her lawyer's arm. 'What are you talking about?'

'A person matching your description was spotted at the hotel crime scene last night between eleven and half past.'

'I was with Dean.'

'That's very convenient, princess. Shame you weren't dancing or out on an escort gig. You'd have a roomful of reliable witnesses.'

Cullen slumped back in his chair. No winning with Bain.

'Like they'd come forward for me.'

'How come we found you at your mate's flat this morning?'

'Dean came round. Cleared off after we, you know, made love.'

Bain leaned back in the chair, pulling his left index finger until it cracked. He slid a sheet of paper across the table. 'This your number?'

Candy checked it. 'Nope.'

'Sure about that?'

'I've got one phone and that's not it.'

'Let the record state that Ms Broadhurst doesn't recognise the number in question.' Bain took the sheet back. 'You're saying you never had sex with Mr Ferguson?'

'I've no idea who he is.'

'Funny, we've found yours and his DNA in Mr Van de Merwe's sex room. Looks like you were there a few times. You definitely don't know him?'

'No comment.'

'You're sticking to your story, then?'

'Of course I am.'

Bain lifted a shoulder. 'Interview terminated at nineteen forty-seven.' He got up and adjusted his suit jacket. 'Have a word, Al. See if she wants to confess. It'll save us all a lot of time.'

Reynolds snapped his document holder shut. 'I'll do no such thing.'

'Charming.' Bain opened the door, holding it for Cullen before slamming it. 'What do you think?'

'Should've let me handle it.'

'Come on, Sundance, you were getting nowhere.'

'Did Anderson really find Ferguson's DNA there?'

'Aye, he did.'

'Was it at the same time as Candy?'

'No idea. She's definitely hiding something, Sundance.'

'What was that phone number?'

'We found a text message on Ferguson's phone about meeting up in that room.' Bain gave a shrug. 'Number wasn't in his contacts list. Tommy Smith's confirmed it was a disposable phone.'

'So someone lured Ferguson to the hotel?'

'Looks like it.' Bain stroked his moustache. 'Let's have a word with Vardy, see if he tears her story a third arsehole.'

'Better be quick. I'm supposed to be taking Buxton out for a beer. He got his tenure.'

'Wonders will never fuckin' cease.' Bain shook his head, adjusting the micro-quiff. 'This you inviting me out?'

'No.'

'Cheeky fucker.' Bain pushed into the adjacent interview room. 'Evening, Campbell. Surprised you've not sent an underling along. Usually turn into a pumpkin at about half six, don't you?'

McLintock rested his fountain pen on his legal pad. 'I'm here when my clients need me, Brian. You know that.'

'When they're ready and willing to pay through the nose for it, maybe.'

'I charge a competitive rate, Inspector.' McLintock raised his hands, his mouth forming an O. 'Sorry, I should have said Sergeant.' He grinned.

Cullen sat next to Bain and cleared his throat. 'Shall we get this started?'

McLintock whispered something in Vardy's ear, getting a nod. 'We're good to go.'

Cullen leaned across the table and started the digital recorder. 'Interview commenced at twenty oh two on Friday the twenty-second of May, 2014. Present are DS Scott Cullen and DS Brian Bain. Also present is Dean Malcolm Vardy, with his legal representative, Campbell McLintock.' He held Vardy's gaze for a few seconds. 'Do you know a Martin Ferguson?'

'Never heard of him.'

'That the truth?'

'Calling me a liar?'

'Mr Ferguson was murdered last night.'

'No idea who you're talking about.' Vardy snorted and folded his arms. 'Campbell, I don't have to stay here, do I?'

'This is entirely at your discretion.'

Vardy got to his feet. 'Cheers, lads. It's been—'

'We found DNA traces from Mr Ferguson and your bird in Van de Merwe's sex room.' Bain drummed his thumbs on the table. 'Looks like they'd been—'

'I don't know who you're talking about.' Vardy rested against the chair back.

'I want to—'

Cullen raised a hand to Bain. 'Dean, can we talk about the burner?'

'What, CDs and that?'

'Don't get cute. You know what I'm talking about.'

Vardy smirked at McLintock. 'Boy here's watched *The Wire* and thinks he's an expert on the criminal underworld.'

'You've never used a disposable mobile?'

'Got a Nokia Lumia. Suits my needs.'

'That the only phone you've got?'

'Not answering that.'

'Mr Vardy, someone in your line of work has a lot of use for anonymity, right?'

'Excuse me?'

'Discretion. Secrecy. Whatever you want to call it. You try to distance yourself from your illicit activities.'

'Back to this shit, is it? Listen to me — I've no idea who this guy was.'

'Martin Ferguson.'

'Aye, him. Never met the boy.'

'Doesn't mean you didn't have someone kill him, does it?'

'Only guy I ever heard of in relation to Candy was Van de Merwe.'

Bain leaned forward. 'Going to open up about that, are you?'

'There's nothing here. You boys know me. At least this one does.' Vardy flicked a hand at Cullen. 'I never attach myself to a bit of skirt. Soon as they've served their purpose, that's it. Move on. Get the fuck out of Dodge.'

Cullen got in first. 'Like with Pauline Quigley?'

Vardy looked away. 'Aye, like her.'

'So you'll just move on from Candy?'

'Of course.'

'If you think so little of our female friends, why did you ask Candy to move in with you?'

'Eh?'

'That's very caring for someone who just wants out of Dodge.'

'Piss off.'

'Has a girl ever got that close to you before, Dean?'

'No comment.'

'Never melted your heart?'

'No. Comment.'

'Come on, we were getting on so well there.'

'Where were you last night between half past eight and midnight?'

'With Candy. At her mate's flat. Had a nice night in. Got a Chinese in, watched a film.

'Which one?'

'I can't remember. Candy'd bought it in the Co-op. It had Matthew McConaughey in it.'

'You knew we were looking for her, didn't you?'

'News to me, pal. Listen, I've given her the week off cos her back's been sore.' Vardy looked over at McLintock. 'Get me out of here, Cammy.'

Cullen glanced over at Bain and got a shrug. 'Interview terminated at eight fifteen.'

44

M urray stood up and belched. 'Sorry, boys. I'll have to love you and leave you. Got to get back to Garleton to see the other half's old dear.'

Buxton raised his empty glass. 'Cheers for coming, Stu.'

'If you'd told me earlier, I could've got a late pass.' Murray did up his coat. 'Don't stay too late, boys.' He gave a mock salute and left the bar.

Cullen sank back in his armchair, looked around the Elm and took another glug of Punk IPA, bitter and hoppy as fuck, already zapping his brain. The bright lights stung his eyes. 'This is lovely stuff.'

'Tell me about it, mate.' Buxton held up his glass, the liquid inside fizzing away. 'Good enough to grow a beard for.'

'That didn't suit you.' Cullen swallowed more beer, the tension in his shoulders slackening off. 'I've missed this stuff.'

'Can't believe you lasted that long on the wagon. This you off for good?'

'We'll see.' Cullen took another sip, the liquid just below half-way. 'Two pints is my limit tonight.'

'Sharon's got you on a tight lead these days.'

'Self-imposed, Si.'

'Impressive. If you stick to it.'

'Course I will.' Cullen pinged the edge of the glass. 'Then it's home for some more *Super Mario 3D Land*.'

'You're such a child.' Buxton paused and cleared his throat. 'Thanks for getting me the tenure, mate.'

'Nothing to do with me. Well, not much.'

'All right. Piss off, then.'

Cullen laughed. 'You should be thanking Cargill.'

'I did. She wasn't interested in a pint with you and Stuart. Eva and Chantal weren't up for it, either.'

'Your reputation precedes you.'

'What's that supposed to mean?'

'You're a booze hound.'

'Like you're any better.'

'I've knocked it on the head.'

'Says the man who's arsed half a pint of five point six per cent craft beer.'

'Shite.' Cullen looked at his glass. 'It's not that strong, is it?'

'Stronger than Stella. You know how bad you are on that.'

'See, you *are* a liability.'

'How's this my fault?'

'You're pressuring me into drinking.'

'You don't have to go along with it.'

'Alcohol-free beer just doesn't cut it.' Cullen took another drink. 'So. How do you feel about your tenure?'

'I'm okay.' A deep sigh. 'Now the monkey's off my back, I can think more about what I should be doing.'

'Leaving the police?'

'No, mate. Finding a girl and settling down.'

'What about your flatmate?'

'Bugger off, I mean it.'

'Seriously, there's nothing there?'

'Just friends.' Buxton drank some beer and grimaced. 'You know I shagged Chantal, right?'

'She might've let it slip.'

'I think she's the one.'

'She's way out of your league, Si.'

'I'm fed up of being single. I want what you've got with Sharon.'

'You can't have her.'

'Very good. You know what I mean. Just want a nice girl who

puts up with my nonsense.'

'That's how you see it?'

'Isn't that how it is? You're an idiot like me. She's really good for you.'

'I know that.' Cullen folded his arms. 'We've had some tough times recently.'

'The baby stuff?'

'And others.'

'But it's behind you?'

Cullen tightened his grip on the glass. 'Early days.'

'See, that's what I want. A girl who'll put up with my shit.'

'She has to exist first.'

'Very funny.' Buxton drained his glass and slammed it on the table. 'Do you mind if I partake in another, kind sir?'

'Be my guest.' Cullen watched him wander over to the bar, fishing for change and burping into his other hand. He took another swig and checked his phone for messages. Just a couple of texts.

Rich. *Not going to make it along, mate. Got a front page to run.*

He tapped out a reply. *Remember our deal...*

He checked the message from Tom. *Won't get down there. Say hi from me. Heading to Liquid Lounge soon if you fancy it...*

Cullen replied. *Keep your eyes peeled there, mate. Blokes have been getting raped there.*

His phone rattled again. *Doubt they'll be after my fat arse.*

Buxton dumped his fresh glass on the table and tossed a tub of wasabi peas at Cullen. He waved his phone in the air. 'Murray's just missed his train. He's coming back.'

'Sounds like trouble.'

THE BOUNCER NODDED. 'In you go, gentlemen.' Thumbed behind him into the Liquid Lounge. 'Have a good night.'

Cullen strutted inside. 'Not done this in a while.'

Buxton grinned at him. 'Shame you've hit your limit already.'

'We'll see.' Cullen looked around the bar area. Bass drums, shouting, neon lights, short skirts, open shirts. No sign of Tom. 'You sure you're not going for that train, Stuart?'

'I'll get the last one.' Murray glanced at his watch. 'Quarter past eleven, I think.'

'You think?'

'There's a Dunbar one at half past if I miss it. Get a Joe Baksi back to Garleton.' Murray got out his wallet. 'What do you want?'

A voice beside him. 'Scott Cullen.'

Cullen spun around.

A woman pinched his cheek. Dolled up, pretty. Leather skirt, leather boots. Unnecessary spectacles, giant red frames with no prescription.

He frowned. 'Do I know you?'

She grinned, eyes twinkling with mischief. 'It's Lorna?'

'Lorna?'

She took off the glasses. 'Lorna Gilmour? From Alba Bank?'

'Christ, I didn't recognise you.'

'It's these, right?' She held up the specs and waved behind her. 'Tom's back there.'

'You know him?'

'I'm afraid so.' She put the glasses back on and waved a black credit card around. 'This's on the bank.' She winked at Buxton. 'Constable?'

'Yeah, cheers. Lager.'

'I love the way you say it. Like that Underworld song. It's a great accent.'

'Been trying to lose it for years.'

'What about you, Scott?'

Cullen sucked in the air, tasting dry ice. 'Lager. Bottle.'

'I'll get your drinks.' She muscled in next to Murray, smiling at him. 'Another lager?'

CULLEN BATTERED THROUGH THE CROWD, clocking Tom's ruddy face in a booth at the back. Another four people next to him.

Tom made eye contact and raised an almost-empty bottle of Tiger. 'Skinky!'

'Evening, sir.' Cullen wedged in next to him. 'How's it going?'

'Good night so far.' Tom held out a hand to Buxton. 'Congrats, mate. Skinky finally bothered to sort out your promotion, right?'

'Cheers. But it's not a promotion.'

'Aye, aye. Must feel good, though, right?'

'It does.' Buxton grinned. 'Really good.'

Tom took a slug of lager. 'Lorna's just gone to the bar.'

'We saw her.'

Tom made room for Buxton to sit and grabbed a leatherette stool from the next table, dumping it at the end. 'You know Rob, right?'

Rob Thomson swigged from a bottle of Grolsch, the cap rattling. 'What are you doing here?'

Cullen raised his hands. 'Having a drink.'

Thomson pushed his bottle onto the table. 'You framed anyone for Van de Merwe yet?'

'Can't comment on an active investigation.'

'Bullshit.'

'Seriously, we can't.'

'You know who I think it is? One of those fucking Indians. They're all over this programme. Complete disaster.'

'Why would they kill him?'

'I'm just providing the intel. You find the motive and arrest the bastards.'

'I'll bear it in mind.'

Lorna pushed a tray onto the table, a tall glass of rosé and eight shooters. 'Here you are, boys!'

Murray dumped a bucket of six Cobras, snatched a bottle and perched on his stool.

Cullen grabbed a beer, ice cold. 'How much do we owe you?'

'This is on expenses.' Lorna nodded across at Thomson. 'Rob's team ... powered up the first server? Is that right?'

'Aye. Some heavy-duty kit.' Thomson raised a shoulder. 'We had to open another data centre in Linlithgow, otherwise there would've been blackouts in Edinburgh.'

Cullen frowned. 'As in the power going out?'

'It's true.' Tom snatched a Cobra. 'Seriously heavy-duty kit.'

Lorna looked around. 'Oh, there's nowhere to sit.' She sat on Buxton's lap. 'Hope you don't mind.'

Buxton sipped his beer. 'This is fine.'

Cullen mouthed, 'Cougar.'

'Piss off.'

'Lorna, quit twerking the guy.' Thomson picked at the label on his bottle, nodding at Cullen. 'Heard about that Martin Ferguson boy you were asking me about.'

'Look, I'm off duty.'

'Aye, bullshit. Poor guy. Someone said he was into whips and shite like that.' Thomson smirked at Lorna. 'You weren't into that, were you?'

'Piss off. You fucking know he was stalking me.'

'Aye, aye.'

'I mean it, Rob.'

'Sorry.' Thomson took another swig, narrowing his eyes at Cullen. 'You've been asking about UC Partners, right? Bunch of fucking cowboys.'

Buxton peered around Lorna. 'What do you mean, cowboys?'

'I managed the handover to IMC. Basically, they'd have been better starting over again. They'd no idea how to design an application. Just coded shit up, making it up as they went along. Left no documentation, designs, test cases — nothing. They've got a squad out in Pune going through it all. Documenting every line of code. Fucking cowboys...'

'IMC have?'

'Aye. This whole thing's hardly going to deliver two quid of benefit let alone a billion.' Thomson necked his beer and stood up. 'Need to get home. Got my boy staying with me tomorrow.' He waited for Buxton and Lorna to move then set off with a wave. 'See you all on Monday.'

Buxton stole his seat, wriggling free of Lorna. 'He okay?'

She shrugged and put her specs on his nose. 'Think he's found it hard with you lot being here. Reminded him what happened to Kim.' She took a big dent out of her wine. 'It's been tough.'

'Can't begin to imagine.'

'Imagine what?' Rich grabbed a beer from the bucket and sat at the end of their table. 'Evening.'

Cullen tapped his arm. 'Thought you couldn't make it?'

'Time off for good behaviour. Besides, I've done a shitload this week.'

'Aye, and I'm paying for it.' Cullen took a drink, dull compared to the Punk IPA.

'And that's me off.' Murray dumped his empty bottle and

grabbed his coat. 'Have to love you and leave you, I'm afraid. See you tomorrow, guys.' He wandered off through the club.

Lorna watched him go, then dished out shot glasses. 'Right, down this lot.'

Cullen nudged the drink away. His bladder burned. 'I'm not touching that.'

'Just a wee shooter?' Lorna snuggled into Buxton. 'Come on, grow a pair!'

'That's my limit.' Cullen took a drink of water. 'I'm on to soft drinks now.'

'Lightweight!'

'Seriously, stop it. Tom, Rich, one of you take this. And talk sense into her.'

'Come on, it's just a Goldschläger.' Lorna took her glasses off Buxton's nose and rested them on the top of her head. 'It's your turn.'

'My days of shooters are long gone.' He sucked on the beer, avoiding looking at her. He gazed around the club, spotted a couple groping each other at the next table. Time to get home and feed Fluffy. Scoop shit out of his litter tray. Drink a cup of decaf tea. Kip and get in early tomorrow. Maybe catch a murderer.

He put the empty bottle down and got up. 'Off for a slash.' He wandered to the back of the bar, heading for the toilets. Stopped just outside, looking across the rammed dance floor. Music blasted his ears. Lights strobed across the hands in the air. Two pairs of male and female dancers strutted on podiums in the middle.

He pushed into the Gents.

A hand grabbed his shoulder. Harsh voice in his ear, female. 'If you could just come with me, sir.'

He twisted round and jerked his head back. 'Sharon?'

She laughed, her face caked in make-up. Tight jeans, strapless purple top, hair tied up. 'What are you doing here?'

'Meeting Tom for a drink. Rich's just turned up. Had two pints at the Elm and I'm now on Tiger.' He shrugged. 'Might be Cobra, can never remember the difference.'

'That right?'

'I've got everything under control.'

'Is that what you're telling yourself?'

He burped into his hand. 'This is my chance to show I'm in

control. That bottle's the last one, I swear. Home and Mario. And Fluffy.' He tried for his best smile. 'What are you doing here?'

'A barman called in with a suspect an hour ago. There's been a guy hitting on men on the dance floor. Can't see him, though.'

'I'll keep my eyes peeled.'

'Don't.'

'Why?'

'Because you're drunk, Scott.'

'I'm not. Look, I can help.'

'You'll blow our cover. And I don't mind. Just keep a lid on it.'

'See you later.' He pecked her on the cheek and pushed into the toilet, passing the guy with the table of aftershaves. Had to stand between two men at the urinals. As he washed his hands, he noticed one of the cubicle doors hanging open a crack.

'Come on, man. I love the fuck out of you. Let's do it here. Right now.'

'Fuck off. Thanks for the coke and everything, but—'

'You cock tease.'

'What?'

'You fucking knew it wasn't just drugs on offer.'

Shite. Cullen barged past a man at the Dyson Airblade into the bar area. He scanned around. There. He jostled through the crowd. 'Chantal, have you seen—'

'Scott?' Jain raised an eyebrow. Short skirt, white blouse with a plunging neckline. 'Fucking hell, Scott, have you been drinking?'

'A bit. Look, I think your guy's in the cubicles. He's doing coke with some guy in trap one.'

'Trap one?'

'The first cubicle.'

She reached into her purse for her Airwave and held it up to her face. 'Sharon, we've got a suspect.' She listened to the response. 'I'll head in there with him, aye.' She killed the call.

'Me?'

'No, Scott. McKeown. And keep your eyes off my tits.'

'Got no choice when you present them like that.'

She waved at McKeown, then at the toilet door. 'You ready?'

He nodded. 'Always am with you.'

'Shut up, Mac.'

45

C ullen slid into the seat and took a drink of beer, draining the bottle. Definitely time to get home.

'You were a while.' Buxton held Lorna's hand. She stared into space, a smile on her face, glasses back on.

Cullen nodded at Lorna's hand, tucked into his.

Buxton mouthed, 'Shut up.'

Tom looked up from fiddling with his mobile and winked at Cullen.

His phone rumbled in his pocket. Cullen checked the display, a text from Tom. *Your mate's well in there.*

He nodded at Tom and replied. *Tenner says no.*

A notification flashed up on his screen. The *Edinburgh Argus* app.

Alba Bank BDSM Ring

He tapped the message. 'Cheeky fucker.'

Tom frowned. 'Who is?'

Cullen looked around. No sign of Rich. No, wait. There.

Rich swanned through the crowd, dumping a tray of shot glasses on the table. 'Sambuca time!'

Cullen got up and grabbed his shirt, shoving the phone in his face. 'What the fuck's this?'

'It's news, Skinky. Corruption and sexual deviancy at a bank. Just need a paedo and we've got the set.'

'Where did you get it?'

Rich smirked. 'So it's true?'

'We had a deal.'

'No, Skinky. We didn't.'

'You said you'd share what—'

'We said *we*'d share stuff. I had to wait on the press release. First opportunity and you blew it. This is what you get, mate.'

'Come on, Rich. That story could only have come from the police. Both stories.'

'You reckon?'

'Okay, let's play your game. Who's your source?'

'For which story?'

'What do you mean which one?'

'Check your app.'

Cullen flicked down the notifications on his phone.

Consultancy Fraud At Death Bank

'You total wanker.' Cullen prodded his finger at the mobile. 'You got that lead off my phone. In the restaurant at lunchtime, when I went to the bloody toilet.'

'When you were crying?'

'Piss off, Rich. You saw the message come in. It mentioned a name.'

'Should really change your Notification settings, mate. You can stop the whole text showing up.' Rich picked up a Sambuca and downed it. 'Good start, though. I dug into this guy. Took me to UC Partners and what they were up to.'

'You should've come to me.'

'Like fuck I should. They had the same trick going on across a few other projects at Alba Bank.'

'Why didn't you tell me?'

'Because you didn't tell me about Martin Ferguson. That was gold dust, mate. I found out *after* the press release this evening. *You've* let *me* down.'

'I'm going to arrest you. Right now. We'll go down to the

station. You'll tell me who's leaking this shit to you. And we'll charge both of you.'

'Come on, mate.'

'Do you know where he is?'

'Who?'

'Paul Vaccaro. Mr UC Partners. The name you got from my phone.'

'I could ask my source.'

'You're going to tell me their name.'

'Fuck off, Scott.'

'You're really pissing me off.'

'Look, I'm sorry, Skinky, but you don't realise how fucked things are for me.'

'Call your guy.'

'Come o—'

'*Now.*'

'In the morning.' Rich pushed him away and stomped across the club to the toilets.

Cullen glared at him. Cheeky fucker. 'I'm heading home.'

Lorna finished her Sambuca and glanced up at him. 'You sure?' She slurred her words. Eyes weren't staying open. 'What was that all about?'

'He's being a wanker.'

She held Buxton's hand up in the air. 'We should go dancing! Right now! After another round.'

'I'm good.' Cullen finished his beer.

'I've still got the corporate card, Scott. Another round, then you can do whatever you want.'

'No.'

'Come on. Simon's just got promoted—'

'It's *not* a promotion.' Buxton downed his Sambuca and took a suck of lager. 'I'm just saying.'

'Okay, whatever. Still deserves a toast. Come on.'

Cullen exchanged a look with Buxton. 'I'm fine.'

'Simon?'

'Not had a Grolsch in ages.'

'Tom?'

'I'll go for that. Get Rich one too.'

Cullen scowled. 'Only if I can piss in it first.'

'Back in a sec.' Lorna sprang to her feet, grabbed the tray and darted off.

Cullen shook his head. 'Seeing a different side to her tonight.'

'She's quite the girl. Professional as you like during the day, but get a wine inside her, and boom!'

Tap on the shoulder. Whisper in his ear. 'We've caught him.'

Cullen shifted round in the seat and frowned at Sharon, Jain standing next to her. 'The guy in the toilet?'

'Pocketful of roofies.' She kissed him on the lips, lingering. 'I'll see you when I get home. Don't stay too late, okay?'

'I'll head soon.'

'See you.' Sharon squeezed his shoulder and disappeared into the crowd.

Jain reached over and took a glug of Buxton's beer. 'Have another one, you big twat.'

Cullen rolled his eyes at her. 'What's it to you?'

'Come on, you're off the lead. Man up, Scott.'

'Now you realise why I gave you to Sharon.'

'Watch it. Come on. Be thankful you're not working like me and Shaz. Just one. For me?'

'The more you push, the less likely I'll have another one.'

Buxton leaned over to whisper something to Jain. 'Can I fuck you?' Far too loud.

Her eyes darted around. She leaned in and breathed into his ear. 'Fuck off, Simon.' She raced off after Sharon.

Buxton winked at Cullen. 'See? I've got no chance with her.' He stood up. 'Need a slash.'

'Might need to be more subtle, mate.' Tom laughed and took another drink.

Lorna put the tray down, three fancy beer bottles and a glass of rosé. 'Here you go.'

'Cheers.' Tom rattled the open cap and took a slug. 'Fancy bottle, but it's still the usual fizzy pish.'

Lorna sat down across from Cullen. 'Where's Simon?'

Cullen eyed Rich's bottle, his mouth watering. 'He's gone to the toilet.'

'Right.'

Tom took another drink. 'Were you trying it on with him?'

'Maybe.'

'You're such a cougar, Lorna. We'll have to sift through your lair for his bones.'

'Chance'd be a fine thing.' She gulped down wine. 'That your girlfriend?'

Cullen shrugged. 'Just collared a serial rapist, by the looks of things.'

She shook her head. 'Fucking scumbags.'

'Who, the police?'

'No, rapists.'

'Right.' Cullen grabbed Rich's bottle and took a long drink. 'Shame for that to go to waste.'

Lorna rolled her eyes at him. 'So you are drinking, after all?'

Cullen stared at the bottle. 'Aye, fuck it.'

She shook her head. 'Better get Rich another, then.'

'Great idea. You're the one holding the purse.'

She raised her bag. 'Ha, very good.' She put her glasses back on and wandered off towards the bar.

Tom clattered his bottle down, fizz boiling up. 'Rich said you guys had lunch today.'

'Aye, and?'

'Seriously, mate. Are you okay?'

'I'm fine. Just had some...' Another slug of beer. 'Some bad news. That's all.'

'This about Rich writing that book about the Schoolbook killer?'

'What?'

'Shite.' Tom tried to hide behind his bottle. 'It's not, is it?'

'Is that what his crime novel's about?'

'Reckons it'll be a big seller. Some publisher in Glasgow's after it.'

'What a total wanker.'

'Asked me to set up an interview with Rob Thomson.'

'Have you?'

'Of course not.'

Cullen picked up the bottle, clattering the cap off the side, and took a pull of beer.

Lorna sat down with another Grolsch for Rich. 'Here we go.'

Buxton sat next to her. 'That's better.'

She handed him a bottle. 'Here you go.'

'Cheers.' Buxton necked half of it in one go. 'Classy beer, this.'

Lorna tapped her wine glass against Tom's, then Cullen's. 'Come on, boys. Drink up. Time to dance!'

'Jesus.' Cullen took his down to halfway. 'You always like this with some booze in you?'

'Quite a lot, yeah.'

Rich sat down. 'You still got that corporate card?'

'Yes.'

'Can we get some more shooters in?'

'Later, maybe. After we've been dancing!'

Cullen leaned over to Rich. 'Tom told me about the book.'

'What book?'

'The one you're writing about me.'

Rich pinched his nose. 'Jesus.'

'So you are writing it?'

'Maybe.'

'You need to stop, okay? I don't need any more shit at work.'

'You're not stopping me, mate. It's my way out of this shite.'

'I met someone else who's writing one.'

'Bullshit.'

'Guy called Porteous.'

Rich's eyes bulged. 'What?'

'You heard—'

'Would you two please stop arguing!' Lorna bounced to her feet. 'Come, let's dance!'

'Aye, go on.' Rich got up and nodded at a guy at the next table. 'Keep an eye on our drinks, will you? I'll buy you one next round.'

~

CULLEN OPENED HIS EYES. Music thumped from somewhere. Deep thuds like a migraine. Rumbling bassline.

Just him in the booth. Empty table. Where's Tom? Where's Rich? Where's ... thingy. Lorna. Where's Lorna? Where's Budgie?

Fuckers left me.

He swallowed, stomach growling. No food since the pizza at lunchtime. Saliva filled his mouth. Going to be sick.

He lurched to his feet, dizzy. His legs went and he collapsed back down. Stared at the table. Empty bottle of Grolsch in front of him. Empty wine glass opposite. Another empty next to it.

Where the hell were they?

Tom? Bastard.

Rich? Lying fucker.

Took another go at getting up. Swayed a bit. Jesus. His stomach lurched again. He stumbled across to the toilets and pushed the door, leaned against it, forehead touching wood.

What the fuck was going on?

He pushed into the toilet, swaying past the guy with the aftershave. 'Fuck your perfume.'

Lurched over the tiles into trap one. Down to his knees. Opened wide. Vomit hit the pan, sharp in his nostrils. Burnt his throat.

He hugged the toilet bowl. Retched again. Shiiiiiiiiit. And again. Shit. Shite. Shit. Shite.

He rocked back on his heels. Tumbled against the door. Eyes shut, puffing in air.

Tried to get up. Nothing. Fumbled his phone out of his pocket. Dropped it on the tiles. Picked it up and held down the home key. 'Call Sharon.'

'Sorry, I didn't get that.'

'Call Sharon.'

'Sorry, I'm not sure what you said.'

'Call Sharon.'

'I didn't quite get that.'

'Call Sharon.'

'Ok, I didn't think so.'

'Call Sharon.'

'Calling Sharon.'

The line clicked. 'Hello, Scott.'

He held the phone out. 'Help.'

'Scott?'

'Help.'

He dropped the phone. Christ. Shite.

Knock on the door. 'Sir, are you okay in there?'

'I'm fine.'

Another knock. 'Sir?'

Stuffed his phone in his pocket. 'Said I'm fine.'

'You don't sound it. We're—'

'Police.'

'No, we're door staff. We need you to leave, sir.'

'Police.'

'Sir, we're coming in there.'

The door cracked into his back, the edge digging into his side. 'Ow.'

A hand grabbed his arm and pushed him forward. Hauled him up.

He collapsed to his knees again.

'Come on, sir. It's time to leave.'

'F-f-f-four drinks.'

'This isn't four drinks.'

Yanked up, feet off the ground. He opened his eyes, everything swimming around him. 'Police.'

'Sir, we can get the police involved once you're outside.'

'I'm police. Me.'

'What?'

'DS.' Burp. 'Cullen. Scott.'

A pause. 'Let's get you some fresh air.' Another voice.

Eyes shut again. They dragged him through the club.

Cold air hit his face. The drone of traffic. Someone singing the Beach Boys, shouting *"Sloop John B"*. 'Thank you.'

'We'll get you a taxi, sir.'

Cullen rested against something hard. A shoulder, rock solid under the T-shirt.

'Aye, it's fifty quid if he chucks his ringer, okay?' A warm hand on his back. 'I'll take him home. Come on, son.'

DAY 7

Saturday
24th May

46

The taxi driver let go of his arm. 'You okay now, mate?'
Cullen grunted, holding out his mobile. Warm air on his face. The flat door in front of him. 'Where's Sharon?'

'Who's Chantal?'

'*Sharon.*'

'Oh, Sharon. No idea, pal. Look, in you go, okay? I've got to get back to work.' Footsteps clattered down the stairs.

Cullen flopped against the stairwell wall and dropped his keys. He reached down to pick them up. Collapsed to his knees, head against the tiles. Christ.

His phone rang. Couldn't focus on it. Just blurry. He swiped the screen. 'Hello?'

'Scott?'

'Mm?'

'Scott, where the hell are you?'

'I'm here?'

'It's Sharon! Where the hell—'

'Mm. Bye.' Cullen frowned through the keys, picking out the front door one. Maybe. Looked up at the doors. Is this the right floor? Maybe. Keys in the lock. Opened the door. Stairwell light crawled across the laminate, the flat dark.

Fluffy cantered through from the living room, blinking into the light. 'Ma-wow!'

Cullen knelt down and stroked him. Tumbled over onto his back.

'Ma-wow!'

'Is your mummy not here?' He eased the door shut with a foot and got up on all fours. Then stood, started creeping through the dark hall into the living room. He flicked the light on. Empty.

'Jesus.' A sweet tang hit his nostrils. 'Fluffy, you dirty—' Burp. 'Boy.'

'Ma-wow!'

'I'll get you some food first.' Cullen scooped the mug into his food tin and tipped biscuits into a clean bowl. They clattered all over the floor. He tumbled over again, cracking his head off the cooker. 'Shite!'

Fluffy cracked biscuits with his teeth, splinters hitting the floor.

'You could say thanks, boy.' Cullen held up his phone, trying to focus on it.

Sharon calling...

The front door thudded open. 'Scott, you're really scaring the shite out of me. Where are you?'

Cullen stared up at the underside of the extractor unit. 'In.' Burp. 'Here.'

Footsteps in the living room. Louder. 'What are you doing?'

'I can't get up.'

'Scott.' A sigh. 'For fuck's sake. You're shit-faced.'

'Not my fault.'

'Whose was it? Tom's? Budgie's?'

'Not my fault.'

'How much did you have?'

'Four.'

'Four bottles of Jägermeister?'

'Beer. Gottles of geer.'

'Why are you so pissed?'

'Mm. Love you, sweety biscuits.'

'You lying bastard.'

'Four gottles of geer.'

'Can't believe this.'

'And if one little bottle should accidentally fall—'

'Scott, how much did you really have?'

'—there'd be no sticks of dynamite and no fucking wall.'

'Scott.' She pinched his cheek. 'How much did you have?'

'Four gottles of geer.'

'Scott, did you leave your drink alone in there?'

'Are you dancing?'

'Scott! Did you—'

'Are you asking?'

'Scott! I asked if you'd—'

'I'm asking.'

'Scott!'

'I'm dancing.'

'Did you go dancing?'

'Mm. Dancing. Don't leave the drinks!'

'Shite.' Silence. 'Chantal? It's me. Aye. Get the duty doctor round here. I think Scott's been roofied.'

∼

CULLEN BLINKED HARD. *Is that Chantal Jain?* 'What, where am I?'

Jain shook his wrist. 'It's okay, Scott.'

'Did you shag Buxton?'

'What?'

'Did you do the nicey nice with Buxton?' Cullen closed his eyes again. 'Mm. Sleepy.'

'This won't hurt, Sergeant.'

'Mm?'

Tightness around his left arm. A sharp prick, just below the left elbow. 'There we go.'

'What?' Cullen blinked his eyes open, struggling to focus on the blurry figure leaning over him, holding up a syringe full of blood. 'Who are you?'

'It's Dr Carnegie, Sergeant. You know me.' He got out another syringe. 'Here we go.'

Another prick. Left wrist. Sharp.

'Ow.'

'That's the Romazicon injected now, Inspector.'

Sharon appeared, frowning. 'That'll counteract the Rohypnol?'

'Five minutes. Assuming he *was* spiked.'

'Spiked?' Cullen rubbed around the tingle in his arm. 'What's going on?'

'Scott, could someone have put something in your drink?'

'Is that why I feel like this?'

'I think so.' Sharon crouched down. Fluffy galloped through to rub against her jeans. 'How much did you drink?'

'Four beers.'

'That's nowhere near enough to get this bad.' Carnegie zipped up his bag. 'He's showing all the symptoms of a Rohypnol attack.'

'Scott, do you know who did this?'

Cullen beamed. 'They played that waterfall song again. Our song.'

'It's not our song, Scott. You like it, I don't.'

'Our song.' Cullen twitched. Again. And again. Eyes wide open. Wooooooosh! 'What the hell's that?'

'The Romazicon kicking in, I suspect.' Carnegie capped the syringe and put it in his bag. 'I'll head back to the station and get this processed.'

Cullen bounced up to his feet. Dizzy. Alive. 'Woah, this is great.'

'Scott, could anyone have spiked your drinks?'

'We were dancing. Rich left our drinks on the table.'

'Did you drink any more when you got back?'

'I've no idea. Woke up at the table. My bottle was empty.'

Sharon looked across the room. 'Chantal, look through the CCTV. There's got to be someone lurking around them.'

'Will do.'

Cullen frowned. 'Did you get the guy in the toilet?'

'It's not him. He was in Dubai for the last three rapes.'

'Shite. I feel bad.'

'It's not your fault. He had a pocket full of Rohypnol on him. You saved that man in the toilets. He's just not our guy.' Sharon walked over to the other side of the room. 'Chantal, when you're over there, get it shut down.'

'It's only half twelve, Shaz.'

'I want it shut. Time we used the sheriff's approval.'

Jain nodded. 'I'll keep the bar staff for questioning.'

'Someone's spiking their drinks. Keep everyone in that club. Don't let anyone leave.'

'Will do.' Jain left the room, the front door clicking shut.

Sharon collapsed onto the sofa and patted the seat beside her. 'Come here.'

Cullen sat next to her, facing away. 'What a twat.'

'You were just in the wrong place at the right time.' She gripped his shoulder and massaged it, her thumb digging into his muscles. 'You've got to give us a statement. How are you feeling?'

'Whatever was in that shot works.'

'How much did you drink? Honestly?'

'We'd had two Punk IPAs in the Elm. Bottle of Tiger or Cobra in there. Then a Grolsch.'

'No shooters?'

'They did, I didn't.'

'Who else was there?'

'Just four of us at the end. Murray went for his train. Tom. Rich. Buxton. Someone Tom works with. Girl called Lorna. She was firing into Budgie.'

'We'll need to speak to them.' She got up and yawned. 'In the morning, though.'

'Jesus Christ. I really need to sleep.'

'Get to bed. I'm going into the station. I'll be back in a few hours.'

47

The front door clicked open. Flat shoes padded from the hall. 'Scott?'

Cullen flicked the bedside light on and sat up, his pillows pushing against the metal frame. 'In here.'

Sharon collapsed on the bed, the frame creaking. She kicked off her shoes, sending them thudding to the floor. 'I am *so* tired.'

He checked the clock. 'Ten to six. Is that all?'

'At least you've been asleep.' She rolled over onto her side, propped up on an elbow. 'How you feeling?'

'Like shite.'

'Could be much worse, you know.'

'Don't remind me.' Cullen clicked his back. 'Assuming it was your guy.'

'Your blood test was positive for Rohypnol.'

'So I was spiked? Jesus.' Cullen chewed his bottom lip. 'Have you spoken to the others?'

'We've been trying to ring them. Not got hold of them yet.'

He yawned. 'I'm getting up.'

'You sure?'

'I'm not really sleeping. Must be the beer.' He stood up and burped, stomach bile leaching into his mouth. He swallowed it down. 'I need to get in. Do some work. I'm so far behind it's not true.'

'You sure you're okay?'

'I've got a fuckton of work on, Sharon.'

'Come on, Scott. Chantal's trying to track them down.'

'I need to help. Find out who's done this.'

'You sure you should?'

'I've not got a choice.'

'Well, I'll be sleeping till nine.' She crawled up to her side of the bed and shrugged off her jeans. 'We'll get him, Scott.'

'Rich, it's Scott. Call me back, okay? It's urgent.' Cullen pocketed his mobile and leaned back against the glass outside the Starbucks. Low sunlight swung over his shoulder, bleaching John Lewis and Alba Bank across the road and the walkway looping over Leith Street. He yawned into his hand. Floaters spun in front of eyes, tracking his gaze. He pressed dial and put his phone to his ear.

'This is Tom. Leave a tone. Beep boop.' Beeep!

Cullen hung up and redialled.

'This is Tom. Leave a tone. Beep boop.' Beeep!

'Tom, it's Scott. Call me when you get this, okay?' He tapped the red button and waited for a few seconds.

The door clunked open to his right. He swung round. A barista undid the top lock, his Starbucks T-shirt riding up.

Cullen entered the café, house music pumping from the speakers, and walked up to the counter.

The barista grinned at him. 'Morning, sir, what can I get you?'

'The biggest and strongest coffee you've got.'

'A latte? Flat white?'

'Americano, black.'

'Coming right up. What's your name, sir?'

Cullen fiddled in his pocket for change. 'Scott.'

'Coming right up, sir.'

Cullen handed over a fiver and waited for his change. He got out his phone and dialled as he walked over to the other side of the counter.

'You've reached the voicemail of Simon Buxton. Leave a message or call back. Thanks.' Beeep!

He hit redial.

'You've reached the voicemail of Simon Buxton. Leave a message or call back. Thanks.' Beeep!

'Si, it's Scott. Give me a call. Cheers.'

He ended the call and rifled through his bulging wallet for recent business cards. Nothing.

Switched to Google and searched "Lorna Gilmour Edinburgh". Hundreds of entries. Christ.

His phone rang.

Tom calling…

He swiped across the screen. 'Hey, Tom.'

'Scott, do you know what time it is?'

'Aye. I'm already working.'

'Fuck me.' Tom paused. 'You sound like shite, Skinky.'

'Feel like it. You sound just as bad.'

'What a night, eh?' Burp. 'Scuse me.'

'Has Chantal called you?'

'Nope.'

'Anyone from Sharon's team?'

'Saw I had a load of missed calls. What's happened?'

'When did you leave last night?'

'Half eleven, maybe? Everyone else had bailed by the time I got back with the last drinks. I think.'

'What?'

'Buxton had gone. Lorna'd gone. Same with Rich. Took me ages to get served, as well. I was completely locked and—'

'Someone spiked my drink.'

'Shut up.'

'I'm serious. What about you?'

'I'm fine.' Another pause. 'You don't think it was me, do you?'

'Mm.'

'Come on, man. How could you think that?'

'A lot of my friends are betraying me just now.'

'What's that supposed to mean?'

'Rich.'

'Right.' Yawn. 'Mate, come on, there's no way I'd do that.'

'Even as a joke?'

'If I did, don't you think I'd at least video it and put it on YouTube?'

'Very good.' Cullen laughed despite himself. 'Is Rich there?'

'Are you guys still speaking?'

'What's that supposed to mean?'

'You had a bit of a barney last night.'

'He deserved everything he got. Is he there?'

'I'm not going into his room after last time. I can't unsee that.'

'Tell him to call me when he gets up, all right?'

'Sure thing.'

'I need to see if Lorna's okay. Do you know where she lives?'

'Broughton Road, I think. Not far from the Tesco. I'll text you the address.'

'Cheers.' Cullen ended the call, grabbed his coffee from the barista and left the café, waiting for the text to arrive. His phone thrummed — Lorna's contact details. He stabbed a finger against the mobile number.

'You've reached Lorna. Can't take your noise just now. Text me, I don't listen to voicemails. Bye!' Beeep!

Cullen passed the big Tesco and drove the pool car along Broughton Road, passing a left turn into an office development. He stopped by a tarmac playground and tried her number again. Voicemail.

He checked Tom's text for the address and clocked her flat — ground-floor, across from the Powderhall Arms. He got out.

His phone rang. Buxton. He swiped to answer the call. 'Cullen.'

'Got your voicemail, mate.' Buxton croaked down the line.

'You okay?'

'Too much booze. I'll have a Berocca, then get in soon.'

'Did you get home okay?'

'Yeah, why?'

'My drink got spiked. Rohypnol.'

'Jesus Christ. Are you okay?'

'I'm fine. I was completely out of it. I can't remember much about last night.'

'Have you got him?'

Cullen gritted his teeth. 'Not yet. Was yours spiked?'

A pause. 'No.'

'You sure? You don't sound good.'

'Positive, mate. Someone had to drink your shots, didn't they?'

'Did you see anyone near our table?'

'I was putting the booze away, mate. I can't remember much. Everyone just disappeared. Tried calling, but nobody was answering.'

Cullen swapped his phone to his other hand. 'Look, I'll need to get a statement when you get in.'

'Why?'

'Because we think it's related to Sharon's attacks.'

'Shit.'

'That motherfucker could've got me. I could've been ... raped.' Cullen tightened his grip on the phone. 'I'll give you a shout later. Bye.' He pocketed it and crossed the road, rapping on the blue door.

It swung open. Lorna folded her arms across her T-shirt, "I'm Sick To Death Of Low". She blinked against the daylight, swaying a bit. 'Scott Cullen?'

'Lorna, are you okay?'

'It's really early.'

'I've tried calling, but you're not answering your phone.'

She yawned. 'Sorry, I sleep like the dead when I've been drinking.'

'I had my drink spiked last night.'

'Shit, you too?'

Cullen frowned. 'What?'

'I got done.' She bit her lip. 'Got spiked when I was a student. I recognised the signs last night and got a taxi back here.'

'Are you okay?'

'I left as soon as I started feeling it. Lots of dodgy blokes hanging around. I downed a coffee when I got home. Think it cleared my system.'

'You should've told me.'

'I thought you were still dancing.'

'What about Buxton?'

'Your mate Simon? He'd left. Couldn't find him anyway.'

'My girlfriend's been investigating male rapes over the last couple of weeks.' Cullen got out a business card and scribbled

Sharon's mobile number on the back. 'I need you to go speak to her. This might be connected.'

'Oh my God.'

'Any idea who could've done it?'

'When we were dancing for a bit, there was that guy sitting near us, kept trying to chat to me and Simon. Rich was flirting with him.'

'Would you be able to describe him?'

'Probably.' She tapped the card. 'I'll get up there now.'

'Do you need a lift?'

'Give me a minute. I need to get changed.'

CULLEN LED Lorna down the corridor in the station. 'How are you feeling?'

No reply.

He swung round.

Ten feet back, she stumbled back against the wall. Hand to her forehead, knees buckling.

'Shite.' He jogged back and grabbed her arms. 'What's happened?'

'Feel wooooooozy.'

He wrapped an arm round her shoulders and helped her along the corridor, taking it slow. He kicked the meeting room door open. Photographs and papers pinned to the walls, case files all over the table.

Jain stood near the window, talking into her mobile, McKeown next to her. 'I'll call you back, okay?' She dumped the phone on the table. 'She was in the club last night, right?'

'One of Tom's mates. She's been drugged as well.'

'Christ.' Jain swung round. 'Mac, can you bring the duty doc up?'

'Aye, sure.' McKeown stormed out of the room.

Cullen winked. 'Bossing people around, Chantal.'

'Someone's got to.'

Lorna collapsed onto a seat. 'What's happened?'

'We'll make sure you're okay.' Jain crouched down, smiling. 'We'll do a blood test. Maybe a rape kit, as well.'

'I didn't get raped. I went home when I felt this kick in.'

'Doesn't mean you were alone.' Jain stood up again. 'Be back in a second.' She nodded at Cullen and left the room.

He followed her out, pulling the door shut behind him. 'What's up?'

'Is she on the level?'

'I think so. Why?'

'She looks pretty fucked. Worse than you did.'

'She didn't get injected with magic juice.'

'True.' Jain sighed. The sigh turned into a yawn. 'I need my bed.'

'You getting anywhere?'

'Just finished interviewing the staff. Again. Still checking out the punters.'

'You're not interviewing them?'

'Just took names and addresses. Got a hit against the sex offenders' register.'

'Sounds positive.'

'Hardly. Guy stuck a traffic cone up his arse ten years ago. We're getting nothing.' Jain leaned against the glass and folded her arms, yawning. 'You were fucked last night when we came round.'

'Not my finest hour.'

'Quite sweet, really.'

'Why did you ask if she was on the level?'

'Well, this guy isn't targeting women.'

'He's been raping men. Might've been targeting men *and* women. Spiking drinks at the bar, scattergun, and seeing who's tottering about.'

'Well, Mac's been through the CCTV and found the guy who looked after your drinks.'

'You bringing him in?'

'When I said found, I mean you can see a grainy face on the screen. That's it so far.'

'Let me know if you need anything.'

She nodded. 'Have you spoken to the others?'

'Tom's clear and Buxton's hungover. I can't find Rich. He might've pulled.'

'Pulled? You sound like an issue of *Loaded* from 1996.'

Cullen checked his watch. 'Shite. I'm late for Methven's briefing.'

48

C ullen took another sip, the Starbucks coffee too cold to drink. Too tired to think. He pushed into the Incident Room.

'—and I expect you to have a—' Methven stopped and frowned at him. 'Good morning, Sergeant.'

'Sorry for being late, sir.'

'DC Murray's just given your update. I was just setting out my expectations from your team. Anything to add?'

Cullen shrugged. 'Please continue.' He rubbed his forehead, trying to get the knitting needles out.

'Anything more from you, Stuart?'

Murray shook his head.

Eva put up her hand. 'Sir, I've finished going through the drug squad case files.'

Methven shot a glare at Cullen. 'Thought we agreed that was a dead end?'

Eva swallowed. 'Shite.'

Methven folded his arms and nodded at Cullen. 'Sergeant, a word after this.'

'Fine.' Cullen stayed focused on Eva. 'Did you get anything?'

'From what I've read, it's ninety per cent certain the coke we found in Mr Van de Merwe's flat came from the batch Vardy's selling.'

'That's a dead end, understood?' Methven glared at Cullen. 'What's today's plan of attack, Sergeant?'

'We need to determine whether Candy's involved or not.' Cullen yawned into his hand, trying to cover it with his cup. 'And find this Vaccaro guy.'

'Very well.' Methven uncapped a different pen and turned back to the whiteboard. 'DS Bain, can you give your team's update, please?'

Cullen shut his eyes, out of sight of Methven.

'Aye, sure thing.' Bain snuffled. 'DC McCrea and the rest of my team were in late last night and we've made solid progress on the Ferguson case.' A sniff. 'Dean Vardy's still not speaking.'

'I expect you to resolve that this morning, Sergeant.'

'See what I can do, Col.'

Methven squeaked a new note on the board. 'Continue.'

'Interviewed everyone connected to him at work and in his private life. No additional suspects identified.'

'None?'

'Sorry.'

'Sodding hell.'

'The question of whether Ferguson topped himself's still open, sir. We've got a statement placing a woman with him, so we think it's murder. Deeley's veering to that side, as well.'

'Do you have an identity for her?'

'I think it's Candy but there's nothing on the CCTV or any of the witness statements.'

'I'd like that identity confirmed.' Methven scored through two actions. 'Anything else?'

'Finished speaking to the Schneider people who worked at Alba Bank last year.'

'Why?'

'Sundance wanted us to ask about these equity partnership rumours. They're all remaining tight-lipped.'

'Do you think that means anything?'

'Not sure, Col.'

'Anything else from you? No? Dismissed.' Methven cut through the throng to Cullen and leaned against the white-painted pillar next to him. 'You were seriously late, Sergeant.'

'Had to drop someone off upstairs. It's related to Sharon's case.'

'Oh?'

Cullen looked away. 'Somebody put Rohypnol in my drink last night.'

'Dear God.' Methven leaned in close. 'What happened?'

'I had four beers. Next thing I know, I wake up in the club and threw up in the toilet. The bouncers chucked me in a cab.'

'Have they finally shut that place down?'

'Too late, but aye. They're still interviewing the staff and punters.'

Methven leaned against the adjacent desk, the wood creaking. 'Sergeant, do you think Sharon's rapist tried it on with you?'

'Maybe.'

'What were you even thinking going to the Liquid Lounge?'

'Thought I was safe, sir.'

'Are you okay to work today?'

'I wouldn't be here otherwise.'

'Don't let me down.' Methven started counting through a handful of change. 'Time for my coffee. Can I fetch you one?'

Cullen held up the Starbucks cup. 'I'll microwave this after I've seen what my team's been up to.'

'Excellent, excellent.' Methven marched off through the Incident Room.

Cullen leaned against the pillar and sucked cold coffee.

'Jesus fuckin' Christ, Sundance.' Bain looked him up and down. 'You look like you went twelve rounds with a bottle of Absinthe.'

Cullen folded his arms. 'Feels like it.'

'What time did you finish up?'

'Midnight, I think.'

'Bullshit. I was fuckin' barrelling home along the M8 at midnight.' A smirk danced across Bain's face. 'Sure you didn't get chucked out of a club at three before finishing a bottle of whisky round Buxton's house?'

Cullen took another swig of coffee, not helping the stomach any. 'Four beers, that's it.'

'Seriously, what did you do?'

'Four. Beers.'

Bain snorted. 'Believe that when I see it.' He walked off.

Cullen clocked Murray and Buxton heading over. 'Morning, boys.'

Murray frowned. 'Not going to thank me for deputising?'

Cullen shrugged. 'Aye, thanks for that.'

'Take it you had a late one?'

'Didn't get much sleep last night.' Cullen looked Buxton up and down. 'How are you doing, Si?'

'Feel like someone's eaten my brain, but I'm raring to go.' Buxton yawned. 'Any ill effects?'

'Not too bad.'

Murray did a double-take. 'What's he talking about.'

Cullen looked away. 'I got my drink spiked.'

'What the fuck? In the club?'

Cullen nodded. 'Did you see anything before you left?'

'There was that guy sitting between Si and that Lorna bird. Skinny boy.'

'It's not him. That's my ex-flatmate.'

'Seemed well dodgy. He brought a round back, didn't he?'

Cullen rubbed his neck. 'Lorna had her drink spiked, too.'

'Gentlemen.' Methven reappeared, glowering at Cullen, Bain lurking behind him. He snapped out a newspaper, the broadsheet sprawl of the *Argus*. 'This Rich McAlpine chap's at it again.'

'You seen this, Sundance? "Consultancy Fraud At Death Bank".' Bain pointed at the headline and shook his head. 'How the fuck did he get that?'

Methven snorted, nostrils flared. 'DS Cullen?'

Cullen winced, eyes on his two DCs. 'I've spoken to him about it. He said—'

Bain pointed at another headline and cackled. 'Check this. "Alba Bank BDSM Ring". The boy's got the inside track.'

'You've both discussed this with him.' Methven folded his arms. 'I want to know how he's getting this stuff. This has to stop. Now.'

'I spoke to him about it when the story went online. I don't think his source is a police officer.'

'Then who the hell is it?'

'Someone at Alba Bank, most likely.'

'Guesswork, Sergeant. I'm disappointed.'

'Look, it's not me.'

'I know it's not you.'

Finally listening... Cullen folded the paper in half. 'I'll go and have a word with him.'

CULLEN TILTED his head to the side. 'You pissed on your own chips?'

Buxton clenched his jaw, hands gripping the wheel. 'Yeah, bought some chips on the way home last night. Went for a slash down a back street and put them on the ground. When I zipped up, I saw I'd pissed all over my chips. Hadn't even eaten any.'

'What did you do?'

'Took me a few seconds to walk away from them. Long seconds.'

'I hope a tramp didn't pick them up.'

'Not going to be the worst thing they've eaten, is it?'

'True.' Buxton pulled in on Portobello High Street and yawned. 'Not sure I should be driving.'

'The breathalyser's clean.' Cullen tightened his grip on the steering wheel and looked at the flat above the kebab shop.

Buxton let his seatbelt slide up. 'Who are we speaking to here?'

'We're not. I am.'

'Come on, mate.'

'You stay here. This is personal. You saw what Crystal was like back there. I'm in the toilet. I need to fix this.'

'Suit yourself. That geezer seemed ... dodgy. Sure you don't need me?'

'I'll give you a call if I need corroboration.' Cullen got out of the car and stood on the pavement, clutching Methven's *Argus*. Two buses hissed as they crawled to a halt at stops on opposite sides of the road.

A man walked past, face covered in scar tissue. Papers and rolls in his blue carrier bag, a three-legged dog following him.

Cullen sucked in breath and pressed the buzzer.

'Hello?'

'Tom, it's Scott. Is Rich back yet?'

'Negative, amigo. Found a text from him at midnight saying he pulled. Gone to some guy's flat.'

'Jesus Christ.'

'Unreal, isn't he?'

'So he's not there?'

'Afraid not. Wasted trip. You should've called.'

'Been trying for the last half an hour.'

'Aye. Sorry, I was just having a du—'

'Catch you later.' Cullen walked over to the car and got in. 'He's not there.'

Buxton locked his phone. 'What?'

'Did Rich leave with you?'

'Don't know. I was a bit pissed.'

'What about Lorna?'

'Thought I was in there. She went home before me. Just bolted.'

'What was I doing?'

'Dancing like you were Hall or Oates.'

'Shite, I don't remember any of this.'

'The joys of Rohypnol.' Buxton leaned back in his chair. 'All I can think of is that geezer hanging around us.'

'I don't remember.'

'Wait, didn't Rich ask this geezer to look after our drinks while we danced?'

'I don't remember.' Cullen looked back up at the flat above. 'Could Rich have done it?'

'You think your mate drugged you?'

'How else do you explain it? Me and Lorna got drugged and now he's missing.'

'I mean, yeah, maybe.'

'Well, if it was him... I need to run this past Crystal.'

49

Cullen staggered into the Incident Room, blinking at the lights as he looked around. No sign of Methven. Murray sat next to Eva, both working at laptops. 'Either of you seen Crystal?'

'Think he's interviewing someone.' She frowned at him. 'I'm not sure what I'm supposed to be working on.'

'Can you find Richard McAlpine?'

Murray frowned. 'Your mate?'

'Aye. Eva, bring him in, okay?'

'Right, I'll try.'

Cullen retreated from the Incident Room, yawning his way to the Obs Suite. He checked the monitors for Methven. There, in Four. With Bain. He left and crossed the hall, knocking on the door. Didn't wait for a response.

Methven and Bain sat at the table.

Opposite was a tall man, hands in pockets, leaning back in the chair. Stone-washed denims tucked into crocodile skin boots, casual shirt hanging loose. He winked at Cullen. 'Well, hello there.' American accent, polished and clipped.

Cullen nodded at Methven. 'Need a word, sir.'

Methven hefted himself up. 'I'll just be a second, sir.' He marched over and yanked the door behind him, folding his arms. 'How did it go with our little Fourth Estate problem?'

'Rich isn't at his flat. Tom reckons he picked someone up last night.'

'Well, you find him. Okay? Nip this in the bud, Sergeant.'

'Sir, I think it could be him drugging people. Drugging me and Lorna.'

'What?'

'I've nothing concrete, sir, but I'm getting worried. He's gone to ground and he had opportunity to do it.'

'Sodding, sodding hell.' Methven glared at the door. 'I need to discuss this with DCI Cargill. Can you take over here?'

'Who's that in there?'

'Wayne Broussard.'

'The Schneider guy?'

'He's just flown in from the States, claiming he's jet-lagged, though I suspect lying's part of his professional training.' Methven started off. 'Ensure DS Bain doesn't tear his head off, okay?'

'Fine.' Cullen watched him storm off down the corridor, prodding his Airwave. Jesus. He pushed open the door.

Bain leaned over to the microphone. 'DS Cullen has entered the room.'

'I assure you, officer, my firm's clean as the pure-driven snow.' Wayne Broussard crossed one leg over the other. 'We're audited by four global institutions. Plus, we're benchmarked on a whole heap of metrics every single quarter. Takes a lot out of us, but I can put my hand on my heart,' he thumped his chest, 'and say we're clean.'

Bain scribbled something in his notebook. 'What about IMC? Are they as clean?'

'Oh, those guys. Tell me, how do you think they got a gig this big?'

Cullen frowned. 'A tender process?'

'Very naïve.' Wayne nodded at Cullen. 'Who are you?'

'DS Cullen. We spoke on the phone the other day.'

'Right, the little guy.' Wayne looked him up and down. 'You're bigger than I expected.'

Bain smirked. 'You were saying about IMC...?'

'Yeah, yeah.' Wayne tapped his nose. 'I'll let you in on a secret. Offshoring's been a complete waste of time since the mid-nineties. Too expensive and the distance causes too many communication problems. Everything sloooooows down.'

'I bet you've made a lot of money advising on it, though.'

'Look, we know how to make it work, but nobody's interested in spending the time or money. You need to get people over there, establish the relationships. You wouldn't believe how many times I've been to Bangalore or Chennai. Whether they choose to heed our advice is another matter.'

'Was it Jonathan van de Merwe who didn't heed your advice?'

'Him and Yardley. Desperate men trying to cover their asses. Real rootin', tootin' cowboys. Alan Henderson busted his balls on a daily basis. Doing that shows they're trying to save costs.'

'Were ICM better or worse than UC?'

Wayne sat upright and jabbed a finger in the air. 'Don't start me on them.'

'Struck a nerve, have I?'

'Just don't get me started on those guys.'

'I'm afraid I just have, sir. What does it stand for?'

'I've no idea.'

'Nobody seems to. Please, continue.'

'Look, there was a murky grey area around that whole thing.' Wayne drummed on the table. 'You know something? One of the outlaws is joining IMC once his golden handcuffs with UC are off.'

'Who?'

'Paul Vaccaro.'

'He's an equity partner, right?'

'Hence the handcuffs. Got six months to sit on his ass, then poof! He can join a competitor. Supposed to be heading up the UK operation. High six-figure salary's what I hear.'

'How does this relate to what you were telling us about how much they were creaming off the top at Alba Bank?'

'I'm not following you?'

'Your deputy told us they made about twenty million. Why bother having another job if you've made that sort of figure?'

'I wouldn't expect a little ant like you to—'

'A little *ant*?'

'Sure. You're just skirting round for crumbs. Do you know how much—'

'You can't call me an ant.'

'Course I can. Just avoid aardvarks.' Wayne shook his head.

'This game's all about power. Money's secondary, shows how much power you got. You know how much I took home—'

'Do you know where we can find him?'

'Paul's fishing, drinking and fucking.'

'Where?'

'He's renting a farmhouse near Edinburgh. Place called Cramond.'

~

SOMETHING NUDGED CULLEN'S ARM. 'Wake up.'

'Mmf?' Cullen blinked his eyes open. Bright sunlight. They were bouncing down a farm track, cows in a field to the left, opposite neon-yellow oil seed rape. 'Where are we?'

'Vaccaro's house.' Murray pulled up in front of a gate, a mishmash of trees and shrubs behind a gap in the leylandii. 'Nice sleep?'

'Feels like I'm coming down with something.' Cullen stretched out and yawned. 'This where—'

'What was that?'

'What?'

'Loads of stuff came out of your mouth when you yawned. You're a snake.'

'It's just this thing I've got.' Cullen unclipped his seatbelt and shrugged it off. Loosened his shoulders. 'Let's get this shit started.' He got out of the car and yawned again. 'Christ.'

'Sure you're okay?'

'Aye.'

'Your funeral.' Murray opened the gate and crunched up the path to the big old farmhouse, stone with a rendered extension. He knocked on the door. 'Better be in.'

A man pulled open the front door, head tilted to the side. He tightened the belt of his cream dressing gown, cut up with green stripes. Silver hair but a boyish face underneath. Rounded. Chubby. Just like George Clooney. 'Yes?'

'Police. DC Murray, DS Cullen.' Murray flashed his warrant card. 'Paul Vaccaro?'

'That's me. What do you want?'

'Need a word inside, if it's all the same.'

Vaccaro held the door open. 'In you come.' He trudged through the hall, adjusting his belt. 'What's this about, gents?'

Cullen followed him into a living room, his eyes itching.

Vaccaro sat on a sofa and checked his watch. 'I've got to head up to Dundee in about an hour.'

'We'll be quick.' Cullen perched on a winged armchair. 'Do you know a Martin Ferguson?'

Vaccaro sniffed. 'Worked with him at Alba Bank.'

'You were the UC Partners lead there, right?'

Vaccaro frowned. 'I headed up the HR programme. Martin was on the Ops programme.'

'We found his body yesterday afternoon.'

'What?'

'You didn't know?'

'He's dead? Really?'

'I'm afraid so. Surprised you haven't heard.'

'Sorry, I'm on a sabbatical just now. Trying to switch off from all that.'

'We understand you engaged in certain activities with him?'

'That's very euphemistic. Come, come, Sergeant, BDSM isn't a crime. We were conducting consensual acts. Among adults, I hasten to add.'

'Mr Ferguson seemingly died during one of these acts.'

'Jesus Christ.'

'Where were you on Thursday night?'

'Here.' Vaccaro sniffed. 'Some ladies came round to keep me company.'

'Prostitutes?'

'Did I say that? It was an entirely innocent visit.'

'I'll get some officers to corroborate your story, if you give us their names.'

'Shall I just print the email?'

'Whatever works.' Cullen leaned forward, clasping his hands in front of him. 'Did Mr Ferguson participate in these activities?'

A deep frown twitched on Vaccaro's forehead. 'Martin was a very enthusiastic occupant of a gimp suit.'

'We also found Jonathan van de Merwe's body on Sunday morning.'

'Jesus Christ. Nobody told me. What happened?'

'Pushed from Dean Bridge. Other than that, we don't know.'

Vaccaro bit his lip.

'We found his sex room. Mr Ferguson had been there.' Cullen gave a smile. 'Will we find your DNA there?'

'Probably. We were in the same ring.' Vaccaro leaned back, the dressing gown riding up. 'That sounds so seedy.'

'Where were you on Saturday night?'

'Same story as two nights ago. Here, balls deep in—'

'Again, I'd appreciate some proof.'

'Sure thing.'

Cullen made a note. 'We understand you were an equity partner in UC.'

Vaccaro frowned. 'Why are murder detectives interested in who owns what?'

'There may be a financial motive to his death. Are you a partner?'

'Why are you interested?'

'We believe Mr Van de Merwe was engaged in fraudulent activities.'

'Well, I don't know anything about that.' Another frown, held this time. 'I was just the Managing Director, just an employee. I didn't own any equity.'

'Who did?'

'Jonathan had a third.'

'We know that. Who else?'

'I only know one of them.' Vaccaro sighed. 'Wayne Broussard.'

CULLEN LEANED against the wall of the interview room and glanced at his mobile. He looked at Wayne Broussard, then over Bain's shoulder at the recorder winking on the desk. 'Mr Broussard, I'm suggesting you take legal counsel here.'

'And I refuse it.' Wayne put a boot up on the table. He tapped at a frat ring on his right pinkie, arcane symbols scored into the metal. 'I studied at Harvard Law School. I know my way around the law.'

'Can you put your foot down, please?' Cullen waited until he complied. 'American law's very different from Scots.'

'Just get on with it.'

'If that's how you want to play it.'

'I've got a conference call in half an hour. Be quick.'

'You're not getting out of here until we're done.'

'That so?'

'Mr Broussard, we believe you're an equity partner in UC.'

'That's good.' He laughed. 'Vaccaro told you this, right?'

'I can neither confirm nor deny that.'

'He's lying. I'm not involved.' Wayne licked his lips. 'What evidence have you got?'

'We're assimilating it as we speak.'

'You know Vaccaro has a share, right?'

'Our understanding is that isn't the case.'

'Bullshit it is.' Wayne clamped his lips together. 'Look, son. I'm a partner of Schneider Consulting LLP. It'd be more than my job's worth if I got into bed with a bunch of cowboys like UC. The other partners could sue me.'

'What about for a third share of twenty million pounds?'

'You little ant, do you know how much I make—'

'Are you a co-owner of UC or not?'

'Of course I'm not.'

'But Mr Van de Merwe was?'

'Absolutely.'

'So he used his position to rip off his employers?'

'That's right.'

'How could he get away with it?'

'Politics.' Wayne shone a smile at them. 'Jon's boss, Alan Henderson, sponsored the programme. That disaster happened on his watch. Sacking Jon would show how little attention he'd devoted to three hundred million.'

'We understand the CEO sacked them?'

'*I* kicked them out of Alba. Sir Ronald just listened to my advice. He heard what he asked to hear. Replace UC with my firm.'

'And you used it to your advantage?'

'That's not a crime. It was all signed off by Jon.'

'I hear he wasn't the most diligent.'

'Not my problem. I submit into their process. What they do's nothing to do with me.'

'You've no guilt about exploiting this situation?'

'It's what I do for a living. I'm the best at what I do.'

'We've found some transactions Mr Van de Merwe received from an IMC subsidiary called Indus Consulting.'

Broussard gave a shrug. 'Greedy men take anything from anyone.'

'Thought you said it's only about power?'

He shrugged. 'Jon was a bit different.'

'Who else is an equity partner?'

Wayne glanced at his watch. 'Look, I really need to get on this call soon.'

'Tell us who else owns equity in UC.'

Broussard licked his lips. 'William Yardley.'

50

Methven stopped outside the top-floor flat and tightened his stab-proof vest. 'I shall lead here, Sergeant.'

'Fine with me.' Cullen sucked in breath and waited for the two black-suited uniforms to join him. 'Right, here we go.' He knocked on the red door and waited.

It flew open. William Yardley stood there, frowning and red-faced. Lines creased his eyes, looking like he'd aged a year in a week. 'What?'

Methven stepped forward into the doorway. 'We need a word with you about your interest in UC Partners.'

He snorted and widened the door. 'Come in.'

'I'd rather do this down the station on the record.'

'Look, Sergeant, I'm stretched to breaking here. I'm trying to hold this programme together with my bare hands.'

Cullen glanced over at Methven. Got a shrug. He nodded at the uniforms. 'Stay here. Nobody leaves, okay?' He followed Yardley through to a library, oak shelves filled with dusty books. A large table dominated the middle, just a laptop and green reading light on top. Sheets of flip chart paper covered the opposite wall.

Methven unstrapped his vest as they walked. 'This is quite some place, sir.'

'It does me during the week.' Yardley pointed at a sofa by the window. 'Please, have a seat.'

Methven sat on it.

Cullen stayed by the door, near the uniform blocking the exit. 'I thought you lived in Peebles?'

'Just at the weekend. My wife's taken the kids back to the States for a couple of weeks.'

'Is this a recent thing?'

'Left on Tuesday.' Yardley sat at his desk and shut the laptop. 'Let me get this straight, you think I've got an equity share in UC Partners?'

'We believe you and Jonathan van de Merwe co-owned the company.'

'Have you got any evidence?'

'Just two witness statements naming you as an equity partner.'

'That's not a whole heap of beans.'

'You should talk to us.'

'No.'

Methven got up. 'This is getting us nowhere. Let's do this down the station.'

'Officer, I seriously can't spare the time.' Yardley waved a hand at the wall. 'Can't you see how busy I am?'

Methven gripped his arm. 'Come on, sir.'

'Look, I'll tell you what you want to know. I just need to work. *Please.*'

Methven let go of Yardley's arm and tapped his watch. 'I'm giving you a minute to explain.'

'What do you want to know?'

Cullen locked his gaze, holding it for a few seconds. 'How much have you made through this scheme?'

'Aren't you listening? I've no idea who owns UC.'

'What about Mr Van de Merwe?'

'Well, maybe I heard a few things about that.'

'What, that he owned the company?'

'Maybe.' Yardley collapsed into his desk chair. 'You guys think I killed Jon, right? Why would I do that?'

'Killing him allowed you to take ownership of the UC bank account in the Caymans.'

'Where are you getting this from?'

'We can't say.'

'I just want to deliver this programme. That's it.'

'Are you denying you knew about this fraud?'

'Listen, I found out what Jon was doing last year. I tried to get him to stop, but he wouldn't. I went to Alan Henderson about it. Tried to get Jon sacked.'

'What happened?'

'Henderson knocked me back, said Jon's too ingrained in the bank. I don't know what went on between them, but, next thing I know, UC got kicked out. Schneider were running things and IMC got brought in. Made my life a lot harder.'

'Not sure I believe you weren't involved.' Cullen smiled. 'Big house down in Peebles. Nice flat here.'

'Alba pay for these. I get a decent salary, but it's all going on the mortgage on our place near Sevenoaks.'

'So you're saying you don't co-own UC?'

'Of course I don't.'

'If it's not you, then who's the other partner?'

'Wayne Broussard.'

'Right, that's enough.' Methven hauled him to his feet and waved to the uniform at the flat door. 'Constable, can you escort this gentleman down to the station?'

Yardley stood stock still, resisted the tug at his arm. 'You need to speak to Wayne, not me!'

'You're playing games with us, sir. You think he's landed you in the shit, so you're dropping him in it.' Methven folded his arms. 'I'm sick of this. We're going to prosecute you.'

'Listen.' Yardley shrugged off the uniformed officer. 'Look, this won't stand up in court, but... One of the guys I kept on from the UC team saw all this stuff on their walls.'

Cullen frowned. 'On the whiteboards?'

'Right. It was the money trail. How the money went from Alba Bank to their UK account. Then over to the Caymans. Then BVI. Then a few other places.'

'This isn't helping us solve a murder.'

'I know.' Yardley let out a deep sigh. 'Look, I don't know who owned them, but the ultimate owner of the company was in the UK. Based in Canary Wharf. Triple-V Holdings.'

～

METHVEN WAVED his hands around the Obs Suite. 'I remain hopeful this will lead us somewhere.'

'You mean you don't believe him?' Cullen stayed focused on the screen, Bain and McCrea grilling Yardley on low volume.

'We're dealing with a pack of liars here, Sergeant.' Methven tapped the screen. 'We need to get to the truth. He's just going to trot out the same story to DS Bain.'

'Stuart Murray's on with the City cops just now.'

'And I hope we get some evidence.'

The door thumped open.

'Just a second.' Murray held out his mobile, static crackling from the speaker. 'I'm on with DI Coulson of City police.'

Methven snatched it off him. 'Inspector, this is DI Methven of Police Scotland. We need to know the exact ownership of UC Partners LLP.'

'Okay. Well, I've done some work here. I've traced the ultimate ownership to a shell company based in Canary Wharf.'

'Triple-V Holdings?'

'Correct.'

'What have you found?'

'Here we go. I've got the Certificate of Incorporation. I'll send an email with—'

'What does it sodding say?'

'The equity split is fifty-fifty between Jonathan Morten van de Merwe and Wayne Edward Kinski Broussard.'

～

METHVEN SLAMMED his fist on the interview room table. 'Mr Broussard, you've been lying to us.'

'Listen, buddy.' Wayne licked his lips. 'I need to get on that call.'

Cullen sat opposite, rocking forward on the chair. 'You're a co-owner of UC.'

'I've no idea what you're talking about, guys.' Wayne stared to the side and chuckled. 'Guys, I've been candid with you so far. There's no connection between me and that business.'

'We've got proof you're the other partner.'

'Your proof must be wrong, ant man.'

'Why?'

'Because I'm not involved.'

'You are.' Cullen pushed the sheet of paper across the table. 'A Certificate of Incorporation of Triple-V Holdings, the ultimate parent company. See? You and Mr Van de Merwe are named owners.'

'No comment.'

'His death means you're now the sole owner.'

'You can fake documentation.'

'We'll interview everyone at your firm who's worked on any of the programmes with UC.'

'What do you hope to gain from that?'

'The truth.' Cullen rested his hands behind his head. 'City of London police are raiding the Triple-V offices in Canary Wharf as we speak.'

'Look, buddy, I'm not the second equity partner.'

Cullen grinned at Methven. 'I think he's lying, sir.'

'I *know* he's lying.'

'I'm telling you the truth here.'

Cullen stabbed a finger at him. 'You implicated Mr Yardley in this.'

'He owns a third share. Let me out of here and I'll show you proof.'

'You mean you can fabricate something.'

'Look, son—'

'You're in the shit here, Mr Broussard.' Methven hammered a fist on the table. 'Do you want us to speak to the other partners at Schneider?'

Wayne fiddled with his cufflink, resetting it a couple of times. 'What do I get in return?'

'Fired, I'd imagine.' Methven grinned. 'Probably sued by Schneider and Alba Bank. The City police are already raiding a number of addresses in the Greater London area. I've got a call with the Serious Fraud Office at three. They were talking about passing it to the US. Not sure who it'd be over there. The Treasury? SEC? FBI?'

'Look. Guys. What's the deal on the table?'

Cullen glanced over at Methven. 'Depends what he's offering, sir, right?'

'Agreed.'

'This was all Jonathan's idea.'

'So you're involved?'

'Jon came to me needing to offshore money through shell companies. I hooked him up with someone.' Wayne adjusted his left cufflink. 'You guys need to speak to Ollie Cranston. He's the expert.'

'Right. Why did you sack UC?'

Wayne adjusted the other cufflink. 'It was getting messy. Jon was falling apart. Too much coke, too many whores. The longer it ran, the further the milestones slipped. It just looked corrupt, you know?'

'So you stopped taking the money?'

'I never got a dime. It's all Jon and Ollie. I persuaded Sir Ronald to get rid of them.' Wayne's cufflinks clinked together. 'Look, it's my fiduciary responsibility to Schneider to bring more business in. This was a great opportunity.'

'Why bring IMC in?'

'Jon needed a scapegoat.'

'Like Mr Yardley?'

'Like that.'

'Who killed Mr Van de Merwe?'

'I've no fucking idea.'

'You didn't?'

'Why the fuck would I do that? Answer me that. Why?'

'To take over the bank accounts?'

'Fuck off. No. That was Ollie and Jon. Nothing to do with me.'

'So you've no idea why Mr Van de Merwe took a header off the bridge?'

'Will Yardley'd be my bet.' Wayne let out a deep breath. 'So, what do I sign?'

'There isn't a deal.'

'But I've just spilled my guts here.'

'There's nobody else left to prosecute. It's just you. The accounts are frozen. You're deep in the shit.'

'Listen, it's Ollie you need to be speaking to here, not me.'

'I don't believe you.'

'I'm not saying anything more without a lawyer.'

'Then we'll appoint one.' Cullen leaned over. 'Interview terminated at midday.' He clicked stop on the recorder and followed Methven out into the corridor, slamming the door behind him. 'Well?'

'We're no further forward with our cases. Does this mean Yardley's in the clear?'

Cullen folded his arms and leaned against the wall, cold through his shirt. 'The guy's just caught in the middle. He's genuinely trying to deliver this programme. He's just not very good at his job.'

'You might have a point. We don't know who killed Van de Merwe, we just know he was a crook. Sometimes we take the results we can get, Sergeant.' Methven patted Cullen on the shoulder. 'Looks like there's a couple of hundred million in fraudulent assets to be reclaimed here. Brownie points with the NCA and City.'

'We should interview Cranston.'

'I'll get Bain and McCrea on it.' Methven jangled his keys. 'I'm off to brief Alison.'

'Good luck with that.'

'Can I borrow DC Murray?'

'Why?'

'He's got the connections with the City.'

Cullen sighed. 'Sure thing.'

'You should take a break, Sergeant.'

'We're still nowhere with Van de Merwe's murder. We need to sort out the loose ends. Candy and Vardy.'

'Fine. I'll leave it in your hands.'

'Cheers.' Cullen got out his phone and found Anderson's number. 'I'll keep you updated, sir.' He put his phone to his ear, watching Methven pound away down the corridor. 'James, it's Cullen.'

'Can you keep Bain away from me?'

'Not until you finish the sex room analysis.'

'I finished that this morning. Fuck's sake. Confirmed your pal, Candy, was "there" a few times, if you catch my drift.'

'Who else have you got?'

'Ferguson, Vaccaro, Van de Merwe. And a few males we don't have on file.'

'Vardy?'

'Boy's got a record so he would've shown up.'

'So, nothing?'

'Got one other female, though. She's been there at least ten times.'

'Who is it?'

'No idea, DNA's not on file.'

51

Cullen leaned back in his chair and looked at Candy and her lawyer. Eva sat next to him, scribbling away. 'Candy, we still think you could've killed either of them. Or Dean paid someone.'

'He was in a club on George Street! He couldn't have pushed VDM off the bridge.'

'True, but he's got money and a lot of influence. A lot of people willing to gain favours and his approval.'

She spat at Cullen, a thick glob spattering his cheek. 'You've got fuck all on him, you prick.'

'Charming.' Cullen tore a page from Eva's pad and wiped his face clean. 'We know Mr Van de Merwe was in a BDSM ring. Were you?'

'No.'

'But you know what I'm talking about, right?'

'Stop it.'

'Why did you have a cloak covered in his semen in your wardrobe? He's hardly Bill Clinton.'

'I don't know anything about that.'

'Persuade me.'

'About what?'

'When was the last time you saw him?'

She looked around at Reynolds, getting a shrug. 'I was at an orgy there about six weeks ago.'

'Did he pay you?'

'Quite a lot.' She nibbled her lip. 'Didn't know I was pregnant, otherwise I wouldn't have let them...' She wiped at a tear.

'What did they do?'

'Whatever they wanted. Whips. Chains. Sticking things in me. Getting me to kick them in the balls.'

'Who's "them", Candy?'

'I don't know. I only knew VDM.'

'Men? Women?'

'Mostly men. There was an older woman, late forties maybe. She was vicious. South African, I think. Another woman was maybe your age. Getting on a bit, but still had something about her.'

'Any others?'

'A couple of girls like me.'

'Prostitutes?'

'Escorts.' She folded her arms. 'There was a guy there with a goatee beard. He had a tiny cock, even smaller than VDM's. This guy loved getting the shit kicked out of him.'

Cullen showed her a photo on his phone. 'Was this him?'

Reynolds raised a hand. 'Candy...'

She looked away. 'I'm not saying.'

'Why? Because it's Martin Ferguson? A man we found dead in a hotel room?'

'Listen, this woman.' She leaned over the table, tanned arms crossed. 'The one your age. She had this big fight with VDM.'

'Isn't that part of the fun?'

'Not like that.' Candy ran a hand through her hair. 'They had a huge argument. She called him a needle dick, started shouting stuff about tops and bottoms.'

'Which was Mr Van de Merwe?'

'He was a bottom. For definite. Took a lot of punishment.'

'How do you know that?'

'I kicked his balls a few times. Tied him up. Strangled him. Stuck things up his fucking arsehole.'

'What did she say to him?'

'Said she was stopping it.'

'Stopping what?'

'I don't know. He was pleading with her, said she needed him more than he needed her.'

'Had you ever seen this woman before?'

'Never.'

Cullen flicked to the previous photo and held up his phone. 'Was Mr Ferguson there?'

She raised her hands. 'Fine, he was there.'

'He was the one tied up?'

'That's right. Someone was sticking molten wax on his scrotum.'

'Who was the girl my age?'

She nibbled her lips. 'No idea. Sorry.'

'Anyone who might know?'

'Look. There was a guy who looked like George Clooney.'

'MR VACCARO, why does everything on this case seem to come back to you?' Cullen crunched back in the chair and watched the recorder flashing away, Eva next to him. 'I'll start by saying we don't think you're an equity partner in UC.'

'Excellent.' Vaccaro let out a deep breath. 'Can I get on up to Dundee?'

'Not so fast. We need to ask you a few more questions.'

'Will you let me go if I help?'

'Who owned UC Partners?'

'Like I said, Messrs Van de Merwe and Broussard.'

'Was it just the two of them?'

'As far as I know.'

'Not Ollie Cranston?'

'Him?' Vaccaro stared straight up and let out a laugh. 'Guy only just rocked up here in January after we left.'

'So why's Mr Broussard saying he's involved?'

'Guess he forgets what the lies are and what the truth is.'

Cullen flicked to a new page in his notebook. 'We believe you were at an orgy at Mr Van de Merwe's house. Is that right?'

'"Orgy" sounds very old-fashioned. Can we call it a black sheet party, please?'

'Fine. So, were you there?'

'This the one about six weeks ago, right?'

'Are there others?'

'I was there. That's all I'll say.'

'Was Martin Ferguson there?'

Vaccaro shrugged. 'He might've been.'

'Did Mr Van de Merwe get into a fight with a woman at this orgy?'

'Maybe. Something blew up in the middle of the evening, I don't know what.'

'What did you see?'

'I think Half-inch's top was inserting a—'

'Half-inch?'

'It's what we called Jon. He wasn't very well-endowed.'

'What happened?'

'She just walked away. Just left him tied to the wall.'

'That not part of the fun?'

'It can be.'

'But this wasn't?'

'One of the whores let Jon go and he ran after her.' Vaccaro laughed. 'His butt plug was still hanging out. Must've hurt.'

'Do you have any idea who she was?'

'Just some girl.'

Cullen showed him the photo of Candy. 'Was it her?'

'No.'

'Sure about that?'

'Positive. She was there, but it wasn't her. I think it's the same one Fergie fell in love with.'

Cullen frowned, his buttocks clenching. 'Say that again?'

'The girl Martin fell in love with. Got himself sacked over it.'

52

C ullen bombed up the stairs, two at a time, and jogged down the corridor, Airwave pinned to his head. *Beeeep!* 'Sharon, can you call me back? Airwave or mobile. It's urgent. Cheers.'

He pushed into Methven's office, the door rattling.

Bain glanced over at Cullen. 'Aye, so Cranston's denying it all.'

Methven leaned over his desk phone, Murray in front of the desk, laptop out, Bain lurking in the corner. 'Sergeant, we're just about to get on a conference call with the NCA.'

'This is important.'

Methven rolled his eyes. 'What's the latest emergency?'

'Usual shite, Col.' Bain patted the back of Methven's chair. 'Bet your bottom fuckin' dollar.'

Cullen ignored him. 'Lorna Gilmour had a relationship with Van de Merwe.'

'What?'

'Sounds like fuckin' bullshit to me.'

Cullen shot a glare at Bain. 'We've got Vaccaro on record.'

'Aye, cos he's so fuckin' reliable.'

'I believe him this time. Said there'd been an argument about tops and bottoms. She ran off, he followed.'

'Fuck's sake, Sundance, that's a load of shite he's feeding you there.'

'He's put himself in the firing line over this.'

Methven raised a hand. 'What do you want to do, Sergeant?'

'We need to get her in.'

'So get her in.'

'I can't find Lorna. The rape team aren't in their meeting room and Sharon's not answering her phone.'

'Telling you, Col, this is a disaster.'

Cullen's phone burst into life. Calvin Harris. "Feel So Close".

'I need to take this.' Cullen stuck it to his ear and turned away. 'Hey.'

'Scott, what's up?'

'Is Lorna still with your team?'

'Chantal sent her home. I'm at the Liquid Lounge just now.'

'Shite. When did she go?'

'Hours ago. Back of twelve.'

'Right, better go.' Cullen ended the call and spun round. 'They let her go.'

'Sodding hell.'

'Col, we really need to fuckin' get a hold of all this shite.'

～

CULLEN PULLED in on Broughton Street, a smoker outside the pub frowning at him as he got out of the pool car. He checked over the road. There, the blue door.

Bain's purple Mondeo screeched to a halt in front of him. Bain got out, nodding at Cullen as he straightened up. 'This it here?'

'Aye.' Cullen jogged across the street, skipping between the traffic, his warrant card out.

Bain hammered a fist against the door. 'Police! Open up!'

Nothing.

'You okay, Sundance?'

'No.'

'What's up with you?'

'She's been lying to us.' Cullen wheezed, hammers drilling into his head. 'She was involved with Van de Merwe.'

Bain banged on the door again. And another thump. 'Fuck it. Let's do this old school, Sundance.' He snapped on a pair of blue nitrile gloves and lashed out with a high foot. The door rocked back on the hinges. He kicked it again, sending it flying. 'Come on.'

Cullen jogged inside, head thudding. The hall was empty. Into the bedroom next, dark as night. He flicked the switch by the door. A double bed, maybe bigger. Fluffy pink handcuffs tied to the bedpost. Red and white bedding. And—

What the fuck?

A poster loomed above the bed, a dark-red circle in the middle, three stars inside a crest. He squinted. *Hamilton Academical Football Club.*

Christ on a bike. He checked under the bed. An empty suitcase.

Nothing in the en suite, either. The tiles were slightly damp.

He tore out a drawer. Handcuffs, vibrators, butt plugs. 'Jesus Christ.'

Bain smacked the door against the wall. 'Anything?'

'She's not here.' Cullen tapped the sex toys with a foot. 'See all this?'

'Racy stuff, Sundance.' Bain laughed at the poster. 'An Accies fan? Christ, it gets worse.'

'She's not here.'

'Sure this is the first time you've been here?'

'What's that supposed to mean?'

'Heard about your little bullshit story about getting date raped.'

'It's not bullshit.'

'Reckon you were hiding the sausage with Lorna.' Bain let out a peal of laughter. 'Lorna sausage!'

'Shut the fuck up.' Cullen jabbed a finger in Bain's chest. 'I've had it up to here with your shite.'

'Don't you fuckin' touch me again, Sundance.'

'I got my drink spiked. That's not funny. I could've been raped!'

'Bullshit.'

'I'm warning you. Shut your mouth.'

'Warn away, you stupid prick. Slipping it to someone on the case. How fuckin' stupid are you, Sundance?'

'Fuck off.' Cullen stormed out of the flat, into the sunlight. He glared at Bain. 'Can you call in backup? Man-mark this place.'

'Aye, boss. Three bags full, boss. What are you doing?'

'I need to speak to Sharon.'

'What, to tell her about fuckin' that Lorna bi—'

Cullen took a step forward and rested his forehead against Bain's. 'Shut up before I boot the fuck out of you.'

Bain swallowed. He retreated a pace and sniffed. 'You better call Methven, Cullen, cos I'm about to.'

'Be my guest.'

~

CULLEN HELD the lift open and stomped down the corridor to the meeting room. 'Lorna's not at her flat.'

Sharon stared at a laptop, twirling her hair in her hand. She looked over and smiled. 'Crystal was in here about ten minutes ago. Spitting teeth.'

Cullen slumped next to her. 'What was he after?'

'Scott, did you hit Bain?'

'What? No!'

'Crystal wasn't happy.'

'Fuck him.'

'Is there any chance you can help me?'

'What with?'

'I'm so tired I can't focus on the screen.' Sharon tossed him a package. A brown Jiffy bag, meticulous handwriting. LIQ LNG 22.00–03.00. 'This is the CCTV from last night at the Liquid Lounge. I'm trying to see if Rich did it.'

'It can't be him, can it?' His gut plunged a few levels as he tore it open. 'I've known him since school. There's no way.'

'Just look at it and try not to overthink it.' She pushed her laptop over to him and yawned. 'Here. You drive.'

Cullen leaned in to slot in the first DVD. He waited for the app to load up, then adjusted the speed hard to the right until it hit 22:40. 'There we go.' He slowed it down.

Figures darted into the club, a few staggering out. The bouncers chucked someone out, getting a volley of abuse and spittle in return. Stuart Murray left just before eleven.

Cullen pointed at the screen. 'This matched what I remember and what I've pieced together.' He shuttled the speed down at 00:00. The bouncers hauled him out, stumbling all over the place, speaking into his phone. They led him over to a taxi, where they had a long conversation with the driver. Then they chucked him in the back. 'Believe me now?'

'It's good to see the proof.'

He wound it back to 23:50.

Buxton staggered out, on his phone, looking around. He walked off to the right of the shot.

Cullen tapped the monitor. 'His story's checking out.'

Customers left on double-speed over the next ten or so minutes, mainly to the left of the camera.

Cullen sat up straight and wound it back to 23:45. 'Here we go.'

A woman staggered out of the club. She glanced up at the camera and walked over to the right.

'That's Lorna.' Cullen tapped the screen. 'She left when she started feeling it.'

'Where's Rich, Scott?'

'He can't be the rapist. He just can't.' Cullen swallowed and checked his phone. Nothing. 'There's no way. No way at all.'

'When was the last time you heard from him?'

'Last night. Tom got a text. Said he'd pulled.' Cullen hit play. 'He's got to have left the club, right?'

'There's no back door access until half four and that was one of the staff.'

At 00:12, Rich lurched out of the door, spilling a glass of wine across a bouncer. He sank to his knees, just his head visible, and vomited. The bouncer marched into the shot, helping Rich to his feet and escorted him up the steps, out of the frame.

Cullen let out a deep breath. 'So it's not Rich.'

'Then who is it?'

'Have you got footage from the other rapes?'

'Aye.' Sharon logged onto the machine next to him, CCTV footage filled the screen. 'This is from the nineteenth. Monday. When Kyle Graham was attacked.' She started playing it.

Graham stumbled out onto the street, the sole bouncer staying at his post as he collapsed in a drunken heap. He shouted something, then lay on the street for a minute, resting his head against the paving slabs. Ten minutes later, he crawled off the left of the screen.

Sharon tapped the mouse against the desk. 'This was all we had.'

'What if you wind it back?'

She slid the footage back ten minutes. A ghost emerged from the club, arms wrapped around her body, glancing up at the camera.

Cullen frowned, his gut descending another few flights. 'What about her? She knows where the cameras are.'

'So?'

'Wait a sec.' Cullen wound his own footage back and let it run from 23:45. The same ghost appeared on the screen. 'No, no, no.'

'What?'

'It's Lorna. She's your rapist.'

53

Cullen got up and paced over to the corner of Sharon's meeting room, Airwave to his ear. 'Control, is Lorna Gilmour at her flat yet?'

Hiss of static. 'I've got a negative on that.'

'She's behind the rapes DI McNeill's been investigating.'

'Do you want me to escalate the search?'

'Please.'

'We've got a team up at Alba Bank and one through in Hamilton.'

'Call the second you find her.' Cullen pocketed the Airwave and looked at Sharon. 'Getting anywhere?'

'She was there last Friday when that guy in Leith was assaulted. She left the club before Egan got chucked out. This is good shit, Scott.'

The door shuddered open. DC McKeown entered, Buxton lurking outside.

'Si, what are you doing here?'

'Just giving my statement about last night.' Buxton glanced at the screen in the room. 'What's that?'

'Lorna's the rapist.'

Buxton swallowed hard. 'She was on my bloody lap.'

Sharon tapped Cullen on the arm. 'You need to see this.'

Cullen perched next to her on the desk.

'This is from the RBS ATM just round the corner.' She slapped the spacebar on her laptop.

Rich staggered into the shot, across Hanover Street. Lorna trotted after him, stopping him and holding him tight, whispering into his ears. Then she flagged down a passing taxi.

Buxton reached across Sharon and stabbed a finger at the screen. 'We need to get hold of that taxi.'

                                 ∽

CULLEN PUT the phone to his ear, looked across the Incident Room. 'Aye, it was at twelve, maybe thirteen minutes past midnight this morning.'

'*That'll be a lot of pick-ups, son.*'

'On the corner of Hanover Street and George Street.'

'That narrows it a wee bitty. Just a sec.' Clattering of keyboard.

Methven stormed into the room. 'What on earth's going on?'

Cullen put the mobile to his chest. 'We've found out who's—'

'Sergeant, I've had a formal complaint raised against you by DS Bain.'

'Sir, that's a load of shite.'

'A load of *what*?' Methven turned purple. 'Get off the phone now!'

'Bain's being a cock. Look, this is urgent.'

'This is more—'

'Hello?'

Cullen raised a finger. 'I need to take this.' Turned away and gripped his phone tighter. 'Sorry, what have you got?'

'There you are. Right. Got two fares from George Street at that time.'

'Where were they dropped off?'

'Just a sec.' More clattering. 'First was North Berwick. Marly Green.'

'And the other?'

More clattering. 'Not sure.'

Cullen swallowed. 'Can you put me through to the driver?'

'Let me see... Aye, Peem's on today.'

Cullen poised his pen over his notebook. 'What's his full name?'

'James Hunter. Just connecting you now.'

A click. 'Aye?'

'Mr Hunter, this is DS Scott Cullen of Police Scotland. I believe you had a fare from George Street last night.'

'Aye?'

'Who was in the car?'

'Eh. A boy and a lassie, I think.'

'Notice anything unusual about them?'

'Let me think. Aye. The boy was blotto. Completely out of his skull. Had to warn him about chucking his ringer in— Hang on a sec.' Honk! Honk! 'You can get a bus through that, you fucking numpty!' Hooooooonk! 'Aye, sorry. Warned him about—'

'Did you catch a name?'

'Naw.' Honk! Honk! 'The girl paid cash, I'm afraid.'

'What did she look like?'

'Tall. Not bad. Maybe a six or a seven.'

'Anything distinct about her?'

'Nothing. Look, do you mind—'

'She wasn't wearing glasses?'

'Oh. Aye, now you mention it. Had big stupid ones on her head. Like that snooker boy. Dennis Taylor. You know, huge. Red.'

Cullen swallowed hard. 'Where did you drop them off?'

'End of Belford Road.'

Right by Van de Merwe's house.

~

CULLEN DROVE DOWN QUEENSFERRY STREET, away from the centre of Edinburgh. He grabbed his Airwave and called Buxton. 'You on your way yet?'

'Sorry, Sarge, just about there.'

'How many with you?'

'Squad of four. Is she there?'

Cullen took a sharp left. 'I'm just about at Belford Road now.'

'I see you now.'

'Secure the road.' Cullen tossed the Airwave onto the passenger seat and parked by the bollards. He tore out of the car and bombed down the street.

A squad car trundled over to block the road farther down.

Buxton stood at the open gate outside the town house. Uniformed officers lurked round the corner, out of sight of the house.

Cullen powered up the path. The police tape flapped in the breeze, cut in half. 'Is she in there?'

'I wasn't entering until I got support.' Buxton jogged to catch up. 'Been burnt too many times.'

Cullen stopped outside the door and held up two fingers, waving for the nearest uniforms to follow. 'Right, one of you guard the front door, the other's guarding the staircase inside. Okay?'

Both nodded.

Then at the taller of the other two. 'You're with me.' He gestured at the last uniform. 'You're with DC Buxton. Body Worn Videos on now.'

They both tapped a button on their vests, starting them recording.

'Come on.' Cullen snapped out his baton and stepped into the house. 'The place should've been locked down. Any tramps been in here?'

Buxton got out his pepper spray. 'Supposed to have been a security guard checking in.'

'Stay here. I think I know where she's gone.' Cullen started up the stairs. The boards squeaked. He sighed and continued up.

His uniform followed him, heavy boots clattering on the wood.

Cullen took the first door on the left, waved for the uniform to take the other room and entered the bedroom. The panel was still wedged open. He took it slow as he crossed the room, torch out. He click it on, lighting up the sex room. He crawled through, swinging the light around. Nothing.

Wait, what was that?

He swung it back. There. A figure lay on the floor. He crept over, light trained on the body.

It was Rich. Naked, huddled in a ball.

Cullen stuck a finger to his neck. Still had a pulse. He shone the light in his eyes.

Rich's pupils dilated, though he didn't flinch. His eyes rolled and he let out a groan.

'In here!' Cullen got out his Airwave. 'Control, I need urgent medical back-up to thirty-two Belford Road.'

'Affirmative. It'll be five minutes.'

Cullen swung the light around again. What the fuck was that smell? Shit. He took another look. Stopped the beam over a long object. White, plastic. A strap-on dildo, at least twelve inches. White cotton straps. A condom stretched partway down the shaft, blood and excrement covering it.

He looked over at the uniform as they entered the bedroom. 'Can you bag this up?'

'Aye, Sarge.'

Cullen knelt down and waved a hand in front of Rich's face. 'It's Scott. You're safe.'

'Fuck off, you cunt.'

'Are you okay?'

'I'm fucking burst open.'

Cullen jolted upright and nodded at the uniform. 'Stay here.' He climbed the stepladder and swung his torch around the attic room. Nothing. He slid down, his jaw tightening as he passed Rich.

'Fucking hell, Sarge, he's bleeding out of his arse.'

'Stay with him.' Cullen shone his torch at the uniform. 'Did you check the other room?'

'Aye, Sarge. She's not here.'

'Wait with him till the ambulance gets here.' Cullen crept through the passageway into the bedroom and thudded down the stairs. 'Anything down here?'

Buxton came out of the living room. 'Nothing here, Sarge.'

Cullen looked around. Where the hell was she? He held the handset up to his mouth. 'Control, have we got an update on her location yet?'

'Negative.'

Cullen stomped across the parquet, putting his Airwave away, and went back into the cold air outside. His Airwave chimed again. Bain.

He answered it facing away from the house. 'Cullen.'

'Sundance, you near a computer?'

'Why?'

'You'll want to see this.'

'Right.' Cullen logged in to his police email on his phone. 'What am I looking for?'

'Link's in your inbox.'

'Aye, what is it?'

'Given how much of a fanjo you were earlier, you should be thankful I'm giving you this.' A pause. 'It's a Body Worn Video feed. I'm out in Hamilton looking for this bird you porked.'

Cullen found the email and clicked the link. 'Here we go.'

Grainy video filled the screen. The resolution sharpened, showing the inside of a dark flat.

'I can't see much.'

The camera swivelled round. Bain snorted at it. 'You should fuckin' smell this, Sundance. Like a granny's—'

'Where are you?'

'Here, point at the bed.'

The camera switched over to the far side of the room. A fat man lay on the bed, naked and bloated, covered in flies, skin pale except for purple blotches.

'Who's that?'

'We think it's Eric Gilmour. Her uncle.'

'Why kill him?'

'Fuck knows. Boy's been dead a few weeks.'

Down the street, Methven's Range Rover pulled in.

'Cheers. I have to go.' Cullen marched over to the end of the path as he pocketed his Airwave. 'Sir, she's not there.'

'Then where the sodding hell is she?'

'She's raped Rich. He's out of his skull.'

'Sodding, sodding hell.'

Cullen stared back at the house, spotting the ambulance crawling up the brae. 'Can't believe she brought him here.' He gazed up at the sky, dark grey clouds billowing, rain definitely on the way. 'She's behind all this, sir. She raped those men, spiked my drink. Raped Rich. Killed Ferguson. Killed Van de Merwe.'

'I don't get the why, Sergeant.'

'Me neither.' Cullen shook his head and gritted his teeth. 'She's lost control.'

Methven waved at Van de Merwe's town house. 'Why did she do that to him?'

'Shite, I think I know.' Cullen frowned and reached for his phone, dialling Tom.

'Yo. Hearing a lot from you today, Skinkster.'

'We've found Rich. He's been raped.'

'Fuck me. Is he okay?'

'Not really. Listen, do you know who his source was?'

'No you don't. He swore me to secrecy.'

'This is serious, Tom. I think it's why he's been attacked.'

'Skinky, if you're recording this—'

'Who was the source?'

A pause. 'Lorna.'

'That figures.' Cullen spun round to Methven and mouthed her name. 'How did they meet?'

'Night out a few weeks ago. Went dancing. After that, they started chatting.'

'Why didn't you tell me?'

'He swore me to secrecy, mate. Come on—'

Cullen ended the call and pocketed the phone. 'Lorna was Rich's source.'

Methven held his Airwave away from his head. 'I'll phone you back.' He stabbed a finger on the screen. 'So why do this to him?'

'She overheard Rich and me arguing about his source last night in the club. He was about to give me her name. Just before she spiked our drinks. Fuck, I grabbed his beer.'

'So she did this to him?'

Cullen swallowed hard. 'She must've killed Ferguson because he was giving us too much information about what was going on at the bank. This BDSM ring. Everything.'

'Why give all that information to Rich, though?'

Cullen shrugged. 'To avoid any suspicion falling on her?'

'Why not frame someone for Van de Merwe's death?'

'She was trying to frame Candy. She didn't know about the cloak. It was Lorna's. Fuck.'

Methven frowned. 'Did she say anything useful in the text she used to lure Ferguson to the hotel?'

'Not sure.' Cullen fumbled for his Airwave and hit dial. 'Tommy, it's Cullen. Have you done any work on the burner used to call Martin Ferguson?'

'I can only trace it when it's on and calling. It's off.'

'When was it last on?'

'Last night.'

'Can you check it again?'

A pause. 'Give me a minute.'

'Sergeant, we need to have a word about DS Bain's complaint.'

'Ignore it. It's bullshit, sir.'

'I can't just ignore it.'

'You know what he's like. He can give it out, but he can't take it.'

A tinny voice came from his Airwave. 'Cullen?'

Cullen put it to his head. 'Sorry, Tommy. Got anything?'

'The phone's on.'

'Now?'

'Aye, just hit a cell tower on Chester Street in the West End.'

'So where is she?'

'That's all I can give you until tomorrow.'

'Cheers.' Cullen ended the call. He typed in the mobile number and hit dial.

'What are you doing, Sergeant?'

'Trying something.'

A crackle of static burst out of the speaker. 'Aye?'

'Lorna?'

'You know it's me then, Scott Cullen. Top points. Meet me on Dean Bridge. Now.'

54

Cullen darted over the mouth of Bell's Brae. Shit.

Lorna stood in the middle of the bridge, leaning over the side and staring at the water.

His Airwave chimed. *'Control to Cullen.'*

'Receiving.'

'Alpha six is in position. Over.'

Up ahead, flashing lights cut across the oncoming traffic, blocking both lanes. Two figures got out, keeping their distance.

Cullen continued on towards her, his heart thudding in his chest. He took a backwards glance at the squad car behind him. 'Lorna! It's me!'

She swung round to face him. 'Stay there!'

'What do you want from me?'

She put her knee on the ledge and hoisted herself up, her leather coat flapping in the wind. 'Stay back!'

Cullen came to a halt and raised his hands. 'I'm not moving.'

'Get back.'

'Here's just fine.' Cullen tossed his baton to the ground and waved at the approaching uniform, getting him to stop. He pointed at the BWV camera and got a thumbs up. 'If you jump, you'll most likely survive the fall.'

'That's a lie.'

'You were lucky Jonathan died when you pushed him.'

'I didn't do anything!'

'We know you killed him. We know you've been raping those men.' Cullen inched his right foot forward. 'Why did you do it?'

'You wouldn't understand.'

'Try me.'

'You really want to know?' Tears flooded down her cheeks, twisted out of recognition. 'My uncle fucked me when I was little. I was just a child!'

'That doesn't make it right for you to rape people. One of my best friends.'

'Rich *enjoyed* it.'

'He's in hospital with a ruptured arsehole. You didn't give him a choice.'

'My fucking uncle never gave me a choice. Is that fair? Is any of this fair?'

'Why did you attack Rich?'

She just shook her head.

'What about Kyle Graham or Callum Egan?'

'Who?'

'Your victims, Lorna. Young men who've done nothing. You've torn them apart and they've done nothing to deserve it.'

She swallowed. Said nothing.

'How did you fake the Rohypnol test?'

She grinned, still kept quiet.

'Wait, you did yourself when I let you get changed?'

'Maybe.' She stared down into the water. 'I thought I was over what happened. Then I started sleeping with Jonathan.'

Cullen took another step.

'He kept our relationship a secret from everyone at work.'

Another shuffle forward.

She glared at him, fists clenched, fire in her eyes. 'I couldn't keep a lid on it. It made me feel things I'd not felt for years.'

'You broke up with him at the orgy, right?'

'How do you know that?'

'What do you think I do all day?' Cullen flashed up his hands, eyes locked with hers. 'Why did you start raping men?'

'Deep things came out of my skull.' She stared back at the water. 'I missed Jon. *Hurting* him.'

'So you hurt other men?'

'I didn't mean to. Not at first.'

'You couldn't stop, though, could you?' A long stride forward. Not far away now. 'What happened on Saturday night?'

'He invited me round and we ended up doing it one last time. I told him I didn't want to see him again. *Couldn't* see him again.'

Another stride, wind whipping Cullen's hair. 'And?'

'He didn't take it well. Started crying, clawing at me. I ran off and he followed me out here. Pathetic bastard was in his pants.' She leaned over the side. 'Right here.'

A long step. Not far now. Keep her talking. 'Why did you kill Martin Ferguson?'

'Because he was talking to you, like Rich in the club last night. It was only a matter of time before one of them told you about me.'

'You framed Candy.'

'Now she deserved it. The little witch had her claws into Jonathan.'

Cullen took another step. 'Come on, Lorna—'

She jumped.

Cullen lurched forward. Reached out, catching her jacket. Tugging hard.

The weight of her body fell away, leaving her jacket. She tumbled down, twisting around, eyes locked onto Cullen, screaming. Her back crunched against the rocks, her head on the fake otter.

She screamed out, curdling Cullen's gut.

He shut his eyes, collapsing to his knees, clutching her jacket tight.

55

Cullen handed the clipboard back to the uniform. 'Type that up and I'll sign it when I get back to the station.'

'Sarge.' The uniform nodded and walked off.

The wind blowing down the Water of Leith valley cut into Cullen. He started across the bridge, traffic now rumbling past. Rubberneckers craned their necks to watch him.

He stared at his hands, fingers not strong enough. He shoved them deep in his pockets and powered through the sheet of early-summer rain. Stopped near where—

He looked down. Lorna lay on a gurney, just by the rocks, mouth covered in breathing apparatus. Body arched back. Eyes wide open. Two paramedics wheeled her over to the ambulance.

Blood spilled over the rocks where she'd landed, dyeing the fake otter red.

Cullen sucked in breath.

'Sergeant!'

Cullen twisted round and nodded at Methven. He let out a deep breath. 'Sir.'

Methven patted him on the back. 'Are you okay?'

'I'm a bit shaken up, to be honest.'

'Hell of a business. Can't believe she jumped.'

'I tried to reach her, sir, I was—'

'You couldn't've stopped her. She wanted to die.'

'She still might.'

'This isn't your fault, Sergeant. You've saved lives. Your friend's, for one.'

'Thanks, sir.'

'DC Murray's been a credit to our team. The NCA are hopeful they can claw back those funds.' Methven cleared his throat. 'We need to talk about this scuffle with DS Bain.'

Cullen leaned against the wall, looking over at the ambulance trundling up the brae. 'Now?'

'You can't punch people, Sergeant.'

'We locked horns. That's it.'

'Not what he's saying.'

'He's a lying bastard.'

'He's asked me to take you off active duty.'

'Nobody witnessed it.'

'You're lucky.'

'So that's it?'

'Of course it's not. It never is for him.' Methven leaned against the wall. 'I've had the Chief Constable phoning me up about one of my sergeants scuppering a high-profile drug investigation.'

'I can only apologise.'

'That didn't get us anywhere, Sergeant.'

'Vardy's hauled his guys off the street, sir. Candy could still testify against him.'

'I very much doubt it.'

'Stopping selling the drugs isn't enough?'

'There's no conviction.' Methven thrust his hands into his pockets. 'Let me be clear on this — you've got away with a lot in the past. It stops now, okay?'

'It stopped a long time ago.'

'Am I making myself clear?'

Cullen stared at his feet. 'You are.'

'Once we get the paperwork for this arranged, you're reporting to DI Wilkinson on Monday.'

'Christ.'

'DCS Soutar's reallocated DS Bain to my team to cover. I suspect she wants one of her people on the inside.'

'You're kidding—'

'Scott?' Sharon pushed past Methven. 'Are you okay?'

'I'll live.' Cullen leaned against the wall, arms folded. 'She slipped out of my grasp.'

'Turns out your profile wasn't worth the paper it was written on.' Methven smoothed down his eyebrows. 'It said she would never confess.'

Sharon frowned at Cullen. 'Did she?'

'Got it on BWV. Not sure how much of it'll be admissible...'

'We should have—'

'Colin.' Sharon raised a hand to Methven. 'Back off. Now.'

Methven nodded at Cullen. 'Report to DI Wilkinson on Monday, okay?'

'Will do, sir.' Cullen watched him storm off across the bridge. 'What an arsehole.'

'What does he mean about Wilkinson?'

'He's seconded me. Punishment for all the shite I've been pulling, I suppose.'

'Because you hit Bain?'

'I didn't.'

'He seems to think so.'

'I wish I'd battered the fuck out of him. He's been asking for it for years.'

'You can't just punch him, though.'

'I didn't. He was threatening me.'

'How badly?'

'Just the usual shite with him. He thought I'd been shagging Lorna. You know what he's like. He gets in there and fucks with you. I've had enough. Can't believe Methven brought him back. I'm the one who's had to deal with him. Chipping away at me all the time.'

She put her hand on his arm. 'Scott, are you okay?'

'I don't know.'

'What happened?'

'I fucked up. Tried to grab her, but she just... She slipped through my grasp.'

'Scott, it's—'

He locked his eyes on hers. 'If I hadn't let her go. If—'

'Scott, it's okay.' She put an arm round him and hugged him close. 'It's not your fault. She'll still pay for what she's done.'

~

CULLEN STOPPED outside the operating theatre.

Doctors in scrubs marched around, looking purposeful.

A uniform perched on a chair, nose stuck in a Stuart MacBride novel. "Broken Skin". Gave Cullen a nod and raised the book.

Cullen took a step away from him.

'There you are.'

'Chantal.'

Jain handed him a coffee. 'Got this for Shaz, but she didn't show up.'

'She's outside, briefing your DCI.' Cullen tore off the lid. 'Thanks for this. Assuming you've not put Rohypnol in.'

'Don't even joke.'

Cullen took a burning sip. 'What's the latest on Lorna?'

'She's just going into surgery.' Jain gulped at the foam. 'The doctor gave me two minutes with her.'

'Any use?'

'Completely out of it. Sorry.'

'We've got BWV evidence against her.'

'That's a relief.'

'She'll face two cases. She's going away for a long time.'

Jain patted his arm. 'You okay, Scott?'

'I'm not bad. Need to have a chat with you about your future when this is all over.'

'Sounds ominous.'

'I mean it in a good way.'

~

THE DOCTOR OPENED the door and waved her hand at Rich. 'We've had to administer a severe painkiller.'

Cullen couldn't keep his focus on the bony figure in the bed, facing away from them, his arms out in front of him. 'Take it that means he's been badly injured?'

'Suffered a torn rectum and a perforated colon.' The doctor shut her eyes and flared her nostrils. 'This is the worst of the cases your partner's been investigating.'

'Can I get a minute with him?'

'Just don't get him excited, okay?'

Cullen stepped across the room and sat next to the bed. 'You okay, mate?'

Rich just stared at him.

'I'm really sorry. I didn't catch her in time.'

Rich rolled over, his blotchy eyes glaring at Cullen.

'If she hadn't overheard our argument in the club—'

'Skinky, I thought I was in control of it. She was just playing me. Feeding me stories.'

'You got caught up in it.'

'It's my arrogance that's got me here. If I hadn't chased the story, I'd not be here.' Rich shook his head, wiping the back of his hand across his eyes. He sat and picked up a cup from the stand. He swallowed down water, slivers running down his cheeks, soaking his gown and the bed. 'Can't believe it. I'm *broken*. She spiked my drink, took me to that house and fucking raped me. What sort of person does that?'

'She jumped off Dean Bridge.'

'She's dead?'

'In surgery. Chantal reckons she'll survive.'

Rich stared up at the ceiling. 'I don't know if that's good news or bad.'

'Me neither.'

'I'd like ten minutes in a room with her.' Rich scrunched up the bed sheet. 'I shouldn't have lied to you.'

'You shouldn't.' Cullen smiled. 'But then I'm never the most honest.'

'No, you're a lying bastard.' Rich rubbed his face and winced. 'Look, I'm sorry about the book.'

'It's okay, mate. Really. Just stop writing it.'

Rich laughed. 'You're such a fucker, Skinky.'

'You need anything?'

'A new arsehole.'

～

CULLEN OPENED the door of Sharon's car and got in the passenger seat. He yanked down his seatbelt. It caught halfway. He tugged it again. Nothing. 'Jesus Christ.'

Sharon leaned over and eased it down. 'There you go.'

He let out a deep sigh. 'Thanks.'

'How did it go?'

'Shite.' He shut his eyes and ran a hand across his forehead. 'We're trained to deal with these things, but it's never easy, is it?'

'How is he?'

'Broken. Poor guy. I can't believe this.'

She shook her head and gripped the steering wheel tight. 'Rich sent me a text yesterday. Said you'd been crying.'

'Right.'

'Was it about Becky?'

'We were having lunch. It all just hit me.'

'Me not being able to have kids?'

'The stress we've been under. My promotion, your promotion. Bain. Methven. Everything that's been happening.'

'But mainly Becky?'

Cullen rubbed his damp eyes. 'I couldn't deal with it.'

'You're dealing with it, Scott. Better than most.'

'Maybe I should go back to my counselling.'

'Maybe.'

Cullen reached over to kiss her. 'Look, I'm sorry.'

'What about?'

'I've been such an insensitive wanker. Treating you like the enemy. Pushing you away.'

She wiped the misted-up windscreen and started the car. 'We just need to talk more. Deal?'

Cullen grabbed her hand and clutched it tight. 'Deal.'

SCOTT CULLEN WILL RETURN IN

"HEROES AND VILLAINS"

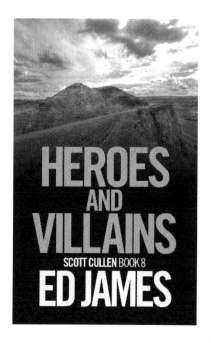

Out now!

If you enjoyed this book, please consider leaving a review on Amazon.

The eighth book in the series, HEROES AND VILLAINS, is out now — keep reading to the end of this book for a sneak preview. You can buy a copy at Amazon.

If you would like to be kept up to date with new releases from Ed James, please fill out a contact form.

AFTERWORD

A monster. There's no other way to put it.

Sincere thanks for buying this book, I hope the reading was as enjoyable as clicking Buy on Amazon.

Thanks this time go to Kitty for the cover, the alpha reading, the harsh criticism and the brilliant copy editing, especially as it was an emergency; to Ginty and Rhona for the incisive alpha reading; Victoria Pepe for the brutal structural and line editing; and Len Wanner for stepping in for the emergency proofing and doing such a grand job in tight timescales.

This was one of the most personal books I've written. IT projects, with their corruption and ineptitude, paid my bills for many years. Now it's time to write about them. I got a lot out of my system with that. Where there's money, there's usually the stench of corruption and people wasting their time on politics and games instead of just doing stuff. Of course, it's all fictional, even if based on real experiences.

Anyway, Cullen will be back late next year in HEROES & VILLAINS. It's shaping up to be pretty interesting, in my head at least. You've probably noticed, but I'm slowing down production of Cullens as he's taken up most of my time over the last eighteen months. I want to devote energies to DS Vicky Dodds and DI Simon Fenchurch, among other projects. That said, I've got an idea for a Sharon McNeill short novel, so we'll see how that goes. And HEROES is already eating at my synapses.

One final note, if you could find time to leave a review where you bought this, I'd really appreciate it — reviews really help indie authors like myself.

-- Ed James
  East Lothian, August 2015

ABOUT THE AUTHOR

Ed James is the author of the bestselling DI Simon Fenchurch novels, Seattle-based FBI thrillers starring Max Carter, and the self-published Detective Scott Cullen series and its Craig Hunter spin-off books.

During his time in IT project management, Ed spent every moment he could writing and has now traded in his weekly commute to London in order to write full-time. He lives in the Scottish Borders with far too many rescued animals.

If you would like to be kept up to date with new releases from Ed James, please contact a contact form.

Connect with Ed online:

Amazon Author page

Website

OTHER BOOKS BY ED JAMES

MAX CARTER SERIES

1. TELL ME LIES

SUPERNATURE SERIES

1. BAD BLOOD
2. COLD BLOOD

HEROES AND VILLAINS

EXCERPT

PROLOGUE

Detective Sergeant Scott Cullen kept his gaze on the silver Range Rover three cars ahead as they followed it past the Scottish Parliament, which still looked like a municipal swimming baths from provincial Scotland, just with some Catalan window dressing stapled on. Showed where the country was these days.

DC Paul 'Elvis' Gordon was behind the pool car's wheel, giving off the vibe of his namesake's final hours in Vegas, rather than his Hollywood pomp. He scratched at his massive sideburns, keeping the car a steady thirty as they passed through two roundabouts and two sweeping bends along the busy road from the city's political heart to its social armpit, Dumbiedykes. He stopped to wait for an old man to cross, drumming his thumbs off the wheel, then headed into the former council estate. The high-rise blocks still seemed like a junkie haven, even though the flats were mostly leased to MSPs and bankers, and filled with designer furniture and bespoke kitchens. Mostly.

The Range Rover pulled up outside a beige-and-grey tower block, the blacked-out windows hiding the driver.

Cullen gestured for Elvis to drive on by the target – no slowing down, no turned heads, no suspicious behaviour. As they passed, Cullen angled the wing mirror.

Dean Vardy hopped out of his pimp ride, his disco muscles

and skin-tight T-shirt a cocky challenge to the afternoon's fourteen degrees, the Edinburgh wind lowering the temperature. He strutted up to the front door like he owned the place. Not far off the truth – his legal businesses owned twenty flats inside. God knows how many his illegal ones did.

Elvis cruised around the turning point at the end, doubled back to the neighbouring block and slowed to a halt at the side of the street. He killed the ignition and yawned, releasing a blast of coffee breath. 'Hope you're pleased I haven't made a joke about you being the dumb guy in Dumbiedykes?'

'Very pleased.' Cullen reached for his Airwave radio and put it to his ear. 'Suspect has entered premises at Holyrood Court, Dumbiedykes. Want us to follow him in?'

'Negative, Sundance.' DS Brian Bain's Glasgow rasp hissed out. 'We've got eyes on you from up here, so sit tight. Your front-left headlight is buggered, by the way.'

'Look, she's in that flat alone.' Cullen tightened his grip on the 'oh-shit' handle even though they weren't moving. 'We're just letting Vardy walk up there?'

'It's called a fuckin' plan for a reason, Sundance. Boss's orders. Now you make sure he doesn't leave without us knowing.'

Bloody hell.

Cullen ended the call and slid the Airwave back into the sleeve pocket of his battered green bomber jacket.

Across the street, by the entrance, some neds were playing football – none of them looking any older than ten.

Nothing else happening.

Elvis was stroking his lamb chops, a look of puzzled constipation stuck on his face, like the King of Rock 'n' Roll on his resting toilet. 'So we're just to sit here?'

'Those are the orders, aye.'

'Tell you, this undercover stakeout's been dragging on longer than one of Wilko's morning briefings.' Elvis shook his head. 'Here we are, sitting on our arses, while that Vardy bastard runs around like he owns the place, raping and killing. And I'm only here because you pissed off the boss.'

'You don't need to remind me.' Cullen gave him a glare, hoping it would warn him that a constable should watch what he says to a sergeant. Elvis looked the other way. 'Fine, I'll say it if it makes you happy. You're here because I messed up Wilko's case, but I did solve a murder in the process. And, for my troubles, I got a secondment to Operation Venus. Along with the rest of the Special Needs class.'

'Very funny.' Elvis chuckled despite himself. 'Just saying, that's all.'

'You could put in for a transfer, you know.'

'How did you...?' Elvis settled even deeper into his seat, blushing. Something groaned. Could've been the back rest, could've been his stomach. 'Sorry, Sarge. Might want to open a window.'

Cullen held his breath as he got out into the blustery wind and leaned against the car.

The sky looked like it had been in a fight. Hard winds from the North Sea pummelled grey clouds across the horizon. One seemed beaten up, a lumbering purple mass like a bloody bruise.

Edinburgh in August. Got to love it.

The car rocked as Elvis got out. He stepped around and settled his bulk on the bonnet, upwind of Cullen. 'Look on the bright side, though. You've got me for company. Dragged me into this unexpected career development opportunity and I haven't resented you for one moment. Must be my sunny deposition.'

'You mean disposition.' Cullen stuck his hands into his jeans pockets. 'And you don't mind this new gig because it means you're not gawping at CCTV all day.'

Elvis pushed himself off the bonnet and puffed up his chest. 'Hold on a—'

'Alright, Scotty?' A big guy in a shiny blue muscle-shirt slapped Cullen's shoulder with one hand, holding a two-litre plastic bottle with the other. 'Alright, my man?'

'Aye, just walking the daftie here. What's up?'

'Your daftie looks fair exhausted, Scotty.' Big Rob grinned at Elvis, killing any attempt at a witty comeback with a confused wink. 'You boys doing interval sprints?'

Elvis rolled his eyes. 'Aye, that's what we're doing out here.'

'Good effort, my man.' Big Rob waved the bottle around, splashing water on the pavement. 'Been working hard myself all morning. Today's target is ten litres.' He flexed a pair of bulging biceps. 'Need to hydrate these bad boys.'

'Ten litres?' Cullen smirked at him. 'Isn't that going to dehydrate you?'

'Science.' Big Rob tapped his nose and wandered off.

Elvis watched him go. 'That your ex-boyfriend?'

'Just some old CHIS.'

Elvis did that particular frown, his features squishing up like a used chip wrapper. Usually meant he was thinking of something funny. 'There's nothing covert, human or intelligent about him, is there?'

Cullen glanced at the heavy clouds pressing down on the tower blocks. 'Elvis, you'll need to drive me to A&E, I think I've split my sides.'

'Come on, mate. That was funny. Got to admit.' Elvis crossed his arms and did his best impression of a petulant toddler, huffing and puffing.

Cullen closed his eyes, wondering what he'd done to deserve this. Then he remembered, in exact detail. When he opened them again, the dreich weather made him sigh for the four hundredth time that day.

'Looks like a right cloudburst's on the way.' Elvis elbowed Cullen in the ribs. 'Bet you've pulled yourself off so much in the shower, you get a hard-on every time it rains.'

Cullen couldn't even muster the energy to turn the radio back up. *I need out of here. Or to get shot of this clown.* 'Me and Craig Hunter busted a steroid ring in a gym a few years back.'

'Sounds like a great excuse for you pair to hang around with a load of naked blokes.'

'That's Craig's thing, not mine.' The first raindrops battered off the pavement, so he got back in the car and scanned the radio. Had to settle for *TalkSport*. Even though the caller sounded off his head, it was better than listening to *Elvis in the Afternoon*.

Elvis got behind the wheel again, stroking his sideburns as he turned off the radio. 'Load of pish.'

In one of the towers, Dean Vardy was meeting a young woman. Unprotected, unguarded, and alone. With *his* record.

It didn't feel right.

Elvis cleared his throat and spat out of the open window. 'I was reading this article in the New Yorker by this boy called Art Oscar. Heard of him?' He took Cullen's silence as an instruction to keep talking. 'Said the war on drugs was a political ploy cooked up by Nixon to take out people who weren't going to vote for him. You know, blacks and anti-war lefties. Think that's true?'

Cullen cocked an eyebrow. 'I didn't know that.'

'Said it was heroin and marijuana at the start. Makes you wonder what this war on drugs is all for, eh?'

Cullen paused. 'I mean, I didn't know you could read.'

Elvis rolled his eyes.

Sod this for a game of soldiers.

Cullen opened the door and pointed at Elvis. 'Stay here and wait for Vardy. I'm going upstairs.'

∼

CULLEN KNOCKED on the door three times, the secret signal that was about as subtle as a brick in the balls. Or one of Elvis's jokes.

The door cracked open and half a face appeared in the gap: round suedehead, receding hairline, deep frown, squinty eyes, and a limp moustache. DS Brian Bain. 'Sundance, I fuckin' told you to wait downstairs, you tube.'

'You did.' Cullen looked down at him, letting Bain feel his height disadvantage. 'How about you go and babysit Elvis?'

'How about you fuck off?'

Cullen stared at him, then lowered his eyes and unzipped his jacket to give his hands something to do other than punch the little bastard. 'I need to speak to the boss. Move.'

'You could ask nicely.'

'You wouldn't understand nicely.'

Bain stared at him, an uneasy smile twitching under his moist moustache. He recovered his cool, stepped back and swung the door open. 'You charming fucker.'

Cullen walked straight past him into the flat. Boarded-up windows, grotty old furniture, cold strip lighting making the place feel as inviting as a mortuary. Must be the last place in the tower block that hadn't been turned into an IKEA showroom.

In the kitchen, an Armed Response Unit loitered with intent. Four men, two women, dressed head to toe in black tactical gear, handguns strapped to their thighs, semi-automatic rifles slung tightly over their chests, index fingers resting idly on the trigger guards. The sight alone made Cullen twitchy.

DI Paul Wilkinson sat at the kitchen table, fussing over some recording equipment. Well, one of his hands was. The other was busy stuffing his mouth with chocolate raisins. A pong of stale sweat radiated off him. He caught sight of Cullen and dropped the smudgy paw to give his balls a good scratch. The guy seemed to gain at least a stone of flab every week, his manboobs straining at his latest checked farmer's shirt. 'Well done, Cullen. You found us all the way up here.' His Yorkshire accent was hiding behind an acquired Scottish one, just a few syllables off here and there. He gathered another handful of raisins and hoovered his wee sweeties up with a wet sucking noise. 'Despite being told to stay down there.' He chewed open-mouthed, a mess of brown and pink and purple.

'I'm worried about Amy Forrest, sir.' Cullen looked away from his jowly face. 'More specifically, about Vardy murdering her.'

Wilkinson stared at him for a few seconds. 'We're sticking to the plan. End of.' He popped another chocolate raisin in his gob.

Cullen glanced at the men and women standing to attention. 'Come on, you've got this lot hanging around with their thumbs up their arses, while Vardy's downstairs, right below our feet. With *her*. She's alone. With *him*. We know where he is, what he's capable of, and what he'll do if we don't stop him.'

Wilkinson snorted, then rolled his eyes at the figures in black. 'I said no.'

'Come on, let's just get in there. We can pick him up for the assault charge and collect evidence on the murder allegations while he's in custody.'

'Cullen...' Wilkinson took another mouthful and chewed slowly, really taking his time with it, like he was provoking Cullen to do something rash. And get himself kicked off another case. 'This isn't a simple murder investigation, the sort you're used to. You're in the drugs squad now and you need a bit more of this.' He tapped his temple, repeatedly, then kept his finger there.

Even the ARU cops became so restless they started running unnecessary checks of their equipment, rustling in the awkward silence.

'You need strategic thinking in this game.' Wilkinson dropped his hand and leaned back on his chair. 'That girl is risking her life for this operation, seducing Vardy into some dirty pillow talk, while we record it. You want to do him for some assault that'll get him, what? Five years? Out in two? I want him bragging about his drug deals, I want him off the streets for life.' He gave Cullen a stern look, then reached for his raisins and popped another load into his mouth. 'That little enterprise nets him seven million quid a year, right? And you want him inside on assault charges. Leave the thinking to the big boys, yeah?'

Cullen stared at him. *Playing power games while an untrained mark lured a violent misogynist into a honey trap.* He flexed his fingers and zipped up his bomber jacket. 'Understood. Sir.' He turned away and stepped over to the wall to await orders.

I know all about your kind of 'strategic thinking'. Throw bait to a shark, then wash your hands of any responsibility if the shark kills the bait, just as long as you catch the predator.

The audio recorder on the table burst into noise. A door creaking, followed by a female voice: 'Why... why don't we slow things down a wee bit, eh?'

'Slow down? *Slow down?*' Vardy's voice, guttural and deep. 'You having a laugh? Thought this was a booty call.'

'Sure, but I want to get to know you first, Dean. I see you at the club all the time, but you're my boss. You're so distant. I mean you're cool and that, but I want to get to know you. What you're thinking.'

'Right now, I'm thinking that I want to smash your back doors in before I get back to work. How about you get to work on this rager, eh?'

'Okay, then. But I've got a wee surprise for you.' Amy Forrest's voice was close to the mic. Sounded like a door opening.

'Now we're talking!' Bed springs creaked, followed by some slobbery noises. 'Aye, that's the game. Cup the balls, nice and hard. Work the shaft. Just like that. Oooh. Bite it. Aye, you too.'

Cullen left Wilko glued to his recorder and stepped out of the flat into the dank corridor.

'Here, Sundance.' The door closed behind Bain. 'What a fuckin' farce.'

'We need to stop it. Right now.' Cullen powered over to the stairwell. One floor down, Vardy was in a flat with Amy Forrest.

'We've got way more than enough on Vardy. We should be arresting him.'

'Wilko's having a fuckin' laugh if he thinks that wee lassie will get Vardy to incriminate himself.' Bain was up close, moaning into his ear. 'I should still be running this. Load of—'

A gun shot, echoing up the stairwell. Cullen froze. Felt the pressure in his chest, took a sharp breath, glanced around, tried to—

Another shot.

Down there.

And another.

Shite, Amy's flat.

Cullen sprinted down the stairs, a rush of blood like static in his ears, disembodied voices shouting, then along Amy's floor, combat boots hammering along the corridor behind him, the door rushing towards him, his shoulder crashing through it, the force carrying him several paces into the flat before he stumbled to a halt. He jerked his head around to get his bearings.

There – bedroom door wide open, Dean Vardy's back framed by the doorway, motionless, head bowed, arms loose by his sides, trousers round his ankles, a gun dangling from his right hand.

Cullen felt like he was staring at a picture – a perfectly composed still life.

Then Vardy spun around. His eyes shot to Cullen, fury flashing. But, just like that, it was over. He dropped the gun, grinning. 'I found her like that.'

Cullen charged at him just as the first ARU cops piled into the flat, their shouts deafening in the confined space. He flew through the bedroom doorway, pushing Vardy sprawling onto the floor.

But Cullen's gaze was drawn to the bed.

A woman lay tangled in the blood-soaked sheets, naked but for her torn underwear. It felt wrong to look at her exposed body, even more wrong that her chest was burst open by a gunshot wound. Her head was like some overripe piece of fruit used for shooting practice.

Amy Forrest.

Cullen's mark.

Cullen's fault.

He grabbed Vardy's T-shirt and yanked him up. Fist poised,

ready to strike – but didn't. It took all his strength to stop himself from smacking that smug, smug face. 'You're going away for a long time.'

Vardy glanced around to make sure no one else was looking at him. Then he winked at Cullen, whispering, 'Sure, sweetheart, you keep telling yourself that.'

∾

THE EIGHTH SCOTT CULLEN BOOK, HEROES AND VILLAINS, is out now. You can get a copy at Amazon.

If you would like to be kept up to date with new releases from Ed James, please fill out a contact form.